OF FEAR AND FAITH

Death and Destiny Trilogy, Book 1

N. D. Jones

Copyright © 2019 by **N.D. Jones**

All rights reserved. No part of this publication may be reproduced, distributed, or transmitted in any form or by any means without prior written permission.

Kuumba Publishing
Maryland
www.kuumbapublishing.com

Publisher's Note: This is a work of fiction. Names, characters, places, and incidents are a product of the author's imagination. Locales and public names are sometimes used for atmospheric purposes. Any resemblance to actual people, living or dead, or to businesses, companies, events, institutions, or locales is completely coincidental.

Book Layout © 2014 BookDesignTemplates.com
Cover design by Atlantis Book Design
All art and logo copyright © 2016 by Kuumba Publishing

Siren-Bookstrand-1st Edition (2014)

Of Fear and Faith/ N.D. Jones. – 2nd Edition
ISBN-13: 978-1-7325567-9-9

DEDICATION

Nathaniel Jones Jr. (1944-1999)
Peace.
Blessing.
Love.

PROLOGUE

Oyo Empire, 1500

The sky over the ancient land of Yoruba darkened as the thunderstorm approached, growing mile by mile, village by village, blanketing the sky in unforgiving clouds of anger and loneliness.

Thunder raged behind the clouds, its agonized roar sending animals and humans fleeing for safety.

Crack.

Crack.

Crack.

More thunder, loud and menacing.

Crack.

Crack.

Crack.

Sàngó, the god of fire, lightning, and thunder, appeared in the sky. Bolts of burning, ragged heat surrounded him, setting him apart from the blackness of the caustic sky.

Lifting nothing more than his chin, Sàngó unleashed his bolts.

They spiraled in sonic white waves southward, breaking off in rapid sparks. A moment later, the first shock hit, a second, a third, then far too many for Sàngó to count.

Within minutes, rivers and lakes erupted from their puny depths, a wasted plea to the god who would compel them to free his wife.

More bolts, stronger this time, charged through pathetic watery defenses, finding lakes and riverbeds and exploding in guttural cries of fury.

"Return. What. You. Have. Taken."

The only words Sàngó had ever deemed to speak on this unholy of anniversaries.

The day she was taken from me and locked in an inescapable watery prison.

But the lakes and rivers didn't respond. No, they only ever heeded the commands of Yemaya, their mother. For all Sàngó's might, his will was but an insignificant drop of rainwater.

Then the watery voice he knew, all too well, restored the destruction he'd wrought and whispered, in his mind, with neither gentleness nor malice. And Sàngó's heart was already drowning in the familiar words—a dousing reply to his fiery entreaty.

Every five hundred years, in the year of Ra, a fire witch born to the Temple of Oya and a water witch born to the Temple of Mami Wata will mark the beginning of the end but also rebirth. Ma'at demands balance, and these witches will bring both destruction and another five hundred years of peace for humans. The old will be washed away like sand after an early morning tide. Pray for Oya's fire witch and her invincible Mngwa, for they will be all that stands between humans and a liquid serpent grave. Pray for Mami Wata's water witch whose desire for power will know no bounds. Humans cannot know love without hate, good without evil, fire without water, Oya without Mami Wata. The Day of the Serpents will be upon you. Relinquish your fears and embrace the power of faith.

Those words, the ones inscribed on the most ancient caves of the Oyo Empire, were meant for fire and water witches. They were the ones who carried the tale of Oya and Mami Wata. Some of the more foolish among the witches secretly harbored a dream of being the next fire or water witch of legend. But those unfortunate witches wouldn't be birthed for nearly five centuries.

How many more battles had to be waged before Oya would be returned to him? When would the sun god be done with his game of fear and faith? Sàngó didn't know. The only truth that had ever meant anything to him was his love for his wife, his Oya. And like the fire he wielded so effortlessly, love was an eternal flame.

Rain began to fall, slowly quenching the deprived land below, and Sàngó refused to call them tears, yet from the mix of rain and dirt sprouted a flower of hope.

There will be two, my dear Sàngó, *a mighty union capable of saving us from ourselves. Only then will Oya be returned to you. Have faith.*

CHAPTER ONE

Baltimore, Maryland, Present Day

Silence.
Darkness.
Footsteps.
Growl.

"I can smell you, child. You can't hide from me," whispered a mangled voice on the other side of the closet door.

Elizabeth Ferrell thought her heart would burst from her chest as those dreaded words smashed through the darkness and found her hiding spot. But, instead, sweaty fear rolled down her tiny back, legs cramped and tight from being wedged between the closet wall, dirty clothes hamper, and a toy chest she'd had since she was a girl of five. She was now a big girl of eight, and big girls didn't hide in closets from imaginary monsters, or so she told herself during the safe light of day.

Elizabeth closed her eyes and tried to reconcile this new reality to what she'd been led to believe. Unbidden memories flowed forth. Her mother's soothing words rang in her head, a dead, flat note.

"There are no such things as ghosts, Betsy. So come out of that closet and get back into bed."

"But Ma, I saw a monster. It had long, pointy teeth, huge claws, a twisted face, and black eyes."

"Ah, my sweet girl, that's just your imagination, shadows of things in your room like your superhero plushie or your dancing teddy bear. All normal once the lights are on, and you can see them clearly. I promise you, sweetie, ghosts, demons, and monsters are all make-believe, like in the fairy tales I read to you. They don't exist, trust me."

Trust me.

The closet door creaked. Scratching sounds sent a fresh, cold wave of fear through Betsy. Her eyes snapped open in wild terror. She now knew the truth her mother refused to tell her.

Lies, all lies.

Betsy would die because of them. She knew that, as well. Her closet would become her tomb, her sarcophagus. She'd learned those two vocabulary words yesterday from a social studies lesson on ancient Egypt. Yes, a make-believe monster that wasn't make-believe at all would kill her. The police would find her lifeless body next to her favorite possessions, her treasure chest of birthday and Christmas toys. Betsy shivered, and warm tears fell.

What did it matter? Her parents were dead. Betsy was sure of it. She'd heard their awful screams, the ones that woke her, driving her to the closet in search of safety. Yet it was she who now screamed, her cry breaking through the morbid silence of the house when the closet door was suddenly wrenched from its hinges, the monster real, no shadow, no dream, no fairy tale.

"Goddess, save me. P–please."

Scream.

Silence.

FBI Special Agent Assefa Berber sat at his desk looking over the crime scene photos taken a few hours ago at the Ferrell residence. The Ferrell murders were the fourth slaying of this sort since he'd started working the Baltimore angle of the case. But, to his shame and frustration, Assefa had achieved little in the six weeks since his division chief sent him to the city to help the local police.

He flipped through the pictures. Blood-splattered walls. Blood-soaked bed. Broken night lamps and splintered bedroom door. Sliced and diced victims. The photos were nothing more than a reminder of what he had witnessed firsthand a few hours ago when his plans for the evening were interrupted by a terse phone call from Mike.

"There's been another murder, and from initial reports, it's our guy. He left one alive this time, so I'm on my way to the hospital. Get

your ass to the crime scene. The dispatcher has the address to the Ferrells' home."

Then the phone went dead in typical Michael McKutchen fashion—abrupt and rude.

Now Assefa sat in his office, peering down at the photos in his hand and seeing all the reasons for doing this work. Growing up in the flat plains of the Sudan, he'd glimpsed the face of death too many times. Admittedly, Assefa's childhood had been one of privilege and entitlement. As a boy, he'd wanted for nothing. And for far too long, he wore his naïve blinders with pride, unwilling to see the world…and his family through a lens that wasn't as rosy as he'd liked to believe. No, there was nothing rosy about the history of the Berber family or their dominance in the Sudan. With shameful clarity, Assefa knew that evil came in all forms, that monsters often wore the skin and smiles of "civilized" men. Yet even a privileged, spoiled boy grows into a man, and a real man cannot feign blindness to the fragile existence of others. Likewise, a man cannot ignore his calling. This work, protecting innocents from the depraved, was indeed Special Agent Berber's calling.

Leaving the past where it belonged, he reclined in the black executive leather chair that came with the office. He didn't know who the chair belonged to, but its extravagance was a stark contrast to the drab, dingy closet of an office with its off-white paint, dented file cabinets, and a carpet of indeterminate color.

A minute later, Assefa raised his head, looked at his office door and said, "It's definitely our guy, Mike," just as the detective opened the door to his office and entered.

Doorknob in hand, Mike frowned at him, looked at the layers of white paint covering what used to be a window in the wooden door but now served as a cheap form of privacy, and then back at Assefa. "I hate it when you do that," Mike grumbled, then slammed the well-worn but sturdy door behind him.

Assefa only smiled, knowing from Mike's entrance he hadn't had his cup of leftover station coffee—gritty, bland, and hard to swallow.

"You hear and see everything, and don't tell me again it's nothing more than coincidence."

"It's 9:00 a.m. And you've met me in this office at the same time five days a week for the last month and a half. Besides," Assefa continued, opening a desk drawer and pulling out a can of Lysol, "I smell your cigar in the air the same as everyone else who wonders how you get away with smoking in a non-smoking police station."

Ignoring Mike's frown at the familiar pink can, he liberally sprayed the area around his desk.

"It's called seniority, and no one around here dares come between me and a good smoke, especially not a rookie agent who still smells of his mama's tit milk," Mike responded before choking back a cough from the "Summer Breeze" scented spray. "Hell, I only have six months before I retire and have nothing to lose if the captain decides to suspend me for breaking a rule or two. Shit, he would be doing me a favor if he did, kid."

Assefa hated when he called him "kid." He was twenty-eight, and his mother had been dead for almost as long. If he'd ever fed from her breast, that memory was as buried as her remains.

"I don't think so. You don't get to retire until we capture the bastard and put him in prison. Or, better yet, in an anonymous grave." His voice had suddenly turned cold and hard, as cold and hard as the veteran detective sitting across from him.

Assefa knew all about Detective Michael McKutchen, having performed a thorough background check before he set foot in Baltimore. His division chief and uncle, Ulan Berber, had an understanding with Baltimore's Chief of Police, who, unlike most full-humans, knew of the existence of the Preternatural Division of the FBI and the unique nature of its mission—to serve and protect all life forms from dangerous preternatural beings. Calls were typically made, and action was taken when unusual cases arose that needed a "special touch."

Two calls were made two months ago, and Assefa's current assignment was the action, or rather reaction, to the recent Baltimore slayings. Suddenly, he had a temporary partner. One he'd learned was a veteran, earning himself a Medal of Honor. Becoming a police officer for the urban streets of Baltimore, the desire to protect innocents seemed to fit

Mike's personality profile, as did claims of harsh treatment by criminals and officers alike.

Assefa regarded the man with guarded respect, slid to the edge of his chair, and pushed the crime scene photos to him.

Mike plopped his arthritic body in the rickety chair and slowly picked up the photos. Taking the gruesome images before him, his face contorted in a familiar mask of anger.

"This son of a bitch just doesn't know when to stop. He figures he can do whatever he wants in my city and get away with it." Shoving the photos back to him, Mike managed to drop his anger an octave. "The survivor of the Ferrell murders is at Johns Hopkins Hospital. She's awake and physically unharmed. The night nurse suggested we bring in a psychologist. Her two cents' worth of advice wasn't asked for, but I think it's a good idea. I have someone I trust we can use. She's a good friend."

Assefa pondered the man's words a minute, having caught the gentle way he used the word "friend" and the barely-there smile that followed. This was a different side of Mike. One he wanted to explore. Circumstances forced him to work with the man, so the more he learned about the detective, the better.

"I didn't think you trusted anyone outside of…of…Hell, I didn't know you trusted anyone, nor had friends."

"Just because women think you're tall, dark, and handsome doesn't mean you're the only one with friends. Besides, she's more like a daughter to me than a simple friend. And if it weren't for this case, I wouldn't even consider introducing you to her. The last thing she needs is God's gift to women putting the moves on her."

Assefa gave the detective his most charming smile, a familiar mask that hid the depth of his feelings, a necessary protection for him and others. The mask came to life the morning after he'd learned that all the rumors about his family were disgustingly true. Assefa had been eight, and his illusions of normalcy were shredded when he'd overheard his grandfather and father arguing. He hadn't understood everything they'd said that fateful night, but he'd comprehended enough to confirm his greatest fears. When his father stormed from his grandfather's office,

Assefa under the secretary's desk, his father's words of: "You're nothing but a murderer. I'll never take over for you. I'm nothing like you. Nothing!" had stayed with him. One year later, his grandfather was dead. Then, six months after that, Jahi Berber, Assefa's father, had done the one thing he'd sworn he would never do. He'd taken over for his father.

Assefa continued to smile at the detective, angering him the longer Assefa refused to be baited.

"Look, Mr. FBI man, she broke up with her dickhead of a boyfriend a few months back, and I don't want you bothering her. I see the way women swoon all over you. Wherever I take you, women seem to find their way to your side. She doesn't need that shit."

Why did he even bother having a normal conversation with the detective? The man was stubborn at best, irrational at worse. And Assefa was pretty sure the woman in question wouldn't appreciate Mike sharing details of her private life with a stranger.

"You have it all wrong as usual, Mike. Just because women find me attractive doesn't mean I date them, and it sure doesn't mean I have sex with them." He felt his good-natured mask slipping just a bit. He didn't take kindly to being insulted, having his character impugned by someone who knew nothing of him beyond the superficial. "I'm not like that. I haven't even met this mystery woman and you're already warning me to stay away from her."

"Look," this came out as if Mike was speaking to a recalcitrant child, "her name is Dr. Sanura Williams. She's a child psychologist and professor at the University of Maryland. She's the daughter of my deceased best friend and very special to me."

Mike leaned forward and gave Assefa the type of stern glare all males feared when meeting their girlfriend's father for the first time. "Don't let my age and gray hair fool you, son. I won't take shit from any man who hurts my goddaughter, including a hotshot special agent."

Assefa returned the man's glare, breathing deeply. It wouldn't do for him to get into a stupid altercation with the detective. The man enjoyed pushing his buttons and testing the boundaries of his patience and control. But Michael McKutchen would have to do more than insult

Assefa to break his self-control. Many had tried, but none had suc-ceeded.

"Dr. Peterson is waiting for us in the morgue," Assefa said calmly. "His preliminary report is ready, and I don't want to be late." Assefa stood, and walked around his desk and to the closed door. He opened it, glanced out, and then back at Mike. "Let's go, so we can get this over with."

Mike rose slowly, his back and knees clearly bothering him, but Assefa cast his eyes elsewhere, feigning ignorance, a pride-saving gesture for an older man not ready to be cast out to pasture.

"What's the rush, kid? The killer made sure they aren't going any-where."

No, they weren't. Callous but true.

Five minutes later, Assefa entered the morgue, instantly assaulted by its spiritual coldness. It held an eerie stillness that chilled him to the core, reminiscent of too many burials he'd attended before moving to the States. No matter how often he'd rubbed against death, he never got used to it. He just wasn't built that way. His older brother, Razi, viewed this as a weakness, "a character flaw not becoming of a male from the House of Berber." Assefa disagreed, for only a person who despised senseless death, understanding the far-reaching tentacles of its toxic vapors, could battle the malignant forces of the world.

He said a brief prayer to Anubis, the Egyptian god of death and dying, to watch over the lost souls who'd found their way to the emotionally sterile room, where bodies, not people, were dispassionately dissected and discussed like a frog in a high school biology class.

"Dr. Hudson Peterson, you remember Special Agent Berber?" Mike said, having moved into the chilly room and in front of Assefa.

"Of course, I remember him. He's the only one brave or crazy enough to work with you, Mike. Nice to see you again, Agent Berber. I wish the visit were upstairs where it's bright, warm, and free of dead bodies, rather than down here where it's…well, *not*."

"I thought you liked working with the dead, Hudson," Mike said glibly. "The dead can't complain about your bad jokes or poor surgical skills."

The medical examiner laughed, and Mike continued, one inappropriate joke after another.

Assefa observed the interplay; the men were obviously friends on some bizarre level only they could explain. They exchanged a few more jabs before the doctor returned his attention to the purpose of their visit.

Finally, if he had to listen to one more joke that began with "An ME and a homicide detective walked into a funeral home…" he would've been forced to rip their tongues out and throw them in a jar of formaldehyde.

"So, the FBI thinks our guy is a serial killer?" Dr. Peterson asked of Assefa, the doctor's mind back on the case.

"The victims in Maryland fit the profile of other victims up and down the East Coast we've documented over the last three or four years—Central Maine, Cape Cod, Manchester. There are probably more victims than we're aware of, but this killer seems to go on a rampage for a few months, then goes underground for a year before resurfacing in another locale. It's made tracking the murderer near impossible. By the time we realized a string of murders in a state weren't random and were likely our perp, they have sated their appetite and disappeared. If it weren't for Mike and his ability to connect the dots, we would've been too late again. We need to catch the bastard before they disappear again, Dr. Peterson. So, what have you found?"

"As you've probably already surmised, the cause of death of the Ferrells mirrors the other victims. So look at this." Dr. Peterson waved his hand, encouraging Assefa and Mike to move closer to the corpse on the table.

Dr. Peterson pushed a gloved finger into a gaping hole in Mrs. Ferrell's neck. "My finger is where her carotid artery should be. The carotid artery is a paired structure for both sides of the body. The right artery starts at the brachiocephalic trunk, whereas the left originates from the aortic arch in the thoracic region. At the lower part of the neck, the two carotid arteries are—"

"Speak English, Hudson, and stop trying to impress the kid with your medical lingo. If you've forgotten, some of us haven't been to medical school or have an egg fuckin' head."

Unfortunately, this wasn't the first time Assefa had witnessed Mike rudely rebuke a colleague. When Mike joined the force, a high school education had been considered good enough, not the bare-bones, minimal requirement it currently was. Over the years, his street smarts and military experience had made him a prime candidate for a detective. Unfortunately, while Mike was the best detective in his unit, the younger detectives had letters behind their names, giving them knowledge of modern technology and forensics that Mike struggled to stay abreast of. The fact that a few of those guys were arrogant jerks who treated Mike like a useless relic did nothing to endear them to the older detective. Assefa assumed this accounted for the detective's lousy attitude toward any twenty-something with a degree. Of which Assefa was guilty on both counts.

"So, what you're saying, doctor, is that the Ferrells are missing the two common carotid arteries, and judging from the size of the hole, the internal jugular vein and vagus nerve as well."

Assefa stepped closer to the bodies to get a better look.

"Is the kid right, Hudson?"

"Yes, it's as if she was mauled. Here, take a gander at this." Hudson lifted Mrs. Ferrell's right wrist to the men. "The superficial veins of the upper extremity have been ripped and partially removed. Here as well," he noted, pointing to the torn and battered region around the pale woman's heart.

Dr. Peterson covered the body with a white sheet, grabbed a manila folder off his spotless, metal desk, and handed the preliminary report to Mike. "Here's the most interesting part, assuming I can trust my calculations." He gave the bodies a thoughtful look. "Based on their height and clothing size, my estimation of their weight is probably ninety-five percent accurate."

"What in the hell are you babbling on about, Hudson?"

"Ah, yeah, right. Where was I? Oh, yes, while blood makes up about eight to nine percent of a person's body weight, the Ferrells had far less when I examined them. So, for example, a woman weighing, like Mrs. Ferrell here, approximately one hundred and ten pounds, should hold about three point five quarts of blood. But when she was brought in, at least half of that was missing. So even taking into account the blood found at the crime scene, that's still not enough to account for how much is missing."

Dr. Peterson scratched his head, black hair thick and a bit untamed. "Now, what kind of killer removes almost two quarts of blood and takes arteries and veins as souvenirs?"

A sadistic one.

"Your results reflect the division's findings, Dr. Peterson. Unfortunately, I've seen this before." *Too many damn times. Too many kills. Too many victims. Must stop him. Put the beast down like the rabid dog it is.* "I am surprised the girl survived, though. The killer doesn't give a damn about slaughtering children. It's killed minors before, in the same brutal manner. 'Mauled' is apt to describe what happened to the Ferrells and the other victims. Elizabeth Ferrell is one lucky little girl. She—"

"*Lucky*?" interjected Mike. "I don't know how lucky she is after having her parents drained dry like a cold beer by some…some…fuck, I don't even know what to call someone who would do something like that." One thumb gestured in the direction of the two covered bodies. Then that thumb joined the others and formed an angry fist.

"A demon. A monster. The devil. Take your pick, detective, and you'll be right. Elizabeth Ferrell may not feel lucky now and won't for a long time. But her life was returned to her. It has meaning she is too young to appreciate or see."

"Oh, for the love of Nostradamus, don't tell me you're one of those people who believes everything happens for a reason and God works in mysterious ways or some other bullshit."

"I see why you can't keep a partner. Who would pair themselves with a foul-mouthed, I'll-offend-anybody-who-doesn't-think-like-me runt of the litter like you, Mike?"

Assefa knew all too well the pain of losing a parent at a young age and the subsequent despair that gripped a child's heart and mind. Mike may have lived through a war and seen unimaginable atrocities, but he lacked spirituality, faith. In times of great sorrow, faith was often a beacon of light, a critical support used to guide one through the cavernous melancholy of their mind. It happened to Assefa. He believed it could happen to Elizabeth Ferrell.

"My point is, Mike," he said, swallowing the urge to choke the narrow-minded detective with his nineteen-eighties ketchup-stained tie, "we give our lives purpose, and without it, there's no meaning or form to it. Parents help shape and give meaning to the lives of their children. Elizabeth Ferrell's purpose for living was brutally taken from her, and she's probably struggling to find meaning in what's left, questioning why she survived but her parents did not. So don't make light of something you know *nothing* about. I can only hope that your goddaughter can help."

Dr. Peterson grinned and patted Mike on the back. "Well, they finally found someone you can't bully, eh, Mike. And he can walk, talk and think at the same time."

Mike smirked.

Dr. Peterson laughed, showing two rows of gleaming white, perfectly set teeth.

"You're incorrigible, Hudson. I can't have these kids thinking they can show me up. As it is, they call me 'old man Mike' behind my back. I hate being called old. I may not move as well as I used to, but I can still kick ass if I have to. And right now, I feel like kicking some serial killer's ass."

"Finally, something we can agree on," Assefa said, his expression grave, and tone as deadly as the killer they tracked.

The men walked to the door. Mike exited, but something compelled Assefa to turn and take a final look at the serial killer's handiwork. He had told Mike the truth. He knew precisely what he was hunting—a monster, a demon, but most assuredly *not a man*.

"Where's your goddaughter? She's late, and I don't have all day to wait around for her when I could be interviewing the child myself."

Assefa had spent the day gathering reports on the new case and cross-referencing them with the other Baltimore City murders. He and

Mike had interviewed the Ferrells' neighbors, none of whom had heard or seen anything out of the ordinary. No screams, broken glass, or crying. No strange cars or people. Nothing but dead ends.

A complete waste of a day except for the man who found Elizabeth Ferrell walking in the middle of the street late at night. In fact, the elderly man had to swerve his car to avoid hitting her.

"I thought she had been stabbed or shot," Mr. Diamond, the neighbor, had told Assefa. "She was covered in blood when I managed to calm my nerves enough to get out of the car and see what I almost hit. My wife says I'm too old to drive. Bad eyes. Bad reflexes."

Assefa already knew the girl was unharmed. Mike had taken care of that end of the case.

"Why were you out so late, Mr. Diamond?" Assefa had asked, pleased the Diamonds had invited him into their air-conditioned home, providing a temporary escape from the warm April day.

"I forgot to pick up my heart pills. The drive-thru pharmacy on Foster Avenue is open 'til midnight. When you get old like me, son, the mind starts to go. Perhaps my wife is right. I probably shouldn't be driving."

"Well," Assefa had said, taking a long drink from the refreshing iced tea, "if you hadn't been out so late, who knows what would've happened to Elizabeth Ferrell."

A couple of hours later, he was wasting time at Johns Hopkins Hospital, waiting for some crackpot doctor Mike recommended. What was he thinking, trusting the detective to find a decent psychologist? She dared to be late. Didn't she understand the importance of this case, the delicate nature of having a child as the sole witness to a murder? But, of course, she didn't, because if she did, the woman would be there, and he would be in the child's room getting the information he needed.

"Calm your nerves, kid, and don't even think about talking with that girl without a professional. Besides, it's only ten after four. Sanura said she would come here after her last class, and College Park is at least sixty miles away. She doesn't work for us. Try to remember that, big man. She's doing me a favor, and you better tone down that FBI attitude before she gets here."

Assefa scoffed instead of unleashing his impatience on a man incapable of appreciating restraint. "You can wait here. I'm going to take a walk."

"You do that. While you're here, consider having a personality transplant."

Assefa ignored Mike's mockery, deciding to stroll away from him in search of the hospital's cafeteria or any Mike-free zone.

Fifteen minutes later, a bottle of cold water in hand, Assefa rounded the corner to see Mike sitting with an attractively slender, brown-skinned woman with shoulder-length hair that matched her complexion. He nearly dropped his drink.

While Assefa's keen eyes easily made out the woman's—Sanura Williams?—black dress shoes and black and gray pinstriped business casual skirt that fell just above her knees, beautifully accenting long, well-toned legs, it was the wild energy from her aura which held him captive and made him her silent, willing prisoner.

CHAPTER TWO

Sanura rushed off the elevator and down a bright corridor with pink, blue, and yellow balloons decorating the walls of the children's wing, bordering a mural of happy children in a park, the sun above affirming their unique place in the world. An illusion, she thought, a beautiful illusion of how life should be for children. The truth, however, rested behind the closed hospital room doors, where reality had long since claimed their innocence.

Her heels clicked with each long stride, her pace hurried, purposeful. Mike only sought her counsel on cases of a unique nature, counsel that was off the record. And she was late. She hated being late, and Mike would worry. Mike constantly worried. He'd probably already called her mother, Makena, or her best friend, Cynthia, alerting them to her MIA status.

Sanura made a right onto another colorful corridor. At the end of the glistening hallway sat Mike, cell phone in hand and an all-too-familiar scowl gracing his aging features. Then, as if sensing her presence, he looked up from his phone, and their eyes met. His face softened, reminding Sanura of the tender heart encased within the detective's tortoise shell of a body.

"I'm sorry I'm late. The beltway was a beast." She bent to give Mike a heartfelt hug, her long arms circling his taut shoulders.

"It's all right. I was just beginning to worry about you, but you showed up before I could call Cynthia."

"You always worry about me, and I'll tell you the same thing I told Dad, and I tell Mom, I can—"

"Take care of myself. I know, but that won't stop me from worrying, so you might as well accept it."

She kissed Mike on the cheek and sat beside him in one of the wooden chairs lining the hallway, conveniently serving as a family waiting area.

"So, tell me about this case of yours, the girl, and what you need me to do." Sanura leaned back in the chair and crossed her legs, seeking a comfort she knew wouldn't last once Mike began.

Sanura listened to the detailed, unabridged facts of the case, having already read reports of the slayings in the *Baltimore Sun*. The gruesome murders headlined every local news program, from the early morning to the eleven o'clock evening news.

She nodded, listening intently to details about Elizabeth Ferrell's horrific night. While Sanura enjoyed using her training to help Mike, she hated when the case involved children, which didn't make sense since she was a child psychologist. Perhaps that was it, she reasoned, as Mike regaled her with one morbid piece of evidence followed by an even more depressing fact. Maybe it took a person who detested even the thought of an injured child to be such a strong advocate for their rights and protection. Sanura wanted to help those lost souls. No, she *needed* to help them, free them from their pain and misery.

So she sat and listened and fought the urge to cover her mouth and squirm in her chair when Mike described the crime scene photos his temporary partner had shown him earlier in the day. And just when she was about to tell him she didn't need to know the coroner's findings, a wave of energy slammed into her, shredding her concentration and dissolving all thoughts of the child and the case. The energy rode Sanura hard. It forced her eyes to close, mouth slightly parting, aura open and alert, searching for the source.

Deep breaths, Sanura. Deep, calming breaths.

With embarrassed concentration, she slowly opened her eyes. A smiling stranger stood before her, a bottle of water in his right hand.

Their eyes met, and another blast of energy assaulted her senses. She didn't close her eyes this time and refused to look away. Instead, Sanura simply absorbed the magical energy, opening her senses and pulling the scent to her. It swirled about her, strong but gentle. While it should have felt strange, as if her body had been invaded by a foreign substance, it simply felt—*right*.

The man's eyes widened almost as much as his nostrils when he inhaled deeply. Still, he only stared, gaze unwavering, eyes sparkling with unasked questions. She had questions of her own, like, had he experienced the odd sensation too? Sanura didn't know. But she had felt it, as strongly as she now felt the heat of his gaze roaming her body, slow and sensual, ratcheting up the indescribable energy between them tenfold.

Damn.

Mike placed himself between Sanura and the fine stranger with the most tantalizing aura she had ever sensed. Mike faced the man, his head craned up to meet the taller man's eyes, a snarl seeping through his lips when he said, "We talked about this, remember what I said."

Frowning, the stranger gave Mike a hard you're-not-worth-my-time look before gazing over Mike's shoulder and at her. His smile returned and settled firmly on her still-seated form. Angling from behind her godfather, the stranger extended his right hand.

"Hi, I'm Special Agent Assefa Berber. I assume you're Dr. Williams, the child psychologist and professor."

Sanura stood and returned the smile. She took the offered hand and shook, trying to ignore his unique masculine scent. The scent went straight to all the right places, subtly finding her genetic code and adding his. *Impossible.* "Yes, it's nice to meet you, Special Agent Berber. Mike's told me so much about you." *But not everything. Not nearly.*

In fact, Mike complained about the agent a lot. To hear him tell the story, his "jackass of a captain" maliciously assigned him to work with "an anal-retentive, smart-ass upstart from a secret division of the FBI." But Sanura knew that was Mike-speak for he was young, intelligent, talented, and didn't put up with the older man's grumpy ways.

The agent gave Mike a shallow smile and nod. Then his penetrating eyes were back on her, the odd warmth of recognition radiating from him too strong to discount. "Call me Assefa," he said, upping the wattage of his smile. And, damn, had any man ever smiled at her like that before, all white teeth and unabashed interest?

She returned his smile. How could she not? "Then you must call me Sanura. Only my patients and students call me Dr. Williams."

By the gods, she tried not to stare, but Sanura couldn't help but notice how tall he was and how devastatingly attractive he looked in his

. . . Ermenegildo Zegna suit? Sanura matched his height with her two-inch heels, making him six feet. She usually removed her pumps as soon as the last student exited the lecture hall, but she'd been in a rush, leaving them on as she made her way across campus and to the faculty parking lot. Now she was pleased she'd forgotten, for the extra lift allowed her to look directly into eyes so brown and luscious they reminded Sanura of chocolate ice cream on a sweltering summer's day—delicious, cool, and never enough.

Sanura made a quick mental inventory of the shamelessly grinning man. Broad nose and strong chin. Check. Long arms and big hands. Check. Full lips and high cheekbones. Check. Muscular form no suit could mask or do justice. Double-check.

Then there was his deep, confident voice and the cultured accent of an intelligent man from northeastern Africa, she surmised. *Maybe Ethiopia or Sudan.* They were a heady combination, reminding Sanura of why she avoided men like Assefa Berber. *Powerful. Relentless. Passionate.*

Sanura swallowed. Hard. She'd never considered herself a vain or shallow woman, but, damn, the agent knew how to make a fine good first impression.

Mike stepped between the two again and cleared his throat. "Now that the niceties are over, can we get back to business?"

With effort, Sanura managed to break the spell she'd found herself immersed in and looked down at her godfather. "Of course. Of course. I'm ready to speak with the girl if she's willing to speak with me."

"Let me check with the nurse before we go in." Assefa granted Sanura one last broad, silly smile before turning and walking to the nurse's station, an adorable swagger to his step.

Sanura glanced quickly to ensure Assefa was preoccupied with the nurse before whirling on Mike, her voice a hiss of sound. "You know what he is, don't you?" It was a statement, not a question. He nodded. "And you weren't going to tell me?" He shook his head. "Is that all you're going to do? Move your head?" He shrugged. Sanura opened her mouth to argue but closed it when she saw Assefa walking back toward them.

"The nurse said Elizabeth Ferrell is awake and calm. So now is as good a time as any to speak with her."

"Good, then let's go," Mike responded, moving surprisingly quickly toward the child's room.

Assefa stepped aside, allowing Sanura to walk in front of him. She sensed his eyes on her and smiled, hoping the view was as lovely to him as he had been when she'd watched him walk to the nurse's station.

A woman could lose herself in such a man, but not her. No, that required something she wasn't prepared to give again—trust. Pity, that. Special Agent Berber seemed like the kind of man who would make a woman *want*…so much more. Too much.

She gave herself a mental shake. Now wasn't the time. No, now was about business, a child, a murderer.

When Sanura entered, young Elizabeth Ferrell wasn't in bed as she'd expected. Confused, she scanned the small hospital room. It was Assefa, however, who found the child. His deep voice cut through the silence, strong chin gesturing toward the closed closet. "She's in there."

"And how do you know that?" came Mike's sarcastic voice, a gritty edge Sanura knew unsettled most men. "Wait, wait, don't tell me. You can hear her breathing, right, Agent Berber?"

"Well, Detective McKutchen, the bathroom door is wide open, and unless the girl leaped out of an unopenable window or is a ghost, it's a safe bet she's hiding in the closet." A calm response from the special agent, a reply that held controlled steel Mike would be best to take note of. But they didn't have time for this.

Sanura shushed the feuding men, walked to the closet, and slowly opened it. Inside, a small girl no older than eight or nine sat. Liberally sprinkled freckles dotted ivory skin. Her curly red, shoulder-length hair looked too much like Little Orphan Annie. The irony of the resemblance was not lost on Sanura. The little girl wore duck-print pajamas, probably supplied by a kind hospital staffer to replace her bloody ones. Mike had shared that grisly detail as well. Elizabeth was discovered bathed in her parents' blood but with no visible injuries to her person.

Poor kid. Her body trembled in the comfortably temperate room. Sanura took her high heels and blazer off and sat beside the fearful girl,

Sanura's back to the men. She reached for her purse and took out a sparkling silver bracelet that hung charms of various sizes and colors. A blue dolphin, pink flamingo, white rabbit, and multicolored beach balls, a vibrant visual meant to tempt, tease, and bring joyful light to the heart of a child.

"Would you like to have this?" Sanura held the bracelet in the palm of her hand. Then, so as not to startle the child, she slowly extended her arm until the hand with the bracelet was right beneath Elizabeth's chin and lowered eyes.

The girl stared at the bracelet.

Sanura waited, knowing nothing good came from rushing a traumatized child, especially an eyewitness to a brutal crime. After all, Sanura was a stranger to Elizabeth Ferrell. And hadn't a stranger just destroyed the girl's world?

Watery eyes gazed upward, pained but hopeful.

Sanura brushed loose curls from Elizabeth's face. "You have beautiful gray eyes."

A timid smile formed, barely there but quite lovely.

"If you wear this bracelet, the killer won't be able to find you."

A shaky, pale hand reached for it, then stopped. "Are you sure? I–I don't want it to find me. It found me before. Nowhere to hide. Nowhere to hide."

Her shaking worsened, punctuated by glistening tears and shuddering shoulders.

With only thoughts of comfort, Sanura pulled Elizabeth Ferrell from the closet and onto her lap. She didn't resist, didn't scream, didn't flail about, didn't do anything other than cry and let a stranger soothe her.

Cradling the child's head against her shoulder, Sanura was reminded of how overcome she'd been as a child when she would scream herself awake from one of her many nightmares. Her parents would come running, worry and fatigue adding premature age lines. Her mother, Makena Williams, would hold Sanura just as she held Elizabeth Ferrell now. Makena would place one thumb at Sanura's nape, the other at her temple, and then press gently while saying, "I've got you, little one. Listen to my heart and breathe."

Sanura repeated those soothing words now, and Elizabeth Ferrell did as she said. The same as the child Sanura had done, following Makena's calming voice, forcing her mind to a task and away from what most frightened her. "I've got you, little one," she repeated. "Listen to your heart, feel it, hold it, see how strongly it beats for you."

No longer crying and shaking, Elizabeth Ferrell's breathing slowed even more. When the child wrapped one arm around Sanura's waist, she silently spoke the final words. The words that always managed to locate a rainbow just beyond her emotional storm. The child in her arms was no different.

They stayed like that for long, uninterrupted minutes, talking in low tones, Sanura pumping soothing energy through their shared touch. It was a small gift but an even smaller sacrifice. Sanura gladly accepted the child's pain and fear, taking it within herself and replacing it with positive, life-affirming energy from Mother Earth. She would dispose of the crippling energy later when she was outside and closer to nature.

Sanura caught Assefa's intense eyes when she and the child finally stood. They were no longer bright with flirtatious mischief but cool and serious.

The eyes of a man who wants answers.

"She likes to be called Betsy," Sanura informed the men, holding Betsy's hand as they made their way to the bed.

Sanura lifted Betsy to the bed and helped her pull the covers up her chest. Little hands gripped them, tightly holding the sheets to her chest, a shield of woven cotton and little-girl faith.

Sanura wished she didn't have to do this now. However, she'd learned from Mike that the sooner a witness was questioned the better. Their memory would be more trustworthy hours versus days later. Yet a child was a special kind of witness, their immature minds more fragile than that of an adult. But the men behind Sanura needed information, and Betsy was the only one who could give it to them, no matter how fragile and frightened she may be.

Sanura retrieved her purse from the floor and fished out a four-by-five notepad and a golf pencil, giving both to Betsy. "Can you draw me a picture of the person who hurt your mommy and daddy?" Sanura asked in her best soothing voice. The one reserved for her most delicate of patients.

Betsy tentatively took the items from Sanura. Then, with all the enthusiasm of a student sent to the principal's office, the child drew her parents' killer. Once finished, Sanura handed the drawing to Assefa. "Give me a few minutes alone with her. I won't be long." She gestured for the door and waited for it to close before returning her focus to the little girl.

"You're a strong and brave girl, Miss Betsy Ferrell. Your parents would be very proud of you. I can see you're special."

Her little nose wrinkled, and her eyes squinted, giving Sanura an appraising look. Then, after a few seconds, she hunched her shoulders, satisfied with whatever she saw in Sanura's eyes.

"I'm not supposed to tell or show," Betsy said in a soft, unsure tone.

Sanura touched Betsy's baby soft cheek. "I know. My parents told me the same thing when I was your age."

The girl's eyes piqued at the admission. This time, her smile was wide and reached her eyes. "You're like me?"

"Yes. When it's safe, I'll take you to a school where there are others like us. So you'll be among friends. My sister is the principal of the lower school, and she'll make sure you continue your training." She pulled Betsy into an embrace, then made her a promise she damned well intended to keep. No matter what she had to do. "I won't let anything happen to you. Wear the charm, sweetie, and never take it off, not even when you bathe."

Betsy nodded in relief but clung to Sanura. "She saved me." A whisper.

"Who saved you?"

"The goddess. She protected me from the monster."

Sanura pulled back to look into her eyes. Betsy's gray orbs were as clear and sure as her voice. "Which goddess came to you?" she questioned, thinking a child's active imagination combined with great fear could cause such an illusion.

"Sekhmet," she answered in a low, conspiratorial tone, although it was only the two of them in the room. "She told me to not be afraid. That demons and ghosts exist, but she would protect me."

Sanura believed in the goddess Sekhmet, of course. The same way Christians believed in God or Muslims in Allah. But she'd never seen or spoken with the goddess. Sanura smiled at Betsy and kissed her forehead. It was about faith. Who was she to question the child's story? Betsy Ferrell survived the attack, and no one, not Mike or Assefa, had an explanation. "Get some rest. I'll check on you tomorrow."

It was getting late, and the child appeared exhausted. While she slept, the charm bracelet would keep the monster away. But nothing could stave off Betsy's nightmares. Nightmares Sanura knew would come for the child.

The way mine used to come for me.

"Tell me a story."

"A what?"

"A story. My ma always tells me a bedtime story before tucking me in and…"

Lower lip trembling, Betsy stalled.

Sanura knew the choke of such pain, the hole a parent's death left, the emptiness and hunger that followed. Betsy's eyes started to water. Sanura glanced at the closed door. She was stuck between a child in mourning and the emotional freedom the hallway offered. Unwilling to leave the little girl in such a wretched state, Sanura moved back to Betsy's side.

"I don't know any bedtime stories."

Betsy gave Sanura a pleading smile, irresistible for the desperate heartache behind the sweet appeal. "All grownups know bedtime stories. Didn't your ma ever tell you a story when you were a kid?"

"Yes." There was one story she knew far too well. "Okay, there's a story my mother used to tell me."

Looking pleased with the response, Betsy slid her tiny frame over in the bed, glanced at the now-vacated space, then back to Sanura.

Taking the hint, Sanura moved into the abandoned space. She propped her back against the elevated bed and soon found the curly-red-haired girl snuggled against her. This was as close as Sanura wanted to get to motherhood. There were certain places she just wasn't ready to go. Hell, forget motherhood; she didn't think she was even prepared for a serious relationship. Being burned by a guy tended to have that effect on a woman.

Sanura smiled down at the child and began her tale. "Once upon a time, in a faraway land, there were many gods and goddesses. They created all that is and would be. The gods wielded immense power, some more wisely than others. However, there was one among them who was lonely. Her name was Yemaya, the goddess of all the oceans. She yearned for a family of her own, so she blessed herself with a daughter and named her Mami Wata. Like her mother, Mami Wata had the power to control bodies of water and the creatures therein."

She looked down at Betsy again and noticed that the child's eyes were closed. She started to roll her over when the girl shifted. "Tell me what happened next with the water goddess."

Remembering how she used to wrap her arms around her mother's waist and refuse to go to sleep until she regaled her with at least one story, Sanura figured Betsy wouldn't allow her to leave until she finished. So, she forged ahead like a new mother wading in knee-high water.

"Five hundred years passed, and Mami Wata became extremely powerful, encouraging mortals to turn away from other gods and worship only her. Sometimes this was achieved through the granting of prayers, but other times it was accomplished through force. Another five hundred years passed, and Yemaya created another daughter to balance out her first. This daughter she named Oya, goddess of wind, thunderbolts, and fire.

But Mami Wata wasn't pleased with her younger sister because humans began to flock to Oya. Viewing this as an act of betrayal, Mami Wata sought revenge against the humans. She brought forth floods to destroy their civilizations and caused droughts, denying the much-needed life source for themselves, their crops, and their livestock. This

angered Oya, who, in turn, used her powers to return peace to the ravaged lands. With this, war broke out between the sisters, each trying to
control the other, the land, and its people. The war raged for years until
Ra, the sun god, and his daughter, Sekhmet, intervened. It was decreed
that every five hundred years, a servant of Mami Wata and a servant of
Oya would be born to finish the goddesses' battle for Earth.

According to the legend, each goddess selected a strong witch family to pour her power into. Each woman born into that family was
endowed with powerful magic that remains dormant until passed to that
one witch who will serve the goddesses when the time comes. In the
case of the fire witch, her natural ability to cast fire spells would be
greater than the average fire witch's. And because she is a servant of
Oya, she would also have the ability to cast wind and lightning spells.
As far as the water witch, legend notes the monstrous power of this
witch. She doesn't acquire control over any other earth element. Still,
her ability to manipulate water spells was five times that of any other
water witch, more than enough to flood a city the size of Baltimore."

This time when she looked down, Betsy was asleep, her deep, heavy
breathing a sign Sanura could cautiously dislodge her body from the
child's firm grip. Sanura placed a pillow where she'd been, and Betsy
snuggled tight around it.

Sanura placed one finger on the bracelet and another against the
pulse point of Betsy's wrist and then shifted into her second sight. The
magical vision allowed her to see the aura signature of another preternatural. Elizabeth Ferrell's aura was thin but steady, typical for a witch
as young as she. As she grew older, her aura would strengthen and
thicken, able to hold and sustain her increased magical energy. But right
now, it was just a thin white layer, almost translucent in its paleness.

Focusing on the pulse point and the underdeveloped aura, Sanura
closed her eyes, called up an old but familiar spell, and whispered the
words of protection. The bracelet began to heat, magic slipping from
Sanura into the dangling charms. The warming magic slinked around
Betsy's wrist, sizzled, hissed, and then disappeared into the jewelry,
now tuned to the girl's aura, making for an even more potent charm.

Satisfied, Sanura pulled the covers up Betsy's shoulders and quietly walked toward the door. Dimming the lights, Sanura whispered a soft, "Goodnight, little sister. May the gods continue to bless and watch over you."

When she exited the room, Assefa and Mike were staring at the picture Betsy had drawn, their faces grave, no words needed. They knew what it was.

"We need to talk," she told the men.

"I know," Mike quickly responded. "How about we meet Makena for dinner, and the three of us discuss the case?" He reached for Sanura's arm, making a clear effort to exclude Assefa.

She moved her arm out of his reach. "No, Mike, all of us need to talk. Mom's house is a good idea. We can speak freely there."

"Are you sure you want to do this, Sanura? For the love of Dr. Phil, you only just met the guy, and you want to bring him into our inner circle. You're taking a huge risk, and for what? Because you think he's good-looking with all those muscles and fancy clothes?" Mike snorted. "Well, let me tell you what, there's a whole station full of women who would agree with you. That doesn't mean you drop your common sense and start thinking with your girlie parts."

She did find the special agent attractive, disturbingly so, but that didn't mean she'd lost perspective. "You know me better than that, and I don't appreciate the deliberate insult."

She looked at the man they were talking about, and that damn wickedly pleasant scent came again, smacking against all of Sanura's well-fashioned walls. She shook it off and refocused on Mike. "Assefa can be trusted." And how she knew that as fact, Sanura couldn't reason. But every pulse point in her body responded to his. Her aura tingled, and her mind reeled from the possible implication of the introduction of this stranger into her life. But he could be trusted. That she knew with eerie certainty.

"We need to speak candidly, and this hospital isn't a safe place for us to do that. My mother lives about twenty-five minutes from here. If you're free, I would like to invite you to dinner."

Assefa glanced at a disgruntled Mike, irritation clear in his cool, brown eyes. But when he turned his gaze back to her, there was a softness, warmth even. "Thanks. I haven't had a home-cooked meal in a long time."

Mike shot boulder-sized daggers at them, but Sanura and Assefa turned away from him. Neither spoke a word as they walked to the elevator, not about Mike, Betsy, the killer, or the energy pulsing between them. Sometimes when there was just too much to say, it was often best to say nothing.

CHAPTER THREE

Two hours later, Assefa arrived at the Williams residence in Mount Washington, a small suburb of Baltimore City. Among the tree-lined, winding streets Assefa drove down were professional offices, shops, boutiques, galleries, and cafes. At the intersection of Falls Road and Kelly Avenue, he saw a sign for a natural food market. He took a left onto Kelly Avenue and made a mental note to check out the market on his way home. Assefa needed groceries, and he wasn't so much of a bachelor that he couldn't cook a decent meal.

The monotone female voice of the GPS alerted him to his arrival. Assefa pulled in behind what he knew to be Mike's please-wash-me-I'm-owned-by-a-slob mobile. The car was a beautiful dark-green 1972 Mustang Convertible that, unfortunately, had Mike McKutchen as its owner. Assefa shook his head, closing the door to his car when he exited. *What a waste.*

Assefa hustled up the steps and to the front door. He rang the doorbell, feeling late, although Sanura hadn't given him an exact dinner time. In case he got lost, her mother's address and Sanura's cell phone number were all she'd given him before Mike virtually dragged her away from him and toward her car. But it was now almost seven o'clock. He grimaced, thinking he'd probably taken too much time in the shower and finding something to wear that wasn't one of his standard blue or black suits.

Assefa reasoned he'd lost all his cool points earlier in the day when he'd mindlessly found himself staring at Sanura Williams. Even now, he could feel the residual energy from her aura tempting him with its rhythm, causing his own to respond in a primal mating dance. No woman had ever tapped into that special part of him. The part that was sacred and dangerous. It wanted more, wanted the dance Sanura's aura dangled in front of him like a sensually gyrating Hula dancer, lei about her neck, arms open wide and inviting.

Assefa raised his finger to ring the doorbell for a second time when it slowly opened. The flood of light from the inside settled upon an attractive woman in her mid-fifties. She could easily pass as an older version of Sanura in height and body structure. The woman smiled warmly, eyes reflecting the same quiet strength as Sanura's.

"I'm Makena Williams. You must be Agent Berber." Makena stepped aside and allowed him to enter the single-family, brick home.

"I am. Thanks for having me to your home." He took the offered hand in a soft handshake.

Makena frowned and looked at their joined hands. Then, belatedly realizing his unintentional insult, he tightened his grip, giving her a respectfully firm handshake. Appeased, she gave a slight nod and smiled.

Makena Williams was a beautiful woman, her full-tooth smile reminding him of a toothpaste commercial actress. *Definitely one of her finer features, but far from her only one.* Like Sanura, she had long, unprocessed dark-brown hair that framed an oval face and fell over lean shoulders in a thick wave of barely-tamed curls. Dressed in gray dress slacks and a black and gray abstract designed blouse, the professional clothing did nothing to conceal the older woman's full-body appeal. An appeal his widower of an uncle, even his uptight father, would find impossible to resist. Yet, her knowing brown eyes and powerful aura signature gave him pause. She knew. *Two minutes in her presence, and she knows what I am. Damn.*

He followed Makena into the dining room where they joined Mike and Sanura. Mike extended Assefa his usual frown, but Sanura greeted him with a pleasant, sensuous smile. With that, he knew his manly primping wasn't wasted.

She bit her bottom lip and gazed at him with unguarded attraction, then immediately lowered her eyes when she realized she'd been caught. Clearly discomfited, Sanura looked away, excused herself, and walked into the kitchen, followed by her mother a minute later.

"So?" Makena asked, turning the sink faucet on full blast before taking a seat at the kitchen table across from Sanura.

"Don't start, Mom."

"What? Start what, Sanura? I only said one word." Amusement glinted in Makena's eyes.

"Don't play innocent with me. I know you."

"And I know you." Makena pointed toward the dining room. "We both know what he is. I assume you invited Assefa here to tell him who and what you are, so you and Mike can drop the façade and get on with capturing the monster responsible for killing our sisters."

"That was the plan, but—"

"No buts, it must be done. He's the one, and you know it."

"I also thought Richard was the one, and look how that turned out."

Makena scoffed. "Richard was never the one. You only wanted him to be. He's a nice man, and he made you happy for a while, which made me happy. But I never once thought he was the one. If you're honest, you'll admit this and allow yourself to move on. For Oya's sake, Sanura, he isn't even one of us. It would've been impossible."

Sanura sighed, conceding the last point. In fact, it was the reason why they were no longer together. Sanura hadn't dated anyone since Richard had broken up with her. Her trust factor was low, and the thought of opening herself up again to get to know someone new, taking with it the possibility of having him hurt her too, was a risk Sanura wasn't sure she could take.

"For our people, sweetheart, there's only one other. We can spend a lifetime trying to find that one. It's built into our DNA, whether we like it or not. And once we've found our other half, we cannot deny it. You feel the pull as much as he does. If he didn't, he wouldn't be here. Working in concert, it'll take both of you to capture and vanquish the predator."

Makena reached across the table and covered Sanura's hand with her own. "Your father was my one, and I was his. I had to leave my home in Nigeria, and your father had to leave Trinidad before we found each other in America. Circumstances will always draw the two together. It's the way of our kind. The reason why we've survived. The two of you are destined to save the world from the one who would see us all in a watery grave."

"I know, but what if he doesn't understand or accept the truth?" Not that she truly accepted the truth herself.

"You think he doesn't understand, Sanura, but I'm sure he understands more than you're giving him credit. His inner spirit is as powerful and fierce as your own. I could sense that the minute I opened the door and let him in. Of course, you must go through with the ritual to be sure, but you know this already."

She did know, but her mother always had a gentle yet unrelenting way of helping her shine light in corners she would otherwise leave dark and unexcavated.

"Give him a chance. If you don't, you may not live to regret it," Makena said, sounding far too prophetic.

" 'Live to regret it'?" Sanura repeated, arching an eyebrow. "Don't be so dramatic, Mom. Having been an attorney, I would've thought you could come up with a better cliché than that."

Makena arched an eyebrow of her own before bestowing Sanura with her haughtiest judge glare.

Sanura smiled and squeezed her mother's hand. "What would I ever do without you?"

"Let's hope, for both our sakes, you won't have to find out for a very long time." Makena returned the smile. She looked at her daughter thoughtfully, then a wickedly playful grin crossed her lovely face. "So what does he smell like? And don't tell me he isn't emitting his pheromones, or you haven't detected it because I won't believe you."

She rolled her eyes at Makena's annoyingly smug smile, not wanting to admit her almost overpowering physical attraction to a man she'd met a few hours ago. Finally, after a few silent moments, Sanura huffed and gave in. "Fine. He smells of a sweet spice."

To Makena's credit and Sanura's relief, her mother allowed the subject of pheromones to drop, chucking Sanura under the chin instead in a way that told her she was pleased with her response. "Now, let's rejoin the men before Mike burns a hole in Assefa with his overprotective eyes and sends the man running."

Doubtful.

Nothing about Assefa screamed "coward," although, she admitted, retaking her seat at the table, his aura thrummed with the tempo of a sensitive soul. But a sensitive soul was not the same as the soul of a coward. A man with a coward's soul would turn tail and run, whereas a man with a sensitive soul would search out every avenue of peace, using violence as a last resort, then praying for his soul and the soul of his enemy when he delivered the killing blow.

After dinner, Makena discreetly excused both herself and Mike, leaving Sanura and Assefa alone in the dining room. Assefa had caught the show of motherly matchmaking, but he was unwilling to complain. Makena had created an opportunity for him to get to know Sanura better without Mike's watchful and intruding eyes. Obviously, Sanura also picked up on her mother's intention, her lively conversation at dinner now replaced by uncomfortable silence.

"Would you like to go for a walk?" Assefa asked. He stood then moved away from the table.

"Yes." Her relief was immediate and clear. She stood, leading the way from the dining room to the front door.

It was a balmy spring night, stars overhead casting a hypnotic glow, making Assefa feel as if he was the right man, in the right place, at the right time. He spared Sanura a quick glance. *With the right woman.*

They walked the block length in silence, Assefa patiently waiting for Sanura to work out whatever was on her mind. He had a good idea of what she wanted to say to him. Assefa had, after all, overheard most of her conversation with Makena. However, he would've heard more of the discussion if Mike hadn't diverted his attention with station gossip. The detective knew all—affairs, financial troubles, health problems. Apparently, nothing escaped the man's keen eyes and ears, and it was equally as apparent that Detective McKutchen enjoyed being the teller of other people's not-so-secret secrets.

And then there was the running water. Assefa almost laughed at that trick. Makena Williams really did know what he was, and apparently, she'd learned a lot being married to a man just like him. He wondered how many times she'd used that strategy on her husband. Many, Assefa assumed, for the water pressure in the kitchen faucet was abnormally strong, the sound distractingly high. But he'd managed. He always managed.

As they made their way back toward the house, Sanura finally spoke. "I gave Betsy Ferrell a charm bracelet today to hide her scent so the killer can't find her." She paused, nervously biting her bottom lip, then tucking an errant strand of hair behind her ear.

"I know."

Apparently, that wasn't the answer she expected to hear from him, her arched eyebrows and frown saying as much. "You know?"

"Of course, I know, Sanura. When I first entered the room, I cataloged her scent and knew she was in the closet. Deductive reasoning aside, my sense of smell is almost 100 percent accurate. When she came out of the closet, her scent had changed, and a sparkling charm bracelet dangled from her wrist."

"What do you know of charms, Assefa?"

He smiled a little more than necessary, then took her hand and softly kissed the top. "I know Mike wears a silver necklace he tries to hide under his shirt to cover the unique scent all dwarfs emit. I know Dr. Peterson wears a silver watch to cover his were-leopard scent." Although Assefa's other talent allowed him to figure the ME out, there was no need to get into all of that tonight. *Keep it simple, Berber. Don't frighten the woman.*

Sanura jerked her hand from his. "You seem to know a lot, Agent Berber." Then, after a brief pause, she asked, "Do you have a profile of me?"

They stopped at the bottom of the steps to Makena's home. At 10:00 p.m., the street was quiet and free of people. Save for the porch lights from the neighboring houses and a few streetlamps, it was dark and still, just the two of them. But Assefa didn't need light to see

Sanura's beautifully unsure face. He had excellent night vision. All of his kind did.

Assefa purposefully reclaimed her hand, hoping she would relax and open up to him. But she didn't know him. No more than he knew her. Yet there was something unexplainable between them, something that, upon first seeing her, had forced its way into him and had refused to leave. So it was with him now, lurking deep within, setting up stakes as if it planned to lay claim and never leave. The most disturbing thing was that it didn't feel like an uninvited guest. It had knocked, and without conscious thought, Assefa had opened his soul and let it in. *Let her in. Insane.*

"I know you value your privacy and safety against those who may harm you or your loved ones," he said, pleased she hadn't yanked her hand away from him again. "I know you use your knowledge and skill to create charms to protect the prey from the predators. Your mother probably wears one as well, but not in her home. Or maybe," he said, scratching his head, "she took it off to test me. I'm sure you told her about me before I arrived."

She briefly lowered her eyes. He was right.

"I also know that while I can't see it, you also wear a charm. Although, I suspect it does more than cover your scent." The last part was a guess. He had no idea why that baseless claim poured from his mouth, although something within him knew it to be true. "Finally, I know only one species can make charms like the one you gave to Elizabeth Ferrell."

She tensed.

He paused.

A car sped up the street, making a rolling stop when it reached the stop sign.

Assefa tightened his grip on Sanura's hand and gave her his most charming smile. "Only a witch could make such a charm. And only a powerful witch could make a charm potent enough to fool the predator we're after." He wanted to say more but knew tonight was too soon for full disclosure. Sanura was already skittish. He didn't think it wise to push.

Keeping her hand firmly in his own, he began walking the few steps to the front door, eyes, nose, and ears alert to any potential danger. He sensed nothing but the now-familiar magical energy wafting from Sanura—his witch. *Not yet, but soon.*

"You figured all that out about me in the short time we spent together at the hospital?" she asked when they'd reached the last step, the house quiet, serene energy surrounding it. *Witch magic. Subtle but effective.*

"You smelled wrong. I was drawn to you the minute I saw you, and there's only one reason to explain our instant connection."

She gave him a guarded but sincere smile, which Assefa latched on to as a good sign. He leaned in close and gave her a short peck on the cheek. "Prepare the ritual, and I'll be there." He gave Sanura his "friend plus" smile. The plus was whatever she wanted to add to what he hoped was the beginning of a friendship.

Sanura said nothing, just stared at him.

He nodded to the front door. "Go in, so I can make sure you're safe."

Without a word, Sanura dug in a metallic leather handbag she wore crossed over her body and removed a ring of keys. Then, unlocking the wrought iron security door, she entered the house and closed the door behind her. But she didn't move; she simply stood there watching him with big, brown eyes. And Assefa couldn't help but wonder what she saw when she looked at him. *A threat? A protector? Her mate?*

Assefa could still feel her eyes on him as he walked down the steps and got into his car. Once settled, he turned around to see the front door closed and Sanura gone. He put his key in the ignition, turned it to the right and the engine came to life, strong and smooth. He touched his lips, still feeling the warmth of her cheek, and wondered if he'd finally found his witch. He then grimaced, knowing everything in their world would change if she were his witch—*the* witch. Then again, maybe not. *Perhaps it's just a myth, a story passed down through generations and told to children as bedtime stories.*

The presence of the goddesses in the skies above the Eastern Seaboard of the United States stilled to a slow, churning trot. The temperature rose and fell with each spoken word. The clouds performed a waltz, gliding counterclockwise around the newly formed electrical discharges all gods emitted while in their natural, fluid state. There were no bodies, human, animal, or otherwise, just neutrons, protons, and electrons, forming the basis of all that was, is, and will be. The gods were life, down to the tiniest atom and molecule, and mortals, their creations, were life incarnate, born from their essence, their breath. But the essence was borrowed, limited, and once the last of it flickered, stilled, and then returned from whence it came, the body it inhabited was no more.

"The child told Sanura I saved her." The voice was hard, barren, and dry, not unlike the hyper-arid region of the Sahara Desert with its infrequent rainfall, dry valleys, salt flats, gravel plains, and stone plateaus. It was the voice of a formidable military commander who had seen much, done much and did not give a damn about either beyond the rules of engagement and the win.

"We knew she would. Was that the only reason you saved Elizabeth Ferrell, Sekhmet, when you allowed all the others to perish at the hands of that monster?" Unlike the first, this voice was gentle and soothing, emphasizing each word with wispy leisure that had nothing to do with age but cold, wet power.

"They died for a good cause, Yemaya, you know that. But it took a child, a mere fairy of a girl, to do what all the others failed to do."

"And what was that?"

"She displayed proper respect as all good children should. Prayer and faith, Yemaya, saved the child, nothing more, nothing less."

"I should have known."

"Yes, it is why we are here and continue to exist."

"How long before Sanura and Assefa are ready?" Yemaya asked of Sekhmet.

"Give them a few weeks to get to know each other and bond. Then we will start."

"My daughters are growing anxious. It has been five hundred years, and they have waited patiently, but I fear they will not wait much longer."

"I know. Tell them to set the board with their pieces and make a move or two, but nothing more than that."

"But you just said Assefa and Sanura are not ready."

"They are not. Yet no explicit rule says we cannot intervene as we see fit. Ra set this in place and charged the two of us to serve as referees, but I take no true pleasure in using good witches and their familiars this way."

The goddesses vanished before the clouds finished the last rise and fall of the waltz, taking their electrical energy pulses with them.

CHAPTER FOUR

"It's an adze," Assefa said once he closed his office door behind Mike and Sanura, assured no one would overhear their conversation. And this conversation, the one that had nothing to do with hunting a human serial killer, was a discussion best left to those who understood the world the way it truly was. To date, Assefa hadn't bothered with full disclosure, he and Mike dancing around each other and the truth. *Time for that to end.*

Mike and Sanura both nodded their heads at his proclamation.

He gestured to the two wooden chairs in front of his desk. They sat, Mike's face hard and grim, Sanura's beautiful but equally grim.

"What do you know about adzes?" Sanura asked Assefa after he rounded his desk and settled in his leather chair.

The image drawn by Betsy Ferrell of her parents' killer was on his desk between them. They all stared down at the grotesque creature. The girl's drawing was surprisingly detailed and lifelike, a natural artistic ability her parents probably encouraged. But who would encourage young Elizabeth Ferrell now? Who would watch her grow and marvel at the critical milestones yet to come?

Anger suddenly surged within Assefa. He wanted the adze dead. Not caught, not locked up, just dead, as dead and cold as all its victims. His inner cat snarled, reflecting Assefa's vicious thoughts of death and loss of control. But he wouldn't lose control. He was no longer a boy unable to master the beast within. No, those days were long behind him.

Assefa leaned back in his chair and forced his mind and body to relax. "The adzes of folklore were vampiric beings described in tales of the Ewe people of Ghana and Togo. They were said to have the body of a large bat, but they could also transform into a human form which, I'm sure, helped them blend into society or escape capture when they hurt or killed someone."

He sat forward, thinking, forearms going to the desk. Then he looked at Sanura, the beauty who had invaded his dreams last night, who was invading his rational mind right now. He kept looking at her, and then she subtly shifted. Assefa's eyes slid from her face, down her breast, and to her thighs. Bad idea.

Sanura crossed long, delectable legs, her ivory dress formfitting and sexy as hell. It was bad enough the woman wore her hair up today, revealing the slender column of her neck, the sweet-smelling body oil she'd apparently dashed there affecting more than just his nose. So, he pretended not to notice how appealing she looked today, how mouth-wateringly delicious she smelled, and how much he wanted to mark her tender neck with tiny nips of shifter possession. But she'd said something, adding to the conversation he'd started. He should probably listen.

"My Nana told me adzes once could possess witches with or without their consent. For some reason, the adze could only possess a witch, never a warlock. These adzes would commit horrible crimes while in the witch's body. This resulted in claims of witchcraft in every village an adze would pass through. The witches were hunted and persecuted, but the adze would take leave of the body before the witch was captured, leaving the witch to pay for the crimes committed by the adze."

"Our killer can't be an adze, Sanura," Mike said, grabbing the drawing from Assefa's desk and glaring down at it. "Based on our interviews of family, friends, neighbors, and coworkers, there's no evidence any of the victims did or said anything or went anywhere that would've been considered uncharacteristic prior to death." He raised his eyes to Sanura. "I know the girl's drawing may look like an adze, but she's clearly mistaken."

"No, Mike, it's you who's mistaken. Don't forget that I spent most of my teenage years studying under my grandmother in Nigeria. She taught me the old ways of my people, making sure I knew all the popular and obscure legends. There is more to the adze myth that's not found in most of the texts witches study today."

"I believe I know the extended version of the adze story." Sanura gave Assefa a puzzled look, and he understood her confusion. Not wanting to reveal too much of his heritage in front of Mike, Assefa added, "I'll explain everything to you after the ritual. For now, listen to my version of the story and feel free to jump in if I miss something important."

"After the ritual," Sanura repeated, confirming his statement as a promise.

"If the ritual goes the way I believe it will, we both will have a lot to share, starting with where on your body you keep your charm hidden." This he said with a flirtatious grin, followed by an open, lazy gaze of appreciation at those enchanting, crossed legs of hers. Damn, the woman needed to stop waving those mile-highs in front of him or start wearing pants. Instead, she uncrossed her legs and demurely returned his smile.

"Would you two stop that?" Mike slammed his fist on the desk to get their attention. "Just tell me the damn story before I get any older or throw the hell up."

"I've known my share of dwarfs, Mike, and none of them were as rude and impatient as you. If we didn't have to work together, this scene would play out very differently."

Assefa never had in the month and a half he'd known and worked with the detective led on that he knew Mike was anything other than the full-human he pretended to be. Assefa knew it wasn't a good idea to antagonize a dwarf, especially one who carried a sidearm, but he was tired of all the cloak-and-dagger nonsense. Assefa was convinced Mike knew he was more than an ordinary FBI agent, and if they were to capture the adze he had to be himself, even if that meant going toe-to-toe with an old war veteran.

The room suddenly filled with hearty laughter. To Assefa's surprise, the snorts were coming from Mike. He slapped the desk again with his strong fist. "Well, it's about damn time you stopped pussyfooting around with me and manned up. I wondered how long it would take you to play that card. Hudson and I have a running bet on how long it would take you to admit you knew what we were, revealing your own secret in the process. I knew Sanura's father too long not to be able to spot one of you. You had me the first two weeks. You're exceptionally good at covering your tracks, pretending you don't hear, smell, and see things you shouldn't. But I haven't survived this long, kid, without having picked up a thing or two along the way." He laughed again.

Astonished by Mike's reaction, Assefa rubbed his temples in disbelief. The man was annoying as hell. True, he was an excellent detective but also a pain in the ass.

It was unusual for dwarves to take jobs that kept them out during the daylight, preferring night jobs, which suited their light-sensitive eyes. Mike was different from an ordinary dwarf in so many ways, which was probably why he was friends with a leopard shifter posing as a full-human medical examiner and had a witch as a goddaughter. Assefa knew he could trust Mike with his secret no matter the frostiness between them. Dwarves would go to their graves fighting before they would betray their friends or dishonor themselves with weakness.

Finally getting his laughing and coughing under control, Mike asked with more interest than Assefa knew he meant to reveal, "How did you know about Hudson and me? No one makes a finer scent disguise charm than Sanura, yet you made us. And I want to know how you did it."

Taking pleasure in Mike's discomfort with being "outed" by someone he considered a rookie, Assefa made the man squirm by refusing to give him what he wanted. It was petty, he knew, but the dwarf needed to learn a lesson.

Ignoring Mike, Assefa returned his focus to Sanura and his story. "After the witches went underground, no one was left for the adzes to possess or spiritually feed off. So most of them died out. When only a handful remained, the witches finally felt free to resurface. They formed secret societies and developed ways to hide their scent from all predators, especially the adzes. However, a few determined adzes survived, as the myth goes, and they kidnapped a young witch. They tortured the poor girl, demanding she reveal the whereabouts of her sisters, but she refused. As punishment, they bled her to death and drank her blood."

Assefa paused, waiting to see if there was something Sanura wanted to add. She said nothing, just continued to sit quietly, her hands clasped in her lap, lips glossy and full, legs crossing yet again.

Assefa sat back in his chair, the desk hiding Sanura's runner's legs from him, all sleek muscle and unstated strength. "The strangest things started happening to the adzes once they tasted witch blood for the first time. They became stronger, bigger, and more aggressive. They were suddenly able to do all that the witch could do whose blood they consumed. They could cast spells and turn curses. They realized they had the world at their fingertips, and it was all due to the blood of the very beings they'd possessed for years."

"Okay, I think I see where you're going with this," said Mike, "but why keep killing witches if one or two would do?"

"Because," Sanura interjected, "the effect is temporary. Only a true witch can hold and wield such power permanently. For them to maintain the level of strength they probably desired, they had to keep going back to the source. You see, Mike, adzes can live for a very long time. Witch blood sustains them, increasing their lifespan to a near-immortal state. An adze can live hundreds of years with a regular supply of our blood. But such a long life comes at a price. From what I was told, they must hibernate once or twice a year, and the bloodsucking adzes we know today are all that's left of their race. The younger adzes have forgotten how to possess a witch, which would allow them to live a relatively normal life. Now all they know is the blood. They will seek it out at all costs."

Mike snapped his fingers. "That is why there have been lulls in the murders, and the FBI struggled linking victims from different states and over long periods."

"Exactly. Adzes only need to feed for a few months at a time, but it's enough to maintain them throughout their hibernation. The blood also enables them to take human form, so they can walk among us and hunt," Sanura said, her voice clear, words precise as if she was delivering a mini-lecture.

"They hunt independently of each other and are very competitive," Assefa said. "They know no loyalty and have been known to kill their own during a blood frenzy. They believe blood and bone marrow contains a witch's essence, which is why Dr. Peterson found wounds to the victims' neck, wrists, and chest. All major blood arteries that can be easily ripped while in bat form."

Assefa grabbed a bottle of spring water from a side drawer, twisted off the cap, and drank. He pulled out a second bottle and a BCPD mug and offered them to Sanura. She took both, her soft, dainty fingers coming into contact with his, sending a spark of magic through him.

"Aren't you going to offer me a bottle of your precious water, kid? Or do I have to bat my eyelids and cross my legs to get your attention and a bit of hospitality?"

Assefa wondered how upset Mike's chief would be if he snapped the detective in two, shoved him in the trunk of his Mustang, and sank both in the Chesapeake Bay.

"The Preternatural Division of the FBI," he said, not offering Mike a anything, "has been tracking this thing for a while, building up a reliable profile. Unfortunately, this is the closest we've come to capturing it. We must catch and destroy the adze before it goes underground for hibernation, and we're forced to wait months before it reappears."

They all sat back in their chairs.

Assefa contemplated what lay before them. Until the last few years, all the adze attacks he'd ever heard of or read about had been mere attacks. It made no sense for them to kill off their primary source of blood and power. No witches meant no more adzes. This change in the adze's hunting pattern bothered Assefa. Adzes were depraved creatures, sure, but they were also survivalists. And survivalists never threatened their own future with shortsighted acts. *No, there must be more to this. I just need to figure out what.*

The next day, Sanura was back in Assefa's office. But, surprisingly, Mike was nowhere to be found, and neither was the good-looking special agent. He'd stepped out ten minutes ago and had yet to return.

She sat in the same chair as she had yesterday. It was wooden but not as uncomfortable as it looked. Besides, she didn't want to get too comfortable. She didn't particularly like coming to the police station or the courthouse where Makena worked, for that matter. *Too much resid-ual energy from the auras of criminals and the mentally unstable.*

Sanura reached into her satchel and removed her iPad. She might as well get some work done while she waited for Assefa to return.

Five minutes later, there was a knock at the door. Sanura stood. "Enter."

The door opened, revealing a surprised and pretty Latina with jet-black hair pulled into a tidy bun at her nape. No necklaces. No rings. No earrings, not even studs, just a sturdy leather watch that looked as if it could take a beating adorned her stalwart frame. Dressed in navy-blue dress slacks and a white button-up blouse, the woman's large brown eyes skated over Sanura, taking her measure in a quick but thorough perusal.

"Where's Special Agent Berber?" the woman asked. But Sanura heard the unspoken question of, "Who are you?"

From a badge she'd seen most of her life, like Mike, the woman was a detective, her shield attached to the side of her belt. Almost as tall as Sanura, the detective radiated self-assurance, her posture steel-pole perfect.

"I'm not sure, but you can leave him a message."

"With *you*?"

Ah, tone there. The detective may have carried a weapon, but the full-human would do well to not awaken Sanura's fire spirit.

Sanura grabbed a pad and pen from Assefa's desk, then turned back to the detective. "I was thinking you could just write him a note." She extended the items to the woman.

Apparently, that steel pole went beyond her back because the detective didn't move, smile, take the items, or do anything other than stare at her. Sanura smiled. The woman clearly had no job-related busi-ness with Assefa. The attractive detective was on a different sort of business that apparently required a fresh coat of lipstick and too much perfume.

"Please let him know Detective Pilar Salazar stopped by."

"No problem, detective, nice to meet you." *Not that we introduced ourselves.* But Sanura knew when a woman thought another was encroaching on her territory, whether she could rightfully claim the male in question or not. And Sanura couldn't help but wonder if she was referring to herself or Detective Salazar. Because no, she didn't like the crestfallen way the detective looked when she'd discovered it was Sanura, not Assefa, on the other side of his office door.

After the detective finally left, two more females came in search of the special agent, one a secretary, the other a sergeant, both gorgeous, both disappointed Assefa wasn't in his office. But, like Detective Salazar, no real message other than that they had "stopped by" and would "return later."

Nearly fifteen minutes later, Sanura sensed Assefa. His energy reached her before his words of, "I apologize for having kept you waiting."

Assefa breezed through the open door that Sanura had decided to leave open after the fourth woman had come and gone. Assefa's office, a revolving door of Baltimore's finest beauties, she thought with an unreasonable flint of annoyed jealousy.

"You know," he said, closing the door, "Mike McKutchen may not last until his retirement."

Sanura didn't even want to know what her godfather had done.

Instead of sitting in what looked to be a comfortable leather chair, Assefa sat in the wooden chair beside her.

"By the time I reached the men's locker room, Mike already had Lieutenant Ramsey on the ground and in a chokehold. Mind you, Sanura, Ramsey could pass as a thirty-something Bubba Smith." Assefa smiled, a faint dimple coming to life as he told his story. "Mike was on Ramsey's back, a speck of snarling, cursing detective. I didn't wait to hear how it started. I knew I had to end it before Mike did something he would later regret."

Sanura closed her mouth when she realized it hung open. Gods, Assefa was right; Mike wouldn't make it to retirement if he kept getting into fights with men half his age and triple his size. As much as she hated that Mike had managed to get himself into yet another altercation, Sanura had to admit how pleased she was to have this moment of alone time with Assefa.

"Anyway, I managed to get Mike to let Ramsey go."

"You what?" No way had he talked Mike down from the ledge. The only person she'd ever known capable of pulling the dwarf back from the brink had been her father.

Smiling at her, Assefa wrapped a lock of her hair around two of his fingers and twirled. A naughty twinkle appeared in his eyes, and Sanura knew this was what had drawn all those women to this tiny, tackily furnished office. This man, this amazingly handsome man who, when he smiled at a woman, made her feel as if she were the only star that mattered in a world full of beauty and wonder.

"I told Mike that if he didn't let the lieutenant go, I would whisk you away to my secret lair, seduce you, and name our tenth child after him."

Who knew a jaw could drop so far or blood could rush so fast to a witch's face?

He tightened his fingers in her hair. "Would you like that? To go away together and forget all this madness with the adze?"

Gods, the man's voice was breathy sex, his fingers masterful negotiators. His lips were warm and soft when he leaned in and kissed her cheek. "Maybe not ten children, though. Two or three would do nicely. By the way"—he released her hair— "you blush so prettily you make a man want to beat his chest, throw you over his shoulder, and find the nearest cave."

She shoved against him, all hard chest and immovable body. The man was unbelievable, taking far too much delight in unsettling her.

He jumped to his feet and was behind his desk and sitting in his chair before Sanura could reel in her thoughts of being seduced by Assefa Berber.

"I asked you here today to talk to you about the magical wards I sensed around Makena's house when I was there for dinner."

How did he switch gears so fast, flirty and fun one minute, all about business the next? Hell, Sanura would swear she still felt his fingers in her hair, gently tugging, pulling her closer. "Umm, yes, the wards. What about them?"

"With very few exceptions, all of the murders we've been able to link to the adze have taken place at a witch's residence."

Sanura sorely hoped he wasn't about to ask her for the names and addresses of her sisters. Even for their own safety, that she absolutely could not do. The Witch Council of Elders would bind her magic for such a betrayal, no matter how well-intentioned.

She crossed her legs. "Not all witches are capable of setting magical wards, Assefa. We don't all have the same interest in magic or the same level of spellcasting ability."

"Exactly my point. It's my theory that this adze hunts not only witches but magically weak witches."

She'd had the same thought. No way should the Ferrells have been killed in their own home.

"From the coroner's findings and my own suppositions, I think it's safe to conclude that Mr. Ferrell was killed first. Fast and first."

That made a lot of sense.

"From my experience, even witches who don't practice the craft still use magical wards to keep evil from entering their home."

"True. High-level witches often aid their lower-level sisters in magical workings. It's a given in our community."

"Exactly, yet that only holds true if a low-level witch is part of a network that includes strong witches. But I sensed no magical wards while in the Ferrell residence."

"So, you think the adze targets weaker and isolated witches because they have little to offer by way of defense? And, of course, they would be more vulnerable in their home and at night."

"Yes, you see where I'm going with this." His smile said he was pleased but not surprised by her quick deduction. "Any were-cat worth his fangs would've put up one hell of a fight. Even the smallest cat shifters, the clouded leopard, would've damaged the adze."

But Mr. Ferrell had been found in his human form. She'd seen the photos. When were-cats died, they stayed in their final form—human or cat.

"I'll probably never know precisely what happened that night with the Ferrells, but my gut tells me the adze went for Mr. Ferrell first, not giving him the chance to shift. He was the biggest threat, the only object standing between the adze and its prey. In human form and without a weapon, a shifter would be easy enough to kill."

The frown that followed said that fact didn't sit well with the special agent.

"Adzes are swift and not without stealth. By the time Mr. Ferrell heard or smelled the monster, it was probably already in the house, if not his bedroom. There was evidence that Mrs. Ferrell fled, but it caught and dragged her back into her bedroom."

Sanura had seen those photos. Streaks of blood had led from the Ferrell's bedroom and halfway down the hall. *She'd gotten no farther.* Sanura knew what was at the end of the hallway. *Betsy's room. She was trying to protect her daughter.*

"What I'm getting to, Sanura, is that you have an in with the local witches. That's your community, your family, and your friends. I don't know how long it will take us to track down the adze. But, in the meantime, I don't want more victims."

"So, what exactly are you asking?"

Assefa took a sip from a mug sitting on his desk. "I want you to get the word out in your community. Wherever your sisters live or congregate, the buildings need to be protected by magical wards. The scent disguise charms are useless if the witch removes them in her home, thinking she's safe behind locked doors and windows."

"Nowhere to hide." Betsy's words. Betsy's horror.

"You're right; people become lax in their home."

Another sip. "I know I'm asking a lot."

No, he wasn't. It was a good plan, one the Witch Council of Elders should've thought of. Makena was the exception. She'd never taken any chances with her family's safety. For as long as Sanura could remember, Makena always used magical wards, even when the family went on vacation and stayed in hotels. As a child, Sanura always thought her mother a tad paranoid. Now, however, Makena's inherently cautious nature just might save lives.

"I really think—"

"I'll take care of it."

He put his mug down. "Just like that?"

She nodded.

"And here I thought I would have to sweet talk you."

"No sweet-talking necessary, special agent." Although Assefa did it exceedingly well. *Too well.*

"So, we have a plan." They did. "Good." He stood, then walked around his desk and to her. "I'm starving; what about you? Have you had dinner yet?"

She shook her head, tongue and stomach suddenly tied in knots. Had he just asked her out on a dinner date, or was he simply a hungry shifter who wanted to eat while discussing the case?

He looked down at her expectantly. "Unless you have other plans, Dr. Williams."

"Well, umm, I don't. I really thought we would just—"

"Good. Then, unless you're opposed to my company, I'd suggest we leave now."

He grabbed his suit jacket off the back of his chair and a manila folder from his desk.

"Why are you in such a rush?" She put her iPad back in her satchel and slung it over her shoulder when she stood.

"Do you know how long it takes a dwarf to get out of handcuffs?"

"Huh?"

"Approximately twenty minutes." He glanced at the black-and-white clock on the wall. "It's been exactly seventeen, and I intend not to be here three minutes from now when your godfather breaks free."

"Y-you locked Mike in handcuffs?"

Assefa opened the door and quickly ushered her out, taking her hand in his.

"Of course, I locked the detective in handcuffs. How else do you think I prevented him from going for my…?" He glanced down at his pants. "Maybe not ten, Sanura, but I intend to become a father one day." He winked at her.

Sanura blushed. Again.

Still holding her hand, Assefa led her onto an elevator.

"Oh, there you are, special agent."

And that was the voice of the lovely Detective Pilar Salazar, standing in the back of the elevator, lipstick still shiny, perfume still cloyingly strong.

"Is there something I can help you with, detective? I was just heading out for dinner."

"Well, I…" She glanced down at the hand Assefa still had interlocked with Sanura's. "Umm, well, it was nothing important, Special Agent Berber. My mistake. I didn't understand earlier."

"Mistake? Understand what?"

The elevator stopped on the second floor. Detective Salazar got off, but not before taking one last admiring look at Assefa.

"What in the hell was that all about? And why did my office smell like a Macy's perfume counter?" He nearly snarled the words. "I can't stand all those scents. They drive me crazy."

The elevator dinged, and they got off on the first level.

Oblivious to the women in the lobby giving him sidelong glances, Assefa pulled Sanura to him. "Your scent, on the other hand, I could breathe in all day. Even if it isn't your true scent."

Unsure what to say to that, Sanura said the only thing she could think of, revealing none of what she truly felt. "I know of a charming Italian restaurant not far from here. Let's go."

CHAPTER FIVE

"Remember, oral reports are due in two weeks. Check the Blackboard site for additional resources. It's been updated, and I expect you all to use the discussion forums to run ideas by each other. Some of you are still trolling and need to join the discussion before I start docking points. It isn't much of a community if all of you don't participate and participate often." Sanura smiled at the sea of youthful faces, hoping she'd kept the annoyance out of her voice. Her students, while technically adults, were still young, some on their own for the first time, not quite ready for the responsibility of being college students. But the semester was nearly over, and she'd made the same announcement and warning many times. Not that she would lower grades, but that wasn't the point. With her gentle, albeit repetitive chide, she dismissed the class, only to see a smiling Assefa at the back of the lecture hall.

"How long have you been standing there?"

"Long enough," was his playful reply, smile as broad and charming as ever. His walk down the steps and toward her was full of a were-cat's confidence. A confidence that was endearing and sexy without being arrogant or manipulative. Nothing was calculating about Assefa Berber. On the contrary, his aura radiated honesty and integrity in equal measure. But there was also a controlled fierceness about him that left an indelible streak of roaring energy through his aura signature.

"Long enough for what?" Sanura asked, warming to his game, squelching her initial surge of embarrassment at being caught in teacher mode.

"Long enough to see you're a woman of many talents and that ninety percent of your students are male." He gave her a flirtatious wink, snagged her short-sleeve suit jacket from the back of her chair, and helped her into it.

"Are you always so observant?" She began packing her leather satchel, storing a heavy Introduction to Psychology text on the bottom before sliding several of her students' papers on Sensation and Perception on top.

Sanura knew all about sensation and perception. Assefa's striking eyes and voice sent way too many sensations through Sanura, feelings she wasn't sure she was ready to explore. Yet the more she was around him, the more she wanted to…well, the more she wanted.

"You know I am, and if I were eighteen again, I would definitely enroll in your class, Dr. Williams."

She gazed at the tall man in his dark-brown eyes, overtly glistening with humor and attraction. "And you would flunk my class, Special Agent Berber, because you prefer your own rules and like to be in charge."

Assefa relieved her of the satchel and gave Sanura one of his award-winning smiles. "On the contrary, Professor Williams, I was an excellent student and always received straight A's. Besides, I can follow the rules quite well when provided by the right person, under the right circumstances, while wearing little to no clothing. And"—he leaned in to whisper— "I don't always have to be in charge. In fact, it's better when the woman takes the lead. Don't you agree?"

His question burned against her ear, heating her body and mocking the lie she kept telling herself. *He's just a nice guy. I don't want him for myself. Liar. Liar.*

Sanura gently pushed Assefa aside and walked past him, hiding a flushed smile. He had a way of getting to her, taking obvious delight in embarrassing her with his blatant flirting. And Sanura had a way of bashfully diverting her eyes and nervously tucking a strand of hair behind her ear whenever he did so. This was their game. They'd been playing it for the last two weeks while they searched for the adze's hideout.

But she couldn't bring herself to move beyond the flirting stage, no matter how her body reacted to him. He seemed perfect, perhaps too perfect. Too good-looking. Too charming. Too intelligent. Too…Hell, Sanura was making excuses, and she knew it. No one was perfect, and Assefa wasn't the problem. *I am.* No matter how much she enjoyed his company, Sanura used the light flirting to keep Assefa at arm's length without closing the door of possibility. She may have been gun-shy, but her parents hadn't raised a fool.

"Are you coming, Don Juan?" Sanura reached back to grab his hand.

Assefa happily took the offer and gave it a soft, teasing kiss. Sanura stared into his eyes again, feeling the heat between them rise, their shared energy starting to coalesce around them. He stepped nearer, closing the short distance between them. By the gods, the man was handsome, with a rugged body that fit enticingly into an exquisite suit.

A hand going to her waist, he drew her even closer, and she went, too caught up in their shared energy to do anything but follow his lead. A large, gentle hand rose to a shoulder, a cheek, her nape. Sanura wet her lips, unconsciously mimicking Assefa. She stood there, frozen, mesmerized by the man. His intention was clear—Assefa's lips just a silent wish away.

Their lips met, and magic whipped across her senses, flooding her aura with sweet, hot pulses of pleasure and power. But it was just a barely-there taste, a flirtatious tease, like the man himself. Yet that little bit made her feel—

The doors to the lecture hall opened. Assefa pulled back, followed by an unmistakable growl, all his sweetness and softness evaporating like an untamable mist.

Moment lost.

Sanura stepped back from Assefa and looked over her shoulder to see who had interrupted them. Perhaps one of the freshmen had left a cell phone or iPad. But when she turned, it was no freshman standing at the top of the stairs who'd let in the intrusive beam of light. No, it was the man she'd least wanted to see, especially now.

Assefa released her hand, stood tall and firm, and turned into the stoic FBI agent right before her eyes. Sanura knew the look, the posture, the attitude. She'd seen it many times over the last two weeks, never directed at her but at others. Shifters were proud, protective, cautious, always sniffing out danger, preparing to defend themselves or those under their care. But the visitor wasn't dangerous, just Sanura's ex. The man Mike disdainfully referred to as a "dickhead." Unfortunately, he'd turned out to be precisely that, though she'd sooner walk over broken glass than admit that to Mike.

Sanura watched Richard Houghton walk down the steps. He was a light brown-skinned African American dressed in black khakis and a red, black, and white Maryland Terrapins polo shirt. Houghton's face was a poor mask for the bothered look Sanura could see in his pale brown eyes. She'd avoided his phone calls for the last couple of months, failing to return his messages requesting to speak with her. So today was the first time he'd taken the initiative to make the trek across campus. Now that he had, Richard was suddenly face-to-face with a man he'd never seen his former girlfriend with before, jealousy evident in his stiff frame and quizzical eyes. Those eyes kept moving from Sanura to Assefa and back again.

I really don't need this, not now, not when I have bigger things to deal with than a jealous ex who has no right to be jealous at all.

Seconds crawled by, and Sanura realized neither man intended to make the first move by way of introductions. Now she was the one who felt bothered, but good manners kept her from telling Richard to go the hell away. Sighing, she stepped between the men. "Special Agent Assefa Berber, this is Professor Richard Houghton. Richard works at the university in the math department. Richard, Assefa is an FBI agent temporarily assigned to the Baltimore City Police Department. He works with Mike."

Sanura continued speaking, filling the silence with her rambling, then wondered why she was nervous and acting like a woman in a love triangle. She'd only just met Assefa, and they weren't officially dating. Nor was she still involved with Richard. This was stupid.

The men grumbled something Sanura couldn't make out, and honestly, based on the glares that passed between them, she'd rather not know.

Assefa looked dangerous in his custom-made suit, the jacket perfectly covering his sidearm, with no lump or bulge to reveal what lay beneath. But it was there, she knew. The agent was on duty and would have his weapon on him. But Assefa was a weapon with or without a gun. *Claws and fangs.* Yet the concealed firearm posed no true threat to Richard. Assefa was the real threat, his dignified calm scarier than a big cat's roar of possession, marking, and claiming, none of which he'd done to her.

Did she want him to? Was that what she truly desired? To be marked by his beast? And would his beast be strong enough to accept her own? *To get close to the fire and not fear it...fear me?*

"Sanura, I was hoping to speak with you, but I see you're busy," Richard finally managed to say. "Maybe we could talk over dinner tonight? I could make reservations at your favorite restaurant. We could go dancing afterward if you like. I remember how much you like to dance. How well we danced together." It was a hopeful, if not arrogant, request. Richard's eyes slid to Assefa and then back to her, a proprietary gleam that leisurely swept over her.

Sanura narrowed her gaze at Richard, not appreciating what he was attempting to do. Yet, before she could think of a polite way to decline and prevent Richard from further antagonizing a man who could rip his throat out with one well-placed swipe, Assefa whispered a quick, "Don't let me interrupt. I'll see myself out," in Sanura's ear. No, that wasn't what she wanted, but Assefa had returned Sanura's satchel to her. She wanted to say something to him, to replace the ice wafting from his aura with the heat they'd shared only five minutes before.

But she said nothing, just stood there numbly and watched as Assefa walked up the stairs and out of the lecture hall as quietly as he'd entered. He'd driven to College Park to see her and hadn't even had a chance to tell her why, and now he was gone. And the special agent had taken something with him, something fragile, new, and wholly unexpected.

But he *had* left. Assefa had looked at Richard and turned into an unemotional slab of marble. Territorial by nature, were-cats ceded to no one unless it was in their best interest to do so, or they had no genuine stake in the claim. Perhaps the special agent had no genuine interest in pursuing a witch who dated full-human males. A full-human male, like Richard, who'd just deliberately taunted Assefa with their past relationship, implying that perhaps it wasn't past at all.

Angry, Sanura swung her gaze back to a smugly smiling Richard. "What can I do for you, Professor Houghton, that couldn't be accomplished with a phone call?" And it was all there, in Richard's pompous gaze. She'd been such a fool. *Should've listened to Mom and Cyn. And, damn it, I shouldn't have let Assefa walk out of here thinking there is something more between Richard and me than there actually is.* Glaring up at Richard, Sanura could no longer deny the source of the barrier she'd erected around her heart, keeping fear in and Assefa out.

"Don't be angry, Sanura. I only wanted to talk with you, and I didn't think what I had to say should be said over the phone. In-person is always the best approach for these things, especially since you haven't found the time to return not one of my phone calls."

No, she hadn't. If Richard hadn't shown up today, Sanura would've continued to avoid the man and his calls. *So why in the hell has he been calling me anyway? Guess I'll find out whether I want to or not.*

"What things? We haven't spoken in months, and suddenly you want to talk. If I remember correctly, you are the one who decided we shouldn't speak anymore. In fact," she said bitterly, "you were the one who decided we shouldn't do *anything* together anymore."

Richard seemed to shift uncomfortably at having his sentiments returned, but his words were milder than Sanura's when he spoke. "I know what I said, but I regret my decision to break up with you. I wasn't thinking straight when I made that decision. I've spent the last few months kicking myself for being such a dumbass."

Sanura had spent the last ten months trying to forget about the man standing before her. She'd analyzed their entire relationship, regretting her choice to be honest with him about who and what she was. *Stupid. Stupid. Stupid.* She suddenly felt weak and hurriedly found a chair to sit in before her legs betrayed her.

Richard followed, sitting next to Sanura and taking her hands in his. They were soft and long like a pianist—delicate and fine, whereas Assefa's hands were large and hardened with old and healing calluses. The type of hands that could tend soil, hold a gun, or soothe a woman's fragile heart and fiery spirit.

"I'm sorry I overreacted." Richard rubbed a thumb over the back of Sanura's hand, the gesture sweet but far too late. "I wasn't prepared for what you told or showed me, and I responded badly. I've had time to process it since then, and now know I have what it takes to make it work. We may be different, but we're alike in ways that matter."

Those were the right words, but she remembered the horrified look in his eyes when she told him she was a witch. *Like I was a crazed monster who ate little children for dessert.* Sanura snatched her hands away, the same as he'd done her when she'd reached for him, trying to convince Richard that being a witch was as normal as being a full-human. That she wasn't evil or hurt people with her magic. But he didn't believe her, his words of, "I don't think I can handle being in a relationship with a person like you," stinging Sanura to her core, shredding any illusions she had of being accepted. *Too different. I'm not even a typical witch.*

"Please forgive me, Sanura. I shouldn't have broken up with you over something so unimportant."

Her mind was whirling, but she heard Richard clearly, the desperation in his voice, the lack of understanding in his words. "Unimportant?" she repeated in a low, angry voice. He had no clue what his rejection had done to her. How hard it had been for Sanura to reveal her secret to a full-human, baring herself for him to see and judge. *And reject.* And now he had the nerve to call it unimportant. More upset than was healthy for either of them, she stood, retrieved her satchel, and started up the stairs, intending to get as far away from Richard Houghton as possible.

Richard scrambled to his feet and rushed after her. "Come on, Sanura, I said I was sorry. Won't you forgive me for this one thing? I know it'll take time, but the least you could do is say something."

Sanura spun on her heels to face her former lover. "Trust me, my silence is far nicer than what I want to say to you. You don't get it, and I won't waste my breath trying to explain it to you." She walked out of the lecture hall, hoping he wouldn't follow but knowing he would.

"Sanura, don't be like that." Richard's long strides made it easy for him to keep up with her.

Not wanting to make a scene now that they were in public, Sanura stopped. She'd run from this for too long, and the psychologist in her knew what had to be done. So she turned and faced her past.

"Damn you, Richard, I was in love with you. I thought I knew your soul. I trusted you. I've never trusted any man other than my father and Mike, certainly not a full-human. But you trampled all over the trust and love I gave so freely. I can handle a man not wanting to date me. But what truly hurt was being rejected by the man I loved for simply being *me*. What you call unimportant is who I am. I broke one of the most cardinal rules of my people by revealing my true identity to someone outside of our society."

And her mother had been royally pissed at Sanura, angrier than she'd ever seen Makena Williams. According to their rules, Makena should've reported Sanura to the Witch Council of Elders. She should've been punished, and Richard's mind magically wiped of the memory. But Makena had kept her daughter's secret. For as much of a stickler of rules as the judge may be, Makena Williams would permit no one to sanction her daughter. Not even the women who governed them. So Sanura was able to keep her shameful secret and Richard his memories. And that was a kindness for both of them, for a magical mind wipe wasn't so precise as to remove a single memory. No, it took chunks, no less than six months. Sanura would've gladly taken her punishment, but why should Richard suffer for her misplaced trust and poor judgment of character?

With unshed tears, she admitted, "As much as I believe in forgiveness, I can never forgive you. And I will never forget the look on your face when you walked away from me, from us."

"Is this about that agent?" Richard asked as if he hadn't heard a word Sanura had just spoken. "I know that type of guy. He's attractive and probably has a horde of women running after him. Those guys don't care about women beyond the joy of the chase and the conquest. They use women and discard them like trash once they've had their fill."

"Like you did me?" Sanura shot back with a wave of anger that told her she needed to calm down. Her loud response garnered them a few glances from passersby. She ignored them, not caring what they thought. She knew she would later, but not now. "You know nothing about Assefa, and don't insult me by presuming the only reason I don't want to rekindle a relationship with you is because of another man. If you'd come to me two weeks ago, before I met Assefa, with the same attitude and misguided thoughts, my reaction would've been the same."

"But—"

"No, Richard, this time I will make the decision, and I've decided you were right all those months ago. We're not suited for each other. You did me a favor, but I was too blinded by love or stupid to realize it. But now I see the truth as clearly as I see you. It's over. Don't come to see me again. Don't call me. Just pretend we never happened."

Sanura walked away from a stunned Richard, a weight slowly lifting off her shoulders. She smiled. The sun was out, and she had only one more class to teach today. But that wasn't until two o'clock. It was a beautiful spring day, and she was ready for lunch. If only her special agent had stuck around, she would've liked to have had lunch with him. Sanura's smile dimmed then, the sun suddenly not as bright, warm, or restorative. And she couldn't help but wonder when or if she would see Assefa again.

He'd waited too long. Dammit, Richard had waited too long to set things right with Sanura. He slammed his office door shut, still seeing Sanura's back when she'd stalked away from him. *Away from me, as if she's the Queen of Sheba. Like I'm nothing but a lowly fuckin' human not worthy of her witch time.*

A second chance. Yeah, that was all Richard had wanted. He'd messed things up with Sanura, he knew. But he'd wanted to give her space, time to calm down and get past the hurt before he sought her out. Hell, for a minute there, he'd considered begging the woman to take him back. *Won't beg. I refuse to beg some stuck-up bitch to take me back.*

Then there was the special agent. The man oozed money and contempt. He'd need to be careful there. His eyes radiated danger. Richard knew the look. *Know it too well.* But he wasn't done with Dr. Sanura Williams yet. *Not even close.*

Richard pushed his desk chair aside, cursing the day Sanura had made her big reveal. *A goddamn witch.* He'd had no idea. They'd dated for months, and Richard had no clue. *The woman sure knows how to keep a secret. And what a secret.*

But he'd played it cool, showed the appropriate amount of shock, even revulsion. Now, however, Richard knew he'd overdone the whole what-the-fuck-you're-not-quite-human response. *Yeah, definitely over the top.*

He should just let her be. Leave Sanura to her coven and her GQ special agent.

Richard slumped in his chair, head going back and reclining against the worn leather. *Can't let her go. I should've never broken up with Sanura. Mistake..*

He closed his eyes, a slow throb beginning to pulse in his head. The warning thump always came first, followed by a stronger, more insistent thud, and ended with an excruciating screech for relief. *Always needing relief. Too much. Never-ending.*

Richard leaned forward and opened the long center drawer of his desk. He rummaged through the desk, shuffling papers and pens, moving aside old flash drives and even older granola bars. *Gotta be in here some—ah, here it is.*

He lifted the red-and-white bottle of aspirin, the paltry weight a pathetic reminder of his painful and odious fate. Richard thumbed the top off, popped three pills straight from the bottle into his mouth, and swallowed the capsules dry. Frustrated, he threw the empty bottle across the room and at—

"Something bothering you, Dr. Houghton?"

Richard's head snapped up. Special Agent Berber filled Richard's doorway, the tiny red-and-white bottle in his large hand, the man's face as stern and intimidating as his voice. Oh, but Richard so did not need to have the FBI on his doorstep. Not good. Not good at all.

Richard swallowed hard, not liking that the man had apparently followed him to his office. Nor the fact that his too-large frame had just casually slid inside the room, closing the brown, wooden door silently behind him as if he was an invited guest.

He was not. *What in the hell does he want?*

Unwilling to be cowed in his own damn office, Richard stood, legs shaky but doing their job. "I didn't hear you knock, Agent Berber."

The man moved deeper into the office, his cold, dark eyes unblinking and focused entirely on Richard. Oh, yes, definitely dangerous.

"That's because I didn't."

Of course, he hadn't, but Richard should've heard something. A footstep. The turning of the knob. Something. *Quiet, sneaky bastard.*

Recalling they were in his domain and that he was a respected professor, Richard squared his shoulders, told his heart to slow the hell down, and returned the agent's unwavering gaze. "If you're looking for Sanura"—he gestured to the shoebox office— "as you can see, she isn't here." Richard gave the agent his best insincere smile. "But I'll be sure to let her know you were looking for her when I see Sanura for our dinner date tonight."

The lie rolled effortlessly off his tongue. But, of course, they always did.

Then the agent smiled—dark, hostile, and all too knowing. But, like Richard's fake smile a moment ago, it did not reach Agent Berber's eyes. It was then Richard realized that he'd underestimated the man. Dangerous wasn't a strong enough word. Not nearly.

Lethal. Yeah, definitely that. Got to be careful.

The agent moved even closer, the wooden desk all that stood between Richard and the deadly predator. And Richard knew a predator when he saw one. Paltry as it was, Richard had never been so grateful for an old piece of furniture.

Agent Berber shook his head before saying with too much certainty, "You're lying." Those dark eyes narrowed. "Try to refrain from doing that again." One large hand landed palm-down on the desk, a soft but resolute movement. "I really don't enjoy such games. A waste of time."

The migraine thudded painfully now. Richard had things to do, none involving an impromptu FBI interrogation. *Play it cool. Just answer the man's questions, so he can leave.*

"What can I do for you, Agent Berber?"

"You can start by telling me what you want from Sanura Williams."

Ah, personal, not FBI business. Good. Richard laughed. "I think that's pretty obvious but also very personal."

The agent didn't move, didn't speak, and just stared at Richard, obviously with no intention of leaving just yet. Okay. Richard shrugged. "If you must know, Sanura and I used to have a thing. We were in a relationship until I screwed it up."

"You want her back." His words weren't a question but a grittily enunciated statement of fact. Hell yes, Richard wanted Sanura back. He'd waited a long time for a woman like her, a woman who could understand a man like him and his unique heritage. "But she doesn't want you back."

Their gazes held, and Richard sensed the tiniest bit of self-doubt for the first time since the agent entered his office. *Good. Chew on that, you big bastard.*

Another shrug. "She'll come around. I'm a patient man, Agent Berber. She's a special lady, but I'm sure you know that already."

No response, not a twitch of the lips, flared nostrils, balled fists, or stiffening of the back, nothing but those damned black eyes of his, relentless in their unforgiving appraisal. *Shit.*

"What are you hiding, Dr. Houghton?"

W-what?

"Not hiding anything, agent; I'm just a man who messed things up with his lady. I want her back, so I guess I'll have to do a bit of groveling." Richard hoped he sounded casual, nonchalant even. "You know how women like to make us jump through their damn hoops just to get them into bed."

Damn, did he growl at me? What in the hell did I say to piss him off?

"Sanura Williams isn't for you, Houghton."

Stern. Final.

"And I guess she's for you?" *Hell no, asshole, she's mine.*

The agent leaned over the desk, his face too damn close for comfort, that growl coming again, low but there. "She was *made* for me."

No, Sanura wasn't. She was Richard's. But the agent's frosty, onyx eyes dared Richard to contradict him.

He didn't. Richard hadn't made it this far being stupid. And to challenge the special agent right now would've been undeniably foolhardy. But, as he'd told Berber, Richard could be very patient.

Agent Berber walked toward the door—*finally*—but turned back to Richard, hand on the doorknob. Chin lifted and the agent . . . sniffed the air? "I don't like liars, Houghton." Another sniff. "And you"—a third sniff— "smell of lies, secrets, and"—a fourth sniff— "something else."

Something else? No way could he smell that. Unless…

Richard maintained his blank expression and sturdy posture until the agent opened and closed the door behind him. Finally, he collapsed, the chair catching him. But there was no comfort there, just cold, stiff leather.

Yes, Agent Berber was dangerous indeed. *Lethal. If he ever found out.* Richard slumped deeper into the chair, unwilling to think what the man would do to him.

But I'm not defenseless. Not some meek, little math geek that can be bullied into submission by the big, bad FBI agent.

Richard sat up. No, he wasn't helpless, and Sanura didn't belong to the arrogant agent. And if Berber thought that macho bullshit would work with a woman like Sanura…well, that showed how little the agent knew the witch. *He doesn't know her at all.*

But Richard bet the agent thought he could protect her, and Sanura was, after all, due for a lesson. He could do that. *I'll show them both.*

Richard smiled, the headache beginning to subside. Soon it would be gone, sated, until the next time. There was always a next time.

CHAPTER SIX

Warily, Sanura approached her mother's home after seeing Assefa's silver Mercedes-Benz parked in front of the house. She wondered if there'd been another murder. Gods, she hoped not. But, expecting the worst, she let herself in, dropping her satchel in the corner of the foyer.

To her surprise, she heard laughter coming from the dining room. Sanura followed the sound of her mother's laughter only to find Assefa sitting at the head of the table, her mother to the right of him. Samuel Williams' chair. *No one has sat in that spot since Dad's death, not Mike and certainly not Richard.*

"There she is, the other half of my heart," Sanura heard her father say, an old memory that haunted and hurt. *"Your mother once claimed the organ as her own, but she had to relinquish half of it when you were born. I'm the luckiest man in the world to have two beautiful fire witches taking good care of me. So don't just stand there; give your mother and me a hug, make a plate for yourself, and then tell us about your day."*

Sanura pushed back the tears that threatened her whenever she thought of her father. It had been three years since his death, the pain of his passing still ripe, still raw. The slow breath she took in was necessary to calm her pounding heart.

Assefa noticed her first, standing when Sanura fully entered the dining room. Although, being a were-cat, she knew he'd had to sense her long before she'd approached. Then she wondered about the acuity of his senses, trying to gauge the strength of the beast within the man. And there was plenty of strength there. *So much power it strums along his aura, a thick, resounding vibration. And his smell is so damn tempting.*

"I didn't expect to see you tonight." Assefa pulled the chair to his left out for her, his words forcing Sanura's mind off of him and back to the realization that her mother had allowed Assefa to occupy her deceased husband's favorite chair.

"Well, that makes two of us." Sanura gave her mother a look she hoped expressed her level of irritation with her interfering.

Her mother smiled prettily. "I invited Assefa to dinner." Makena's innocent smile and tone were wasted on Sanura. "You rarely visit during the workweek, and Assefa has no family in town, so I thought we could share a meal and get to know each other better. Did you know Assefa has an M.A. in biochemistry and just earned his doctorate in criminal justice?"

Sanura returned her mother's smile while cursing Makena's blatant attempt at playing matchmaker. The woman could smooth talk a jury, deescalate a family feud in her courtroom without raising her voice, the use of magic, or the aid of a deputy sheriff, but Judge Williams couldn't begin to spell the word subtle.

"No, but I suspect there's quite a bit about our agent I don't know."

"You only have to ask, Sanura. I'll tell you whatever you want to know. I don't want to erect barriers, but the ritual is necessary before more delicate details can be freely shared."

Sanura nodded. She knew that, of course, she knew. The ritual came first. Secrets. Their kind always kept secrets. They had to be so damn careful. Couldn't let the full-humans know. But she had let one know her secret. *Richard. Damn him.*

"I'll be right back." Sanura walked to the powder room to wash her hands before joining Makena and Assefa for dinner. Everything looked and smelled good. Her mother was an excellent cook. Too bad Sanura hadn't inherited her mother's culinary skills. Because being able to heat up microwaveable meals did not count as cooking. It barely counted as preparation.

"So," she said to Assefa, taking the plate Makena had filled for her. "Thanks, Mom. Tell me about your doctoral program. What was your dissertation topic?"

For the first time since meeting Assefa, Sanura relaxed completely in his company, freely discussing topics she couldn't with a full-human male. Assefa was widely read, possessing a wealth of knowledge from the mundane to the obscure. But, to her surprise, he also had a dry wit. He was charming but not shallow. And he seemed not to notice exactly how even more attractive and appealing he became when he allowed himself to loosen up. But Sanura noticed, finally granting herself permission to give in to the hard-to-deny energy that flowed between them.

She wanted to lay the entire sorry situation with Richard to rest. Yet it kept popping up at the most inconvenient times, preventing her from letting go and moving on. Well, she had let go of Richard. It had taken her some time, but she no longer loved him. Sanura didn't want to be with him. She'd proven that to herself today.

He was wrong for you. But who was right? A were-cat? Assefa? *Only one is ever right, Sanura. You know how it works.* Yes, she did. So did the man with the warm, chocolate eyes laughing at something Makena had just said. If nothing else, Sanura thought, pretending to be paying attention to the conversation and not simply enjoying watching Assefa Berber shed his FBI mask. *The man is walking cotton candy.* Sanura smiled at another joke she'd missed and wondered if she was ready to take a bite out of Assefa's sugary goodness, knowing any cavity she got would be so much worse than anything she'd experienced with Richard. Because she could easily see herself falling—*hard and heavy*—for Assefa Berber. And that sobering thought scared the hell out of her.

Twenty minutes after dessert, ndizi kaanga, made with fried plantains, lemon juice, nutmeg, and brown sugar, Makena cleared the table, refusing the offer of assistance from Sanura and Assefa.

When she rejoined them, Makena gave Assefa and Sanura a more calculating look than cunning. "I'm off to bed, you two. I'm finally going to read *Their Eyes Were Watching God.* That book's been sitting on my dresser for a month, gathering dust. Richard Wright said of the book, 'The sensory sweep of Zora Neale Hurston's novel carries no theme, no message, no thought. In the main, her novel is not addressed to the Negro, but to a white audience whose chauvinistic tastes she knows how to satisfy.' Well," she said, throwing a sly grin over her shoulder as she started to leave the dining room, "I intend to put a little Sweet Honey in the Rock on, read about Janie Mae Crawford, and determine for myself if Wright's criticism of the discussion of race and the use of black dialect in Hurston's work was overly critical or an astute analysis."

Sanura could only shake her head. Makena's words reminded her too much of an African American lit class she'd taken her senior year in college. Makena never failed to amaze Sanura. Depending on how and on whom she used them, her mother's intelligence and near-photographic memory were gifts to be treasured or irritations to be endured.

She watched Makena exit the room and make a right. The hallway led to the stairs that would take Makena to the second level and her bedroom. Two minutes later, a solidly shut door was heard, a door that never required that much force to close.

After the clear dramatics, they moved to the living room, Sanura acutely aware there was no third person for her to play off of. Then the guilt came. She'd ignored it all evening, but with Assefa's sweet, brown eyes gazing down at her, Sanura had to say, "I'm sorry about today. You drove from Baltimore to pay me a visit, and we didn't even have time to talk before we were interrupted." She didn't want to rehash the uncomfortable moment in the lecture hall, but she also didn't want Richard hanging between them. Whatever was happening between them—and, yes, something was happening—Sanura needed Assefa to understand that Richard no longer mattered.

"No need to apologize. I had a status meeting with my division chief in DC, and College Park is almost around the corner. I should be the one to apologize for showing up unannounced and expecting you to drop everything to have a bite to eat with me."

Calm. Flatly stated.

"Lunch would've been nice, but still—"

Assefa waved another apology away and made his way to the front door, grabbing his suit jacket off the coat hook once he reached the foyer. He slid into the fine garment. The movement was graceful yet quick.

He didn't seem upset, but the good humor he'd displayed earlier was gone, the beginnings of that damn mask reforming and slipping back into place. Walls. Sanura hated them. Helped her patients dismantle them. Hell, she had her own. Yet the wall Assefa was so carefully constructing bothered her.

She'd followed him to the door. "Since you refuse my apology, let me take you to dinner tomorrow. Have you been to the Inner Harbor?"

"I haven't had time to take in Charm City, too busy trying to catch that damn adze and too tired to do anything other than sleep on my days off."

"I'll be happy to show you downtown Baltimore, avoiding the strip clubs, of course. Unless you're into that type of thing," she teased, hoping to break through his wall. His shocked expression told her she'd scored a direct hit. "You aren't the only one who can—"

He kissed her.

Spontaneous and shocking, the kiss left her unresponsive.

But as his soft lips gently caressed hers, her lower brain functions finally took over, compelling Sanura to return the unexpected—*but so damn lovely*—kiss. It was a short, undemanding kiss that served more to test the waters than ignite a flame. But he tasted better than any man had a right to. Spice and mint mingled in an exotic cocktail of irresistible were-cat maleness.

Assefa leaned further into her and kissed her cheek like he'd done on the front porch two weeks ago. Then he trailed those plump, sensuous lips down her neck and deeply inhaled.

Sanura's hands flew to his waist and pulled him closer with each maddening lungful he took of her. And he took many deep, arousing breaths that sent an electrical charge cascading through Sanura's body, settling in her core—heavy and hot.

"You still smell wrong," he finally said, head tucked in the crook of her neck, hot breath inviting more than a verbal response. "I need to know what the real you smell like." Not quite a demand but neither a plea.

"That's part of the ritual." She nearly moaned the words as the intensity of their auras so close together increased with every second they stayed in each other's arms. Made worse or better, depending on how she looked at it, each time his tantalizing lips found her pulsing neck.

Basking in their shared energy, she whispered, "Let me see the eyes of your inner cat?" Her tone echoed his earlier request, neither plea nor demand, but an indescribable need.

He pulled her closer to him as if they could get any nearer while fully clothed. Another deep intake of breath and then a slow release before his husky voice said, "That's also part of the ritual, sweetheart."

Sweetheart? Was that a slip? Or had their relationship just gone from idling to second gear? But, more importantly, why did it flow so naturally from his lips and sound so wonderful to her ears?

Not yet ready to release her, Assefa absorbed the magical energy swirling between them for a few seconds longer, wanting nothing more than to give in to his cat's desire to claim, take, and mark. But that wasn't his way, not the way of the man. And for him, the man was always in control. "How much longer, Sanura?" He slid his hands into his pockets, so he wouldn't touch her again. If he did… "How long do I have to wait before we perform the ritual to confirm our biological compatibility?"

"The next full moon."

"There will be a full moon one week from tomorrow."

"I know," she said, the nervous smile that followed a pleasant surprise.

Sanura was different tonight, he'd noticed, more relaxed and comfortable. He'd been taking it slow, not wanting to scare her with his overpowering need to be near her. So, he simply enjoyed flirting and getting to know the mind doctor. He was making slow progress. Today's impromptu visit to her academic lair was a test of his patience and her receptivity.

Then there had been the unexpected arrival of Dr. Richard Houghton. He assumed Richard was the "dickhead" Mike had told him about. The man was fit, built like a swimmer, with long, gangly arms that housed strength and endurance. He could also be considered handsome,

Assefa supposed, if women went for the angular jaw and dimpled chin look. *Obviously, Sanura had.*

It had taken all of his self-control to leave the lecture hall, his inner cat goading him to mark his territory and destroy the challenger. So, the man had walked away. But the cat—yes, the hunter—returned, finding its prey alone and vulnerable.

"After the handfasting ritual, and after we've captured the adze, I want us to take some time to get to know each other." He opened the door for them. They walked out of the house and to his car. "I don't need a ritual to tell me we have a biological connection or that the gods have already decided we complement each other. Even with that, Sanura, we have our own free will. If we decide to begin a relationship, I want it to be because we want to be together, not because biology or the gods say we should be together."

She's made for me. He hadn't meant to say those words to Houghton, but it was all he could do to stop himself from ripping into the lying bastard. And Richard Houghton was most definitely a liar. He'd lied about having a date with Sanura tonight, and Assefa couldn't help but wonder what other lies the man was capable of. What secrets did the professor hold within his mathematical mind? *I'll find out. Know them all.*

Then there was the scent of the man. Something more than human lingered in his pores. This the cat in him knew. But what? *I'll find that out, too. In a few days, I'll know all there is to know about Dr. Richard Houghton.*

Assefa was too good of an agent to delude himself into believing that the investigation he'd begin as soon as he returned home was business instead of personal. Everything with this woman, this witch, was personal. *She's made for me.* Yes, she was.

Assefa drew her to him again, and Sanura casually placed her arms around his neck. "I've never experienced anything like this before, Sanura. I feel a loss of self-control when I'm with you. It feels as if my emotions are in overdrive. I'm used to order and logic, but nothing about this feels logical, but it feels damn right. Do you understand what I'm trying to tell you?"

Sanura stroked the back of his head and neck, intensifying the flood of energy hurdling through him. "I do understand. I can tell you everything there is to know about the ritual from a factual and intellectual perspective, but nothing more. Regarding practical experience, I'll be in uncharted territory, the same as you. My parents shared their ritual experiences with me, but they also told me each couple's experience is unique to the two of them. I can guide us through the technical phases, but the emotional part will have to be dealt with as it comes."

More stroking, then he forced down a purr. His cat was enjoying the beguiling touch way too much.

At least she had that, Assefa thought. His father had told him nothing about his handfasting ritual. There were many things his father would rather take to his grave than reveal to another, even Assefa. Besides, when it came to courting a witch, the Berber men tended to only tolerate the handfasting ritual. By now, a Berber male would've simply bitten, marked, and claimed his witch and mate. But such a strong-arm tactic was never wise with a witch. Especially not one as powerful as Sanura, despite his beast's constant growls for him to do just that. But Assefa trusted Sanura to guide them through the ritual, knew from the way she kept touching him that she wasn't as unaffected by him as he'd initially thought. *As she acted.*

Sanura slid her hands from his head to rest on each cheek and started to caress his rugged face. "You feel a loss of self-control around me for the same reason I do. We are indeed compatible, and because we haven't gone through the ritual, we haven't aligned our auras to each other's frequency. Once we do that, you won't feel a sense of loss. In fact, you'll have even more control over your inner cat and be more in tune with your chi. There's much more, but it's getting late. I'll stay here tonight but must get up early and visit Betsy before I drive back to College Park for my first class."

Assefa tightened his arms around Sanura's waist, not ready to end the evening. She felt way too good for Assefa to let her go. *Not yet.*

Despite her words, Sanura made no attempt to move either. Instead, she leaned in close to his ear. "Despite the intensity of the energy we create and how good it makes my body feel, that alone doesn't account for the feelings I've developed for you. I want to get to know you for many reasons, none of which have anything to do with biological compatibility. And if I wasn't so tired, I would make you a list."

Relieved, Assefa smiled, thinking he could probably coax her into making that list for him at a later date. He had a list of his own, the top three having to do with brains, compassion, and family values. "I just needed to know what you feel originated in your mind and not simply your body."

"You mean to tell me you want me for my mind and not my body?" Her flirtatious laughter aroused the inner cat and the man. "You're a rare man, Special Agent Berber."

Assefa crushed her body against his. "I want your mind to want me first, then your body. But make no mistake, if you're offering—"

Sanura playfully swatted Assefa on his shoulder and then kissed him. She melted into his tight embrace, pressing her breasts against his hard chest. Oh, yes, the cat purred now. The beginnings of a demanding roar threatened.

Encouraged by this openly sensual side of Sanura, Assefa gently probed her mouth with his tongue, sliding in deep and finding her own waiting. So sweet, the woman tasted so sweet, her tongue lively, soft, and skilled.

And he took all she offered, sucking and nipping and tasting. Playing, teasing, and wrenching a moan from her.

Assefa's large hands chartered a path from her back, down her toned waist, and farther south to her ripe ass. He squeezed—both cheeks—then pulled her forward, sliding her against his unrepentant erection.

She gasped.

He groaned.

And he kissed her deeper, taking and giving and wanting more from Sanura than he knew she was ready to give. But, damn, the way she was kissing him back, rubbing enticingly against him, it was clear there was at least one thing she wanted from him. But Assefa desired more than that. *Want all of Sanura, not just her body.*

But he had a plan. Winning a witch was not for the faint of heart.

CHAPTER SEVEN

"Let's try this again."

Sanura looked up from the laptop and saw Assefa standing at the door to the lecture hall, her students noisily filing past him, clearly relieved to have one final exam out of the way.

"I believe this is what is called déjà vu."

With the grace of a stalking feline, Assefa made his way down the steps, the jacket of his dark-gray suit slung over one shoulder, a brown bag held in his other hand.

Sanura finished closing out her file, safely removed her flash drive, and logged off the computer before shutting it down.

"Not exactly déjà vu," Assefa said. "We actually never got around to the lunch part."

Sanura nodded to the brown bag in his left hand. "Smells good."

"So do you, a secret garden meant only for my pleasure, my indulgence."

Sanura couldn't help but smile. Assefa was all unabashed shifter flirtiness. And he made her feel ridiculously charmed.

He placed the bag on the metal table next to the lectern, pulled one chair out for her, waited for Sanura to sit, and then grabbed the chair on the opposite end of the table, placing it next to her.

"I stopped by a deli on my way here. Knew if I got here while class was still in session, I would catch you before you darted off somewhere. Wherever little witch professors go during their break." He eyed his watch, a gold-and-onyx timepiece that looked like it cost more than she made in three months. "You have nearly two hours before your next class."

Sanura didn't bother to ask how Assefa had known her Tuesday schedule. He would probably consider it an insult to his FBI investigative skills if she did so.

Smoothing out invisible wrinkles from a well-pressed suit jacket, Assefa primly hung the garment over the back of his chair. Then he deftly swung his blue-and-gray tie over his shoulder before digging into the bag and pulling out a one-ounce bottle of unscented hand sanitizer. He handed the clear bottle to Sanura, and she couldn't resist smiling at the special agent. Gods, the man was unbelievably proper, bordering on anal-retentive. She kept sanitizing wipes in her satchel and her car, but she'd never known a guy to be as fastidious about what he put on and in his body as Assefa Berber.

"There's nothing funny about germs, Sanura," he said, tone prickly and all too serious.

Because he was too adorable and outrageously uptight, Sanura found herself laughing.

"Do you know how many germs full-humans transmit every second of the day? They're either sick, getting over an illness, or preparing for the next infirmity."

She howled now, not very ladylike, but she couldn't help it. During his speech about full-humans and germs, he'd squeezed two squirts of hand sanitizer into the palm of one hand and rubbed them vigorously together. Then, apparently for good measure, he did it again.

Sanura wiped the tears from her eyes. "By the gods, Assefa, you're a were-cat. When was the last time you were sick?"

His eyes narrowed to brown slits of annoyed male huffiness. "That's not the point."

No, that was precisely her point. Were-cats had the immune system of a tank. Most full-human diseases couldn't touch them. Witches weren't quite that durable, but they also had constitutions much stronger than full-humans. All preternaturals did.

"Can you spell OCD, Special Agent Berber?"

"Maybe, but I can spell spanking, which I'll give you if you don't start showing a bit more appreciation for this romantic gesture."

"Ohhh, is that what this is supposed to be?"

Napkins, plates, utensils, spring water, fruit bowls, and two chicken salad wraps were pulled from the bag, neatly and equally distributed before them. Assefa was a surprisingly good waiter.

"You know, Sanura, it's a good thing I enjoy looking at your legs so much or I would take my hard-ordered lunch and leave."

She laughed again, then blushed when she realized what he'd said about her legs and where his eyes had settled.

"Do you ever wear pants, woman?" Ravenous eyes were fixed on the objects of his pleasure. "Or do you like torturing men?"

She crossed her legs, a slow, gliding movement that brought her rose-design skirt mid-thigh. "Am I torturing you, Special Agent Berber?"

He reached out and placed one of his huge hands on her knee. And just as slowly as she'd crossed them, his hand made a languid trek from her knee to her thigh, the touch gentle, the skin he stroked undeniably receptive. Then that hand extended his expedition farther north, traveling under her skirt and claiming his newfound land with massaging fingers.

Sanura bit back a moan. Who was doing the torturing now?

"I love it when you wear skirts and dresses, especially without stockings."

She could tell. His hand still worked her leg, stirring the unaligned magical energy between them.

She sucked in a breath and forced herself to say, "M–maybe we should eat the lunch you brought. It looks delicious."

"When I was a kid," Assefa began, leaning into her, his face enticingly close, "I used to eat my dessert first." His lips lightly touched hers. "What about you, my leggy witch? Would you like to have dessert first?"

Gods, yes.

Assefa's other hand came up to a shoulder, stroked, then slid down to her waist, and then pulled Sanura onto his lap. She went, wrapping her arms around his neck.

"I thought about you all weekend. About you and the handfasting."

She'd also thought about him, wanting to see Assefa but not daring to call. He had last-minute bureau business that required his immediate attention. He hadn't gone into detail. But that also meant she hadn't seen or spoken to him in four days. And, to her surprise, she'd found herself thinking about and missing the special agent. Now it was Tuesday, only three days before the handfasting.

"A phone call would've been nice."

"It would've," he too amiably agreed. "So why didn't you call me?" *Touché.*

"I know how dedicated you are to your work. I didn't want to take time away from your assignment." *And it had unnerved me how much I wanted to hear your deep, sensual voice, see your smiling, seductive eyes.* "Why didn't you call me?"

Assefa tightened his arms around her waist. "I didn't want to seem too forward, too pushy." He moved one hand to her face. A single finger found her nose, lips, and rapidly pulsing neck. He kissed her there. "Besides, before I left, Mike made it his business to call and tell me that you only date full-humans. Is that true?" He lifted his head, gaze questioning and intense.

Damn the dwarf and his interfering ways. Why in the hell would he tell Assefa such a thing? Ah, that's right, because he thinks no one is good enough for me. Insufferable busybody.

"Not anymore," she said smoothly, hoping he wouldn't pry further or was offended. Because she could see how Assefa could be righteously insulted. Heck, she would be if he'd told her he'd never dated a witch before, as if there was something so awful about witches that he couldn't bring himself to date one. Yes, he had every right to be offended. But no one understood why Sanura didn't date shifters. She had her reasons, and they were her own.

Yet there had been one person who'd, while not knowing the specifics of her decision, had posed a critical question to her one day. *"How do you expect to find your true mate if you limit your dating pool to full-humans?"* She should've confided in her father that day. He would've listened, understood, and given her advice on how best to handle a were-cat of Assefa's caliber. *"Whatever frightens you, precious, you can't outrun your destiny. It simply isn't done."* Sage words, Sanura was beginning to hesitantly admit.

"So, I'm the exception to your 'no shifter' rule?"

She didn't like how he said that, so she took it as a rhetorical question. Sanura enjoyed his company too much to let Mike and her so-called "no shifter rule" spoil their time together.

"Why me?" he asked, filling the silence with another question.

Never the easy questions from her special agent, but this one she didn't mind answering.

"Because I'm attracted to you. Because you're the poster child for contradictions, and I enjoy each one of them. You're funny when you're being so damn serious. You have a kind heart and protective nature that reminds me so much of my father." *Too much.* "You're insanely bright and wickedly handsome." *You're my dream posing as reality.*

He winked at her. "I knew I could get you to make that list for me."

She shook her head, lips lifting up in amusement.

"Now for my dessert." He kissed her.

And she kissed him back, glad he was probing her mouth instead of her mind, her heart. She relaxed in his arms and luxuriated in the scent of the man. Pheromones tempted her senses, and hands aroused her body.

She could do this for the whole of her break. Let him mold her body to his, ravaging her mouth with his masterful tongue. Then, deeper under his spell, she sank, his kisses and hands magical talismans promising devotion, love, and protection. Everything a were-cat willingly gave to his witch and all a witch granted in return to her cat, her mate. The thought delighted and frightened, mixed emotions she conveniently ignored. Assefa's sensual attentions demanded nothing less from Sanura.

Abruptly, Assefa broke the kiss and looked behind him and up the stairs. "Did you hear that?"

My heart doing double-time? "I didn't hear anything."

"It sounded as if someone opened then closed the door." His eyes were still cast away from her, his focus on the door and the sound he thought he'd heard. "Maybe I should check."

"It's probably nothing, Assefa." She touched his cheek, encouraging his attention away from the door and back to her. "You make for a comfortable chair and a more divine first-course meal."

His smile told her, along with the hand that had reappeared on her thigh, that she'd succeeded in reclaiming his attention. *Good.*

"I'll be here Wednesday, Thursday, and Friday for lunch. Don't make any other plans. I'll bring the dessert; you wear the skirts."

The man had a leg fetish. But Sanura did like to wear skirts, even during the cold winter months. More importantly, she'd found she couldn't resist Assefa's scrumptious dessert choice.

She reclaimed his mouth, not done with her meal.

Richard stood statue-still, making sure to not make a sound. That had been close. And damn Sanura Williams. What did she think she was doing with that agent? She had been all over him, sitting on his lap, tongue buried in his mouth.

And Richard didn't even want to think about where the big bastard's hands had been. *Touching her as if she were his. Like he owned her. Don't think so, asshole. You're just the rebound guy.*

Richard rushed away from the building, pushing past throngs of end-of-year happy students. Their good cheer made him want to vomit. He was the one who was supposed to be happy. He'd given Sanura a little more time to think about what he had said to her. He'd waited, been patient. Knew she would see the error in her thinking and take him back.

But all the while, she's been screwing the special agent behind my back, trying to make a fool of me.

Richard popped two aspirin in his mouth as soon as he'd reached his office. He would teach her, make her pay for playing him for a fool. Today sealed it. After Friday, Sanura would know that her special agent couldn't protect her or her family. No, Richard held all the power. And she would find out, learn what true love was all about.

Genji Zhou-Garvey watched her friends as they laughed and played. Reisterstown Road Plaza was one of their hangout spots. It wasn't as big as Towson Commons Mall, nor did it have a theater. Instead, it was just a tiny plaza with stores that fit the budget of working-class and middle-class northwest Baltimoreans. Nothing special, but it had a decent enough pizza joint, and Gen and her girlfriends loved the greasy, cheesy stuff.

"Gen, do you wanna go half on a pepperoni pizza, or are you avoiding pork like Malcolm X over there?" Jalia asked, jutting her thumb in their friend Keisha's direction.

"Hey, I'm no Muslim. I just don't do pig. They eat any damn thing, and I don't wanna eat something that has no dietary standard." Keisha shooed an annoying fly from her face, looking at Jalia as if she wanted to shoo her.

"'Dietary standards,'" Jalia mocked. "You sound like Mrs. Etheridge."

"Hey, health is my favorite subject. Maybe if you paid more attention in class, you wouldn't put so much crap in your big, fat mouth. Now," Keisha said to Gen, "hand me one of those chocolate donuts with sprinkles."

Gen laughed. "Look, let's just grab a cheese pizza and some soda. This place is starting to get crowded, and I can't be out too late. Curfew, you know."

"Yeah, I know." Keisha pulled her cell phone from a back pants pocket. "My mom got me on lockdown with this thing. I begged and begged, thinking I could use it to keep in touch with you guys and Andre, but she uses it to track my behind wherever I go."

"Hell, yeah, a regular GPS, and she pays the bills, so she knows every call you make, including when you text Andre, which is usually during last period when you should be learning U.S. history." Gen handed the cashier her portion of the bill. A five. No change.

The three friends sat in a booth, greasy cheese pizza soaking through the too-thin paper plates.

"So, Gen, how are the foster parents? They seem pretty cool, as far as adults go, and they're not that old." Jalia washed down a bite of pizza she'd just taken with a swallow of half-and-half. How anyone liked the taste of tea and lemonade mixed together, Gen would never know. For her, it was one or the other, not both.

"They're good people. I really like Cyn, cool, like you said."

"I can't believe you get to call Principal Garvey by her first name," Keisha said. "Aren't you afraid she'll give you detention if you call her that at school? Not that she's actually the principal of the upper school, but adults don't seem to care about little details like that."

The threesome chuckled, and Gen felt happy, the kind of happiness that had abandoned her when her mother had died eighteen months ago. Cynthia and Eric Garvey had opened their home to her, treating Gen with genuine kindness and affection. With them, she could be herself, no longer forced to hide her witch identity.

The same was true with her new friends. In fact, The Witch Council of Elders formed private schools throughout the U.S., where witches and were-cats could attend and learn their craft without the threat of discovery. The educational institutions were havens for her kind. The school Gen and her friends attended, Sankofa Preparatory School, served grades K-12, accepting residential and non-residential students from the Maryland, DC, and Virginia areas. Life in Baltimore had turned out to be infinitely better than her years in San Francisco.

Gen looked up at the black circular clock on the wall, then focused her gaze to the mural behind it. The painting was of a couple relaxing in a gondola, taking in the sights of old Italy. The colors were faded, and the images lacked true talent, but she still found the painting beautiful. It made Gen wish to see such a place in person and feel the warmth of the Tuscan sun on her skin. Then Gen wondered how many Chinese witches actually lived in Italy. Probably none, she concluded, now thinking how nice it would be to visit China, her mother's home. But would China be any more accepting of a witch than Italy would be of a Chinese girl? *Probably not.*

"I have to get home before it gets too late. Curfew," Gen said, by way of explanation, an hour and a half after she and her friends had stuffed themselves, gossiped, and flirted with a few guys from Northwestern High School.

"Me, too," her friends answered in unison.

They made their way through the bustling Friday night crowd, moving to the glass doors and exit. Once outside and at the southbound bus stop, Jalia touched the bracelet on her wrist and then looked at Gen.

"Are you sure? None of us should be out without a protective charm. It's dangerous."

"Yeah, Gen, maybe you should call Mrs. Garvey and have her pick you up. We'll wait with you," Keisha said, her brown eyes full of a friend's concern.

Gen shook her head. "I'll be fine. I don't live far. If I walk fast or jog, I'll be home in less than fifteen minutes."

"But—"

"Don't worry about me, Jalia. You two are the ones who have to catch the bus home. You keep the charm. My Aunt Sanura will make me another one."

"Shit, if I hadn't lost mine, you wouldn't have had to loan me yours."

Gen waved Jalia's worry away. "Look, don't worry about it."

Gen dashed across Reisterstown Road without waiting for the red light or more arguments from Jalia and Keisha. Once across the street, she turned back around and waved at her friends. "I'll see you guys at school Monday. So don't worry about me. I'll have my Cali ass home in no time."

Gen hustled away from the bright lights of the mall and the worried gazes of her best friends. She turned onto Clarks Lane, the residential street a mix of urban and suburban, quiet and peaceful, with a throbbing pulse of energy that only came with living among a diverse group of people. If the full-humans of Baltimore knew how diverse their city truly was…Gen shook her head and smiled.

The sun had started to descend, and Gen figured she would reach her front door before darkness officially blanketed the city, tucking it in for the night.

iPod strapped around her arm and buds in her ears, the teenager sang and danced her way down one side street and up another. When she reached Fallstaff Road, unknown energy caused her to pause. She'd spent too much time looking over her shoulder on the streets of San Francisco not to know when something vile or dangerous was near.

She quickly spun around and looked down the street from whence she came. Gen peered into the darkness but saw no one. The goosebumps on her arms and pounding heartbeat told her she sensed a presence, but her eyes and ears picked up nothing.

Now regretting not calling her foster parents for a ride home, as they requested, she turned her music down to a melodic hush. Then, casting another glance behind her, she made a left onto her street. House in sight, she picked up her pace to outrun whatever her instincts detected.

Stay calm. Just stay calm.

The sickening energy increased. The stench of the malevolent aura clogged her throat, making her want to puke.

It struck.

Darkness with wings and fangs appeared, swooping down toward her, covering Gen with its frightening form. Hungry, glowing, red eyes clashed with alarmed brown ones. Gen let out a glass-shattering scream before the night flyer trapped her underneath its body.

Lights in the neighborhood went ablaze, doors opened by concerned and nosey neighbors alike.

Gen struggled with the adze, her arms wedged between their bodies and pushing upward with all her might. *Not enough. Too strong for me. Way too strong.*

Rancid, hot breath.

Deadly, sharp fangs.

Pierced skin, flowing blood, terrified witch.

Adze.

No! Stop! Her mind screamed.

It didn't.

Gen knew of the death dealer. Her foster parents had talked to her about it. They had class discussions about the monster in Gen's Introduction to Defensive Incantations class. She'd even met a third-grader in Cyn's office whose parents were killed by the monster. Still, she never thought it would come after her.

What do I do now? Dear goddess, what do I do?

Neck burning with each pull from the adze's gluttonous mouth, its weight suffocating and crushing, she focused on gasping out the most advanced defensive spell she knew. It wasn't much, but it was enough to send the bloodsucking serial killer flying off her.

Warm blood ran from her neck, down her shoulder, and onto her pink Beyonce graphic tee. She knew she should move, get up and run away before the bat came back for her. It couldn't be far. Gen's magic was too early in the pubescent stage of development to have done more than give her a few feet of breathing room. The adze would come back for her. She was sure of it. *I gotta get out of here. I gotta do something. I gotta—*

Strong, familiar arms grabbed her like she was an infant, cradling Gen's weakened body to his reassuring chest. She tried to say his name, but no words came. The simple effort wrenched a cry from the teen. Warm blood ran unobstructed from her neck, down her shoulder, and onto her pink Beyonce graphic tee. And she had never felt so scared or relieved.

The arms holding her tightened with ferocious protectiveness. Eric Garvey maneuvered them behind his wife. Gen could make out the words her foster mother whispered. From the soft incantation, a force field, invisible to full-humans, formed from the earth's electrical energy, surging up and over, an ocean-blue haze separating the family from the monster.

The neighbors were out in force, cell phones up to ears and calling 911. Screams bellowed into the night air, a church bell alerting the townspeople to danger. Like Gen, the astonished neighbors had glimpsed the seven-foot brown humanoid bat with a four-foot wingspan and piercing red eyes. While many people wisely hid in their homes from the batlike creature, those who did venture out, guns in hand, probably wanted to mount the hideous thing to their wall.

But there were others, the fortune seekers in the bunch whose cell phone flashes nearly blinded the dazed and bleeding Gen. They, more than likely, hoped to sell the pics to whatever newspaper or cable news show that printed such outlandish features with titles like, "Man-Bat Takes on Baltimore," or "Baltimore Really Sucks."

Regardless of the reason for the neighbors forming an impromptu neighborhood watch, the adze couldn't finish the kill with so many onlookers. Hovering in a human neighborhood, mouth dripping with the blood of an innocent, the monster did something Gen was told adzes never did. It retreated into the shielding darkness of the night sky, followed by bullets from a few of her male neighbors with more bullets than brains, who hooped and hollered that they had "tagged that ugly son of a bitch."

Seeing the retreating silhouette of her attacker, Gen exhaled, taking comfort in Eric's warm embrace and Cynthia's resolute forcefield. Gen could hear sirens and excited chatter in the background and wondered how long before she would pass out or if that only happened in the movies.

Darkness closed in around her; this time, Gen knew it wasn't from the adze.

CHAPTER EIGHT

Hunger. Pain. Fatigue. Anger.

Heavy wings glided stiffly on stale currents of gnawing defeat. So close. The adze's engorged tongue and malevolent teeth could still feel the succulent witch's flesh. Hypnotic drops of blood clung, the taste beautiful and cruel. It wasn't enough. She needed more.

Much, much more.

Grave red eyes scanned the checkered landscape below, leathery wings taking it farther away. The night grew deeper, darker, and unforgiving, mimicking the fierce stab of hunger clawing at the adze, begging for rich, crimson fulfillment or a quick, painless death.

Hunger. Pain. Fatigue. Anger.

She flew, guided by scent, need, and nature. This was what she was, what she was born to do. How the gods had made her kind.

Hunt. Kill. Eat. Live.

Finally, she landed when rancid odors and crammed city living gave way to sprawling greenery and blessed silence. Wings slowly lowered as she made her graceful descent. Claws, sharpened to staggering points, grasped a large branch. The solidly formed, thickly bloomed American Beech was no more fazed by her meager weight or bloody intentions than the ravages done to its glorious bark. A child's well-worn swing, with rusted chains, dangled below her stolen perch.

Pushing back the painful abdominal churning of too many missed meals, she used the barest of efforts to move aside a clump of orange-and-green leaves. There. It was faint. So weak in its sweet allure, she questioned her senses. But the unfaithful clenching of muscles and the sudden quickening of her blood-deprived, blackened heart told another story. A familiar tale that could only end one way—deliciously full.

She pulled the ebbing blood memory of the one that got away. *The one that tasted of an odd mixture of cumulus rainfall and reptilian innocence.*

The shift began, slow and agonizing, body weak, malnourished. But it wouldn't be for long. Not if she could make the transformation work and maintain it long enough. Yes, long enough.

Three minutes later, silent, bare feet rubbed against prickly, fresh-cut grass. The scent tickled her nostrils, and a sneeze threatened. She was human, or as close as she would ever come.

"Who's out there?" The man's voice was high and loud. An edge to it whispered in the wind that this territory was his domain. The man was wrong, of course.

The adze came forward, showing herself in the light that beamed heavy and bright from the wraparound porch. "H–help me," her small, satiny, feminine voice pleaded. "Help me, p–please!"

"Explain it to me again, Makena?" Mike asked for the third time in two days.

"We've gone over this. I don't understand why you don't understand. Or are you choosing not to understand because you feel you're losing Sanura to Assefa?"

Taking a seat on the sofa, Mike ran a hand through salt-and-pepper hair before scratching his two-day-old stubble. "You and Sanura are the only family I have, and with Sam gone, I don't have too many friends left."

Makena stood before her old, dear friend and placed a comforting hand on his shoulder. "This changes nothing of substance. You must know that. Sanura loves you. You have a place in her heart that no one could ever replace and a home with us. Some things change, Mike, but others never will. Besides, Assefa is good for her, and he's the only young man who's ever come to visit that you couldn't scare away. He's not afraid of you, Mike, and I think that's what got you so upset."

She laughed when he pouted and sucked his teeth as if he were a seven-year-old who was just told he couldn't watch his favorite cartoon. Then, she walked into the kitchen chuckling at his juvenile behavior, knowing dwarfs to be a jealous, possessive lot. "You can't intimidate this one, my friend," Makena loudly said so he could hear her, "so you simply need to accept that he'll be around."

"You aren't the one who must work with Mr. Perfect and then have to see his annoyingly cheerful face during off-hours," Mike yelled after her, his smoke-roughened throat sounding harsher than usual. As much as Makena hated the smell of smoke and what it did to the body, she didn't worry about her friend getting cancer. There were very few human illnesses that afflicted dwarves, or witches for that matter, and cancer, no matter the type, wasn't one of them. Knowing Mike McKutchen, he would live to a ripe old age, making Anubis await his leisure.

Makena turned to see that Mike had followed her into the kitchen. "I thought you said you found his intellect and self-assured nature a boon in your line of work. You told me he was courageous and calm under pressure."

"Well," he grumbled, "don't listen to everything I say. I was probably drunk when I made those ridiculous comments."

Makena laughed again, knowing a dwarf's metabolism made it impossible for them to get drunk. The young agent was obviously, if not annoyingly, growing on him. She'd known Mike long enough to know he only bitched about people he liked. But by making such an admission, in his mind, his reputation as a hard-ass would be ruined. For a dwarf who was five feet on a good day with insoles, his I'll-kick-your-ass-rather-than-shake-your-hand attitude had served him well over the years. *More or less.*

"And dammit, Makena, the man still hasn't told me how he knew I was a dwarf."

The fact that Assefa was a member of a secret division of the FBI, devoted to finding dangerous preternatural creatures, and the idea that said division wouldn't have performed a detailed background check on the very man who'd brought the case to their attention before sending in one of their agents to work with him, clearly eluded the detective. Perhaps Mike simply believed that since he'd managed to fool full-humans for so long, he could fool anyone, even a were-cat trained to sniff out killers and lies.

"And," Mike said, scowling, "did I tell you the kid handcuffed me?"

No, but Sanura had, and they'd laughed long and hard. Tears included.

"He's supposed to be my partner but turned on me." Mike raised a black pant leg, revealing a slouched brown sock. "He handcuffed me to my own ankle. Wrist to damn ankle, Makena."

Oh, hell, Sanura hadn't told her that part. Makena howled.

"It's not funny, damn you. Why do you always find humor in my pain?" He dropped his pant leg. "Assefa was gone by the time I got myself free. Probably afraid I would kick his highbrow ass."

"Yeah, I'm sure that was it, Mike."

"You know, Makena Williams, you may be beautiful on the outside, but you're an ugly, ugly woman on the inside."

She batted long, dark lashes at him and said in her sweetest voice, "So you find me beautiful, do you, Detective McKutchen?"

Mike snorted. "Damn, I can't even insult you without you turning the tables on me." Small but strong hands grasped hers. "Of course, you're beautiful, inside and out. Sam always said so, and I agree."

Makena swallowed a sudden lump. She didn't want to talk about her deceased husband, not even with Mike.

"And I'm not the only one who thinks so. Look, I know a couple of decent were-cats on the force. Good, solid guys I could introduce— Come on, Makena, don't shake your head like that. I haven't even— Fine. But—"

"No!"

She said nothing more. Mike knew her feelings on the matter, and she knew his. He thought she should start getting out…date. She disagreed. Positions clear.

He let her hands go, reclined in his chair, and sighed. "One of these days, you're gonna have to…never mind. Just never mind. Tonight's not about that. It's about the kids downstairs and their future. Just…just explain it to me one more time."

Grateful Mike hadn't ruined the evening by pushing her on something she would not be moved on, Makena finished preparing their drinks. She handed a steaming cup of arpeggio coffee to the detective.

Mike pulled out two chairs from the kitchen table, and they sat. The dwarf truly was a dear man, and he missed Sam nearly as much as she and Sanura did. But he was no further along in "moving on" from Sam's death than she. So perhaps if she recommended that Mike get himself a new best friend, he would understand. Or maybe he would agree. And where would that leave Makena?

"I'm sure you're familiar with the typical figure of the witch and her black cat," she began.

Mike nodded.

"Witches have used animals to help them with their magical works for a long time. The familiar assists the witch in her magical works. Traditionally, cats are associated with witches. Yet other animals, dogs, rabbits, horses, and snakes can also be familiars." Raising the coffee cup to her mouth, Makena blew, then took a cautious sip. "When the witches of antiquity went underground to escape persecution by humans and unwilling possession by adzes, the males—warlocks— banded together and devised a plan to protect their women."

"Okay, I remember Sanura saying only female witches could be possessed by an adze, so that meant male witches…I mean, warlocks were never targets of witch hunters or adzes."

"Correct. After years on the run, the group eventually settled in Mennefer, Egypt. Soon after their arrival, the warlocks went to the temple of Sekhmet and hashed out a deal with her. The goddess Sekhmet is the daughter of the sun god Ra. Her name comes from the Egyptian word sekhem, which means power or might. She's the patron of physicians, priests, and healers, but she's also known as the goddess of war and destruction. Sekhmet removes threats and punishes those who go against Ma'at."

"I'm not interested in a mythology lesson, Makena, but what in the hell is Ma'at?"

Makena shook her head. "Is there anything you believe in, Mike, greater than yourself?"

"No. Now spill."

She rolled her eyes. The man could try the patience of the Dalai Lama and wouldn't give a damn as long as he found out what he wanted to know. Makena rubbed her temples, feeling a Mike-induced migraine coming on. "Ma'at is an ancient Egyptian concept based on truth, law, justice, morality, and order. Now that I think about it, as a cop, these are the same principles you believe in. So perhaps there's hope for you yet, Mike. Anyway," she said, seeing Mike wasn't impressed with the idea of having principles beyond the thrill of kicking the asses of criminals. "Sekhmet helps maintain order in the world. So, when the men went to her temple for help, she was more than willing to aid their efforts in restoring the balance between adzes and witches."

"What kind of deal did the men make with the goddess?" He took a gulp of his hot coffee, wincing and cursing when it burned his tongue, glaring viciously at the drink as if his carelessness was the coffee's fault.

Makena stood and went to the counter where she'd pulled a pie from the fridge earlier. Lifting the lid off the see-through Pie Keeper, Makena cut into the pie and then placed a slice on a bread plate. Then, grabbing a fork, she returned to the table, handed Mike a slice of guava cheese, sat, and picked up where she'd left off.

"The men promised to worship Sekhmet for all time and do her bidding if she gave them the ability to protect their women from the adzes. In return, for an eternity of strong males who would pass down the knowledge and wisdom of the warrior goddess, she granted the men the power to transform their bodies into fierce cats. Not only could they shift shape while in human form, but they also possessed an increased sense of smell, sight, taste, and hearing. The type of cat each male can turn into now depends on the cat his forefather chose. Thus, some families can turn into cheetahs, while others leopards and others still tigers, and so on."

"But that doesn't account for were-cats in other parts of the world who had nothing to do with the pact."

Makena couldn't help but nod approvingly at her friend. Behind Mike's wrinkled clothes, bad attitude, and grumpy demeanor was a dwarf with a keen mind. He hadn't made detective by age thirty because of his charming personality or willingness to kiss bureaucratic ass. No, it was his seafoam eyes people often dismissed that told the true story.

Dwarves were many things, but unintelligent and naïve weren't among them. This is what Makena loved about him and what her husband first saw in Mike too many years ago to count.

"I've asked myself the same question and have found no record to support what I believe to be true."

"Which is?"

"That Sekhmet used the pact as an opportunity to create a personal army of were-cats. She is, after all, the goddess of war and destruction. Such a selfish act wouldn't be above her."

"I've never heard you talk about your gods in this way. Aren't you afraid she'll zap your blasphemous ass for talking like that?"

"Perhaps, but faith doesn't have to be blind, my friend," Makena answered, knowing even a disbelieving cynic like Mike could agree.

"So, if you and Sam had a son, he would've been able to turn into a jaguar like his father?"

Makena nodded, causing strands of hair to fall from her limp bun and into her right eye. She pushed them back, suppressing the urge to release the mass of black waves, knowing if she did so she would be too relaxed to appease Mike's quizzical mind. It could wait.

"However, Sekhmet being a protector of Ma'at and the idea of balance, the men eventually discovered an undisclosed price to their bargain. Over the years, the ability of the warlocks to cast spells decreased as their ability to commune with the goddess as her servants, increased until they could no longer cast at all. Thus, we now have two intertwined but distinct biological strands—magic-casting witches and magic-holding were-cats. Two different breeds and each breed is further delineated into type of witch—earth, wind, fire, or water, or were-cat—lion, tiger, etcetera."

Mike's furry eyebrows pinched, mouth tightened, his mind clearly trying to process all she'd shared. "Is the biological distinction the reason for the ritual?" he asked, tense facial muscles relaxing but voice sharp with genuine interest.

"Yes. Two generations after the pact, it was discovered that while we're still fundamentally the same species, we were no longer all compatible with each other. For some reason, the goddess sought to guide our mating choices. I've long since concluded that it probably had something to do with producing the strongest offspring possible."

She waved away a question Mike almost couldn't contain.

"Anyway, there were terrible instances of a male or female choosing to ignore the biological calling necessary for appropriate mating and mating with another. As a result, the children were born horribly deformed, living only a few months, if they survived the delivery at all. More often than not, the witch would simply miscarry, her body unable to provide the necessary support for a child she wasn't meant to carry to term. It's as if our bodies don't possess the proper..." She paused, searching for the right word, but found none. "I don't know, Mike. Any healthy shifter can impregnate a witch because we share about ninety-eight percent of the same DNA necessary for reproduction. But the last two percent makes all the difference in determining whether the two are a perfect biological match or a genetic impossibility."

"So, you mean to tell me you guys are bound to a random biological imperative?" The question bubbled from Mike in a tide of disapproving anger, his cultural norms preventing him from understanding Makena's. But Mike's cultural insensitivity didn't offend her. As far as she was concerned, dwarf society was equally baffling to her. And she didn't even want to think about their mating rituals—a cave, a warthog, and clubs, if she recalled correctly.

Makena shuddered.

"No, we aren't bound by it emotionally, but physically, yes. We can select another mate to spend our life with, but children would be out of the question."

"That doesn't sound like a good deal the men entered into." Mike finished the last bite of pie and wiped his mouth with the sleeve of his shirt instead of the napkin Makena had set next to his plate.

"Well, I doubt they foresaw their deal's side effects, but it saved our lives and made us stronger. Of course, the deal has had other side effects, but I can't get into that with you, Mike. You understand why, so please don't be offended."

Mike snorted. "I've never known a dwarf to be offended. We're typically on the other side, offending any and everyone." He laughed, then turned serious. "But what if the person you're compatible with isn't the one you want to be with?"

"That's happened. Just because a witch finds her biological half, that doesn't necessarily make them mates. It just means they can safely have children. Mating involves the heart and mind, Mike, neither of which has anything to do with biological compatibility. I know several witches who are compatible with their other half on only the biological level, nothing more. In fact, a witch in my yoga class has children by the were-cat with whom she is biologically linked, but they aren't married, not even a couple. She eventually married a different shifter."

"What the hell, Makena? You're hanging around swingers now?"

"Of course not, you judgmental blockhead." She laughed. "They just really wanted to have children and knew they needed each other to make that happen."

"But they aren't together?"

She shook her head. "Like I said, they weren't emotionally compatible, but they're good parents, and their twins are well-adjusted fifteen-year-olds."

"I think your yoga instructor, her husband, and her babies' daddy are into some kinky cat-witch shit you just don't want to cop to. But I'll let it go because, really, it's giving me a damn headache."

"Okay, okay, Mike, I can see how, to an outsider, it sounds rather strange."

"Let me see if I got this right. So"—Mike tested the temperature of his drink by dipping a finger in it— "Assefa and Sanura could be biologically compatible, which would also make him her familiar. Or they could be biologically incompatible, making it impossible for Assefa to be Sanura's familiar. In either instance, they could decide to become mates."

"Well, Detective McKutchen, I believe you've just passed Hand-fasting for Dummies."

"Smart-ass witch." Mike swiveled in his chair and then pointed to the closed door that led to the basement. "How do you think things are going down there?"

"I'm sure they're fine, but if something unforeseen happens, we're here and will remain until they tell us otherwise. Don't worry, Mike; Sanura knows exactly what she's doing, but they may be a couple of hours."

Standing, then grabbing a DVD from the kitchen television stand, Makena held up the movie and smiled. She shook it teasingly at Mike until he grabbed it from her, a pleased smile on an otherwise grumpy face. "*Lord of the Rings*. You're a woman after my heart. They don't make many movies with a dwarf as a hero," he complained, with all the righteous indignation of an unfulfilled moviegoer.

Mike dragged Makena out of the kitchen, down a short hallway, and to the living room. He plopped his load in the middle of the sofa, snatched the universal remote next to him, and clicked one button, turning on the forty-two-inch flat-screen television mounted on the wall across from the sofa. Then he looked at Makena, his face adorably boyish when he said, "All we need now is some popcorn."

CHAPTER NINE

Assefa returned from the bathroom to find the patio door to the basement ajar. He walked to the door only to find Sanura standing next to a hot tub wearing a two-piece blue-and-black bathing suit. He tried not to stare. In fact, he told his eyes not to move farther than her lovely face. Then he commanded it to stop at her perfectly shaped, full breasts, which the top struggled to contain, then he was horrified when his eyes disobeyed him and continued their descent to her long, smooth legs held up only by the inviting curve of her hips and ass. His eyes ignored every command of his weakening mind as they unabashedly drank in her enchanting form, daring him to deny the building of raw emotional energy surging through his body.

"It's impolite to stare," Sanura casually stated, not bothering to lift her head away from her work.

Unwilling to admit to such a display of stereotypical male behavior, he asked, "What are you doing?"

"I'm preparing the purification part of the ritual. Before doing a working, it's important to be in a state of purity, both in a spiritual and a bodily sense. A purification ritual is a cleansing of the spirit and body, a way of replacing negative energy or energy that is out of harmony with the purpose of the working."

"Are we to submerge ourselves in the hot tub? Is that why you asked me to bring a pair of swimming trunks to change into?" He asked this last question more out of nerves than ignorance. Obviously, she intended for them to get into the tub, and he inwardly kicked himself for acting like a braindead fool in front of her.

"Yes. Water has played a part in purification rites for thousands of years in myriad cultures worldwide. From Christian baptism to ritual washings in Judaism to ritual ablutions in the Bahá'í Faith to Msogi in Shinto ritual purification, the act of washing the hands, face, and body to remove physical impurities is as important for cleanliness as it is a symbol of religious or spiritual purity."

Assefa held back a laugh of relief. That unnecessary lecture proved to him that the woman was just as nervous. She tended to ramble when she was, or worse, stayed silent and refused to meet his eyes. *Like she's doing now.*

Continuing her work, Sanura poured out a cup of what smelled like salt into a ceramic shell bowl. She raised her hands over the salts and spoke. "Goddess, bless these salts." She poured the contents of the bowl into the hot tub, followed by a few drops of lavender oil, the fragrance as sweetly delicate as the hand holding the glass vial.

Sanura walked around the hot tub and lit three blue candles.

Assefa believed he understood her selection of the color blue but didn't know if the color had the same symbolic meaning in her culture as in his own. For Sudanese witches, the color blue signified healing, devotion, peace, relaxation, and justice, which seemed to fit perfectly with the spirit of the evening. In addition, the candles would help produce the proper state of being for effective spell casting, as would the full moon that shone brightly in the clear May sky.

Sanura finally looked up at Assefa, and they smiled awkwardly, having never seen each other in so few clothes before. Assefa wasn't an arrogant man, but he was well aware of the effect his body had on women. Were-cats were naturally strong, which didn't equate to being naturally muscular. He was both. For years, boxing, weightlifting, swimming, and running were integral to his weekly regime.

He wore a pair of knee-length, gray Speedos with a thick, black line that ran down each side of the trunks. Assefa specifically purchased them after Sanura had made her request for him to bring swimwear to the ritual. They were comfortable enough, but they also left little to the imagination. Hell, he was there to win her, and if that meant highlighting his package to do it, then so be it. Women had their little sexual ploys, as did men.

Even though he could turn into a furry beast at will, Assefa preferred the sleek feel of flesh, unencumbered by hair. So, his chest and legs were bare. Not a hint of scruffy hair covered the rippled effect of years of bodybuilding. Assefa was pleased with his physique, and from the jaw-dropping, embarrassed look on Sanura's face, so was she.

Glad to know I'm not the only one with Neanderthal thoughts.

Sanura finally managed, "It's ready." And in a much lower tone, "Damn."

He swallowed the ego boost of laughter that wanted to escape and followed her into the hot tub.

Her heated stare was intense, hotter than the water in the tub. Then she licked her lips, swore softly, and tucked a loose curl behind her ear. Finally, she looked briefly away and settled fully into the tub. "As you soak," she began, turning back to him, "inhale the fragrance and visualize yourself becoming physically and spiritually cleansed by the light of the goddess Isis."

Making sure not to hit Sanura with his long legs when he stretched out, Assefa did as she suggested, meditating on the handfasting ritual to come, the first and most crucial level of the tri-ritual marriage ceremony. He began by slowing his breathing—rhythmic, measured breaths.

Ten minutes later, Assefa felt Sanura's hand on his arm. Grasping him lightly, she helped him to a standing position. A sponge in her other hand, she dipped it in the purified water and gently squeezed it over his head. She did this three times, his eyes closed, a soft prayer on his lips.

When she'd finished, Sanura handed Assefa the sponge. "Now me," she said.

Assefa returned the favor, dripping water over her head—three times—blessing her with his continuous prayer.

As he watched the water flow down Sanura's curvaceous form, he noticed a gemstone in her belly button and smiled at his discovery. Then, pointing, he asked, "Is that it, Sanura?" But her eyes were closed, so he waited for her to open them. When she did, he pointed again and asked, "Does that gem do what I think it does?"

"It depends. What do you think it does?" The woman was messing with him. He liked that, but he gave her a mock-exasperated frown, and Sanura gave in, laughing at him when she said, "Yes, it does."

Then the laughter slowly spilled away, leaving an uncomfortable-looking witch standing before him. Damn it, she was nervous again, her gaze focused on the rippling water below instead of the man before her. Assefa refused to rush her. Sanura had to learn that she could trust him. Otherwise, he might as well change back into his suit and go home. He hoped, however, that if he patiently waited, she would reveal her secret.

Giving her the space, he felt she needed, Assefa took three steps back but didn't retake his seat.

Three minutes later, Sanura lifted her eyes and chin, squared her shoulders, and sighed with what Assefa hoped was faith. *In me. In us.*

"This is a moonstone," she explained, laying one finger over the gem in her belly, "it's the birthstone for those, like me, born during June. Through trial and error, I've learned that using a person's birthstone when creating a talisman helps strengthen the spell's potency. That's why I always use jewelry for my scent disguise amulets, especially jewelry made of silver. The properties of silver make it good at holding in a witch's magic, and it rarely needs to be recharged or reset."

Assefa smiled to himself. This was an excellent start. He could see her begin to relax as she spoke of her craft.

"Since you're wearing a moonstone instead of a silver bracelet or necklace, what else does it do besides conceal your witch scent?"

"You said it yourself, Assefa, three weeks ago."

He knew his face went blank because he had no idea what Sanura was talking about. Assefa stepped closer. "What did I say three weeks ago?" Had it only been three weeks since he'd met Sanura Williams? When he was with her, it felt new yet familiar, immeasurable yet finite, empowering yet cautious.

He took another step.

"You told me you thought the charm I wore did more than hide my scent. You were right, which is why I use my birthstone instead of the standard silver. Like I said, using a more personal gem to the wearer enables a witch to increase the potency and complexity of the spell."

"Meaning what?"

Her pause was even longer, and he felt he knew the source of her angst. Makena had taken him into her confidence and told him why

Houghton had broken things off with Sanura. When Houghton learned Sanura was more than human, he'd rejected her. Such a reaction didn't surprise him. Assefa wondered if Sanura feared he would reject her too when she revealed what her moonstone hid. Of course, he wouldn't, but her apprehension made sense, for he harbored his own fears. Who was he to judge?

Assefa took another step, putting him squarely in front of Sanura. He wanted to lift her head, hating how hard she was on herself. Hating Richard for sowing the insecurity Assefa could so easily see and feel.

Head cast down, she whispered to herself, "He's nothing like Richard." Then, she removed the vibrant green, unnaturally shaped gemstone from her belly button.

Assefa stepped back into the water to better look at the woman before him. His head was still down, and his heart pounded so hard it was audible, but Sanura refused to meet his eyes. His gentle yet commanding voice broke through the moonlit silence. "Hold your head high, sweetheart, for this is who you are, how the gods made you."

Cautiously, slowly, she did as he requested.

Assefa saw her completely for the first time, the moonstone no longer blocking her true essence. Sanura's once brown hair, which fell in thick rivulets to her shoulders, was a rich reddish-gold that sparkled as magnificently as Canopus over a sleepy Egyptian village. Then there were her eyes. No longer the flavorful brown that matched her hair of a moment ago, they were now a majestic emerald green.

She tensed when he moved closer, his eyes inspecting and focused. Her heart thudded, his sensitive ears picking up the anxious rhythm of the beat. From one fearful cadence to the next, Assefa knew this was the crucial moment. It was the moment Houghton had revealed he wasn't the man Sanura believed him to be, the moment the professor drew a line in the sand—full-humans and goodness on his side, witches and evil on Sanura's.

Assefa was but a cushion of insecure air away from Sanura. He closed the distance and pulled her into, what he hoped, was a reassuring embrace. For a second, she tensed, her arms limp at her side, face and legs rigid, unable to accept the security of his body, his soul…accepting her for the remarkable witch she was. But it was only a few heart-stopping seconds, then her resistance crumbled, and she allowed him to truly hold her, comfort her, and protect her.

He twined his hands in her red-gold hair, still wet from the purification ritual, and began to run his fingers through the thick curls. Finally, he angled his head to her neck, breathed her in, and smiled in satisfaction.

"You smell like gardenias—peace, love, and health. This is your scent," he said. Then, because he couldn't hold back any longer, he kissed her rapidly throbbing neck, little nips that saturated his tongue with her perfect, magical taste.

"This is who you are," he mumbled between swipes of his tongue, then raised his head and covered her mouth with his. The kiss, controlled but passionate, was not meant to ignite his growing flame. Yet the potency of the melding of their lips, mouths, and tongues was arousing enough to send a surge of unbound magical energy from Assefa and into Sanura.

She moaned and clutched him hard, pressing pointy, aroused nipples into his bare chest.

Assefa groaned. The woman was killing him. Did she know how close he was to ripping that man-teasing bikini off of her, spinning her around, and claiming her with hard, long thrusts of animal craving and need?

With effort, he released Sanura. And her smile of appreciation almost undid him. "This is who you're meant to be," he said, taking in the unique coloring of her hair and eyes. "You're as stunning and precious as a green South African diamond. Thank you for sharing yourself so fully with me."

Again, her smile was bright and heartbreakingly grateful. A man could get used to being smiled at like that.

He helped Sanura from the hot tub and whispered, "Now it's my turn to do a bit of sharing."

Assefa followed Sanura inside, closing and locking the door behind them. She grabbed a fluffy beige towel for herself and handed him one.

Then, neither speaking, they dried themselves off. Once dry, Sanura disappeared around a corner, returning with two garments.

Sanura passed Assefa one of the items, a white ceremonial robe made of expertly woven silk. The robe had long, wide sleeves that would come to the wearer's wrists and a long body that more than likely reached the ankles. In addition, the robe had a front zipper that was discreetly covered by a gold embroidered flap.

He turned the robe over and held it away to see the garment better. On the back of the robe was a design of a seated Sekhmet, the warrior goddess of Upper Egypt. She held an ankh of life in her hands, while a solar disk rested atop her lion's head.

He flipped the robe over again and noticed something he hadn't the first time. *How could I have missed them?* In the upper left-hand corner, over the heart, was a small print of a spotted jaguar and a black jaguar under that.

He looked to Sanura, and she explained. "That's my father's robe. My mother gave it to him during their handfasting ceremony. It's a family custom for fathers to pass on their robes to their daughter, who then passes it on to her mate."

"What if the father has more than one daughter?"

"I don't know. As far back as my family records go, only a female child has been born to each witch-cat mating. The men in my family only seem to make girls." Sanura shrugged. "It's weird, and I can't begin to explain it."

Pointing to the robe, she continued. "This particular robe has been in my family for four generations. The robe includes the print of the inner cat of the previous wearer. A new print is added only if it isn't already represented on the robe."

"Meaning, if my inner cat isn't one of the two already depicted, then I get to add my own unique print?"

She nodded, reddish-gold hair caressing her bare shoulders. "The robe is a spiritual and physical reminder of my family's bloodline and my connection to my ancestors. It's been magically preserved. It will endure. It has endured. Just like my family."

Seeing the jaguars beautifully displayed on the ceremonial robe, Assefa realized that each female in Sanura's family, for the last four generations, had been biologically compatible with a man with a jaguar as his inner animal spirit. Yet, Assefa's inner animal spirit was not a jaguar. No animal so normal as that. *A beast.* He solemnly wondered if the truth would negatively impact the rest of the ritual and their ultimate joining.

His face must've revealed his distress, for Sanura gently touched his arm. "Don't worry, Assefa, I'm sure your cat spirit will complement my earth spirit, no matter the type of cat you reveal to me during the dreaming."

He smiled, but her kind words held little reassurance. Her otherworldly hair and eyes may have been different, but they were spectacular nonetheless. His cat…well, the only thing spectacular about it was how well it stalked and killed its prey. *A predator of predators.*

No matter. Like Sanura, he was what he was. She would either accept his beast or she wouldn't. Rejection. That was the real beast.

Unzipping the robe, he took great care when he put it on, honored to wear the delicate family heirloom.

When he had it on, he noticed Sanura staring at him, eyes suspiciously moist. They hadn't spoken much about her deceased father, but it was clear that Makena and Sanura were still mourning the death of Samuel Williams. And here she had gifted him with the dead man's handfasting robe. Dammit, he didn't want to disappoint her, ruin what could be a turning point in their lives. But how would she react when she saw what truly slept within him? Would her spirit shriek in horror and abandon the ritual, or would she embrace him the way he'd done her? Only time would tell.

Assefa watched as she slid into her own robe. Hers was crafted much like her father's. It was also white, silk, and had wide flowing sleeves. Sanura's had a hood that hung halfway down the back. But, unlike her father's robe—*my robe*—hers didn't have images of jaguars over her heart. No, there was an inscription instead. In the Yoruba language, if he wasn't mistaken. Assefa knew a little Yoruba, but just beginner stuff, nothing more.

"What does the inscription say?"

Without looking, Sanura said, "'Oya has blessed our family. May our ancestors bless and watch over you in all the dark places you may walk.'"

Sanura slid one index finger over the gold writing. She looked at it then, and Assefa saw pride and fear in her eyes.

He thought he understood one but not the other.

"All females in my family are given their handfasting robes on their eighteenth birthday," Sanura informed. "It's anointed and inscribed by the eldest female member of the family. In my case, my maternal grandmother made this robe and gave it to me ten years ago."

Assefa walked around Sanura to take in the full beauty of the robe. On the back of the garment was an incredible landscape. He ran his fingers over the smoothly raised design. The Niger and Benue Rivers flowed from the northwest to the southern lands through tropical rain forests and swamps to their delta in the Gulf of Guinea. To the south of the great rivers were lowlands merging into central hills and plateaus. The entire design was encircled in what could only be described as a fierce fire of wind—protecting, shielding.

Assefa lowered his suddenly trembling hand and took a step backward. He stared at the design, seeing the truth behind each purposeful stitch. The symbols were so clear, the elements. Oya's elements of power, the elements of the fire witch of legend. *The prophecy can't be true.* It just couldn't, because if it was, hell was about to come calling— in a violent tsunami of water witch destruction.

And if Sanura was the fire witch of legend, he knew what that made him. *More than a shifter with a mythical beast as my cat spirit.* Yes, it would make him…*The cat of legend.* The label he'd run from his entire life. A children's story he refused to acknowledge as anything other than one of Aesop's many fables.

He turned Sanura around to face him. He had to know for sure. "You're an elemental earth witch?"

"A fire earth witch," she corrected, "with the potential to cast wind and thunderbolt spells, or so I've been told by the Council of Witch Elders my entire life."

She shrugged, but Assefa could see there was nothing nonchalant in that movement. Ah, now he understood the pride and fear he'd seen earlier. She should be afraid. They should. And, hell, macho bull aside, Assefa was afraid.

"So, you know this handfasting isn't just about us?"

"Yes, I know," she said, voice low and solemn.

Assefa cursed the cold, twisted hand of irony. Fate and love, power and war, they couldn't have one without the other, not if the prophecy was true, not if they were the witch and cat of legend.

"Let's just get through the first part of the ritual. Besides, I've never cast a wind or lightning spell. My hair and eyes are probably just flukes of nature, nothing more. Weird biology. I'm not the fire witch of legend."

Good thing she didn't follow Makena's footsteps and become a lawyer, for Sanura Williams would have no luck in swaying juries, not with the unconvincing argument she'd just given him.

Wanting too much for her to be correct, Assefa didn't bother challenging Sanura. They would know soon enough. She would turn twenty-nine next month, and his twenty-ninth birthday will follow three months later.

Earth births water. The sun births fire. But the moon, in its crescent state, brings forth the beast, giving away half of itself to make the beast whole in order to birth the man. The opening lines to the Sudanese tale about the fire witch and cat of legend churned in his head. Assefa remembered it well. He remembered it all.

He shoved the memory aside. Sanura had just retrieved her athame, a ritual knife. The black-handled, double-edged iron blade had hieroglyphic symbols engraved on it, symbols he didn't know, except for one. *Fire.* The witch often personalized such knives, and the symbols blended the tool's energy with the witch's magical intentions. Assefa knew the athame could be used to cast the magic circle, which he assumed was how Sanura intended to use it tonight.

Through his own study, Assefa understood that the purpose of the magic circle was to raise magical power, to create an area to serve as a passageway to the spirit realm, and to contain and focus the energy witches create through the casting of spells, to make it more potent. There was also an element of protection to the circle. By casting it, the witch ensured that no malign forces could penetrate and affect the outcome of her spell. Clearly, Sanura was ready to begin.

"Last chance to change your mind, Special Agent Berber."

He gave her smiling lips a quick kiss. "Not a chance, Dr. Williams. I'm at your service."

She winked at him. "Famous last words. I'll remember you said that."

Sanura refocused, and Assefa watched on in silence.

The first step, he knew, in setting a magical circle was to clean the area. This Sanura did with a ritual broom. First, she swept the carpet— *energy field*—of negativity. Second, she used the low table in the center of the room as an altar, on which incense was already placed. She lit all three of them.

She then walked the circle three times clockwise, carrying a censer in her hand. As she slowly walked the circumference of the circle, she incanted, "I conjure you, oh circle of power, to be a wall of protection against malign and negative forces. May you be cleansed of all impurities. May this circle preserve and contain the power I raise within."

When they had been warlocks, his kind could do what Sanura was doing, but no longer. Instead, shifters were conduits of magical power. Without familiars, witches could never become mistresses of any earth element. Yet, a witch stood before him who may have the potential to wield three of the four elemental powers. But it was he, a cat shifter from Sudan, who wasn't a jaguar, lion, cheetah, or any other known and accepted witch's familiar, who possibly held the key to her chest of power. *What will she think when she sees my beast? The cat feared above all others?*

Sanura used her athame to draw a pentagram to invoke the elements. A thin, red wave of magic seemed to bleed from the athame, forming the shape an inch above the carpet. "I invoke you, oh elements, the living earth, the breathing air, the warming fire, the chilling water. I invoke you, great Goddess Isis. I invoke you. Be with me. Smile upon your fire witch."

She moved her athame around the outer limit of the circle, counter-clockwise, and incanted, "This protective circle is open."

Assefa felt an indescribable energy flow up and around them. The magical energy she created, they created, was like diving into a lake in the dead of winter, with all your clothes on, surrounded by a blazing ring of fire. He was bone-cold and spirit-hot. His beast moved closer to the surface, seduced by the power of Sanura's spirit. The beast was already drawn to her, taking in her scent and licking his jowl in approval, in hunger.

"Come kneel with me, Assefa."

He took Sanura's extended hand, and they knelt, facing each other.

"Listen to my words and allow yourself to enter a peaceful state. Listen and follow. Listen and trust. Trust and have faith. In me. In my fire spirit."

He did, so he closed his eyes, listening to her melodic chanting.

CHAPTER TEN

Sanura stood and proceeded to the north quadrant of the circle. "I summon you, living earth, as I light this candle. I summon you, Isis. Bring power and strength to my spell."

She moved to the east quadrant and lit the white candle on the floor. "I summon you, breathing air, as I light this candle. I summon you, Isis. Bring power and strength to my spell."

At the south quadrant, she lit the candle and incanted, "I summon you, warming fire, as I light this candle. I summon you, Isis. Bring power and strength to my spell."

Finally, she walked to the west quadrant and placed a water dish down. "I summon you, chilling water, as I light this candle. I summon you, Isis. Bring power and strength to my spell."

Once finished, she returned to her position in front of a now serene-looking Assefa. His eyes were closed, breathing slow and steady. He was already in a meditative state. Good.

Sanura lifted her hood and covered her head. Except for her mouth, her entire face was concealed. Reaching for him, she found Assefa's large, strong hands and began a silent prayer. It was an ancient Nigerian prayer, passed down through matrilineal descent. Makena had taught it to her as a child, long before Sanura knew the significance of the words. And she recited them now.

The familiar words easily flowed from her, through her, a plea, an invitation to Assefa's animal spirit to join her fire spirit in the astro-physical plane. If his cat spirit didn't answer her call, respond to the magical summons, then there could be nothing more between them than friendship. Because only a witch's true familiar could follow the tracks left by her fire spirit, hear her song of joining.

She recited a soothing and melodic prayer to his inner cat, encouraging him to trust and join her. After five minutes, their spirits were transported to a realm beyond physical comprehension, beyond the theories of men like Isaac Newton and Albert Einstein. Their spirits traveled over the magical speedway to a place of mysticism and wonder, defying all the laws of the universe known to mortal men.

The plane appeared to be a vast space of nothingness as far as the eye could see. Sanura's reddish-gold hair blew in an improbable breeze. Green eyes glistened as she sought to make sense of her surroundings. Right before her eyes, the realm started to take form and purpose. The gray dullness gave way to a hot, bright desert. Yellow-gold rays littered the sky above, a canopy that felt thick and heavy. She bent to touch the sand under her bare feet, the granules like raw salt in her hands. It felt so real, as did the sun beaming down on her brow, causing a trickle of sweat to roll down her moist cheeks.

Her fire spirit came to life in this place of mystery and heat. It fueled her fire beast, and the sizzle of contentment was loud in Sanura's ears. Her fire spirit was elated, and it wanted to be completely set free, to be able to roam and explore. *To hunt*. But Sanura was having none of that. She couldn't let the spirit off her leash, not even here. *Not ever*. But she could let her guide Sanura. Permit the spirit to cast her net for the cat they both sought. The one they both wanted. For once, Sanura and her spirit were in complete agreement.

Unable to wait and do nothing, Sanura set out in search of Assefa's cat. Unfortunately, the prayer she'd been reciting for the last hour hadn't been enough to tempt the elusive cat to her side. In her search, the only other "living" creatures she'd come across had been typical desert dwellers—snakes, scorpions, cacti, all of which added realism to a place meant to bend and contort reality. But Sanura could detect no sound nor smell other than the squishing of sand underfoot and her own perspiration. The realm was stale, devoid of a true essence that could breathe life into its veins like rainfall to a drought-plagued Texas town.

Exhausted, Sanura stopped. She had no idea how long she'd been walking or whether she was even going in the right direction. *If there is a right direction*. Her fire spirit was now agitated, desperate even, and Sanura was lava-hot with the magic it took to keep her on this plane. If she didn't find Assefa soon, or him her, she would have no choice but to release the repressed energy, sending it back to the earth that had birthed it. And that, as the saying went, would be that. *End of ritual. End of a destiny.*

Slowly, she faced each direction; still, her cat was nowhere in sight. It had all been a cruel joke. The attraction, the magical connection she felt with Assefa. *Nothing but an illusion. Just like this place.*

Just as she was about to give up, Sanura saw a glimmer of a shape in the distance. He moved watchfully but nimbly toward her. The form was like a mirage in the middle of the desert, a trick of the mind and heart. But he kept coming, and she was as deeply rooted to the ground as a California Redwood.

Sanura strained her eyes to get a better glimpse, a clue in size, shape, or color as to the cat species, but the picture was fuzzy. More minutes passed, then, finally, the cat came into full view.

She gasped and dropped to her knees. Her fire spirit crackled with excitement. Sanura trembled and could only think about destiny and destruction, their destiny, the world's destruction.

By the gods, Assefa is a Mngwa.

The cat of legend trotted up to her, imposing and massive. He looked down at her, a myth that was no myth at all. According to legend, it was said to be stronger than a lion and deadlier than a leopard. It moved silently, came out only to kill humans, and then disappeared like a ghost ship in the night. The bodies of its victims showed wounds made by razor-sharp claws and huge teeth. The Mngwa was said to be so ferocious it could kill a person with a single bite or swipe of its paws. Under cover of night, the donkey-sized cat stalked its prey without a sound, its padded paws making it a most dangerous predator.

The mystery of the Mngwa had terrified East Africans for hundreds of years. No hunter had ever succeeded in killing one. Only fools even dared to try. Yet five hundred or more years ago, the big cat disappeared, never seen again. And the legend had been born. The stories of the ferocious beast traveled like a sandstorm, with density and over great distances. Exaggeration blended with the truth until no one could discern fact from fiction. In the end, as always, some believed the Mngwa would rise again and save the world from destruction, while others thought it nothing more than a quaint bedtime story.

With the mammoth cat hovering over her, Sanura was forced to lean back to see all of him. And while the desire to meet his gaze haunted her, she wasn't quite ready for that. Instead, she quietly observed the creature of myth and legend. The Mngwa's fur was dark-gray with black stripes, like that of a tabby cat. It looked winter-warm and summer-soft. The snout was long and rounded, head wide and thick, ears pointy and alert. And the body, dear Ra, his body radiated controlled might. Sanura swore she glimpsed rippling, powerful muscles even through the charcoal of snowy hair. Then there were his paws, easily larger than Sanura's head. The claws that extended from them were a good seven inches in length, frightening blades that promised death to any challenger.

Hot breath beat down on her, and she knew it was time to face her familiar. Casting her eyes upward, Sanura met the unwavering stare of the cat of legend. To her heart-stuttering relief, behind the beguiling gold eyes of the beast were the chocolate ones she knew so well. Within the shimmering depths of the most renowned cat known to walk the earth was the man, free, in control, and dominant. *Assefa.*

Whatever fear may have lurked within Sanura vanished when the giant cat lowered his eyes, then head, in an act of not submission but acceptance. Then, more amazingly, he plopped his humongous body on the sand in front of her, nearly tumbling Sanura over.

Like a kitten wanting attention, the Mngwa lifted his head and laid it firmly in Sanura's lap. It was heavy and so wonderful. Reaching down, she rubbed the incredibly soft fur of her familiar. "You're no legend," she said, a heat of awe in her voice.

It's time, her fire spirit whispered. *I want him. Make the warrior-beast mine.* No good had ever come from listening to her fire spirit. But this time, this miraculous moment in time, Sanura and her fire spirit were of the same mind.

She continued to caress the Mngwa, her mouth parting on a spell that would align their auras. "Blessed by the gods, we were cast out into the world as two. Two compassionate hearts, two purposeful souls, two enlightened minds. But this year, the twenty-ninth of our birth, we are no longer two, no longer separate, no longer alone, no longer half of a divine blessing. Instead, we are"—Sanura raised her hands, released her flames, and sank them into the Mngwa's coat— "blessed by the gods."

Sanura's aura exploded like a mushroom cloud over them, white and red with specks of gold throughout. Then, up from her flaming hands, pulled from the depths of the Mngwa's soul, came a whirling tornado of gyrating magic—gray-and-blue with an undertone of green.

When the tornado joined the mushroom cloud, setting off wind gusts and sparks of lightning, their auras gradually, completely, perfectly merged. Each took on certain dimensions of the other. Sanura acquired part of Assefa's blue aura, whereas Assefa's took on Sanura's specks of gold.

Hands still in his fur but no longer on fire, Sanura withdrew her touch, their auras now balanced. It was time for them to return home. *Mission complete.*

Reciting a prayer similar to the one that brought them to this plane, Sanura returned them, the journey fruitful, their spirits content.

Moments later, Sanura felt the rush of her soul being pulled back into her body. It was a wild sensation that neither hurt nor gave her pleasure. With magic tingling in her fingertips, Sanura lifted and removed her hood, only to find Assefa staring at her, face taut with what looked like uncertainty.

"I see I'm not the only one with an interesting family lineage." Before he could reply, she reached across and ran her right hand down his cheek. "Before today, I've never seen anything as ferocious yet beautiful as when your cat spirit revealed itself to me."

Assefa placed his hand over hers and held it to his cheek. Then, he whispered, "I was afraid my Mngwa would frighten you. The stories paint them as monsters, and I didn't know how you would react when you found out I didn't match the profile of your forefathers."

"And I don't match the profile of your foremothers."

"Perhaps that's the reason why we're biologically compatible, because who else would pair with the likes of us?"

Sanura knew Assefa was too smart not to comprehend the significance of what happened on the astrophysical plane. But if he was willing to pretend for tonight, that was fine with her. She didn't want to think about the next steps or in what ways Assefa's magic had enhanced her own. But it was nice to be in the company of someone who knew what it felt like to be different, who understood the heavy burden of having a mighty beast as an inner spirit. *Someone who's not afraid of what I am…of what I could become.*

Remembering her training, Sanura grounded the energy. She engaged in the requisite steps to free the energy and ended with, "Return unto the elements from whence you came." The magical energy was sucked out of the room, concluding the ritual.

"That was interesting."

Sanura removed her hood. "That's one way of putting it."

He blinked a few times and rolled his shoulders and head, probably shaking off the same lingering sensation from the astrophysical plane that Sanura felt. "You were right. I think I have more control over my aura now. I take it you'll explain what happened with our auras later."

"I can explain it to you now." But she had no actual interest in doing so at the moment. Instead, her focus was on her hand making its way through Assefa's springy head of curls.

"Sanura, I'm not in cat form now." A weak complaint. His words were not that of the rigid special agent but the softer man behind the badge. "You don't have to caress my hair like that."

She leaned into him. "Do you not like when I do this to you, regardless of your form?"

With a swift fierceness, he grabbed her waist and growled. "Damn woman, you know how to bring out the animal in me." His mouth slammed into hers. Hungry. Hard. Heavenly. No gentle kiss this. It was rough, demanding, igniting the fire that had been burning inside them since first they'd met, waiting for this moment to be unleashed.

Sucking and biting, the kiss was feral in its intensity, their bodies shifting, impatiently seeking closer contact. Tongues swept in and out of mouths, and hands glided over clothes-covered flesh.

She needed more, much, much more.

Apparently, so did Assefa. Jumping to his feet, Assefa hoisted Sanura into his arms, her legs going around his hips. And…*damn*…was that all him under that robe?

Assefa deposited them onto the white-and-black sofa, Sanura on top of him, their tongues tangling in another irresistible kiss. Needing to feel the man, her hot hands on his hard flesh, Sanura impatiently unzipped his robe. With his assistance, she pushed it down and off his shoulders.

Arms free, he buried his hands into her hair and pulled her in for another kiss. And the man could damn sure kiss. Make a woman feel desired with each stroke of his tongue, grinding of his hips.

Sitting up, Sanura admired his physique. She ran her hands down his marvelous chest, so broad and solid and— "You're unbelievably sexy. So fine."

Chuckling, Assefa reached up to free Sanura of her robe. Once off, he tossed it over the side of the sofa. "You aren't one to talk. I nearly passed out when I first saw you in that thing you call a bathing suit."

One finger slipped between her breasts, stroking ever so softly. A second joined, and then a third, grazing quickly heating skin. Then those fingers were at her back, sliding between her skin and the bikini, locating and undoing the clasp. The clasp at her neck soon followed, and the bikini top went the way of the robe.

Bared to him from the waist up, Sanura nearly imploded from the intoxicating way Assefa made her feel, his eyes eating her alive, one appreciative blink at a time.

"I've never seen anyone as beautiful as you, sweetheart. All supple and voluptuous, a mountain of curves I can't wait to climb."

Oh, hell.

Then his magnificent hands were on her, gliding over breasts aching for his touch, his taste. He didn't disappoint. Thumbs thrummed waiting nipples, each trek sharper than the first, creating peaks on top of peaks.

Hunching forward, Sanura dropped her head, rocking her hips and rubbing against his very aroused, very hard, very impressive erection.

And still, he worked her breasts, squeezing and tugging with just the right amount of pressure, just the right amount of—

He flipped them off the sofa and onto the carpet. In one fluid motion, Sanura was on her back, Assefa above her. "I've never wanted any woman as much as I want you." He tangled his hands in her reddish-gold locks. "I want to love you, make love to you, and build a life with you. Be your familiar as well as your mate."

Sanura didn't know what to say to that, so she touched his lips with her finger and said simply, "Make love to me, the way no man has ever done before. Show me the power of your Mngwa."

With that, Assefa's eyes went from human brown to Mngwa gold. He claimed her mouth again, pushing his muscular body between her legs, forcing them wide, chest smashing against breasts. *Yes.*

Sanura rocked again, lifting her hips to better feel what would soon be in her. By the gods, was there any part of the special agent that wasn't large and hard?

Probing fingers had Sanura moaning into his mouth. She was already so wet. His long, wide fingers just slid inside, stretching and stroking and reminding her how long it had been since she'd let anyone this close to her. *I didn't want another man's touch until Assefa.*

He probed deeper, slow, long thrusts.

"You feel so damn good, Sanura. So wet and responsive. I'm going to take my time with you. Let your body tell me what it likes. Then you're going to come for me. Over and over, screaming my name, begging me to be inside you."

He rose onto his knees, three fingers still working her.

In and out.

In and out.

In. In. In.

Bending, he claimed a breast with his mouth—sucking hard, ripping a scream of, *"By the gods!"* from Sanura.

But this, what he was doing to her, wasn't a matter for the gods, unless it was Oshun, Orisha of love, intimacy, and beauty.

Assefa pulled most of the way out, only the tips remaining. But, oh, they were enough because he crooked those skilled digits upward and renewed his attentions. Stroking the right spot, the one not found in the depths of a woman's sex but the shallow entrance to her vagina.

With a dominance she didn't mind, Assefa controlled Sanura—her breasts, her mouth, her sex. He gave and gave, possessing her through indescribable spasms of pleasure, spasms of delight, spasms of release.

Over and over and over. Just as he'd said.

The man's a beast. Thank the gods.

"Dammit, who in the hell could be calling at this hour? Can't a dwarf watch a movie in peace?" Mike paused the movie before fishing his cell phone out of his pants pocket.

Makena moved away from the swearing detective, slipping into the kitchen to answer the house phone, giving them privacy.

Three minutes later, a worried Makena was back in the living room. "Something has happened."

"There's been another attack. We need to get to Sinai Hospital right away."

As if there was a delay in his hearing and comprehension, Mike paused, then said, "Wait. What has happened? Are we talking about the same thing, Makena?"

"I believe so. I just received a call from Cynthia. Gen was attacked by the adze and taken to Sinai Hospital. We need to get Sanura and Assefa, right now."

Makena knew she was talking too fast, body trembling, fire spirit boiling with concern and rage. The bastard had attacked Gen. Gen was like a granddaughter to Makena, and the adze had come too close to ripping her throat out.

Her fire spirit was so close to the surface now. How easy it would be to let the flames fly. But now wasn't the time to indulge her own revenge fantasy. Eric, Cynthia, and Gen needed them. There was no time to waste.

Having walked to the basement door, Makena placed her hand on the knob when she heard Mike say, "You're just gonna walk in on them?"

Still in a fiery haze, she turned to him. A disapproving frown met her.

"It's been more than two hours. The ritual is probably over by now."

He pulled her hand away from the door.

"That's exactly my point, yet they're still downstairs."

"The ritual is an overwhelming experience. I'm sure they're talking about what happened."

"You mean to tell me the only thing you and Sam did during your ritual was to look into each other's souls and swap stories?"

Makena sobered to his point and took two steps back from the basement door.

"I didn't think so," he snorted, then opened his phone. "I'm calling Assefa."

The phone rang five times before throwing Mike into voice mail. "Damn him, he didn't pick up."

"He probably has it on vibrate."

"I'm sure he does have it on vibrate, but the man can hear every damn thing. I swear, I think he can even hear me when I take a leak. He asked me once if I'd washed my hands, and dammit, I had to go back to the men's room and wash them."

"TMI, Mike, TMI. Just call him again, or I'll be forced to go down there and pray, this one time, that Sanura is nothing like me."

"Come in, sweetheart," the foolish man said, ushering the adze into his precious home. "Dear Lord, child, where are your clothes?"

Before the adze could think of an answer or imitate the immature speech pattern of a pubescent human female, the stupid man hobbled away, awkwardly dragging his right leg behind him.

Too easy. Her lips pulled back and over teeth in a satisfying snarl.

Five minutes later, the sun-kissed man who smelled of fire-cured, dark-leaf tobacco returned, female garments fisted against his chest. He handed the clothing to the adze, then turned away and mumbled, "I don't know what happened to you, sweetheart, but no one has a right to take a girl's clothing and leave her stranded on a stranger's front lawn."

Weak. Compassionate. Foolish human.

The adze sniffed and looked around. The library the human had taken her into felt like a wooden cave—dark, gloomy, confining. *A perfect coffin.* But where was the one she'd scented earlier? Where was the witch who would satiate her pangs of hunger and set her free? The transformation wouldn't hold much longer, and the thought of draining the pathetic crippled human before her was almost enough to quiet her raging appetite. *Almost.*

Not bothering with the lemon-scented clothing, the adze opened her mouth to speak. Inexperienced tongue glided over teeth, saliva pooled and fell. But no words escaped.

But she didn't have to. The man, whose back was still turned to the adze, did, voice inquiring, trembling with anger over whoever was to blame for her abused state.

"I'll call the police. That's what I'll do. They'll take care of you, sweetheart, make sure you get home, capture the swine who hurt you, made you bleed."

Ah, yes, the blood. Even after the transformation, droplets of the girl's blood still stained her mouth. Her teeth. The very teeth that were throbbing to push free of the human gums she now wore and press into the witch's equally throbbing neck. The witch she'd scented from the air, from the gnarled tree, the one she needed to find and devour.

The man's fists balled, then fell away to massage the lame hip. And the adze wanted to laugh.

All that righteous fury, and you're nothing but a neutered dog—leashed and bound and a threat to no one, not even the fleas that suckle from your inconsequential hide.

The man's thin shoulders began to shake. His head moved from one side to the other, short, curly gray hair emphasizing too-large ears.

Without warning, the man turned and exited the room. But not before saying, "I have something to attend to. Give me a few minutes, and I'll be right back."

The adze growled at the closed door, ripping the green dress and ugly white shawl she held in her hands. Angry and impatient, she dropped the shredded pieces, stepping over them when she exited the library.

She was tired of the farce. The blinding ache deep in her soul demanded release, and she would wait no longer. A witch would die tonight, and her exquisite blood would soothe and rejuvenate her body, her life. The way it always did, the way it always would. But first, the adze had to find her.

The house was dimly lit and quiet. The hallway was short but wide, and the smell of witch was mouthwateringly close. Lowering her head like a Basset Hound on the hunt, she followed the scent, moving soundlessly down the hall, around a corner, and up a carpeted flight of steps. The smell of fresh paint hung in the air.

The adze paused in the upstairs hallway, dark-brown eyes scanning. Rows of angled pictures cluttered the walls like a mural done by a fool with too much sentimentality. Children's faces smiled back at her, mismatched shapes, hues, and forms making for the most unlikely of family portraits. There was a toddler in a wheelchair, a teenager guided by a large, brown German Shepherd, and a kid of indeterminate age seated under a tree with the do-gooder next to him. The boy's eyes stared vaguely at the camera, his wilted and misaligned jaw giving way to drool.

The man in the picture didn't seem to mind, though. His arm was wrapped reassuringly around the drooling retard's bony shoulders, the glare from the sun shining off the kid's bald head, reminding the adze why such beings were left in the woods to die. During her day, when adzes roamed unencumbered and were numerous, the weaklings prominently displayed on the *Wall of Shame* would've been shunned, starved, or fed to ravenous giant rats.

Running an index finger over the center photograph, the adze leaned in closer, recognizing the front of the house in the amateurish picture. And a sign she hadn't noticed when she'd entered the home. But one that made her now smile. *Children's House of Hope.* The adze wanted to cackle, to shed her human form and graze her tongue over canine teeth.

Instead, she heightened her senses and renewed the hunt. There were five doors on this level, all closed, no light peeking out from under them—except for one, the wooden door at the end of the hallway, her destination, her café au blood.

Reaching out with trembling, pale hands, long, ebony hair falling over forehead and into brown eyes, the adze turned the bronze-colored knob. The door gave way with a somber creak, and the delectable smell of witch blood filled her anxious nostrils, triggering the most ancient of responses.

The man and—presumably his wife—sitting vigil, turned confused eyes her way when the adze entered the candle-lit room. A twin-canopied bed with pink and white ruffles and lace took up most of the bedroom. A white dresser and chest with hand-drawn flowers flowed like wild vines, merging with the pallid wall.

The neutered dog of a man abruptly stood and placed a hand on his wife's shoulder, bidding her to stay put, to allow him to handle the naked intruder. Again, the adze wanted to laugh. The man was impotent, a pathetic non-obstacle. But, oh, how good it felt to know her belly would soon be filled, no matter the sick stench wafting from the child sleeping in the bed, her human guardians too ignorant to understand that their deathbed ward was a witch.

During her long life, the adze had tasted the blood of witches whose bodies were in varying states of illness, drug addiction, and good health. And while those—like the Baltimore girl tonight—whose body was free of impurities, the sweetness of the rich, thick brew as fine as any Napa Valley wine, was every adze's dream, in the end, however, food was food. The sick and dying girl in the bed, surrounded by glittering white candles, wouldn't make the Wine of the Year list, but, by the gods, she would do.

"What are you doing in here?" the man asked. "I thought you would get dressed and wait for me to return." He began to walk toward the adze and then stopped, his face registering the first horrid embers of fear.

And well he should, for the scent of blood, the pang of hunger, the whisper of animal instinct had the adze in its grip, transforming her. Human skin and limp hair began to slide away, her true self roaring forth. Moon night wings and glorious fangs shimmered in the cloud of deception.

A woman's scream, followed by a ragged hiss from the man, was an elegant symphony that transcended time. And the adze smiled her bat face as wicked as her soul. Her ravenous hunger exploded, the divine smell of fear fueling her craving.

"She's just a c–child, you m–monster, her parents—"

Swipe. Scream. Thud.

The drab, white wall had more appeal now. The shape of an imperfect red rose decorated it, not quite matching the flowers on the dresser and chest, the severed head at the adze's feet an openmouthed soccer ball, still spinning but coming to its last blood-spurting rotation.

A woman's disbelieving bellow of sorrow rang out. The symphony reached its crescendo, then another flower. This one blossomed on the opposite wall, a matching pair. How quaint.

The adze moved to the canopied bed and listened to the labored breathing of its occupant. Fair hair matted to sweaty head; eyes closed in somatic innocence.

Dinner is served. She lunged in for her overdue feast. This time, however, there would be no wallflowers. No, this blood, this sacred elixir of life was too good to waste.

And when the adze fed, she drank every drop, leaving nothing behind but a rotting corpse with hair the color of depleted sunshine.

CHAPTER ELEVEN

Assefa and Mike entered the hospital lobby, followed by Makena and Sanura. Assefa's suit felt uncomfortable, his body wound tight from the interruption and the sexual release denied him. His Mngwa crouched close to the surface, teeth bared, ready to spring forth and take down its prey. But there was no prey to be had in the surprisingly quiet Friday night emergency room that would appease his cat's appetite. Sex or an adze kill was all his Mngwa knew, all he wanted, denied both for too long. He craved either, but right now, after the attack on Sanura's niece, he would settle for the blood of the heinous creature. Yet that particular desire would have to wait—*for us both*. So Assefa strove to calm his cat spirit, telling him to be patient, that their time would come. *Soon, very soon.*

He looked around. Despite bustling nurses, doctors, and general hospital staff moving about like cogs in a well-oiled but overworked machine, the populated, family-friendly emergency room lacked the typical weekend disgruntled chatter that usually accompanied too-long waits. Assefa easily made out the hum of machines, a constant backdrop to the somber mood, a reminder that too many lives depended on the artificial, cold hands of the gods.

Yet, the smell of the hospital, more so than the cry of a bored toddler, the siren of an ambulance, or even the clatter of high heels that caught Assefa by the throat. The stench of death and dying, mixed with disinfectant, assaulted his heightened sense of smell. Unfortunately, he detected everything the weak antiseptic wash and sprays intended to cover—blood, urine, feces, vomit.

He smelled it all, including the diminished scent of Sanura's arousal. But considering where they were and what had happened to Gen, it was a subtle reminder of the arctic water that had doused their sexual flame. Assefa suppressed his cat even more, sending the Mngwa to the underbrush for a nap. Toxic fumes and sexual urges notwithstanding, he had a job to do.

He flashed his badge to the security guard on duty, his tone harder than intended. "I'm Special Agent Berber, and this is Detective McKutchen. We're here to see Miss Genji Zhou-Garvey. She was brought in a couple of hours ago."

"Yeah, I've been expecting you." The guard rose to his feet, thin frame stretching on the way up, cracking muscles as he went. "Umm, sign here and take a visitor's badge. Are the women with you? If they are, they must also show identification and sign in."

The guard's sluggish eyes traveled from Assefa and to Sanura. The green in them sparkled when they dropped to Sanura's breasts. The breasts Assefa could still taste in his mouth, feel in his hands.

Anger flared. His Mngwa stirred.

The guard continued to stare, too foolish to know the danger he was in. Right now, hell, Assefa struggled to ignore his pent-up frustration. Letting his cat out and using the guard as a chew toy would probably not go over well with all the full-humans in the waiting room.

A slow growl started, but before Assefa did something he would regret, Mike slammed his fist on the reception desk. "Unless you want my size-seven foot up your scrawny ass, I suggest you keep your stargazing to the sky."

Caught, the security guard cleared his throat, looked away, and down at the sign-in sheet.

"Look, rent-a-cop, just tell us where we can find the girl's family, so we can be on our way, and you can get back to watching your soap operas or eye groping women through a peephole in the bathroom, or whatever the hell you do here all night to pass the time."

The guard stammered, "S–she's in room 201." He pointed to his right. "The elevators are that way."

"That's all you had to say in the first place, asshole." Mike frowned and then snatched the badges from the guard's hand.

The women took the lead, following the blue lines and engaged in their own conversation. Assefa could hear the worry in their hushed tones, Gen being a loved member of their extended family.

"Thanks, Mike," Assefa said, glancing back at the security guard.

He'd almost lost it back there. That never happened anymore. *Not since I was a pubescent teen.* But he'd wanted to go for the guy's jugular, claw his eyes out for daring to look at *his woman.* And that wasn't like him either. *Damn it, is this what happens after a bonding? Do I have no control over my baser instincts now?* Ra, he prayed that wasn't the case. He wasn't an animal. He was in control. *Always in control.*

"No problem, I hate guys like that. They give all cops a bad name. Besides, I didn't think you wanted to play caveman in front of the women just yet. Sanura can go overboard with her feminism sometimes. So I wanted to spare you."

Assefa slowed so Mike wouldn't have to do double-time to keep up with him.

"The Williams women are used to my crap and won't give it a second thought, but from you, kid, they'd probably expect the ideal gentleman." He snorted. "Yeah, we dwarves aren't exactly known for our"—he wiped his nose on the sleeve of his suit jacket— "manners."

Assefa couldn't agree more. But there was a gentlemanly quality in how Mike protected Sanura and Makena, filling the void, as best he could, left by the death of Samuel Williams.

"What would you have done if I hadn't stepped in with the perv at the desk?"

His Mngwa fast asleep and no longer on the prowl, he stopped, looked down at Mike, gave a smile he knew showed gleaming white with slightly elongated eye teeth, and said without emotion, "I was going to break every bone in his hand when he handed me our visitor passes."

"Damn," Mike said, sounding too pleased with Assefa's response.

He knew it would've been an overreaction, but were-cats were a possessive species, mating for life, protecting their territory with claws and fangs. Their very life, if need be.

Leaving his bestial side behind, Assefa followed Mike and the women onto the elevator. The quartet took the brief ride to the second floor and got off.

They walked down a hallway before rounding a corner, Assefa noting the room numbers as they went. They turned another corner and nearly ran into a woman with dreadlocked hair spiraling over one shoulder. She was a few inches shorter than Sanura but heavier by ten or fifteen pounds, her weight falling nicely to her wide, full hips and thick thighs, filling out tight jeans. Freckles decorated her cinnamon-sugared face, as did gray streak lines, accented by puffy eyes.

He sniffed the air. Her distraught appearance contradicted the aura signature of the powerful witch he detected. It was a natural emission, one he guessed she probably didn't realize she was sending and could be easily managed if she was focused and in control. Right now, however, the witch was neither, which would explain why she wore no scent disguise amulet. But she didn't smell of gardenias like Sanura. No, her aura carried the salt of the sea and something else. *Her true scent.* Yet, he wasn't her familiar. The fragrance was shielded from him, as it should be.

But that barrier didn't stop his prowling senses. Her midnight-blue eyes revealed not only her biracial heritage but also her witch lineage. Moreover, the richness of the near-black color of her irises reminded him of the Blue Nile, confirming the woman as a water witch.

"Oh, watch it there, Cynthia, you almost mowed us down," Mike said, grabbing the young woman.

"Cyn, are you all right?" inquired Sanura, gently removing Mike's chubby hands from her friend's arm and replacing them with her own.

Trembling, the woman finally looked up. "I…I think so. I'm glad you're here."

She then turned to Makena, who was like a second mother to her, and walked into the type of embrace and security only such a woman could give.

Assefa knew Cynthia Garvey's story, one of many conversations he and Sanura had over the past couple of weeks, an attempt, on their part, to get to know each other better.

Cynthia and Sanura had known each other since elementary school. Makena and Sam had taken a personal interest in the girl and her future when her mother died in a fatal car crash, leaving her alone at the vulnerable age of sixteen. With no family to claim or provide for her, the Williams opened their home to Cynthia, affording her the same opportunities and love as their child.

"It's okay, Cynthia, we're here now," Makena soothed. "We'll get through this together. Just tell us about Gen."

Regaining her composure, Cynthia took the handkerchief Assefa offered and dabbed at her eyes. She looked at him, a pretty face giving him a grateful, knowing smile. "You must be Assefa. Sanura told me a lot of nice things about you. I hope you're as good as she says because this adze must be captured before any more of our children are hurt or killed."

What started as a compliment to the man ended as a plea to the special agent.

"Where's Eric?" Mike asked, sweeping the hallway with his shrewd dwarf eyes.

"He's with Gen. He wants to ensure he's there when she wakes up. So he refuses to leave her alone, even though she's sedated."

Makena and Sanura each grabbed one of Cynthia's hands, placing the woman between them, giving her the support she obviously needed.

As they did downstairs, Assefa and Mike followed the women, Cynthia leading them down the hall, then stopping in front of room 201.

Sanura walked up and peered through the small window in the door. "How's she doing?"

"She's as well as can be expected." Cynthia wiped at her eyes again with the loaned handkerchief. "She lost a lot of blood from the bite, but the doctor was able to stop the bleeding and repair the damage done to the artery."

Assefa could tell she was a strong woman, the urge to cry obvious, but she shoved it down, biting her lower lip instead of crying outright the way he knew she wanted to. The way she clearly already had. But she had it together now, at least enough not to break down in the middle of a hospital hallway, with nurses, doctors, and strangers as witnesses.

"If the bite had been three inches deeper, or if Gen hadn't fought as hard as she did, she wouldn't be here." She shuddered at her own words.

"Just another Baltimore homicide statistic in the Charm City, right? Why we haven't moved already, I'll never know."

Sanura hugged Cynthia, pushing her long locks off her shoulder. "I don't know how this could've happened. I gave Gen a scent disguise charm when I brought Betsy to school. It was her first day, and I promised to stay with her until she got settled. You remember."

Cynthia nodded, still clinging to her best friend.

And Assefa sensed magic coming from Sanura. Nothing he could see, but something *was* happening between them. *Just like that first day in Elizabeth Ferrell's hospital room.*

"In fact, while your secretary was enrolling Betsy, I used that time to check in on a couple of the students who were absent the last time I visited. I made sure they were all protected. This shouldn't have happened."

The women parted; Cynthia visibly stronger.

The magic he'd sensed from Sanura had done that. Not that Assefa exactly knew what *that* had been. But the woman was clearly feeling better, the redness and swelling around her eyes already beginning to fade. And Sanura had done that…w*ith a magical hug?*

"She didn't have the charm on her when she returned from the mall. I don't know what happened to it, but Eric made her put it on before she left the house. He's so careful to make sure we both wear the bracelets, ever since this adze started killing again. Maybe she lost it or let a friend borrow it. You know how careless teens can be. I was so frazzled that I didn't even put mine on before I climbed in the ambulance with Gen."

"It doesn't matter," stated Mike. "What concerns me is the attack itself."

"Mike's right," Assefa agreed. "The attack was bold. It goes against everything we know about how this adze hunts. They're one of two reasons for the sudden change. One," he lifted his index finger as a visual, "the adze is becoming desperate, or—"

"We're dealing with a different adze altogether," interjected Mike.

"Right, either scenario is bad. There's nothing worse than a desperate, hungry predator. Except for multiple desperate predators," Assefa said.

"If we don't catch this son of a bitch soon," said Mike, "it will drain whoever it can catch, witch or human."

"No, adzes only have a taste for witch blood," Makena objected.

"Mike's right, Makena," Assefa said. "Adzes may prefer your blood because of the benefits they get from it, but a predator is a predator. Their goal is to survive, and they will do whatever it takes to achieve that end. A lion may prefer to hunt a deer or antelope, but when a lion is hungry and near starvation, it will attack an elephant or hippo and take its chances."

"This may be what we have here, Mom," Sanura added. "There are many of our kind in the Maryland, DC, and Virginia areas. Between the two of us, we know all of them."

Sanura turned to Assefa. "Our network is strong, and we stay in contact. So unless someone is off the grid or entered one of the regions without contacting the local chapter, we know everyone. And one of our cardinal rules is to wear a scent disguise amulet at all times."

"So, by 'chapter' you mean coven?" Assefa asked.

"We don't use that word anymore, but you're essentially correct," stated Makena. "Ever since the Ferrells were murdered, we've been bombarded by local witches we knew nothing about. They were off the grid and living without the protection of one of the chapters, as were the Ferrells. After the murders, they realized they could no longer afford to ignore or deny their identity at the cost of their lives, so they sought us out."

"So, you two have spent the last three weeks charm-proofing the whole damn city," accused Mike. "And you didn't think it was important to tell us?"

"This is witch business, Mike," Makena swiftly responded, her tone reproachful. "No matter how deep our friendship goes, there are certain things I cannot and will not share with you. I don't ask you to divulge the inner workings of your dwarf society, so don't ask me to share what goes on in mine."

Mike grunted; the old man was too intelligent not to understand the finer points of maintaining intraspecies secrets but too stubborn to concede her an inch.

"You should've at least told, Assefa," he snapped back. "He's one of you. Not a bauble-and-broomstick kind of witch, but a bite-your-arm-off-like-catnip kind of witch."

Assefa placed his hand on the shorter man's shoulder. "They're under moral oath to keep their secrets from everyone not sworn to their bonded family, even a trusted friend like you. As for me," he smiled at Sanura, "they couldn't share such details with me until after the hand-fasting ceremony. Now that it's complete, and we know for sure that I'm her familiar, we're now part of each other's inner circle and can share more personal details about each other."

Mike looked at the three women and Assefa. The special agent had a good idea of what was going through the older man's head. Assefa and the women were aware of the rules of a society of which Mike could never and would never be a part. He had severed ties with his dwarf clan years ago, trading it for life among full-humans. Yet, it was Makena and Samuel Williams who had accepted him into their world, claiming a dwarf as family, friend, and godfather to their only child.

Makena bent down to give Mike a reassuring hug and whispered, "Worry not, my dear friend. In all other things, you have my absolute confidence. I trust you as Sam trusted you and as we've raised our daughter to trust you. Don't allow today to make you doubt this essential truth. You're our rock, our stalwart, our special dwarf, and we love you. You're a part of our clan, Mike." She stood tall then and said mock-sternly, "Let us not have this conversation again, Detective McKutchen."

"Yes, ma'am, Judge Williams." There was a relief and a genuine smile on the detective's face.

Well, Judge Makena Williams is a damn snake charmer.

Assefa started to ask Cynthia a question about the attack, but then he smelled it. Smelled *him*. Before he could stop himself, a low growl rumbled in his chest, halting the chatter around him.

Everyone's eyes flashed to Assefa.

But his eyes and words were all for Sanura. "What is he doing here? Did you call him?"

"What are you talking about? What is who doing—"

"The dickhead," Mike said, the smile gone, buried under the dwarf's obvious annoyance.

Her eyes moved away from Assefa and around his body, then quickly skated back to him. "I didn't call Richard. I have no idea why he's here."

Assefa swallowed—hard—balled his fists—even harder—then told his cat to relax and allow him to handle Richard Houghton. How could a day with so much potential end with a teen in a hospital and Assefa ready to drop his control and let his Mngwa have a little mathematical snack?

"Sanura," Houghton called from down the hall, his long arm waving as if they were on a busy street instead of a quiet hospital hallway.

"I didn't call him," Sanura repeated before stepping around Assefa and walking toward the ever-smiling professor.

A snarl. Mike this time. "He's a dickhead. Don't worry about him, kid."

"He's not as bad as all that, Mike." Makena gave Assefa's shoulder a reassuring squeeze. "He's just not right for our Sanura."

"Full-humans never are right for our kind, fun to play with but nothing more."

Fun to play with? Assefa didn't like Cynthia's words. But she and Sanura were best friends, and she probably knew all about Richard and how he and Sanura once *played. Is she playing now? With me? Wants to know what it's like to be with one of her own?*

"He's a nice enough man, but my daughter knows her future isn't with him."

But did Sanura think her future was with Assefa? He thought she did, but maybe not.

Makena and Cynthia joined Sanura and Richard, the women polite, granting him smiles, appreciating his seeming concern over Gen's health.

"The man's a charlatan."

Assefa glanced down at Mike. "I know. What do you know about him?"

Mike shrugged. "Not much. He's always treated Sanura with respect. Said the right things, did the right things. You know, all that bullshit men do to make a good impression."

"So why don't you like him?" Not that Mike liked too many people. Still, if Houghton treated Sanura with respect…

"Why don't *you* like him? And don't give me some bullshit about being jealous of the math geek. He's not even worth one of your expensive-ass ties."

"He smells of lies and secrets."

The detective nodded.

"He also doesn't quite smell human."

"What do you mean?"

Assefa watched Houghton with the women, catching bits and pieces of their conversation. Apparently, the professor was at the hospital visiting a friend. On his way out, he'd seen them get on the elevator and asked the security guard their destination. Being the top cop he thought he was, the incompetent fool provided Gen's room number to a stranger. Maybe on the way out, Assefa would break the idiot's hand anyway.

Mike followed Assefa when he put some distance between himself and the group, his cautious eyes still on Houghton. No way did he believe that story he'd spun for the women. Convenient did not begin to cover it.

"I don't know, Assefa. The dickhead has full-human written all over him."

"I'm not saying Houghton isn't fully human, only that he carries the scent of…something else."

"Something else?" Mike glanced back at the group. "Do you mean something preternatural?"

Their gazes met, and Assefa slowly nodded.

"Shit." Mike rubbed his hands together. "It's always the nice, geeky-looking guys, you know, kid?"

Yeah, Assefa knew. He was one of those nice, geeky-looking guys until he'd hit puberty and discovered weights and a hardcore beast lurking within. Now, well, the geek remained, hidden behind muscles, overpriced suits, and a badge. As for him being nice, a highly overrated trait, unless one happened to be a sexy fire witch with a beast of her own.

"So, what do you want to do about the dickhead?"

Assefa's eyes darted back to the group, then narrowed when Houghton casually touched Sanura's arm. *Rip the lying bastard's throat out.*

Staring at him, an all-too-perceptive Mike laughed. "I can't believe I once thought you were a happy-go-lucky Boy Scout who loved nothing more than being a pain in my ass and dressing like you were too good to do any real police work."

Assefa dropped his gaze to the shorter man. "I do like being a pain in your ass, Mike. But," he leaned closer to the detective, "I also like getting my hands dirty, and I've already dug up some interesting dirt on our Dr. Houghton."

Two bushy brows arched. "Let's talk."

"We will. But first…time to get a little caveman."

As Assefa walked away from Mike and toward Houghton and the ladies made their way toward Gen's recovery room, he heard the detective mutter, "For the love of Larry Talbot, show the dickhead your fangs, kid, and send him running home."

CHAPTER TWELVE

"Absolutely not," Mike said.

"There's no way in hell I'm going to allow you to do this, Sanura. Are you insane?" Mike yelled. "You must be out of your ever-lovin' witch mind if you think any of us will allow you to take such a risk."

"That's the second time you used the word *allow*, Mike," Sanura shot back, tired of going over this. "Whether I have your support or not, I'm doing it, and what you will or will not *allow* doesn't factor into my decision in the least."

Yes, this conversation was past old. Ever since the four of them had returned to her mother's, next steps comprised the entirety of the late-night conversation. After seeing Gen's pale, weak form and bandaged neck, Sanura knew what she had to do.

Mike spun around in Makena's kitchen, his pleading eyes fixed on Assefa. "Tell her she's insane. Tell your mate she can't do what she's considering."

Mate? Hell, Assefa had barely spared a few words for her since Richard had shown up at the hospital. And what was all that about, anyway? Something about being in the area and a friend? She didn't really know. But Assefa hadn't been pleased, even going so far as accusing her of calling Richard. Yeah, like she would do that.

"He's *not my mate*; if he were, he would know better than to try to make my decisions for me."

Okay, maybe she shouldn't have said the first part as if being mated to Assefa was such a loathsome idea. It wasn't. It was just…well, more than she could think about now. And she didn't even want to see how Assefa had reacted to her bold, insensitive declaration. *Gods, how come I can't ever get this right?*

"You see this, Assefa," Mike said, waving his finger at Sanura. "This is what I was talking about earlier. Feminism has ruined this generation of women and the next. It's best you see this side of her before completing the other two parts of the handfasting ceremony and this bra-burning woman's libber becomes your wife. She won't listen to a damn thing you have to say. If you're not careful, she'll wear the pants and put you in a frilly pink dress with garters and lace."

"Stop." The voice was boulder-hard and spoken just above a snarl.

Everyone stared at Assefa, his chocolate eyes shiny marbles of caged displeasure.

"Sit down, detective." He cast those unforgiving eyes at Mike. "You may be Sanura's godfather, but I'm her familiar. If I hear you speak to her like that again, it won't matter how much I respect you. I'll cut your tongue out and feed it back to you."

Mike sat.

Makena stared.

Sanura gulped.

Assefa was in rare form and, from the look of the man, not nearly finished talking.

"Mike's right, Sanura. What you suggest is too dangerous for any witch, especially an untrained one."

She scowled.

He ignored her.

"I'm not saying this because you're a woman or for personal reasons. I wouldn't ask *any* untrained person to do what you're suggesting. There must be another way, sweetheart, and Mike and I will find one."

So, they were back to "sweetheart." She sighed, recalling Assefa's words to Richard when she came out of Gen's room searching for him. *"You're playing games, Houghton, and I won't have it. I thought I made myself clear last week. But in case I didn't, I will destroy you or anyone else who hurts Sanura. Go. Away."*

Richard went. But it was Assefa's eyes when he'd turned and saw her standing there that silenced any cutting words she may have said to him. Under the heat of his unguarded gaze, words about a witch's independence, a shifter's possessive nature had melted on her tongue.

Concern, fear, and affection had stared back at her, his FBI mask discarded, eyes a vulnerable shade of dark brown. And those same fathomless orbs watched her now, waiting with a patience she'd never known.

Taking a deep breath, Sanura reeled in her womanist ideals and said calmly, "There's no other way. I wish there was. I can't allow anyone else to be hurt because we're too afraid to confront this demon. You said it yourself, Assefa. It'll start hunting full-humans if we don't capture this thing soon."

Assefa leaned against the wall in the kitchen, closed his eyes, and then brought his hands up to rub his temples. He appeared exhausted, the case clearly taking its toll, her request now adding to his worries. He shook his head, opened his eyes, and met her gaze. "She's right."

Sanura saw Makena catch Mike before he said something stupid. To her surprise, he actually settled down. That threat of Assefa's must've really gotten to the dwarf. And that was saying something because dwarves did *not* frighten easily.

"We need bait, and she's the perfect witch to lure the adze to us."

She mouthed the words, "Thank you, Assefa." But his arctic expression didn't change. Apparently, the man didn't want her thanks, didn't, in fact, want any part of her plan. Yet he'd given in, seen the merit of her reasoning. If nothing else, Sanura knew Assefa respected her mind and opinions.

No matter her bravado, there was no way Sanura could do this without the men's support. She hated doing this to them but didn't see a better option.

Mike began shaking his head before the words of "Hell, no. I won't do it," came spilling out. "I promised her father that I would keep her safe. I won't voluntarily put Sanura in harm's way."

Makena took hold of Mike's balled fist and slowly, effortlessly, smoothed it out. "You also made an oath to the people of Baltimore City to protect them against all threats. Would you turn your back on that oath? Is your family's safety worth more than the security of innocent full-humans who will assuredly fall prey to the adze if we don't do something now?"

It was a good lawyer's argument. Makena's face betrayed none of the fear Sanura knew her mother was feeling.

"Come on, not you, too, Makena. You can't possibly want Sanura to do this."

"No, Mike, I don't want my daughter to do this. But I trust you and Assefa will keep her safe. Besides, she's not as defenseless as the two of you may believe. Sanura has received extensive training beyond that of a normal witch. Sam saw to it, as did my mother. The three of you will be able to defeat the monster and free the city from its threat. This I believe, Mike, unless you're telling the three of us you're too old, slow, or otherwise infirmed to hold your own against the adze. Perhaps you should retire here and now if this is the case."

Yeah, her mother was good. Sanura needed Mike to be onboard with the plan. Her mother's persuasive words were the only ones he would even consider.

Sanura gave her mother a thankful smile, while Mike treated Makena with a glare that screamed "traitor."

A few tense seconds later, he released a defeated sigh. "For the love of Johnnie Cochran, I see why Sam never won an argument against you. You're the consummate lawyer."

Makena leaned over and placed a loving kiss on Mike's cheek, leaving two shiny lipstick marks behind.

Mike blushed, adding his own pink color to the mix.

It was done.

Three grim but resigned faces met hers, and Sanura forced a smile, wondering if she'd just made herself the adze's next meal. *I will destroy you or anyone else who hurts Sanura.* Of course, she knew Assefa meant it, and catching killers, after all, was his job, which was why the special agent was in Baltimore. Still…the thought of the man…her man, going up against a cold-blooded killer sent chills down her spine.

"We have a lot of planning to do," Makena said. She rose and then moved to the kitchen counter. "I'll make the coffee, Mike will grab the pie from the fridge, and Assefa will sit down before he makes a permanent outline of himself on my wall."

"What do you want me to do, Mom?"

"Pray that you're right."

Sanura nodded instead of admitting she'd offered a prayer to the gods for her safety before suggesting herself as adze bait.

Turning to Assefa, Sanura watched him approach Makena. "I need a few minutes. Mind if I use the heavy bag you have downstairs?"

Makena's fingers went to Assefa's forehead. "You have too much magical energy running through you." She dropped her hand. "Sam's treadmill is also in the basement. It hasn't been used in a while, but it still works. I think a good run will help."

"Thanks. I'll try not to be too long." Then, without a word to Sanura, he made his way to the door that led to the basement, opened it, and descended the stairs.

"What was that all about, Mom?"

"He's running a magical fever. He needs to get it down before fully concentrating on catching the adze."

Magical fever? Assefa didn't seem the least bit sick. No, the special agent had simply retreated behind that damn mask of his again.

Makena approached Sanura, and Mike didn't even have the good manners to pretend he wasn't paying attention to them.

"Are you planning on taking Assefa as your mate?"

Umm. Well, she wasn't expecting that question. Though she shouldn't have been surprised, not when it came to Makena Williams. Besides, she had merged their auras, an act that wasn't necessary to determine whether Assefa was her familiar. Yet such a merging was the way a witch magically bound her familiar to her. But it was the cat's bite that bound the witch to the man. Until both occurred, the mate bond was incomplete.

Without waiting for a reply, Makena just kept going. "Look, I know you've never dated a were-cat before, not that I ever understood the reason why. Anyway, that's old news. But you're a master witch. Your lack of personal experience with a were-cat is no excuse. Your father and I raised you better than this."

"No excuse for what? I'm not at fault here. I told Assefa that I didn't call Richard, and I didn't. Why are the two of you looking at me as if I've done something wrong?"

"Because you're trying to turn a perfectly good FBI agent into a *mangina*. And I don't—"

Whack.

"What the hell, Makena?" Mike rubbed the back of his head. "Did you just sucker punch me with a magical slap to the back of my damn head?"

"Watch your mouth in front of my baby."

"Your *baby* will be thirty next year. And from the sounds I heard when you opened the basement door, she knows all about vaginas and di—"

Whack.

"Dammit, *stop* hitting me."

"Language, Mike, language. Anyway," her mother said, swallowing what was probably another Mike-intended spell, "you left Assefa with too much of your energy. I know you've never had a familiar before, but you should know they need to maintain a magical balance. If they don't have that balance, they will become—"

"Grumpy, irrational, stubborn," she interjected. Yeah, Assefa was all of those. But she wasn't to blame. Why could no one see that?

"Your mother is gently trying to tell you that there are two ways were-cats can best release pent-up magical energy. Hunting and fucking."

Quick as a rabbit, Mike covered his head, but no magical slap came.

Makena sighed. "Or," she said with intense exasperation, "you could've simply siphoned off some of the magic before we left for the hospital. The way I taught you. That's what a witch does for her familiar."

Oh. Damn. How could I have forgotten that?

"Is he in pain?"

"Like I said, Assefa has a magical fever. He's exercising to burn off some of the excess energy. If he could hunt or run in his cat form, that would accelerate the process. But he obviously can't do any of that here."

"Or you could make yourself useful and go down there and apologize for leaving Assefa's side to go talk to the dickhead. And for the love of Heidi Fleiss, Sanura, don't tickle his pickle while I'm still within earshot."

Whack.

"Ow. Fu—If you do that one more time, I swear, I'll lock you up for assaulting an officer." Mike pushed from the kitchen table, his glare all for Makena. "You're an evil, evil woman. A fire-breathing dragon has nothing on you."

"Stop complaining. I didn't hurt you. A dwarf's head is like granite. Besides, it was just a mild spell."

"Mild spell, my ass. Nothing about you is mild, woman. Look, I'm going into the living room to finish watching *Lord of the Rings*. Call me when Assefa's done, so we can chart our next move."

Mike left the kitchen, one hand rubbing the back of his head. Sanura felt sorry for him. He was only looking out for her best interest. And what did he get in return? *A threat from his temporary partner and magical slaps from his friend.* Yeah, that was enough to send any dwarf fleeing to the comfort of Gimli and his ever-faithful battle-ax.

"Maybe I should go after him."

"Mike will be fine. I'll take him a cup of coffee and a slice of pie in a few minutes."

"I'm talking about Assefa."

"Oh, well, in that case, I think you should just give him some breathing space. Because, really, sweetie, there are just some things a mother doesn't need to know about her daughter. And if you go down there now…" She shuddered. "Thank Ra Assefa heard us because your scream is worse than a banshee's. I hate to think what I would've seen him doing to you if he hadn't heard me on the steps." Another shudder.

O…kay. Did her mother have to go there? But, yes, she'd been loud. And Assefa had made her come—three times, twice with his fingers and once with his fingers…and his mouth. *By the gods, the man knows how to work that tongue of his.* Then they were interrupted, and Assefa hadn't gotten his chance to release the excess energy from his newly altered aura. *The way I did.* Then it was all about Gen and the adze and getting to the hospital as fast as possible.

"All will be fine," Makena assured. "Don't worry."

Don't worry? About what? The adze? Assefa? My safety?

"I think I'll join Mike in the living room." Because she could hear every time Assefa's fist connected with her father's heavy bag—hard and harder. She'd make it up to him. *If he'll let me.*

CHAPTER THIRTEEN

Sanura watched Assefa peer out of the living room window, the impressive width of his shoulders not enough to block the rising sun's rays. He was a strong man in many ways, the body the most obvious but not the most important. His mind, loyalty, and faith exceeded that of any muscled form.

She'd never had sexual relations with a were-cat. On a certain level, full-humans were easier to manage. Their knowledge of her world was nonexistent, so they demanded less, allowing her to maintain a safe emotional distance. She'd had to admit that to herself recently. However, were-cats, especially ones like Assefa and her father, were dangerous.

I fell in love with your father because he was disciplined, so in tune with his cat spirit that he understood me when I didn't even understand myself. He was patient and kind, encircling me with his love when I would've run away. He was possessive, like all were-cats, but only for my heart, never controlling, always there, always true. Her mother's words the day her father died were forever engrained in Sanura's mind and heart.

I will destroy you or anyone else who hurts Sanura. Why would Assefa threaten Richard? The man could be pompous on occasion, but nothing more. *No match for a man like Assefa. "You're playing games, Houghton, and I won't have it." What kind of games? With me?*

Sanura ran a hand through what had to be a messy mass of hair. Still enjoying the view of her special agent, she wondered, not for the first time, how her handfasting had gone so terribly wrong. *No, not the handfasting itself, just everything afterward, like Gen's attack and Richard popping up as if we were still together.*

"I don't want Richard, and I didn't ask him to meet me at the hospital." Third time telling him that, and she would say it over and again if Sanura could forget the look of betrayal, then anger that had crossed Assefa's face when he'd sensed Richard's presence.

Assefa turned, and weary eyes settled on her. Sanura was also tired. A day already too long had ended with a two-hour strategy session. Fifteen minutes ago, Makena had led a grumpy Mike out of the kitchen and to the downstairs guest room before dragging herself to her own room.

"I know you didn't invite him. I shouldn't have snapped at you. I apologize. You didn't deserve my paranoia and venom." A hand rubbed over red eyes. "I'm not usually so…so…easily agitated." Another eye rub. "There's just something about the man that makes me want to"—for a second, his eyes flickered Mngwa gold— "protect you from him." He rolled what were probably tense shoulders. "It's late." He glanced at the window and the steadily rising sun, amending, "It's morning. I should go home."

Assefa didn't move.

His hesitation pleased Sanura, stirring memories from the handfasting and Mike and Makena's wretched sense of timing.

Sanura walked over to him. The man was clearly still agitated, and she wondered how much of her magical energy he'd burned off. She hated seeing him this way, off-kilter and on edge. His mask, the one that kept her out and his emotions in, was gnawing the hell out of her.

She touched a cheek, the beginnings of stubble there, his face too warm. *He still has a fever. All my fault. I should've known this would happen. Should've better prepared and taken care of my familiar.*

"I'm sorry." He didn't even bother asking for what she was apologizing for. The way he looked at her, with understanding and forgiveness, Assefa knew precisely what she was talking about. "I won't ever do that to you again." She raised her other hand and stroked his other cheek. "I promise."

Eyes on her, Assefa said nothing. Sanura knew she should siphon off that extra magical energy still swarming through him. Now was perfect. They were alone, she was able, and Assefa seemed willing. Yet she waited and didn't begin the requisite incantation. Instead, Sanura lifted her face while pulling Assefa's down.

She kissed him.

Tender.

Slow.

Lips and tongue worked to coax him from his self-imposed shell, willing him to lower his mask and let her in. Twining fingers in hair, Sanura massaged his scalp, knowing how much Assefa enjoyed the caress even though he refused to admit it.

Deeper. Her kiss.

Harder. Her massage.

Then she heard it, neither roar nor growl—a purr. *Yes, purr for me, baby. Let me know you're alive in there, that you still burn for me, the way I'm burning for you.*

From one purr to the next, Sanura pressed against the nearest wall and Assefa's massively hard body. *Be careful what you ask for.*

He took over the kiss and—*hell, no*—it was no longer tender, no longer slow, but—*thank Oya*—still wonderfully deep. Still delicious. Still wet. Still hot.

Standing on tiptoe, she wrapped arms around broad shoulders. Joined mouths ate at each other with vigor, lust, want, and madness.

On a ragged hiss, Assefa's mouth slid from hers. She instantly missed those lips. But they returned.

He bit a nipple. The slight sting sent a flood of heat through her. He bit again and again.

Each time, each erotic nip through silky blouse had Sanura arching, a silent demand for a larger, harder bite. But he didn't nip her again. Instead, he opened his mouth and devoured as much of her as he could.

Then he began to suck, wetting her blouse and bra as he found her nipple and made it his. So good, Sanura could barely stand. Another sweet purr and then bold hands shoved her bra up and out of his way. His mouth returned, locating naked breasts and aching nipples.

She heard herself moan. The more he sucked, twisted, and bit, the louder her moans became and the more urgent her need grew. Between the lust shrouding her brain, there was one word that broke the spell. *Banshee.* Gods no, there was no way they would have sex in Makena Williams' living room with her mother and Mike in the same house.

"Not here."

Assefa undid the front bra clasp, claimed breasts with both hands, and then kissed her, sending scorch patterns from their mating lips, down her throbbing nipples, and to her quickly moistening sex.

And under she went.

Those wily hands of his moved beneath her skirt, found her wet secret, and began to stroke. And—*yes*—she knew in less than two minutes Assefa would turn her into a raging, shameless banshee on orgasmic crack.

Searching for fortitude she didn't honestly want to find, Sanura squeaked out, "Not here. We can't do this here."

His growl returned. "Where, Sanura? I'll be damned if we have sex in a car, and I don't want to wait until we drive to my place to be inside you."

She didn't want to wait either. But they had a better option than the back seat of one of their cars.

"Come with me." She took his hand and then remembered her skirt was hoisted to her waist and her blouse and bra were askew. Leaving the bra undone, Sanura dropped his hand, so she could straighten her shirt and readjust her skirt. Once done, she reclaimed his hand.

Sanura found her purse and guided them from the living room, through the kitchen, out the back door, and toward a one-level cottage directly behind the main house.

"When my father died," Sanura started to explain, filling the anticipatory silence as they crossed the stone path to the cottage, "I began spending more time at home to be near my mother. Eventually, I let my lease run out on an apartment I was renting in College Park. Now I spend the weekends here. During the week, I stay at a Council-owned house with three other witches who also work for the university. Mom insisted I stay in the guesthouse, so I could have privacy and she wouldn't have to put up with a grown daughter who likes to practice spellcasting at the oddest hours. To be honest"—she used her key to unlock the door and let them in the house—"I think Mom just wanted time and space to grieve in her own private way while having me close enough that she could keep an eye on me, secure in knowing she didn't lose everyone she loved."

"I'm sorry, sweetheart. I know how it feels to lose a parent. My mother died when I was five. My sister and I were too young to understand why she was no longer around. It was as if she was sucked out of our lives as if she never existed. No one in the family, especially my father, ever mentions her. I don't even remember a funeral, though there had to be one."

Some of the light in his eyes dulled when he reminded himself how little he'd retained of his life before his mother's death. But children as young as Assefa had been when his mother passed on typically recalled only bits and pieces of the deceased parent if anything. And as heartbreaking as her father's death had been, Sanura had nearly three decades of fond memories to draw upon. In that respect, she counted herself among the lucky.

This discussion had taken a morbid turn, and while Sanura wanted to know everything about Assefa, talking about dead parents wasn't precisely mood-setting conversation. She blamed herself for that, her nerves causing her to babble.

"You have a sister," she said, picking up on the one clue to his identity she wanted to know more about.

"A twin sister," Assefa clarified, his delectable lips forming the sweetest of smiles. "Her name is Najja, and I would love for you to meet her someday. I think the two of you would get along. You're both smart, strong-willed, sensitive women who value family and friends." As if it was an afterthought, he added, "I also have an older brother, Razi." The look in Assefa's eyes told her all she needed to know about their relationship. The psychologist in her knew when to dig deeper and when best to let a subject drop. Sanura asked no further questions.

She removed her shoes, and he followed, placing them on the shoe rack in the foyer.

Sanura pulled him farther into the guesthouse, then watched as Assefa took in her quaint quarters. They were painted in earth-tone colors of brown, green and blue, offset in clean patterns of white on the ceiling, window frames, and wall paneling. The floor was made of solid

Brazilian cherry wood, which glowed with a deep unworn shine. All care of Samuel Williams, his unknowing last project before his death.

"How was Elizabeth Ferrell placed in a foster home so quickly?"

"We take care of our own. It doesn't hurt having a mother who just happens to be a family court judge."

Makena Williams, a former prosecuting attorney, often used her position as a judge to assist witches in family matters. In fact, all witches used their knowledge and roles in full-human society to lend a hand to their sisters and brothers whenever the need arose. *Who else can we truly trust but each other?* There were many such secret parallel societies, living beside or below that of the full-human one. Full-humans wouldn't be comfortable with the idea of preternatural beings living and working among them. In fact, they would be horrified. The world had witnessed, unfortunately, what it meant for humans to fear the unknown, the different and unexplainable—repulsion, shunning, even genocide.

No, witches did not always play by full-human rules. And when it came to protecting their own, especially the youngest among them, they were led by their own rules. Elizabeth Ferrell, an orphan by full-human standards, now had more family than she would ever need. She was safe, and she would remain that way. In the end, that was all that mattered.

Assefa followed Sanura when she made her way toward the bedroom. "Are the foster parents witches as well?" he asked before he closed the door behind him.

"Of course, they're witches."

Like the outer part of the house, it was redone, but not by her father. *By me.* She had pictures of smiling family and friends on her dresser, desk, and nightstands placed neatly alongside ritual candles of varying colors, sizes, and scents. Her king-size bed had fluffy down pillows covered in a floral print pillowcase, accenting the all-white comforter that hung to the floor.

While she agreed with her mother and Cynthia that the bed was far too large for the size of the room, looking at Assefa's bodybuilder frame, she was now pleased with her decision to purchase the ridiculously large bed. Oh, yeah, the things she could do to him in that spacious bed. Sanura was suddenly pleased Richard had never visited this place, slept in that bed, sullying this moment in any way.

Sanura lightly brushed her fingertips over his face, which sent his eyes fluttering closed. He was being extraordinarily passive, nothing like the aggressive were-cat he'd been in her mother's living room. *"I don't always have to be in charge. In fact, it's better when the woman takes the lead."* She grinned with understanding and remembrance. He was back in control and intent on letting her take the lead.

"Tell me what you want me to do. What will bring you pleasure?"

Sanura did want to give Assefa pleasure. The man had already given her so much. She wanted more, of course, but Sanura had never been a selfish lover.

Eyelids opened, mouth smiled, and arousal bloomed. "We can undress each other. Take it slow. Savor our first time together. Otherwise"—he stroked her hair, a shallow growl following— "we'll tear into each other, searching for the relief denied us earlier instead of enjoying the total experience. And, sweetheart"—he lowered his gaze to her kiss-moistened lips— "I want to give you all you deserve, all you can handle. And more."

A lasciviously confident smirk crossed his sexy features. Sanura gulped, her body tingling in all the right places. He was right. If they continued the way they were going back at the house, they would barrel through the sex, fucking instead of loving. *Just like Mike said.* While Sanura wasn't opposed to the former, she wanted their first night together to be the latter.

Sanura lowered her hands to unbutton Assefa's blue dress shirt. She ran unhurried hands up his chest and to his shoulders, where she slid his shirt off and down his arms to fall at his feet. She kissed first a cheek, then an ear, his neck, stopping just long enough to tickle, taste, and torment. Lips found pectorals, her tongue his dark, ripe nipples, gently biting, sucking, wrenching a soft curse from the special agent.

Curious fingers skimmed over rippling abs, dipping into belly button and circling.

Assefa sucked in a breath.

Sanura smiled, her lips pressed against his chest, still kissing, still enjoying his rich, honeyed flavor. She undid his leather belt, giving her access to the button that held his pants and her resolve together.

Sanura couldn't help but wonder how long he would allow her to torture him.

Finally undoing the button, she slipped her hands in the waistband and pulled dark-blue pants down. She slid down his body with the pants, helping him remove them from his ankles to rest beside the discarded shirt. Then off came the dress socks, long, large feet revealed. And, damn, even the man's feet were sexy. *Or maybe I'm just so turned-on I would find anything about Assefa sexy right now.*

Unable to resist, she ran her hands up his muscled legs as she stood, resting them on lean hips. "I was hoping you'd left those trunks of yours on." Fingers played with the waistband of his burgundy-and-black boxers.

"If you recall, my witchy temptress," he said, the first sign of the return of the playful, flirtatious Assefa, "you could've hung a flag on my dick; it was so hard. No way was I squeezing myself into some spandex torture device. Besides"—he winked— "from the way you tore those trunks off of me, I think they already did their job."

Was that a blush creeping into her cheeks? By the gods, it was. Because, hell yes, she'd wanted Assefa out of those trunks, flesh to flesh, sex to sex. And they were almost there, condom-covered penis at her entrance, ready to take the plunge, bring them both ecstasy.

Lightly, she swept her lips over his, resuming her torture game, wanting her special agent to lose control the way he'd made her do earlier. But like the predator he was, Assefa seized the bait, taking the kiss from a playful taunt to an intense embrace. He kissed her deep and long, prolonging the intimacy, pressing his solid body into her soft form. Enraptured, she wrapped her arms around his neck, the building sensation too much and not nearly enough.

Unexpectedly, Assefa ended the kiss. "Your turn."

Lost in an electrical fog of stimulation, Sanura had to focus to process what Assefa had just said to her. "What?"

"It's my turn to undress you." Assefa reached for her blouse.

"Oh, yeah, right."

She still had clothes on? How could one kiss make her feel like she stood naked in his arms?

With patience and control, Assefa slipped off her blouse and bra. His appreciative eyes landed on breasts and abs by Healthy Body, Strong Mind Fitness Center; Sanura was suddenly glad she hadn't hexed the crazy "Drill Sergeant" Dena during the instructor's military-inspired kickboxing class.

He fingered the underside of her breasts, gentle back-and-forth glides. Then his large hands held her bare breasts, taking their weight before squeezing ever so delicately. She tipped her head back on a moan. His mouth swooped in and took advantage, sucking and nipping, making her lightheaded and unbearably wet.

Masculine hands drifted to her waist before going lower to massage her bottom. The pressure of his wicked fingers worked in concert with his greedy mouth, a double assault that had to be a felony in some state of the Union.

Assefa's tantalizing hands found her skirt. With the same care he'd used to remove her blouse and bra, he unzipped the garment, sliding it over her hips, backside, and down and off her legs. She now stood before his kneeling form in only white laced panties.

Languidly, hands ran from ankles to calves, to thighs and hips, and back down again, claiming her with his rugged hands as much as those golden Mngwa eyes gazing up at her. Mouth and tongue followed hands. Sanura couldn't watch anymore, fearing she would collapse from the sight. Then again, she reminded herself dully, he hadn't done much of anything yet. *And I'm so embarrassingly wet. So close to coming.*

Carefully removing the moonstone from her belly button, he replaced the jewel with his tongue. And, for once, Sanura didn't feel self-conscious about her unique hair and eye coloring. No, if anything, Assefa made her feel beautiful, alive, special.

Kissing her stomach, his smile felt warm and wet. "You're so sexy. Amazing and hot and so goddamn tasty I want to eat—"

"Do you know what you're doing to me?" she rasped, fighting to draw enough air into her lungs.

"The same thing you're doing to me." He stood. "If I don't make love to you right now, I won't be responsible for my Mngwa's actions." This time his voice held the not-so-faint growl of his cat.

Assefa pulled her to the bed, but it was she who pushed him down, straddling him as she'd done earlier. He was hers now, so Sanura eagerly kissed and licked every scrumptious inch of Assefa's neck, shoulders, and chest, pleased when she heard him purr. She slid down his mighty body to free his arousal from the boxers, tossing them to the floor.

Impressed and feeling like she should give a shout-out to Sekhmet for creating such a fine specimen, Sanura stared at Assefa's magnificent, bronzed body, the touch, sound, and taste of him hypnotically unnerving. Animal or male magnetism didn't begin to capture the explosions he set off deep inside her. Unable to speak those binding and fathomless words of commitment, she poured all her emotions into exploring his body, enjoying locating all the spots that most made him purr.

Just when Sanura was about to take him in her mouth and suck him until he squirmed under her mind-blowing ministrations, losing all control, Assefa rolled her over and then effortlessly divested her of her panties. *Damn him.*

"You've tortured me enough, temptress. I see you like to play with fire."

She wiggled teasingly under him, his penis heavy, hard, and not where she wanted it. "I'm a fire witch; that's what I do."

"Is it? Well, I got something for you, my little witch."

Sanura just bet he did, and she couldn't wait. But Assefa jumped from the bed. Less than twenty seconds later, he was back with a triumphant smile and a closed fist. He opened his hand, and gold, sparkling paper unfurled.

"Boy Scout," she said with a smile and then paused, looking closer. "Magnum." Her grin widened. "Braggart."

"Fire and Ice condoms, temptress." He showed her the profile of a warrior of ancient Troy and winked at her, slow and outrageously cute. "We wasted one earlier." He tore one open and put the condom on, rolling it until it covered his magnificent girth. "If you aren't tired, let's see how much fire and ice we can stand."

The glow of his eyes was her only warning before he took Sanura in a hard thrust, ripping a scream of pleasurable shock from her.

"You're so soft and wet," Assefa moaned, every part of their bodies joined in an electrical dance that shot through her like lightning through a tree—powerful and unforgiving. Pulsing, throbbing, white heat invaded the room, captured and released as the rhythm pounded loudly and methodically to a beat of their own making. Passion-filled groans charged the atmosphere. Sacred names broke the sound barrier in a soul-rendering symphony made up of an orchestra of two intertwined bodies of sweat and desire.

"Oh, gods…Yes. Yes!" Sanura yelled, not caring how loud she was. Right now, she felt more than capable of out-screaming even the banshee queen. And for the love of Isis, was Assefa growing inside her? Longer? Thicker? Gods save her. He was. He had. And she was full to overflowing, receiving more than she'd ever dreamed possible.

Eyes a dark shade of gold now, Assefa's fangs slipped a little from his gums, their tips below his top lip. Sanura knew his cat instinct was to claim her, to bite into her flesh and take her as his mate. *His mate.*

Sanura tensed.

Assefa stopped.

Her fire spirit raged, hissing at the woman to complete the joining, to not fear the unknown, the uncontrollable.

He stared down at her, his body trembling. From mating need or halted pleasure, she couldn't determine. With clear effort, if not reluctance, fangs lifted and then disappeared.

The mood threatened to follow.

She watched him, wondering what he would now do. If he would decide he made a mistake taking her to bed.

Then, like replacing a dead battery, Assefa sparked to life, nipping a shoulder. "No worries." He began to move, setting the pace, a slow speed that was no less intense, no less toe-curling for its lack of raw force.

There were no more words, no more attempts at claiming, no more fear, just the heat, passion, and burning pleasure of two bodies in search of unforgettable rapture.

Assefa awoke a couple of hours later to find himself alone in bed. Through the flicker of a candle flame, he saw Sanura kneeling by the foot of the bed in what appeared to be a meditative state. Not wanting to disturb her, he remained silent.

"Did I wake you?" a gentle voice queried three minutes later.

"Not in the way you mean. I reached for you and found a cold, empty spot." He turned the covers down in invitation. "If you're finished, come back to bed."

Sanura blew out the candle and returned it to her dresser. She removed the short, black robe she wore and slid into bed next to him.

"Were you praying or meditating?"

"Praying."

Who wouldn't pray at a time like this? Sanura had to be nervous about facing the adze. There was no shame in that. None at all. He pulled her closer to him. With her head on his shoulder, thick, wavy gold hair tied back in a haphazard ponytail, Assefa ran his hand up and down her back, not to arouse but to soothe the tension he felt in her muscles.

He knew he'd frightened her earlier. Assefa hadn't meant for that to happen, hadn't meant for his fangs to come out. Didn't realize that making love to Sanura would arouse his cat so much, the feline eager to claim his mate. The desire to sink his teeth into Sanura had been so strong, even when she stared up at him with indecisive and scared eyes. With all the strength he possessed, Assefa had forced back the mating magic and his fangs.

But she hadn't kicked him out. No, Sanura had reveled in their love-making as much as himself. So maybe she just wasn't ready for the permanence of the mating mark. It would, after all, make them eternal mates, only death or an anti-bonding spell capable of separating one soul from the other. In that light, Assefa could understand her skittishness. But that didn't necessarily mean Sanura didn't wish to be with him, to move their relationship forward, beyond the case, beyond Baltimore.

Not giving himself a chance to think of all the reasons he shouldn't ask, Assefa blurted out, "Move in with me."

The hand that had been languidly drawing circles on his chest abruptly stopped. While the quiet room hadn't bothered him a moment ago, it was now filled with a mood-killing silence. If it were possible to hear oxygen being sucked from the dark space, Assefa would've detected it at this very moment, the sound competing against the rapid beating of his vulnerable heart.

Sanura leaned on one elbow, clutching the wrinkled flat sheet to her breasts, and stared at him, her green eyes bright with doubt and uncertainty, brows furrowed, lips tight and anxious. His close-set brown eyes never wavered, allowing her to scour the depths of his soul for whatever truth she sought. His request was sincere, and he took comfort in that truth.

Yet the longer she quietly scrutinized him, the more his logical, insecure side had to rebuild its walls. "Just a trial run to see how it works out," he said, squelching the urge to withdraw the offer and patch his fragile ego. "You can still live here with Makena on weekends, if you like. I'm only asking that instead of staying with your witch friends during the week, you stay with me in Virginia. I have a home, and it's more than large enough for the two of us. It's not as close to the university as where you're currently staying, but the commute should be reasonable." He was babbling, but the longer she stared at him, the more he nervously spoke in circles.

Finally, she found her tongue, but her words didn't put him out of his misery. "That's a lot to digest. I need time to think about all you've said and whether we're moving too fast."

It was he who now opted for silence over a verbal response. Assefa kicked himself for pushing, for revealing his hopeful plans too soon.

Yet he wasn't one to play games. Once he knew what he wanted, he went after it. Perhaps this wasn't the best strategy to use with Sanura, but he didn't know any other way to be while being true to himself. Wishing he could turn back the clock five minutes, he shook his head. Then, falling back on his FBI training, Assefa spoke in a tone devoid of the hurt he felt. "Take all the time you need, no pressure. We better get a few more hours of sleep if we want to be at our best when we go after the adze." He gave Sanura a forced smile, a chaste kiss on the forehead, and then turned onto his side, away from her.

He closed his eyes, wondering what she was so afraid of. Hell, she'd just given him her body—twice—and now she was the one retreating. *Even without the moonstone, she's still hiding.* But where did she think they were going with all this? What had been the point of the handfasting ceremony? *Why did she permit her fire spirit to bind my cat spirit to her if not to take our relationship to the next logical level? What had been the point of tonight? To find out if the rumors about were-cats' prowess were true?*

Assefa felt the bed shift before she snuggled against his back, pressing her naked body into him. Sanura slipped her hand between his arm and hip and found what she was looking for. Pressed tightly against his firm back, she slowly kissed his neck while stroking him in the same fashion, gradually increasing the intensity.

He desperately sought to clear his mind of all thoughts of her and the desire she was trying to build in him. Assefa took himself through mental exercises to get his body under control. He told himself the flesh was a fickle creature, like a woman, but a man's well-trained mind was stronger. He told himself this lie and willed it to be true.

Despite Assefa's valiant fight to ignore the sensations swirling throughout his body, he knew he wouldn't hold out much longer. He grew hard and long in her manipulative hand, twitching each time she circled the delicate, moist tip. And when she cupped and massaged his balls, his resolve snapped.

"Damn you, Sanura, you're a fiendish witch," he half growled, half moaned. Sanura sped up her stroking, perfecting her rhythm, learning his body. To his shame, he gave in to her obvious female manipulation, relaxing and submitting to her will.

The beast rushed to the surface, and Assefa flipped Sanura onto her back. She yelped in surprise. He grasped her arms and raised them above her head, holding her wrists with his forceful hands. Assefa plunged deep inside, Sanura wet and ready. With a carnality he'd kept in check earlier, he used his muscled thighs to push her legs wider apart, demanding unlimited access.

If this was all she wanted from him, Assefa thought bitterly, he would give it to her—hard, deep, and unfeeling. He would be the Mngwa of myth, pillaging and taking what he wanted without a civilized man's good sense or heart.

And he did.

Eyes shut, Assefa thrust into Sanura, the beast in him riding her like a cresting wave, his ragged gasps feral, relentless. Sweat pooled and fell. He didn't stop.

Sanura made a sound that could've been a moan of pleasure or groan of dissatisfaction. Reluctantly, Assefa opened his eyes and paused above Sanura. She was staring at him, green eyes trusting and unafraid, even with him holding her down, his heavy bulk trapping her much smaller, infinitely softer frame. *Shit.* This wasn't who he was, wasn't his spirit. And it damn sure wasn't the man who'd just offered Sanura his home, his protection. He was acting no better than a rutting brute.

Assefa resumed his movements, rocking his hips in a repentant cadence, easing his cat spirit into a contented retreat. He lifted Sanura's chin with his right hand and lightly kissed her. "I'm sorry. I don't want to rush you. I won't ever hurt you. But I do need some assurance."

"Like what?" Sanura clenched around his length, forcing Assefa to increase his tempo, pushing into the spirited witch the way her body was demanding.

Strangely, Sanura didn't seem the least bit put off by the more aggressive sex. In fact, Assefa suspected that a part of Sanura preferred this side of him. But that was probably more the influence of her fire spirit than the woman. *One, but also two.* Assefa wanted both sides of her to want him. *In and out of bed.*

"I don't know…b–but…," he stammered, unable to think coherently, Sanura raiding his aura with her sensual magical energy. It flooded him, drowning his senses in the process, urging his sweaty body toward an explosive completion. Then, at the last minute, he withdrew, spilling himself on a milk chocolate thigh.

That had been close, neither one of them in the right frame of mind to think about stopping and sheathing. Assefa knew this, grateful the man was in control and not his beast. The Mngwa wanted to claim Sanura, make her his in every way. But the man would have none of it, needing her to come to him willingly, not because of a poor choice she'd made in the heat of passion while running from a demon. And it was a demon, but not the kind Assefa and his division tracked. No, such a demon would've been easy enough to dispatch. The demon that haunted Sanura was of a personal nature, one she'd have to confront and vanquish if she wanted more out of this than a one-night stand.

"Allowing me to impregnate you wasn't the type of assurance I was looking for." He reached for the box of tissues on the nightstand. After cleaning her, he settled them under the covers.

"That wasn't my intention," Sanura said in hushed tones. "I'm sure neither one of us is ready for that."

No, not yet. But Assefa could already envision the children they could have, the life they could have together. If only…

"I don't like it when you feign ignorance about our feelings for each other, Sanura, when you shield your heart from me as if I intend to rip it to shreds."

"And I don't like it," she said, finding a warm spot against his side, right leg sprawled over his, "when you don your FBI mask, turning all cold and unemotional on me. I don't know what to do when you get like that."

Fair enough. But Sanura was so damn uneasy when it came to the more emotional side of relationships, which didn't exactly encourage a man like Assefa to fully open up to her either.

Why couldn't he just accept what they had? Why couldn't he leave well enough alone? *Because it's not enough. Because she shouldn't have bound my cat to her fire spirit without being willing to take my bite. All or nothing.*

Assefa could sleep for a week, so sated and exhausted was he. But he had to know. He knew that he would never sleep if he didn't.

"Does the thought of being the mate to a Mngwa unsettle you? Do you even want a were-cat...*me* as your mate?"

Sanura didn't answer, didn't so much as acknowledge his words.

Assefa peered down at her. She was sound asleep, her face buried against his chest, his heart beating a love tune for the damned.

He loved her. *But she doesn't love you back.* No, she didn't.

Assefa breathed in her gardenia scent and knew. He would have to let his fire witch go when the case was over. Clearly, what he offered she couldn't bring herself to accept, and what she was willing to give was less than what he was willing to settle for.

But the case wasn't at its end just yet. He still had a few hours before the hunt would begin. A few hours to hold Sanura and pretend this was the first of many nights she would sleep in his arms instead of the only one he would ever have with her. That was a sobering, brutal thought that Assefa wished he was truly too cold of heart, too unemotional, to feel.

He closed his eyes and cursed the Fates for leading him to Baltimore and the dead end that was Sanura Williams' heart.

CHAPTER FOURTEEN

"Let's go over this one more time," Mike suggested.

"Enough already." Sanura plopped down on the lumpy, pinstriped couch in Assefa's office. "I understand the plan perfectly. You're just making everyone more nervous by repeating the same thing."

"Well, if I felt like I had your and Assefa's undivided attention, I wouldn't have to repeat myself," he huffed, looking from one to the other. "What in the hell is wrong with the two of you, anyway? You've been acting funny ever since we got to the station. I would've thought after the two of you…"

He paused and then made an obscene sexual gesture with his fingers. At least that's what Sanura thought he meant when Mike formed a circle with his thumb and index finger before inserting the index finger from his other hand into the hole—repeatedly, his pace increasing with each…thrust?

"Do you have an ounce of common decency in your dwarf body?" Assefa bristled. He stood, towering over the much-shorter Mike in un-hidden irritation, the desk separating the two men a wholly inadequate speed bump. "This is neither the time nor the place, Mike, and I'm re-ally *not* in the mood for our normal games."

Assefa sat back down, no sign of the man-of-leisure persona he nor-mally used to conceal the depth of the man.

"We all know what's expected of us. There's no need to belabor the point. Thanks to Cynthia, Eric, and Gen, I have a fresh adze scent for the first time. The odor was still strong on Gen's shirt and jeans. Eric had the presence of mind to hold onto Gen's clothing and have Cynthia magically preserve them. I brought the clothing back from the hospital and left them in the car until I was ready to head out to hunt. Earlier today, I tracked the adze to Druid Hill Park."

Sanura now knew where Assefa had run off to so fast after they'd eaten a late breakfast. She'd thought it was her inability to give him an answer to his proposal that sent him out the door in such a rush. Now she knew differently, or, she thought solemnly, perhaps it was just a convenient excuse to get away from the woman who had rejected him. Twice.

Then there was the dream—correction—the nightmare. It had been years since Sanura suffered one. Why now? *What in the hell is wrong with me? Assefa is unlike any man I've ever met. He's kind, protective, bright, and outrageously sexy. He's amazing in bed. And wants me to move in with him and become his mate. And I'm having stupid night-mares again while running away from a man who wants to give me the world.*

"Druid Hill Park has tunnels under it that were built during enslave-ment in this country. It was used as a stop on the Underground Railroad for many years, especially after the enactment of the Fugitive Slave Act when slaveholders could retrieve their runaway slaves from any state in the Union. Unlike other Underground Railroad sites in your state, this one hasn't been made into a historical landmark. It was simply boarded up and built over through the years." Assefa stood again, walked around the desk, and sat on the edge of the battered, steel furniture.

"Sounds like a perfect hiding place to me, kid."

"Which was why we couldn't easily find the creature."

"Since we know where it lives now, we can send Sanura home and go in ourselves."

"I wish it were that easy, Mike." Sanura knew he meant that. Assefa wanted nothing more than to keep her safe, and the best way to do that was to keep her as far from the bloodsucking predator as possible. But that wasn't going to happen. "I don't know about you, but going into its lair isn't a risk I'm willing to take. Adzes may like to hunt alone, but that doesn't necessarily mean they live or hibernate alone. We don't know if there's more than the one adze hiding out in those tunnels."

"Mike, I can lure him…or them out into the open where you and Assefa will have a greater chance of taking them on. And if it turns out to be only one, even better." Sanura moved from one uncomfortable lump to an even more uncomfortable one. No wonder Assefa always sat in that nice leather chair of his. "Besides, those tunnels are probably small and cramped. Assefa's cat will need much more room than that to be effective."

Mike examined Assefa, squinting at the special agent as if that would help him divine the truth. "What type of cat are you, kid?"

"The type that doesn't like to be caged with a predator in its home." He shifted, turning more of his body in her direction. "Once the bastard is out of the tunnel, Sanura, I need you to put your moonstone back in, leave the park, and allow us to do our job."

"But—"

"No, Sanura, I promised Makena you wouldn't be there when we take it down. I won't go back on a promise, not even for you, so don't ask."

She didn't like it. But she was only to be the bait. She wasn't, like Assefa had said yesterday, a trained officer. She was a college professor. A powerful witch, sure, but this was the field, not an advanced spellcasting class. She didn't know or understand these rules of engagement. *Bait, not brawn, that's my role, why I'm here.*

"Check to make sure the park has been closed and cordoned off." His words were for the detective, but Assefa's eyes never left Sanura.

"If you wanted me to leave, you could've just said so."

"Then leave, Mike," Sanura said pointedly.

"Settle whatever the hell is happening between the two of you before we head out. Talk, kiss, screw, I don't care, but make it fast."

Mike slammed the door when he left, but that wasn't the only door Sanura knew had closed.

Assefa slid one long leg then the other from his desk, then moved to sit next to Sanura. Once settled, he took her hands in his. "I'm your familiar. It's my responsibility to protect you from adzes. That is why Sekhmet made were-cats. It's why a beast like me exists."

His baritone voice was as smooth and sensual as any Barry White song. He could lull her to sleep with that voice or make her wet with desire. But Sanura refused to let him face the monster on his own. It was as much her duty as his to capture the witch killer.

She placed a hand on his cheek. "And who protects you, Assefa?"

His blank face and chilly silence told her the answer. In that moment, he looked so lost, his seal-brown eyes betraying his normally self-assured nature. She hated that look nearly as much as she despised his FBI mask. Worse, she'd put it there when she'd refused his bite and again when her insecure mind silenced her heart and lips when they would've gladly accepted his offer to move in with him.

The closed door she'd sensed earlier loomed before her. Since waking and showering, Assefa had been pleasant, as usual, sweet-talking Makena into cooking for them. In truth, Makena was pleased to do, enjoying Assefa's appreciation for her Nigerian and Trinidadian cuisine and simply having a full house of guests to dote on, as she did when Sanura, Sam, and Cynthia all lived there. But, more importantly, Makena already considered Assefa a member of the family, whether Sanura became his mate or not.

He was just as charming upon his return, having taken the time to go home and change his clothes, another tailor-made suit, no less. Before leaving for the station, Makena had hugged Assefa, whispering words meant only for him. Then he had looked over Makena's shoulder at Sanura but didn't hold her gaze. Instead, he'd kissed Makena on the cheek and promised, "I won't let harm come to her."

"What about the other matter?" Makena had questioned, with a worried interest not present in her voice last night when she'd asked if Sanura intended to take Assefa as her mate.

Before Assefa could respond, Mike had interrupted them, opening the front door and exclaiming with gusto, "Let's get the show on the road. I have a special spot on my wall for this bastard's head."

"I can take care of myself," Assefa answered Sanura. "I've been doing it for years."

There was that damn mask of his again. When it wasn't the mask of stubborn stoicism, it was frosty detachment or even charming flirt. Yet, somewhere, amidst the masks, resided the true Assefa Berber, a complex amalgam of a man.

"I'll settle this case, once and for all. It'll be done. I'll protect you from the adze."

"I know you will. I trust you."

His smile was little more than a forced lifting of lips. "I know you do. You trust me with your body."

Who knew a man's smile could reveal an ocean of disappointment? The "but you don't trust me with your heart," the unspoken tide carrying Assefa away from her.

"What will you do once you catch the adze?"

"I'm not going to catch the adze, Sanura." He said this with all the lethal intention of a predator ready for the hunt. "I'm going to execute the murdering bastard and send his worthless soul to Anubis."

And, no, that wasn't what Sanura had meant by her question. But, yes, Assefa was deadly serious.

"I mean afterward, once the business with the adze is over. What then?"

Frosty eyes softened but revealed nothing of the inner man's feelings.

"I'll file a satisfactory but fraudulent report with the Chief of Police. The report will mollify his superiors and keep the true nature of my investigation a secret." He stood. "Then I'll go back to Virginia."

Go back to Virginia. Right, Maryland is not his home. He had no reason to stay nor a reason to return. She'd given him none.

"We need to get going." He stalked away from her, stopping only when he reached the door and realized she still sat, dumbfounded by his nonchalant dismissal. She opened her mouth to speak, to let him know this wasn't what she wanted, that she was afraid and a coward. But Assefa shook his head. "I don't want to do this now, Sanura. I *can't* do this now."

No, neither could she. They both needed to have their heads in the game, focused on the adze instead of the crumbling mess their post-handfasting reality had become.

She joined Assefa at the door and reached up and kissed him because she couldn't help herself. For a moment, for timeless seconds, he didn't respond. The bitter tang of rejection coated his lips. Then the sweetness came and wrapped itself around her—yummy, sugary Assefa goodness.

Pressing her back against the door, he kissed her senseless, her moans muffled by his devouring mouth and relentless tongue. She could feel him, his desire, his heat, his anger. By the gods, she wanted him but had no idea how to have a man like Assefa while still keeping some of herself for herself.

He ripped his mouth away. "No more games, Sanura. No. More. Either you want *all* of me, or you don't. Either you want to be my *mate,* or you don't." He moved her from in front of the door and then opened it. "But what you won't do is kiss me like you want all of me while knowing you have no intention of following through with anything more substantive."

Sanura's mind went blank, her personal Titanic sinking before her eyes. She felt paralyzed, unable to do more than watch it fade into watery oblivion.

"Come along, Sanura. The sooner we finish this, the sooner you'll be rid of me and my too-demanding, unemotional were-cat ways."

Sarcasm had never cut so deep, felt so cold, been so well-deserved.

Then he simply walked out of the office and away from her, a soundless, sightless slamming of a door.

She stared after him, and Sanura refused to cry. Fire witches did not cry. *No, we just conjure a blaze around our hearts and burn anyone who dares to enter. Death and destruction, that's all I'm good for.*

Three hours later, Sanura found herself at the south side of Druid Hill Park, stationed where the tunnels let out. The park had been secured to keep people out, but the adze inside the containment area. If the adze was in the tunnels, there was now only one exit.

Assefa and Mike waited several feet from the south gate in a nondescript black van with tinted windows. A white Baltimore City Police license with its customary four-number tag and BC was written in bold, black letters on the back. The city's drug dealers would've preferred to see this van parked in their neighborhood because it was better than any paid lookout. It yelled *cop*. In fact, it screamed *dumbass cop*.

But this wasn't a drug stakeout, and the officers inside the van weren't trying to bust a bunch of lowlife street hustlers out to make money off the misery of others. No, they were trying to catch a different kind of lowlife, one who would kill those so-called hardcore drug dealers if given the opportunity, no matter the taint of the drug dealers' souls. Food was food when starvation was the alternative.

For the last hour, Sanura had walked the path the special agent had mapped out for her. "No sign of the adze," Sanura informed him into her small microphone provided by the BCPD. She'd felt like a real undercover police officer when the female officer had secured her microphone and earpiece. Now, however, she felt like a worm on a hook waiting to be roasted alive. Yeah, a mixed metaphor, but it was better than thinking about being eaten alive, or rather, drained dry.

"I know. I can see you just fine. If you stay on the path, I'll have an unobstructed view of you and the exit."

"When will you shift?" Sanura realized she knew nothing about Assefa's particular transformation. She recalled her father telling her a were-cat's transformation could be painful or prolonged if the male wasn't adequately trained, as a boy, by his father or another trusted male. She knew Assefa loved and respected his uncle and chief but knew nothing of his father and their relationship. But it was reasonable to assume that Assefa's father would've prepared his son well. *His shift will be quick and painless.* She kept telling herself that while walking the path for what felt like the hundredth time.

"I'll shift in a few minutes, and then Mike will take over communication. Although I won't be capable of speaking to you, I'll be able to hear and understand everything that happens and is said. As in the astrophysical plane, you can speak to me in animal form the same way you would when I'm in human form."

"That won't be necessary. You'll be able to speak to me telepathically once you shift. That's one of the side effects of blending our auras." Yet another way her fire spirit had bound his cat spirit to her, claiming without equally giving. Hell, Assefa had every right to be upset with Sanura for refusing his bite.

"I'm sure that's what one of your books probably said, but telepathy between a cat and a witch, even a familiar, isn't possible."

"The witches in my family have always been able to communicate telepathically with their familiars when they were in cat form."

"Only thing I'm saying, Sanura, is that—"

"Oh, for the love of Romeo and Juliet, perhaps the two of you should've had this little but critical discussion last night instead of—"

Sanura heard rustling on the other end of the line and then a growled warning. "Don't go there, Mike."

Twice in twenty-four hours, Sanura thought. Mike was risking his life with his constant waving of raw meat in front of an agitated Assefa. As it was, the special agent, against his better judgment, had agreed to her plan. A plan that could, if it went badly, end with her death. This couldn't be good for Assefa's self-control or for Mike's life expectancy.

Seconds passed. Nothing but silence came from the van. Sanura wondered if it were possible for Assefa to kill Mike without making an incriminating sound. Probably, she concluded, though Sanura knew otherwise. As easily as Mike managed to slip under Assefa's armor, the special agent had an iron will. Even when angry, he never lost control. *Gods, I wouldn't wish that fate on anyone. Not even the adze.*

"Go change; I'll take care of Sanura while you're gone. Make it quick, Casanova."

Mike's voice told her he was back in detective mode, all irritating humor sealed under the men's common goals, keeping Sanura safe and killing the adze. Capture wasn't an option. This thing couldn't be contained or rehabilitated. From what Assefa told her on the drive to the park, the Preternatural Division of the FBI did not do incarceration or medical intervention. By the time a case reached the desk of the division chief, Assefa's uncle, Ulan Berber, only one option was left, one directive given—execute.

Sanura strolled past the tunnel's entrance again before settling on a bench a few feet away. She waited. The silence on the other end of the microphone contrasted with her heart's wild beating.

"Go now, Assefa; I have this covered."

Pause.

"Look, I know you're her familiar, but she was my goddaughter first."

Pause.

"All joking aside, I'll take care of her. Now move your ass before the ugly fucker makes its grand appearance."

Pause.

"You'd better, detective."

Three words uttered in such a menacing snarl Sanura shivered from their vehemence. Then there was nothing. No one spoke. Sanura assumed the officers had come to some "man" agreement. Soft relief swept through her. She would be okay. Assefa would shift into his Mngwa form and ensure nothing happened to her. At least that was the plan.

Simple.

Lethal.

On this dark, humid May night, Sanura sat in the historic park, the wooden bench sturdy despite the sun-faded paint. The trees were in full bloom, tall and strong, rooted to this place where runaway enslaved men and women sought comfort and protection on their long journey to freedom. The North Star guided their ragged, determined movements away from the dehumanizing system, away from government-sanctioned bondage, and away from a bastardized version of Christianity in which plantation sermons were nothing more than opportunities to tell them to "obey their masters."

Sanura closed her eyes, feeling the lingering spirits of the journeymen, their warm tears shed for loved ones left behind absorbed back into the earth, giving life to the trees. It was an odd sensation, a connection to Mother Earth and the past, powerful witches unwilling conduits for mortals who've passed over but not passed on.

A cool breeze encircled the witch, severing Sanura's connection to the spirits of the forgotten trailblazers. It chilled her to the marrow, forcing Sanura from the bench. She started walking toward the path when she heard Mike yell, "Watch. Out!"

Without looking back, Sanura ran. She was in excellent shape and could outrun any full-human mugger or rapist, but this was an adze that was fast on her heels. No matter how swift she was or how many quick cuts she made, Sanura knew this was a race she couldn't win.

Wings flapped overhead like a sail snapping in the wind, shots from a gun a reply echo. The flapping continued, moving closer with each gust of air, stabbing Sanura in the back.

She breathed out a quick incantation. A wind gust knocked the adze back. Using the seconds the attack afforded her, she dug deep and ran faster, putting as much distance as possible between her and the demon.

Her attack had done nothing but momentarily slow the adze's hungry pursuit. It probably hadn't eaten in weeks, her scent and strong aura an enticing mix for the beast. It wanted her, the craving a psychotic tendril of death and destiny reaching out for her. She could sense the creature's desire to tear into her flesh, filling its belly with her blood.

Hunger and bloodlust propelled it forward. It was so fast and too damn close.

It swooped down just as Sanura rounded a tree.

She couldn't think, couldn't put together one spell in her frazzled brain. All she had were her instincts. Those told her to run faster and not to give up, to trust the man who wanted to claim her with heart, body, and fangs.

Sweat flowed heavily down her face and back. Legs were tight from overexertion.

The heat of the adze's breath found her vulnerable neck.

With effort born of countless hours of practice, Sanura reached for her fire magic, not the cage she kept her fire spirit locked away in.

A knife—*no, claws*—raked across her left shoulder, ripping through shirt, flesh, and hope.

She fell face-first. The ground reached up and found her chin, her cheek, her breath.

Afraid but not paralyzed by fear, Sanura turned onto her back.

The adze stood over her, mouth open, baring razor-sharp teeth. A trickle of saliva fell onto Sanura's forehead, marking her as his. She knew this was the face of death—sinister, cruel, and ugly, not from nurture but by nature. There was no pleading with the monster. It wouldn't recognize the appeal or even care. It was doing what it was created to do.

Her fire spirit raged within, demanding her freedom. Sanura denied the heated plea while knowing the adze was mere seconds from sinking its long fangs into her.

Let me out, her fire spirit demanded.

I can't.

He'll kill you. Me. I can help. I can save us.

Sanura reached for her fire spirit's cage with a trembling, unsure hand. Hand on the handle, she met her beast's shimmering, ruby eyes, as hungry and volatile as the adze wanting Sanura's blood. She dropped her hand.

Her fire spirit snapped and hissed.

The adze bared more teeth. Licked fangs. And came for her.

In the space between the darkness and the light, between life and death, another emerged.

A beast.

A predator.

A myth made real. Created by a warrior goddess and sanctified by a witch's fire. Sanura's fire.

Hunt. Kill. Protect.

The words roared in Sanura's head. Then he was there, his tremendous force knocking the adze forty feet away from her.

Go, Sanura. Now! the Mngwa commanded before bounding after the adze with the speed, agility, and ferocity of no other cat known to the modern world.

And, gods, the real-life Mngwa was even more impressive than the one she'd met within the astrophysical plane. *Larger. Stronger. Fiercer.*

Sanura watched as the adze staggered to its feet. It spread its wings, preparing to take flight. Hurt, tired, but still in the fight, she used her fleeting energy to cast a force field, encapsulating the adze and the Mngwa. Trapped. The killer of witches now had to contend with a foe that had never known defeat. *Serves you right.*

The Mngwa was all muscle, claws, and teeth. He had to weigh over 600 pounds, his huge claws striking the ground soundlessly as he stalked his prey.

"Sanura, are you all right?" called a winded Mike as he approached. "Shit, woman, you're fast, and I'm too old for all this running."

She felt old, too. Her body ached all over.

Noticing her bleeding shoulder, Mike swore, spewing dwarf curses as vile as the adze's soul. He went to work, helping her to her feet. Shotgun in one hand and Sanura in the other, Mike pulled her away.

"No, we can't leave Assefa. What if he needs our help?"

Mike glanced back at the ferocious cat that had once been the special agent. "He won't. Besides, I promised him I would get you to safety. So let's go before he turns that snarl on me."

Reluctantly, Sanura allowed herself to be led away, trusting Assefa to return to her alive and unharmed. The thought of him trading his life to save hers, of never feeling the warmth of his loving spirit again, made her shudder, the urge to return to his side so strong she blocked the taste of bile and hysterics that started to boil just below her shaky reserve.

It wouldn't do. It just wouldn't do for her to throw up and start crying and screaming like some reality show lunatic who was just thrown off the island. Besides, she'd be damned if she acted the part of the nervous-wreck girlfriend in front of Mike. Although, with her bleeding shoulder and weak legs, Sanura made for a stereotypical damsel in distress. And damn Mike's sexist dwarf behind. And damn her for not being honest with Assefa or herself.

CHAPTER FIFTEEN

The adze was finally in a cage where it belonged, a magical trap for the winged monster, care of a brave fire witch.

The Mngwa didn't have to lift his nose to smell the blood. *Sanura's blood.* The creature had hurt her. Sanura's precious blood stained the adze's claws. It would die very painfully.

With piercing gold eyes, the Mngwa watched as the adze attempted to escape the enclosure, slamming face-first into the force field.

Again.

Again.

Again.

Magic crackled around them each time the fool used its head as a battering ram. There was no escape, only death.

The adze bolted for the top again only to pivot and fly headlong into the cat of legend. This move may have worked if the Mngwa had been a smaller, weaker, or even slower cat.

But he wasn't.

It didn't.

The Mngwa backed up, reared up on his hind legs, and with a swipe of his mammoth claws sent the adze crashing into the force field. Blood oozed from the gash on the adze's side, flowing oil-slick black. The Mngwa's mouth watered. The scent of his prey was an indescribable confluence of heartlessness, blood, and terror.

He went in for the kill.

Scrambling to its feet, the adze extended its wings and peered at the top of the field, its intention clear. It bent its legs to take off, wings already flapping. It got several feet off the ground. The Mngwa leaped, his jaws opening and catching a dangling leg. He forced the killer of children, mothers, and fathers back down to the cold, pitiless ground.

Thud.

The Mngwa clamped down on the limb, his sharp, white teeth cutting through leathery flesh and robust bone. Visions of the slaughtered Ferrells entered his mind and of an orphaned child hiding in a hospital closet, afraid of her own shadow, terrified of this creature. *No more.* The Mngwa and the man would abide no more witches' deaths at the fangs of this worthless vampiric bat. It had survived too long on the blood, fear, and tears of others. Today that would end.

Too stupid to know when a battle was already lost, the adze used its wings to attack the Mngwa. Fingernail-like claws went for the cat's eyes. *Stupid move.* The Mngwa sidestepped the weak effort and charged the left wing of his target. Then, in a debilitating light of speed, the Mngwa lunged for the lean bat, tackling it to the ground and ripping at the cape-like wing.

The bite started at the shoulder blade, and with the force of a vise, the cat sank in deep, yanking the appendage from north to south.

The adze keened.

The Mngwa didn't let go or stop tearing, pulling, and ripping. His neck bulged from the tense effort until he freed the wing from its owner. The shredding of bones, flesh, veins, and ligaments sounded nothing like tearing paper or ripping cloth. No, it barely made a sound beyond a pop, splat, and squish.

But the visual, well, that was different. The once darkly majestic wing that could elevate the bat above the world in search of prey, while gliding on the cool air currents of the gods, was now nothing more than a grisly, tattered reminder of why the Mngwa was the predator of all predators.

Then there was the anticipated response to the Mngwa's ruthless call—a high-pitched wail of a downed, conquered prey.

But the adze still lived, the Mngwa's and special agent's mission not yet complete.

Blood soaked into the spring-green grass—inky and thick, the ravaged wing twitching a pathetic cadence of defeat.

Their eyes met—gold versus red. *I'll show you no mercy, beast.* It was there in the killer's cruel glare, the bitter stench of fear and hopelessness. The adze understood the big cat's brutal promise. *Good.*

The Mngwa bared his teeth in a belligerent smile, making sure the son of a bitch could see every one of his incisors. Then, with lightning speed, he struck, teeth sinking deep into the adze's neck, savaging the creature like it had mercilessly killed countless witches. He didn't stop biting, gnashing, and clawing until the adze lay lifeless. Then and only then did the Mngwa release his prey, feel satisfied that the hunter of witches was no more.

A mighty roar proclaimed the Mngwa victorious, the trembling ground echoing his win, his superiority. The Mngwa had once again earned his reputation—an undefeated killer of killers.

"We're almost to the van, Sanura." Mike's voice was fatherly smooth but dwarf-hard. She knew he could feel the warmth of her blood on his arm. "Stay with me, firefly. I'll get you to the hospital as soon as I can."

Firefly. He hadn't called her that since she was twelve and almost burned down Makena's kitchen trying to make him a cake for his birthday. If he was calling her that now, the damage to her shoulder must be pretty bad. Maybe all the wetness she was feeling wasn't just from perspiration.

"I'm fine, Mike," she lied. "Don't worry about me."

"What the fuck?" Mike pushed Sanura behind him and then raised his shotgun. "Goddammit, I knew it couldn't be this easy." Loud blasts, one after the other, lit up the bleak spring night.

Peering from behind Mike, Sanura spotted three adzes. One was unmoving on the ground, bleeding from Mike's gunshot wound. Gods, she hoped it was dead because the other two were fast approaching, quicker than Mike could reload.

They flew at them, fast and wild, red eyes glowing with ravenous rage.

"Shields, rise and protect your servant." The magical field blazed to life, sprouting swiftly from the ground to obey its weak and bleeding mistress, mere seconds before the adzes came crashing into her force field. The field shimmered a flushed red, with gauzy underscores of white, gold, and blue. A colorful mix that was more dismally dull than radiantly rigorous. *It should be darker, brighter, stronger. Much stronger.*

The beasts were not as large as the one that had attacked her, but they were no less vicious and determined to make the only witch in the vicinity their next meal. They were also angry, periodically glancing back at the—*thankfully*—still downed adze.

They circled the field, bloodshot eyes searching…*for a weak spot?* Probably. But they wouldn't find one. *Not yet.*

"This shield won't last long, Mike. I'm tired and weak; if they keep hitting it, I won't have enough strength to keep them out."

Digging into his pocket, Mike pulled out two shells and deftly re-loaded his gun, years of military training making his movements automatic, precise.

"What if I shoot them from inside the field?"

"It won't penetrate. It'll ricochet and probably hit one of us in-stead."

"Shit." Mike scratched his head as if in thought, while tracking the adze with clear, gray eyes. "Then lower the field, let me get a shot off, and then raise it again."

"They're too close and too fast for that to work."

"Then call Assefa and tell him to get his big, hairy, cat ass over here, pronto."

She wasn't made for this, Sanura thought. She was a trained psy-chologist and professor who drove a midsized car and lived in a quiet Baltimore neighborhood. She wasn't a warrior or even a fighter. Sure, Sanura had taken Tae Kwon Do, at her father's urging, but that didn't make her anyone's champion.

Sanura was tired, and they needed help. She'd told everyone, even the caustic Mike, that she could handle this assignment. That she was the only one who could. And, for Oya's sake, Sanura would be damned if she allowed self-doubt to blur her vision. She'd already messed things up with Assefa, she wouldn't screw this up, as well, by getting herself and Mike killed.

She closed her eyes and focused on the partial mating bond she shared with Assefa. Sanura could feel it, sense him in her soul, her heart.

She sent the telepathic message to Assefa. He would know what to do. He was trained for this type of lunacy, having built a career on finding and dispatching the gods' more troublesome creations. Beings that refused to live within the rules of civilized society or who couldn't because of their very nature.

I'm coming, Sanura; just let me out of your force field.

"Oh, gods," she moaned in realization. Sanura had forgotten. Dear gods, she'd forgotten. She wasn't an officer, trained like Mike and Assefa to use her powers as a weapon. She was a witch, a well-schooled witch. But this was combat in which all spells had to be thought out and planned before execution. The night before, Sanura had talked a good game, bristling at Mike's overprotective and sexist comments. He was right. She was ill-prepared for this mission. But, Sanura thought, she was also right, for no other witch could do this. She was their best chance, but Sanura would have to do better, much, much better.

She slid down the force field, her shoulder leaving bloody streaks of frustrated awareness. *If I recall your field, Assefa, I'll also recall the one Mike and I are in. Unfortunately, the spell to recall force fields doesn't discriminate. It's a general anti-force field spell and will destroy all fields I created.*

Meaning you and Mike will be left without the protection of your field if you free me of mine. Hell.

Pause. Pause. Pause.

Sanura, I'm your familiar, call me to you.

That's a legend; that doesn't really work. I can't pull you to me. No witch can do that.

She winced from the growing pain in her shoulder but fought to maintain her composure, to not give in to the encroaching blackness. She wouldn't pass out. She refused to be a liability to the men. And the way Mike was gripping that shotgun of his, watching as the adzes continued to try to claw their way inside, she thought the dwarf just might ignore her warning and let one fly.

Listen to me carefully, sweetheart. You can do it, and you will. We are compatible for a reason. Neither one of us should exist, but we do. If the prophecy is true, a fire witch and a Mngwa can perform powerful magic once their auras are aligned and bonded.

Thanks to her, they were only partially bonded. But, even if possible, would a one-sided bond be enough?

Look, I'm sorry about earlier. Your demons are your own, and I have mine. But know this, mated or not, I'll always be there for you. I made a promise to protect you, remember? I never break my promises, Sanura. And I won't start tonight.

I don't know if it's possible. I just don't think—

For once in your life, Sanura, don't use your psychologist's brain. Just trust your heart and let me do the rest.

"Umm, Sanura, we need to do something soon. The force field is beginning to weaken."

Sanura knew that already. With each slowing breath, she knew. She glanced at her godfather, not having to tell Mike to ready his weapon. The man had never lowered it. This had to work, and Mike and Assefa would have to be damn fast. Because if they weren't…well, Makena Williams would never survive the death of her only child.

With that depressing but fortifying thought, Sanura forced herself to her knees. She drew a small magical circle using the blood that had run down her arm to her fingers. She closed her eyes and started chanting in a language she didn't recognize. An incantation she'd never read or heard before flowed from her. Vapors of earth magic surged around her, reaching in and attaching to her second sight.

Sanura opened her mouth and sucked in the vapors, breathing through her nose and swallowing. Then, she reached for her familiar, suddenly knowing what to do. *I need you to help me, Assefa. You have to reach for me as I reach for you.*

She waited, seconds, a minute, more.

Then she felt it, a raw burning in her gut. Not pain. Not discomfort but solar-hot power. Fingers sizzled, heart pounded, and the magic circle glowed fiery gold.

Sanura raised both arms, lifted them skyward, and commanded in a booming, dictatorial voice that sounded nothing like her, "Heed my call. Listen to my demand. Bring my familiar to me."

Silence.

Nothing.

Then…rampaging gallops in the sky.

Thud. Thud. Thud.

The ground outside the force field quaked.

Thud. Thud. Thud.

The adzes stopped their prowling.

Thud. Thud. Thud.

The gallops were getting closer, louder.

Thud. Thud. Thud.

Crackle. Thud. Crackle.

"Bring the cat of legend to me now!"

Crackle. Boom.

A murderous bolt of lightning filled the night sky, shiny, bright, and deadly. The one she needed came from the light, from the magic Sanura had controlled. Her familiar had answered his witch's desperate call.

In all his black-and-gray glory, golden eyes feral and promising death, the Mngwa roared.

The force field collapsed.

Mike fired.

An adze bellowed.

And all hell broke loose.

Mike fired again, right into the chest of the closest adze, the body exploding in gushy shards of black, bubbling up and over in an arc. The adze collapsed on its side, its jaw in a dead snarl, its grayish-black wings crumpled with scarred-over imperfections.

Strong and steady, the Mngwa slashed into the remaining adze, tackling it to the ground with effortless might.

Sanura couldn't look away, riveted by the sheer power of her familiar in action. As fierce as the legends had depicted him, merciless, the dominant cat ripped and tore at the adze until his muzzle was soaked in blood. As graphic as the scene was, the Mngwa wasn't a mindless monster who killed indiscriminately. Assefa wasn't a beast with fur and fangs. He had a heart, a profound wellspring of a heart that beat only to serve and to protect. *To love.*

As Sanura looked upon her savior, her familiar, she realized she was truly in love for the first time. In that crystal-clear moment, Sanura knew she couldn't let him go. He was her other half, her soul mate. Fear or no, insecurity or no, she was not losing Assefa Berber.

Sanura collapsed, and dizzying blackness claimed her.

He had to see her, make sure she was all right. *Dammit, didn't mean for this to happen. Not her, not my Sanura.*

The door to the room creaked when pushed, and Richard slipped inside, quietly closing the door behind him. A relieved sigh. He'd made it. He'd waited nearly an hour for the doctor, Makena, Mike, and that damn FBI agent…correction, scary-as-shit cat shifter, to leave Sanura's room.

He'd witnessed the man go from some big cat breed he'd never seen before to the scowling special agent he knew too well. *Should've trusted my instincts that first day when the big bastard sniffed me and called me a liar.* But Sanura Williams only dated full-humans, he'd foolishly told himself then. Or at least she had. *Guess that changed in a big fuckin' way.*

Richard glanced down at his watch. *Ten minutes.* He only had ten minutes. It wouldn't take the trio long to run down to the hospital cafeteria and come back.

"I think we could all use a mega cup of coffee," Mike had said when they exited Sanura's room. The detective loved his coffee, always glaring over the rim at Richard whenever he saw him, cup pressed firmly to his big, never-shut-the-fuck-up mouth. Mike should be the one in the bed hurt, not Sanura. *Better yet, that agent.*

Nine minutes. He had to move.

The dimly lit room beckoned. He'd always favored the dark, taking pleasure in the strength of the unseen, the unknown, the unknowable.

But he was tired of living in the darkness alone, with no light, no pulse, and no pleasure. No Sanura. *My Sanura.*

He reached her bed, eyes dropping to the white bandage circling her shoulder. Richard desperately wanted to touch her, to let her know he was there. But he refrained, didn't want to wake or startle her. Although, he was pretty sure the doctor would've given her something for her pain and to help her sleep. Still…

Richard sat in the chair already positioned at the side of her bed.

Eight minutes.

"I'm sorry, honey. I'm so damn sorry. I knew I should've found another hunting area for them when I found out you were a witch. But it's so damn hard, scouting just the right spot, ensuring they'd be safe during the day. That there's plenty of food for them all."

It always boiled down to food, to the hunt. He was so tired of it, years of endless hunting and hiding and never knowing happiness. Except for those months with Sanura, an escape he'd craved more than the promise of a long life.

But that, too, was gone, the blood link Richard shared with the adzes his only chance at the fabled Fountain of Youth.

Six minutes.

The Baltimore, D.C., and Virginia regions have so many witches. Good, easy hunting. The hunger headaches disappeared, and the driving ache to feed them ceased. For a time. Then the witches went underground, shielding themselves, bringing back the pain, the uncontrollable urge to hunt, kill, and live.

Five minutes.

"I'm also sorry about the girl. That was out of bounds, uncalled for. I was just…just so angry, frustrated, hurt." Richard leaned closer. "I forgave you for lying to me all the time we were together; why couldn't you forgive me for breaking up with you?" Closer. A whisper. "I didn't mean any of the hurtful things I said to you. I just couldn't be as brave as you, reveal my secret. They wouldn't have liked that. They needed me. The same way they needed my father and his father before that." *And I needed them.*

Richard glanced to the door but heard nothing. Three minutes. He stood.

"I just had to see you one last time. Tell you how much I love you."

One trembling hand stretched out. He had to touch Sanura, her sleeping face so pretty, so precious, so perfect.

A solitary caress. Finger to cheek. *So soft.*

Richard smiled, then sighed sadly. It would have to be enough.

Two minutes.

A familiar hand reached for him, encircling the wrist of the hand still pressed to Sanura's cheek. His smile deepened. *She still knows my touch. Even in sleep, Sanura wants me. Me. Not the animal that killed my family.*

One minute.

Sanura's hand tightened.

And tightened.

And tightened.

Strong. So damn strong. Too strong.

Her eyes flew open.

Gold eyes. Gold fuckin' eyes. No! "Let me go."

Grip hardened; sharp nails dug deep. No, not nails. *Claws!*

Pain.

Understanding.

Fear.

Time's up.

CHAPTER SIXTEEN

"H–how? It can't be. Y–you're not supposed to be here. S–saw you leave."

Assefa's grip constricted, holding the sniveling math professor as hard as he dared without breaking his worthless wrist into insignificant bits of bone. Hard that, when all he wanted was to crush every conniving bone in Houghton's lying body.

"H–how?" Houghton asked again, eyes wide with horror and disbelief.

The special agent slid from the bed, hand holding fiercely to Houghton's wrist, forcing the man to back up when Assefa rose.

"I saw—"

"What Makena Williams wanted you to see—a witch's illusion."

"But I saw *y–you* leave." Houghton shook his head.

No, Houghton had seen his FBI partner, Zareb Osei, walk out of the hospital room with Mike and Makena. The judge's eloquent magic did the rest.

"You set me up." Houghton's disbelieving eyes turned icy, his gaze mirroring that of the monsters he'd helped to hide, hunt, and kill.

Witches. Like Sanura and Gen. Like Elizabeth Ferrell's parents. Innocents.

Thud. Thud.

Houghton's back and head slammed against the nearest wall, Assefa having attacked without conscious thought. He lifted and squeezed one unforgiving hand around the full-human's neck. *Can break it so easily. Deserves to die. Deserves to suffer.*

Fingers lengthened, as did the claws. *So much better to rip into you with.*

Houghton's heart pumped faster, feet dangled, kicking helplessly as Assefa squeezed. Ah, yes, the scent of retribution was strong in the air. The Mngwa wanted more, wanted blood, wanted the kill.

"P–please don't," Houghton pleaded, face taut with fear. Hands futilely pounded against Assefa's outstretched arm, fingers digging but finding only hard, unsympathetic muscles.

"I told you I would destroy anyone who hurt Sanura." A low growl. The Mngwa was so close, Houghton's neck even closer. The large vein beat hard, faster, pulsing with so much blood and terror. *Prey.*

"I–I would never hurt Sanura." A pathetic whine.

"You hurt her when you sent one of your bat friends after her niece."

Claws pierced skin; blood trickled from five puncture wounds. The Mngwa licked his chops. So close. Wanted more.

"All because she didn't want your sorry, hypocritical ass, right, Houghton?"

Claws sank deeper. The professor stopped struggling, throat crying out in pain. Eyes shed banked tears. *Now you know how your victims felt, bastard.*

"You pretended to be horrified when Sanura told you her secret. That revelation probably scared you to death, afraid the witch would unearth your own dirty little secret."

The man tried to speak. His mouth opened, but he could only manage a feeble gulping of air.

Assefa didn't need the professor's admission. He knew all about Dr. Richard Houghton. His background investigation was hurried but enough to put many missing pieces together.

"You should've left Baltimore before things got hot for your adzes. That's your MO; hunt for a time, then leave the area as quietly and quickly as you arrived. But you stayed longer than you should have."

Yes, and Assefa knew why. *Sanura.* Houghton hadn't lied. He did want her. In his own sick way, he probably even loved Sanura.

"You worked at ten different schools in the last eight years, normally small community colleges where adjunct professors come and go."

Houghton sucked in a deep breath, his tall, lean body boneless, leaning forward, Assefa's claws still embedded in his neck—shallow but relentless. The agent's inhuman strength held him firmly against the wall.

"It must've been easy for you, picking up and moving on. No ties. No responsibilities. Just those freaks to keep fed." Assefa lifted Houghton's chin; the man's head had fallen forward. "And you kept them fed, well-protected." A snarl. "A damn *human servant* for those bloodsucking monsters."

The chin Assefa held in his left hand quivered, but the man's eyes remained fixed on him, tears flowing.

Assefa felt no pity for Richard Houghton. He didn't know why the man would choose such a life. Perhaps it wasn't a choice at all but a family inheritance. The agent knew exactly how easy such unwanted and ungodly legacies passed from one generation to the next, his own birthright one he wasn't proud of. *But a man makes his own destiny and lights his own path.*

The professor was pathetic, too pathetic to hate, too pathetic to live, too pathetic to kill. Yet he deserved to die. *Slow and painful, just as Berber men were trained to dispose of prey.* With an inward snarl borne of years of self-imposed control, Assefa released Houghton. The despicable coward fell with a thump. Disappointed, the Mngwa retreated.

The hospital room door opened. Assefa didn't have to turn to know Mike and Zareb now stood behind him.

Assefa walked away from the sobbing, gulping math professor, Houghton's blubbering excuses and apologies unimportant and far too late.

"Damn, kid, what did you do to the dickhead?"

"His throat is still intact; what more do you want from me?"

Mike snorted a laugh, pulled out a shiny pair of cuffs, and moved toward Houghton, a satisfied smile on the dwarf's normally eat-shit-and-die face.

He didn't watch as Mike cuffed the guy and then handed him over to Assefa's partner. He couldn't care less, Assefa's mind more on the recovering witch four doors down the hall than on the man who never deserved her love or trust.

"You can't do this. I have my rights. You can't—Sanura will wonder what's happened to me. She'll—"

"You have no damn rights here, asshole, so shut the hell up before I feed your hide to Assefa's hungry cat." Special Agent Zareb Osei's harsh words mirrored Assefa's sentiments. Between Assefa and Zareb, there was no good cop, bad cop. It was bad cop, worse cop. On any given day, they could be both.

Like the smart man he thought he was, Houghton shut the hell up. Few men challenged Zareb, especially when he glared at them from the height of six and a half feet.

Zareb had come to Baltimore when Assefa needed trusted backup, trailing Richard Houghton for the last two days, watching then reporting back to Assefa. The professor had been there when the adze attacked Sanura, hiding in the darkness, watching, waiting, and then following the surveillance van to Sinai Hospital, never knowing or suspecting that those stolen glimpses of a hurt Sanura would be the last he would ever have of her.

"What you will do, doc, is walk quietly with me out of this hospital. Get in my car, like the obedient human servant you are, and watch the scenery pass as you say goodbye to your former life and hello to hell."

Houghton sucked in a breath but wisely said nothing.

"No one will miss you. No one will think twice about the absence of a professor who's like a rolling stone of the teaching profession," Mike added. "Besides, you've already tendered your resignation, haven't you, dickhead?"

No response.

Mike laughed. "Thought so. All your shit is in the trunk of your car. I checked while you were up here with Assefa."

When Houghton thought I was Sanura.

"Get him out of here, Zareb." Assefa was tired of looking at Houghton's face, which shone so tender when he spoke Sanura's name. *Not the kind of love she needs. Not his. Mine.*

"Let's go, doc; our division chief can't wait to have a long chat with you."

Then they were gone, the door creaking behind the special agent and the dead man. Houghton's sobs drifted back, brushing against Assefa's unsympathetic ears.

Assefa closed his eyes, breathed deeply, and tried to catch the faintest whiff of Sanura's scent. But all he could smell was Houghton's fear and the stench of the betrayal of the woman the professor claimed to love.

"What's gonna happen to the dickhead once your division chief gets hold of him?"

Sighing, Assefa opened his eyes, the dwarf standing in front of him, bushy eyebrows raised, eyes curious.

"Chief Berber will have him interrogated. The interrogating agent will discover all there is to know about being a human servant to an adze. Fill in the blanks. Hopefully, shed light on cold cases."

"And when all your chief's questions are answered?"

Mike had to know the answer. He was an experienced dwarf of the world.

"She must never know." *Sanura wouldn't understand.* "We all agreed she could never learn what happened here tonight." Sanura didn't need to know that the man she'd given her heart and body to was responsible for the cruel slaughter of countless witches. *Her sisters in magic.*

"He's no better than those bat freaks, Assefa." *No, he isn't.* "He deserves his fate and more." *Yes, he does. So much more.*

Houghton's death would be quick; his body never found. It was the way of things with the Preternatural Division of the FBI, hunting killers and disposing of threats; incarceration never an option. *Not our MO.*

"I assume Makena is with Sanura."

Mike nodded. "The best guard a witch could ever ask for."

"Better than us?" Doubtful. Makena was a good witch. She'd demonstrated that with her illusion magic, but—

"You have no idea, kid. Have you ever seen a fire witch protect her cub?"

Fire witches were rare back home. Sudan boasted mainly water and wind witches. His experience with fire witches was limited to the

Williams women and an FBI field agent no one wanted to partner with because she had one hell of a temper, setting the guilty aflame her preferred form of execution.

Assefa frowned.

Mike laughed. "For the love of Sybil, you and Sanura are a pair, both so damn good about being in control, showing the side of yourselves you think is acceptable, ignoring the other side, the other voice, the other you."

Assefa glanced down at his hands. Claws were gone, but the feel of Houghton's neck remained. *A glorious sensation. Flesh so easy to tear, so fragile, so—*

He shook his head, a quick denial of the detective's words. He and Sanura were nothing like Shirley Ardell Mason, their identities firmly established, their totems one with them, controlled, controllable.

"Thanks for your help, Mike," Assefa said, surprised at how deeply he felt those words. "I trust you'll see Makena home safely?"

"Of course, the Williams women are mine to protect." Mike extended one rugged hand. Assefa took it, the shake firm. "*And yours*, Special Agent Berber. Samuel Williams would approve."

Hands still clasped, the moment stretched, an understanding forged, an unspoken vow made, a truce formed. Maybe even a friendship.

"Now get out of here and go see Sanura before I have to kick your lovestruck ass."

Assefa went. He didn't need to be told twice.

She loved the night—dark, cryptic, and full of endless possibilities. It called to her kind, pulling them into the shadows of its generous bosom, shielding them as they hunted and found sustenance of the most exquisite crimson variety.

Glowing red eyes dropped to the man being led by the arm, away from the hospital's glass doors and to a black SUV. The parking lot's lights revealed little from this distance, but she knew the handcuffed man—his walk, his scent, his taste, the feel of his body over top of her…inside of her.

For a fleeting, sentimental moment, she considered swooping down, claws and fangs bared, and killing the man who was taking away her lover. She'd followed Richard to this place, knowing whom he sought within the building. *The witch he ordered me not to kill. The witch he gave his heart to. The witch whose name he moaned when he was fucking me.*

Lifting higher into the sky, she did nothing when the tall, bald man shoved Richard into the truck's backseat. Nor did she follow when the man started the engine and then drove away—destination unknown.

Richard didn't love her. He had never loved her. He'd only ever loved himself and that sweet-smelling witch of his—the one who'd thrown his apology back in his face and brought the wrath of a Mngwa down on the adze's family.

Even after that, even after watching the slaughter of the adzes, Richard still couldn't help seeking out the wounded witch. Worse, he hadn't used their blood link to call to her to see if she was near or far. Richard had watched the battle, the same as she had, so he knew she hadn't been among the dead. So why hadn't he contacted her?

Because it was never about you, don't you know that by now? It was always about him. His needs. His wants. His desires and feelings. You were nothing more than a filler of his many voids. He thought to control you. He wanted to stop the bloodlust, the headaches from our bond, and the killing of witches.

But the bloodlust couldn't be stopped, not once quickening began. Richard knew that. He understood the gestational demands of an adze, as well as his father had. Nominal, infrequent drinks from an unwilling blood donor weren't enough, not when an adze carried her unborn for four long years. The female required more. *So much more than a measly pint's worth of witch blood a month. Two years into my pregnancy and my belly has the barest of roundness. But once I enter the third year, the babe will need much more blood. I'll make sure she gets it as much and as often as possible. To Anubis with Richard Houghton.*

She snarled at the thought, at the feeding restrictions Richard attempted to place on her and the others. He was an arrogant and manipulative human servant, unlike his blindly obedient father or starchily uptight grandfather. *We stupidly followed him from one state to another, trusting Richard to hide and keep us well-fed when we should've devoured the weakling years ago—one scrumptious organ at a time.*

Now, however, she was alone. For the first time in decades, the adze had no human to rely on or adzes to compete with for food. She could hunt when and where she wanted—consuming as much blood as she and her unborn babe required. *No one can stop me. Not Richard. Not his witch. Not even that vicious Mngwa, who had, in his unintentional way, set me free to be the adze I was meant to be.*

But now was too soon to begin hunting witches again. If nothing else, Richard had taught them how to hide, get lost and start life anew. As she became one with the darkening sky, the adze felt the tiny life inside her shift, temporarily sated from her last feeding. The paltry witch had turned out to be a surprisingly filling meal. Too bad the adze didn't have time to sample the other morsels in the children's home. She always wondered how humans tasted. Maybe she would find out. Perhaps their blood would prove succulent and life-sustaining. Many times, Richard had told them to only hunt witches of no consequence, witches who wouldn't be missed if they turned up dead or disappeared without a trace.

For hours, the adze flew, traveling through Maryland and Virginia. Then, as night threatened to give way to day, red eyes narrowed on a luscious figure in a dismal alley. The woman, wet from the misty rain, cried into her hands, shoulders hunched and shaking.

She didn't smell like a witch, but she was alone, which was nearly as good. From her cheap, black-and-red fishnet stockings and red, skin-tight leather dress, the contemptible creature was most likely a sex worker. *Who would miss a sex worker, right Richard? No one. No one indeed.*

With no other thought than feeding her babe, the adze spiraled downward, joining the pellets of rain cascading on the seller of female flesh.

Gurgled gasps followed her entrance into the alley and fangs into tender flesh—soft, shocked, and final.

Standing over the crumpled corpse on the urine-stained ground, the adze waited for her body to reject the foreign, human blood. When her stomach ceased burning and cramping, it settled into greedy satisfaction—the babe was pleased. She smiled and then licked the last of the crimson tonic from her lips.

Not delicious, but quite good. Oh yes, human blood will do nicely. Now, I wonder if I can transform to look like this human. It worked each time I filled my belly with witch's blood—the only form in which Richard would deign to touch me. Perhaps it will work with the fresh blood of a human coursing through me. There's only one way to find out...

Claws ripped her shoulder, flesh peeled back, exposing the tender meat inside. Blood flowed. Dark, thick rivulets coated shirt, arm, and back. Then the fangs came, sharp and lethal. She cried out in protest, her fire totem rising to the fore, protecting her, pushing back the monster with an inner heat, a flame hotter than the sun's surface.

"Wake up, sweetheart, you're dreaming." Soft. Tender.

The flames grew, spreading, an uncontrollable wildfire bent on destruction. She thrashed, compelling the flames forward, needing the monster away from her, wanting the beast to burn.

"Sanura, *wake up*." Husky. Hard. "It's just a dream. You're safe. I'm here; now come back to me."

Familiar. Her mind registered the familiar cadence, recognized the energy signature circling her fire, corralling the flames, cooling the heat, and calming the woman.

"Open your eyes for me."

Slowly and with surprising effort, Sanura's eyes slipped partially open.

"That's good. Now open them all the way, sweetheart." A gentle coax, one she appreciated.

Her eyes opened the rest of the way, finding Assefa staring down at her when she did. *So handsome. But more than that.* Worried, tense lines replaced his normally stoic veneer. *Not in FBI mode. Only Assefa, the man.*

"H–how long?" Dry mouth. Croaky voice. She vaguely remembered waking up a time or two before, but the pain medicine had her mind muddled, doing its job too well.

Thankful for having such an intuitive agent at her side, Sanura gratefully accepted the water Assefa offered and slowly sipped from the white bendable straw. "Thanks." She cleared her throat. "How long have I been asleep?" Better, less Kermit the Frog.

Assefa stood, walked to the window, and opened the white vertical blinds. The bright light had her blinking, then turning away from the morning rays.

"That long?"

"Long enough for me to run home, grab a quick shower and a change of clothes." He returned to her side, the bed dipping when he sat beside her.

"You needed the rest." He moved a strand of hair out of her face, his callused fingers gentle.

"What did I miss while I was out?" *Did we get all of the adzes? Are we safe from the monsters?*

Hand still in her hair, he began to stroke, the movement sensually distracting, brown eyes locked on hers. "It's over, Sanura." She waited, expecting Assefa to add…well, she didn't know…something else. But he said nothing more, just continued to caress her. His hand slipped to the nape of her neck. Energy spread from his fingers, down her neck, and to her sore shoulder, tingling, tempting, teasing.

Sanura closed her eyes and sank into the slightly elevated bed, enjoying Assefa's attentions. The man could turn into a snarling, vicious beast capable of tearing its prey limb from limb. And he had, the adzes easily succumbing to the superior predator. Yet here he sat tending her, his touch as comforting and inviting as a polar fleece blanket on the coldest of Baltimore nights.

Two thuds, then a dip. Sanura didn't have to open her eyes to know that Assefa had divested himself of his fine leather shoes and had fully joined her in bed. He gathered her close, careful not to jostle her shoulder. She sank into the man, head pillowed against hard chest, his heart a steady, reassuring beat.

The simple, protective gesture made Sanura feel cherished. A feeling only her father had ever completely succeeded at evoking. Now there was Assefa Berber, the man, the special agent, and the Mngwa of myth.

She raised her face to him, his eyes already cast to her, staring, seeing more than she'd ever revealed. Her heart newly but cautiously opened to him.

"Ask me again?" She reached for his cheek. Her wandering hand found a regal nose, thick brows, and dark hair. Then her mouth found his, petal-soft pecks of hopefulness.

She'd spurned him before, surprised by the depth of her feelings yet too afraid to risk her heart again. *Damn Richard. And damn me.* But what would she risk if she gave Assefa up, if she continued to wallow in uncertainty and self-doubt? Would he wait for her to get her act together? Or had she wounded his pride too much for him to forgive, understand, and allow them to move forward…together? By all that was magical, she hoped not.

"Ask me again to move in with you." She stilled her trembling hands and forced the eyes that wanted to slink away in fear to hold firm. If she wanted him—*and I do*—Sanura knew she could reveal none of the inner turmoil she felt. She knew if Assefa didn't see certainty in her eyes, he would reject her as she'd so foolishly done him.

For an indescribable instant, when his eyes darkened with an emotion Sanura couldn't quite define, she wondered if he still wanted her now that his business in Baltimore was concluded. Perhaps the offer was made only in the heat of the moment, and he was now grateful that she hadn't accepted.

The urge to withdraw physically from him and her presumptuous words increased the longer he stared, saying nothing but looking deeply. *Too deeply.*

Finally, he broke the constricting silence. "Are you sure?"

Sanura nodded.

"What if," Assefa began, his tone breathtakingly flirty, "I decide you have to earn that question? Nothing in life is free, sweetheart."

"I thought you were a gentleman. You would charge me for the pleasure of hearing you ask that question again?"

"I can be a gentleman at times." He licked her lip before delving his tongue deep inside, an unexpected but most welcome kiss. "Like now, when I want nothing more than to lock the door, strip you naked, and devour the heat between your legs. Although, as you can see," he looked her up and down, "you're still dressed and"—another spine-tingling kiss— "dry."

Dry? Well, not if he kept kissing her like that.

In a flash, he sobered. The sexy, flirty Assefa vanished, giving way to the more serious special agent. "Will you move in with me?"

As steady as that question had come out, Sanura had seen his eyes' briefest flicker of worry. As if she would be so cruel as to reject him again. She wouldn't. Of course, she wouldn't.

"You're what I want, Assefa." She slid an affirming caress across his solid, stubborn jaw. "I only hope I'm truly what you want." Because there was so much more to her than the special agent knew, a flame capable of burning out of control if she wasn't careful. A fire, she knew, that had nothing to do with passion but everything to do with too much power.

Assefa grabbed a hand, placed it to his lips, and kissed. "You're exactly what I want. My destiny. My—"

She kissed him, seeking the sensations behind the words, needing the physical reassurance no flowery sentiments could ever adequately express.

He returned the kiss. Tongue slid inside, an unspoken dance practiced the world over by new lovers beginning the mating bond of lust and love. While lust was sexy, easy, and fun, love…well, required much more. Trust, faith, and vulnerability, none of which Sanura could claim with proficiency. But she would try. For Assefa…and herself, she would try.

"They survived the first test, Sekhmet, and performed admirably." Yemaya smiled at what Sanura and Assefa—their mortal creations— had accomplished thus far.

"They did, but it is still not enough. They have only begun to open up and accept their powers. They must fully embrace each other, their united potential, and their shared destiny."

"So, test two?"

"Yes, on to test two."

CHAPTER SEVENTEEN

"Are you sure you want to move in this weekend?"

"Yes, I'm sure. This is the tenth time you've asked me. Is my special agent having second thoughts?"

A deep, sensual laugh glided over invisible air currents and curled in Sanura's heart like a warm, reassuring kiss. "Not on your witchy life. I wish I was there to help you get settled. I don't know how much longer I'll be in this icebox of a state."

"Too cold for you, Special Agent Berber?"

"You try catching a murderer in freezing weather and see how you like it. Africans aren't meant for frigid weather. I don't care how beautiful the postcards are of Alaska; it's too cold here."

"I'm pretty sure that's a stereotype about Africans not liking cold weather."

"Stereotype or not, this African, or rather this Sudanese, hates cold weather, especially when I don't have a particular fire witch to keep me warm." A low, rumbling purr of masculine pleasure preceded the softly spoken words, "I need you to protect me from Mr. Frost. He's a cruel beast that threatens a certain *delicate* region of my were-cat anatomy."

Sanura blushed. He could make her body temperature rise with little effort, even thousands of miles away and through a cell phone. She shook her head ruefully, forcing herself to remember it would probably be days before she could act on the heat he created in her every time they spoke on the phone.

"Are you sure, Sanura?" No trace of flirtation and good humor. Back was the too-serious special agent who'd managed to work his way into her heart in an amazingly short time.

"I'm already in the limousine and, according to your driver, we'll arrive in less than thirty minutes. Stop being a mother hen. I had enough of that the last two weeks. Between my mother and Mike, they drove me crazy while I was healing. This move is a much-needed respite from their overbearing fussiness." If Mike had driven Sanura home instead of to the hospital, Makena could've used magic to heal Sanura. After being admitted, however, the magic option no longer existed unless they wished to explain Sanura's "miraculous" recovery to the full-human medical staff.

"You were hurt. If my uncle hadn't sent me away on another assignment, only two days after we dealt with the adzes, I would've been there helping them take care of you."

A heavy sigh preceded a long pause. She knew that pause. It was Assefa's guilt pause. Sanura knew it stemmed from him being forced to leave her before she fully recovered. *But that's not entirely true.*

Sanura remembered Assefa's golden eyes when he held her in the surveillance van as Mike drove frantically to get her to the hospital. His eyes reflected concern but also anger. The concern was obvious. At the time, she thought she understood his anger. Sanura had assumed the emotion was directed toward the adze that had hurt her. It was just that simple, or so she'd initially believed.

Unwilling to spare any time getting her medical attention, Assefa had hastily and partially dressed after his transformation from a Mngwa into his human form. With glassy, fatigued eyes, she'd stared at the half-naked special agent. He wore only a pair of black khakis, his gray shirt pressed to her wound to staunch the bleeding. It had been a nasty gash. She could tell from the amount of pain and blood. But through it all, the loving glow of Assefa's golden cat eyes had silently soothed and comforted her.

It wasn't until Sanura was treated by a capable doctor and fussed over by an equally attentive mother that she'd glimpsed him standing stoically in the corner of her hospital room. He'd leaned against the back wall, eyes closed, jaw and fists clenched. Sanura could see not only his guilt-covered aura but sense his inner pain as strongly as she could feel the lingering effects of her own, dulled slightly by whatever medication she'd been given.

Even when his eyes opened, they never met her own. When he thought her asleep, though, he'd come to her bedside. Placing a gentle finger to her scratched cheek, he'd leaned down to her ear and whispered the most genuine apology she had ever heard. Sanura had made sure to remain still and not respond, unwilling to embarrass him. After all, a were-cat's pride was as great as his will, heart, and need to protect.

"I should've been faster," he finally said, unknowingly bringing Sanura back to the present conversation. "I was too slow, and you got hurt. That should've never happened. It *won't* happen again." An affirmation from the man, a promise from the cat.

"I already told you that me getting hurt wasn't your fault. I don't know the average time for a shift, but you caught up to us in three minutes flat. No one else could've done better," she tried to soothe. "You saved my life. So please stop blaming yourself for something no one blames you for."

"I know, but—"

"It's over. It's done and over with. Buried like those four adzes, never to return. So let it stay buried, all right?" Her words were a warmly uttered coax she hoped Assefa would heed and stop needlessly hurting himself.

Then there was the hospice home for children in Allegany County. While recovering, Sanura had caught the six o'clock news, the stoned-faced male reporter barely able to keep his professional composure. All she remembered from the report were words that trampled her mind and gouged at her heart.

Dead child.

Blood.

Beheadings.

Unspeakable crime.

Clicking off the television, she'd added one more word to the list— adze. Sanura and Assefa had yet to talk about the case, but she assumed his division chief, even before the local news crew had made their way out to the sleepy community, interviewing shocked and fearful neighbors, would've made him aware. And Sanura couldn't help but wonder if the adze that had claimed the lives of three people that night had been among the ones Assefa and Mike had killed at Druid Hill Park. Or if that particular murderous adze was still on the loose, adding to Assefa's sense of guilt, his animal instinct to hunt, kill, and protect clawing at him from the inside out.

"Fine, if it stops you from worrying about me, I won't mention it again."

She kept the psychologist in her bottled. For now, the grudging compromise would have to do. She wouldn't push.

"I have to go." Anxious. Abrupt. "The suspect is on the move. Call you later."

The line disconnected before Sanura had a chance to say another word. She slumped against the plush leather seat and closed her eyes, thinking about everything she and Assefa needed to discuss, the luxurious limousine being one.

Half an hour later, when the limo stopped at a twenty-foot security gate, she stared at the magnificent home and grounds before her, realizing they had a hell of a lot to talk about.

"It's about damn time you got off that phone," Special Agent Zareb Osei complained. "You go away on assignment, for less than two months, and come back in love and whipped."

"Don't make me hurt you, Zareb. I'm not in the mood." Assefa cautiously drove his black Range Rover onto an icy road two minutes after a four-door sedan left Anchorage's Northway Mall parking lot.

"I have got to meet the woman who tamed the great, unflappable Assefa Berber."

Assefa maneuvered around a few cars to keep the burgundy Nissan Altima in sight.

"I should be home with my fire witch instead of tracking crazy sirens, with daddy issues, across a frozen state."

Assefa slowed, not wanting to get too close to their prey, alerting her to danger before they pounced.

"Yeah, well, I don't understand why the chief gave us this bullshit assignment."

"Why not?" Not that Assefa's mind was entirely on the case. His thoughts, of late, were of Sanura—her taste, smell, touch, fragile, feminine shoulder the adze tried to rip in two. If he could kill the bastard again, he would.

"Are you out of your mind? The chief should've sent a couple of the female agents to capture these head cases. Have you seen the file and photos? Have you seen what they do to men once they've weakened them with their song? I'm too attached to my johnson to let that happen to me." As if to emphasize his utter distaste at the thought, the six-and-a-half-foot, two-hundred-and-twenty-pound muscled man crossed his legs.

"Your what?" Assefa asked with feigned seriousness. He wasn't so far removed from popular full-human culture that Assefa didn't know their slang, although he hadn't met a full-human until moving to the United States. But Sudan imported movies and music from other countries, so Assefa and Zareb knew quite a bit about American slang.

"My johnson. You know, my pogo stick, lightsaber, thrill ride, scream maker. Some full-humans call it a johnson."

"Why in the hell do they call it that?" he joked, having always thought the term nonsensical.

Zareb shrugged. "Maybe they named it after Earvin 'Magic' Johnson. You know, the famous Lakers basketball player."

"Now your penis is like magic?"

"Well, I don't like to brag," Zareb said with a full grin.

"The hell if you don't. I've never known a man to talk so much about his…*magic johnson* as you."

They laughed.

Zareb had more women awaiting his pleasure than a sheik with a harem. Tall and dark and broad of nose and shoulder, nothing was brooding about his partner. He was just a big bear of a man who Assefa trusted and loved like a brother. He would trade his blood brother for Zareb in a shifter moment.

"Hell, I'd hope every man considers his penis capable of performing magic."

Twisting until he faced Assefa, seat belt straining instead of giving, Zareb said, "So-o-o?" with a devilish tone Assefa had heard since they were boys and discovered that girls weren't just sweeter-smelling versions of them. Yet Sanura's scent was the sweetest of them all.

"She's moving in with me. That says it all about what she thinks of my magic."

"How is she between the shee—"

Assefa growled.

"You're such a Boy Scout. Come on, give me something. We're in this frigid ass state. The least you could do is share a pornographic detail or two."

Assefa surveyed the quiet, austere neighborhood he'd followed the perp to. Scouring local bars and clubs, showing photos of the four siren sisters to any and every one, two nights ago they'd lucked up. One sleepy but sure bartender had recognized one of the women. She'd been in a couple of times, the last only three nights prior when she'd left with a white male in his late thirties. Assefa and Zareb had no way of knowing if the male she'd left with was still alive, which was the only reason they hadn't pounced when they'd spotted her this afternoon, standing across the street from a strip club, hard gaze on the dancers going in, far too early for customers.

The men would be in after sunset when people felt more at ease to play, to let loose and feed their inner beast. In that respect, full-humans were no different from preternaturals. However, after an hour of surveillance, the siren walked away, jumping into a car and driving to the nearest mall. So, they'd followed and waited, hoping she would lead them to her sisters or victim.

"What does she look like? Unfortunately, I didn't get a good look at her when you and the Baltimore detective rushed her into the emergency room. Does she have a figure that makes Assefa Jr. stand and salute when she walks into a room?"

Even with the reminder of one of the worse nights of his life, Assefa couldn't help but smile. His mind wandered to Sanura in her itsy-bitsy handfasting bathing suit. Assefa Jr. had definitely snapped to attention. His smile grew wider.

Zareb slapped him on the back as if he'd just scored the winning goal of a fútbol match. "Damn, that hot. Yeah, I definitely got to meet this woman."

Assefa's eyes narrowed, not liking Zareb's sudden interest in Sanura. "You keep your playboy charms to yourself when you're around her."

"Afraid of a little competition?"

Assefa returned the shoulder slap. "Trust me. My Sanura is way too much witch for you."

While they talked and caught up, they also scanned the darkness for danger or the inconvenient full-human out when they should be inside where it was warm and safe. Well, relatively safe because sometimes the monsters knocked and were invited in.

"Okay, okay, but seriously, what about this siren?"

"We'll be fine."

"I'm sure those other agents, who had the misfortune of chasing the sirens all over this country, would disagree. Besides, I'm charged with protecting you."

"I don't need your protection. I can take care of myself."

Assefa slowed and then parked four houses down from the driveway the siren had just driven into.

"I know, partner, but try telling that to your father. I'm not complaining, mind you. If it weren't for this assignment, I would be at home like every other Sudanese, ignorant of the beauty and diversity of the world. So I'm glad to be here with you, as your shield and friend."

Assefa nodded, not liking when Zareb reminded him of his official duty to the Berber family. Back home, *Medja* was an honored position, but here, so far away from titles and status, Zareb Osei was a partner and friend. One friend did not serve another.

Assefa watched as the siren opened and exited her car. Maneuvering on impossibly high heels, she made her way up the driveway and to a house. Digging into a silver, sparkling bag, she pulled out a set of keys and let herself into the dwelling.

Assefa pulled out his cell phone, pressed one button and waited.

Three rings later, then a crisp, "Yes, Agent Berber, what can I do for you?"

"I have an address I need you to run for me, Special Agent Huntington." Assefa rattled off the address to the agent, a wind witch with minimal magical ability. But, with Huntington's brilliance, especially in forensics and computer systems, she didn't need much witch magic.

"Give me a few minutes, Berber. I'll text you the info when I'm done."

"Thanks. See you when we get back." Assefa ended the call.

"You have to know," Zareb began as if they'd been no break in their conversation, "sirens are as crazy as they come. So if you want to see your pretty witch again, you had better come up with a damn good plan and quick. Or do you think your Sanura has made you immune to the draw and beauty of other women?"

"I don't know. Maybe."

"Dammit, Assefa, that was a joke."

"I know, but I'm deadly serious. Sanura wasn't afraid of my Mngwa. Hell, she treated him like some fluffy, housebroken cat." He shook his head, still amazed at how her eyes had gone from shock to wariness to cautious pleasure, all within seconds. "We can communicate telepathically while I'm in cat form, and she can call me to her through a thunderbolt."

That had stunned the hell out of him. Even now, after having her pull him from one place and planting him in another, Assefa was unsure how she'd done it. He'd envisioned running to her, seeing through Sanura's eyes as the adzes raged and pummeled her force field. He had run as fast as he could to reach her. Then he was there, in front of the adzes, all claws and fangs and roaring shield for his witch.

"No Sudanese witch can do that, not even Mistress Kemraha, and her magic is the best in the nation."

"You only think that because you haven't met Sanura yet," he said with an unabashed pride in his professor. Despite her lack of law enforcement training, Sanura had performed admirably. Amid chaos and danger, she'd kept her cool, defended herself wisely, and relied on the strength of others. Now she was on her way to his home...*our home.*

Assefa had no clue what had prompted her to change her mind, and he didn't care.

"Is she the fire witch of legend?" Zareb asked. "Do you even believe in the prophecy?"

Assefa didn't want to have this conversation with Zareb before he and Sanura had a chance to talk.

"I don't know what to believe anymore. Time will tell."

"True enough." Zareb ran a hand over his bald head, eyes suddenly filled with concern. "Have you told her about your father?"

Something else they needed to discuss. The topics were mounting but hopefully not insurmountable. "No, if it wasn't for this ridiculous assignment, I would've had time to tell her everything. As it is, she's probably at the estate wondering if she made a mistake entrusting me with her heart."

"You think she'll be upset when she learns the truth?"

Assefa shrugged. He wasn't ready to think about the possibility of losing Sanura so soon after having found her.

"Incoming," Assefa said when his cell phone dinged, alerting him to a text message. He read it and swore. It was as he'd suspected. The siren wasn't renting the home despite the key she'd used to let herself into the house. Instead, the place belonged to one Mr. Jason Vaughn—a divorced aircraft cargo handling supervisor. And, Assefa thought with growing certainty, the man the siren had left the bar with two nights ago.

He showed Zareb the message, then checked his firearm. Securing the truck keys in his coat pocket, Assefa climbed out of the vehicle, followed by his soundless partner.

"You take point," Zareb whispered. "Let's get this man-hating siren and see how well your witch has bonded you to her."

The limousine driver punched in a code. The towering metal security gate effortlessly drew back, permitting them to enter. They drove up a long, winding driveway circled in front of a Georgian Colonial-style home. And if Sanura wasn't mistaken, the Potomac River bordered Assefa's backyard, a stirringly beautiful but foreboding water element that awakened her fire spirit.

"The private, five-acre estate has a dock, five bedrooms, elevator, an apartment with private entrance and catering kitchen, a pool, and cabana," the driver informed Sanura, his voice blithe as if most people lived the way Assefa obviously did.

By the time he'd parked the limo in one of seven garages, he'd finished telling Sanura all there was to know about the house and the name of the company Assefa had hired to have her car transported to his home. The third garage had been cleared out and assigned for her use. In fact, her car was already parked in the garage with a fresh wash and sparkling shine that Sanura could never get by going through one of those gas station car washes.

The lean driver of average height, with the beginning of gray showing at his temples, finally took a breath, and Sanura couldn't help but think he sounded like a realtor, telling her stuff she couldn't care less about. But the man was pleasant, even if verbose, and had kind, fatherly eyes.

She could see why Assefa had sent him—Mr. Siddig—to retrieve her. On the surface, he came off as a happy-go-lucky middle-aged man, friendly in the extreme. But Sanura wasn't fooled. Her ability to read the strength of auras, full-human and preternatural, gave her a different lens through which to view the driver. While she had no idea what inner cat he held, she could feel the power of his cat spirit.

When Mr. Siddig let her into the house, Sanura's mouth dropped. She quickly closed it but couldn't keep the awe out of her eyes. The home was even more stunning on the inside. Vaulted ceilings, glossy wooden floors, African artifacts—a beaded seashell and wooden Kuba mask from the Democratic Republic of the Congo, a colorfully patterned Yoruba chair from Nigeria, a small leather Dinka shield from Sudan. Photographs of the Serengeti and its wildlife, particularly the large cats, led from the foyer and down a long hallway to Oya knew where.

Yes, she and Assefa definitely had a lot to discuss.

"I'll take your luggage to the master bedroom, Dr. Williams, if that's fine with you."

Sanura nodded to Mr. Siddig as she continued to take in her surroundings, wondering if she knew her special agent.

"He owns Berber Pharmaceutical International," Mr. Siddig said by way of answering her unasked question. He shrugged. "He knows a lot about many different things, especially what economically disadvantaged people need."

Sanura had known from Assefa's expensive clothing and car that he had more money than he could possibly make working for the government, but she'd never expected all this. *He's a millionaire who works for the FBI. What in the hell?*

Too exhausted to think about the strange turn of events, Sanura allowed Mr. Siddig to show her to the room she would share with Assefa. As she'd expected, it was a palatial suite, elegant and formal, like the man to whom it belonged. Grays and blues dominated the color scheme, as did artwork of dark, brooding skies and majestic mountains hidden under layers of untouched snow, the contrast exquisite in its emotional symmetry. Again, like the man himself.

Falling into bed after a late dinner and soothing bath, Sanura snuggled under the insanely soft sheets. She was relaxed, warm, and lonely. But, a bed the size of this one wasn't meant for one. Such a bed was designed with a man like Assefa in mind and all the wicked, wonderful ways he could use its expanse to bring a woman endless pleasure.

Sanura grabbed a pillow from the vacant side of the bed, squeezed it to her, and closed her eyes, wishing she was holding Assefa instead. With a needful sigh, Sanura allowed sleep to overtake her.

Startled, the following day she awoke to running water. She soon realized the sound was coming from the bathroom at the end of the bedroom. She grabbed the sheets to cover her partial nudity, wondering who had entered the suite after she'd fallen asleep. Sanura reached for her cell on the nightstand, so she could call the housekeeper, Mrs. Livingston, when the bathroom door opened. A burst of steam flooded the main area, followed by a form she hadn't seen in two weeks but would recognize anywhere.

"Good morning, sweetheart." Wiping water from his wet hair, Assefa smiled at her, warm and delicious. He walked toward her, stopping when he reached the bed. "Did I surprise you?" He sat on the bed next to her, a knowing twinkle of mischief in his eyes.

"You nearly gave me a heart attack," she said, then punched him in the arm.

"Hey, I thought you would be glad to see me. If I'd known I'd be assaulted, I wouldn't have chartered a flight home so I could be here when you awoke."

He put the damp towel around her neck and drew her to him. "I thought you'd be happy to see me."

By the gods, she was. Sanura inhaled his scent. The fragrance of magic, power, and man clung to him in a heady wave of were-cat temptation. "I missed you," she admitted in a whisper, leaning in to taste his sexy lips.

Unrushed and tender, Assefa kissed her back. Rediscovering his feel and taste, she held on tight to damp shoulders, openly exploring with tongue, mouth, and lips. Yes, she definitely missed her special agent.

Without breaking the kiss, Assefa climbed into the bed with Sanura, reminding her of her wish from last night. He was there and in her arms.

Pulling back from her, Assefa smiled when he realized she wore one of his FBI T-shirts and nothing else. "I see you raided my T-shirt drawer. Although, I must admit, this look is right up there with your handfasting bikini."

Unthinking, Sanura had gotten up at night and searched for something of Assefa's. She'd initially wrapped herself in his robe but thinking it would be uncomfortable to sleep in, she'd decided on one of his shirts. Despite it being laundered, Sanura could still make out the faintest scent of her familiar. Then, when she'd slipped it on, and it had touched her skin the same way it had touched his, Sanura could finally sleep.

"I really did miss you," she admitted with pure, unguarded honesty.

She kissed him again, taking what she wanted and what he always willingly gave. Moving her right hand down his battle-honed body, she removed the towel that covered his lower half, moaning in anticipation and pleasure when her hand grazed his steel-hard erection.

Too busy stroking him, delighting in how he gloriously overflowed her hand, Sanura barely noticed when he'd ripped his shirt, slinging the shredded pieces to the carpeted floor. But then soft breasts met solid chest, and she was glad to be free of the encumbrance.

"Much better," he breathed against her lips.

Yes, yes, it was.

"You aren't wearing your moonstone." She felt rather than heard him breathe in her gardenia scent. "You never have to wear that birth-stone around me. I like you the way the gods intended."

She pulled his face closer to hers and eagerly took possession of his lips, no longer surprised by the effect this man had on her. She wanted him, his mouth, his hands, his tongue, his everything.

"Mmm," she purred, Assefa finding a nipple and sucking, pulling it in his wet mouth, then releasing, only to swirl his tongue around the tip, teasing and playing, then sucking again. "Yes. More."

He gave her more. Burying his face between her breasts, hands gripped, massaged, and pleasured her mounds while he kissed and nib-bled, moving from one to the other, running his face over them and biting with spine-tingling nips of were-cat possession.

She hadn't made love with Assefa since the morning before they set out with Mike to capture the adze. Between her shoulder injury and Assefa's last-minute assignment to Alaska, they hadn't spent much time alone. They spoke on the phone every day, but his voice, no matter how sexy, was a poor substitute for this, the man burning her alive with his overwhelming presence, overwhelming desire, and overwhelming sex appeal.

"Oh, baby, you make me feel so good. *I love you so much*," Sanura softly, mindlessly moaned. But the unintended declaration hadn't been soft enough, for Assefa halted his loving and stared with stunned, owl-ish eyes.

Sanura cradled his face in her hands, suddenly wanting him to know, to understand. "I've been waiting for the right moment to tell you. Admittedly, I didn't mean to blurt it out at such an embarrassing moment, but I can't help how you make me feel when we're this close, when you touch me like you do, making me feel so incredible that I forget myself."

Assefa said nothing, as he often did when the world tilted in a direction he hadn't anticipated. But, she didn't miss the relieved look that crossed his face as he absorbed and accepted her words. Then the shock and doubt were gone, and he smiled at her with white teeth and big, brown eyes. She'd never seen him smile at anyone the way he smiled at her. And, like always, Assefa managed to bring a flutter to her heart by just being himself. No pretense. No games. No false modesty.

"Thank you. I love you, too."

That sounded so damn nice. Perfect, in fact.

She knew the grin she gave Assefa was all witch devilment, but she didn't care. Sanura was in too good of a mood to worry about her normal emotional shields. "Show me."

"What?"

She moved seductively under him. "Show me how much a cat can love his witch."

"You know, Sanura," he said, slinking down her hot, eager body, "I've perfected the art of changing certain parts of my body without transforming completely."

He kissed and bit her inner thighs. Oh, yeah, this was nice, just the way to start a morning.

Slinging the covers entirely off them, Sanura reveled in seeing Assefa's muscled body between her legs, bare, sexy ass on display, face buried between her thighs.

He kissed her center, a deep, no-foreplay type of kiss, all lips and tongue. And tongue. And tongue. And, *gods, yes*, and tongue. It kept going and going and going, wide and long with ridges that brought indescribable gasps of disbelief...*and pleasure*.

"Oh, dear g–gods, that should not be p–possible." The words came out as a trembling jolt of decadence. "But damn—" She finished on a moan, hands going to the sheets and twisting, hips frantically thrusting to meet the firm, wet slide of his cat's powerful tongue.

She couldn't look anymore. Sanura could only squeeze her eyes shut and ride out the body-wracking wave. But it kept cresting, taking her higher, harder.

He was so damn deep. His hands held her wide open for his ravenous tongue, lapping at her wetness, a starving kitten with a fresh bowl of milk, whipping whirlpools of magic between them.

And he didn't stop, even after he brought her twice. He kept going, taking her clit into his mouth, sucking with an intensity that had her bucking and screaming. But he held her tight, held her down, made her submit.

Submit she did, unashamed and loud.

Then her mind snapped, her body in a perpetual state of brazen bliss, Assefa's mouth taking her to Elysian Fields.

She crashed back to earth, deep, ragged breaths, overheated skin, and vibrating sex. That had been amazing. *He* was amazing.

Somewhere between sanity and sexual delirium, Sanura watched as Assefa rose above her, reached into the nightstand drawer, and pulled out a condom.

"I'm on the pill," she said, her breathy, hoarse voice stopping him from sheathing. Sanura wanted nothing between them, just her, just him, just this.

"Since when?"

"When I was in the hospital." She'd taken care of that little personal business before she was discharged, her gynecologist, a water witch, seeing to the matter.

"Thank Ra," Assefa said, then slid home, his hard, demanding penetration worth the two-week wait. "Oh, hell yes, that's good. So damn good. I was thinking about this the entire flight home." He stole her gasping breath with a kiss, murmuring, "I hope you got a good night's sleep because I'm just getting started on your sweet body."

Then he began to move, fueling the flame, stoking the fire, bringing the bliss, trapping her mind and body in a vortex of erotic thrust and withdraw, thrust and withdraw, thrust and withdraw.

Two hours later, exhausted, sated, and aching in the most wonderful places, Sanura had never felt so glorious. The man was thorough in the extreme, a passionate lover who took and gave, reading her every movement, moan and whimper then responding with the right amount of gentleness or roughness, whatever her body desired, pleasing both the woman and the fire spirit.

Now that she'd gorged herself on Assefa's special dessert, her mind cleared. Stroking his chest with exploring fingers, Sanura lifted her head from his shoulder. "So, Special Agent Berber, tell me about Berber Pharmaceutical International and anything else you've left out of our conversations."

CHAPTER EIGHTEEN

Cynthia turned to Eric, her too-pale, sweat-drenched husband. He was getting worse. He was … *dying*. "We need to call Sanura. She's the only one who can help when you get like this."

"No, I don't want to bother her," he managed before his breath left him again. With a chest-rattling wheeze, Eric Garvey reclined in their bed, in a partial fetal position, where he'd been since mid-afternoon of the previous day. Struggling with each breath, he stubbornly shook his head, his defiant eyes boring into her. "I'll be fine; I just need—"

Cynthia didn't wait for him to finish his absurd statement. He would not be fine. He was *not fine*. If she listened to Eric, Cynthia was sure she'd be a widow in a matter of days. She stalked away from him and to the nightstand. With desperate resolution, she picked up the phone. "I'm calling her, and that's all there is to it."

"I think our conversation is overdue, Assefa, don't you?"

From his perch on the bed, Assefa watched Sanura slip into a knee-length, red robe that she tied at the waist. She grabbed a hairbrush from an unpacked bag near the closet before venturing back to the bed. Sitting next to him, she caught his appreciative eye. He still couldn't believe she was there, that she'd agreed, despite her initial misgivings, to move in with him.

Assefa surveyed his bedroom. The masculine colors suited him, as did every piece of bedroom furniture he'd hand-selected. They all reflected his taste. The rest of the house was no different. But it needed a feminine touch. *Sanura's touch*. She could change whatever she wanted to make herself feel like this home was hers as it was his. That is, if Assefa could convince her to stay after he revealed his secret.

Forcing himself to stop staring at her, he glanced down at his still-naked form and groaned. He needed to put something on. Revealing his soul would be bad enough. He sure as hell wasn't going to do it with his boys hanging out.

He rose from the bed and took long strides across the room to his solid hardwood Ambrosia Maple Chateau Philippe Armoire, whose design was inspired by 18th-century artisanship. It was a birthday gift from his father, along with the matching one on the other side of the room. Assefa swung the hefty doors to the wardrobe open. One hanging rod, two shelves, and two drawers greeted him. He pulled the top drawer open and rustled inside. A few seconds later, he removed a pair of white-and-black cotton mesh boxers and put them on.

"You're right," he said after he returned to the bed. "We might as well have that discussion now." *Get it all out into the open and off my chest.*

Sanura's hair was wild from their bed play, long, thick, and naturally gorgeous. He took the brush from her hand and proceeded to brush her hair in long, slow strokes. They were sitting so close, his hot breath finding her neck. With deliberate movements, his fingers swam through her hair just as his knee rubbed ever so enticingly against her thigh, increasing the magical energy that always flowed between them.

"I love your hair," he whispered in her ear, massaging her scalp and nape. She turned to him, eyes an aroused shade of dark green, lips slightly parted. He kissed her in that instant, between restraint and lust, giving into their shared desire to touch and be touched.

Assefa ran his hands through her hair before resting them on her waist. Like alcohol and cigarettes, Sanura was intoxicating. Addictive. Assefa was convinced this explained why his brain went on hiatus whenever she was in his arms, as she was now, body calling for him, luring him in, a siren in her own right. With every whimper and moan, she drew him in deeper, and Assefa knew he was in danger of burning in a fire of his own making.

He forced himself to withdraw from the kiss and then release Sanura. He returned her brush and crawled to the other end of the expansive bed. "I think it best I don't touch you until we finish our talk."

Flustered but agreeable, Sanura nodded.

Ignoring the demand from his body to finish what he'd started, Assefa propped himself against the wall, took a controlled breath and tried to figure out where to begin. Sex was such an easy method of escape and avoidance, as was running away. Yet Assefa knew he could no longer run from the truth. He didn't want to hide from Sanura, from himself, not any longer, not today, not ever again.

"I wanted a normal life," he began, "and knew for me to get it, I'd have to move away from home, away from my father. I wanted to build something that was all mine."

"Is that the reason you founded your company?"

He wasn't surprised she'd learned about that. Of course, in the presence of a beautiful woman, Siddig was bound to open that big, overly friendly mouth of his.

"In part, but more importantly, there was a need on the continent for safe, affordable medicine. You know as well as I do that many multinational corporations and pharmaceutical companies don't care about economically disenfranchised people outside of making a quick pound. So they take and take, giving nothing in return but debt and woes," he argued, his passion for his work, the plight of the impoverished and the power challenged coming through in the tremor of his voice.

He didn't care. She wanted to talk. They were talking.

"I perform research others think is too costly or not worth the time and effort. I patent my medicine and sell it to large pharmaceutical companies, while supplying the same medicine free of charge to people too impoverished to pay steep medical costs or who lack medical insurance. And there's a special research and design department devoted to preternaturals, the gods' first creations." *First mistakes.*

"That's honorable, but I suspect there's more you want to tell me. I can't imagine why you would keep that from me. If anything, most men would use such humanitarian acts to wiggle their way into a woman's good graces."

She gave him her doctor voice—patient, soothing, subtly pressing. Sanura would make an excellent interrogator, Assefa mused, lulling criminals into a false sense of security, encouraging them to spill all just to make her happy. And he did want to make Sanura happy.

Assefa paused, knowing what came next should've been shared during part one of the handfasting ritual. Yet the other two parts weren't guaranteed, despite the success of the first. During the mating rituals, either party could end the courting, thereby dissolving the relationship. While biology and the gods deemed them soul mates, the heart wasn't bound to follow such ordained dictates. In the end, even the gods respected the omnipotence of their creations' hearts.

"I already told you I'm from Sudan and about my parents and siblings."

She nodded.

"What I didn't tell you is that my father is the ruler of Sudan."

Sanura's countenance dropped. The doctor personae did nothing to hide her surprise. She shifted on the bed and began wringing her hands. Two nervous gestures Assefa had never seen from her.

"You're the son of the President of the Republic of the Sudan? Your father is General Jahi Berber?"

The questions were one and the same, but Assefa wasn't going to mention the redundancy, not with the uneasy way she stared at him.

"Yes, he's my father." Watching her closely, Assefa waited for the judgment.

"He's *a dictator, a warlord*." The coarseness of her voice was rich, hard, and thick with bile.

There it was. The judgment, the condemnation he knew so well.

"He's *not* a dictator, and he certainly *isn't* a warlord. He doesn't run the country by might or use the military to enforce his will. My father rules the nation with the help of his legislative cabinet. They're all elected officials," he defended, the way any good son would. The way he invariably had to.

He knew his response was too quick and sounded rehearsed. But he'd had a lot of practice, always defending and justifying the Berber name, the Berber legacy. Over the years, he'd perfected comebacks for a myriad of reactions, the typical ones ranging from absolute horror and revulsion to morbid curiosity and intrigue to contemptible greed and sympathy.

"Elected in name only," Sanura said with a brittle tone, taking the horror and revulsion route. "At most, Sudan is an oligarchy. But it's most definitely *not* a democratic state."

Sanura paused, shook her head, and then gave Assefa a pensive look. A few seconds later, she picked up her moral argument, firmly rooted on her soapbox. "Sudan doesn't even allow full-humans within its borders. They were all thrown out, and those who refused to leave were killed. From what I understand, they didn't even know why they were being singled out."

As if she truly understood anything. Assefa had heard this all before. Hell, he could probably rattle off her objections better than she could. And women wondered why men kept their damn secrets. Who in their right mind would subject themselves to such ethical snobbery?

"That happened over fifty years ago," he shot back, tense, irritable. "You can't blame my father for that, Sanura. He was only a boy, too young to be held responsible for his father's actions."

"But he hasn't rescinded the decree."

The need to have her comprehend his precarious position and the urge to defend his father waged within Assefa. In truth, he'd made the same arguments and had the exact thoughts. But it was decidedly different to hear his witch, his mate-to-be, spit them at him. To have his family strung up on a rack and flogged for old crimes.

"While I don't agree with banning full-humans from Sudan or how it was done, I can understand my grandfather's motivation."

"What? I can't believe you would support such a thing. I can't—"

"We *shouldn't* have to stalk around in the dark, hiding our true selves from full-humans. Don't we have a right to stand in the light the way they do? That's what Sudan offers to our kind, Sanura. It's a place where witches can openly practice magic and were-cats can roam the land without fear of being shot or carted off to the nearest zoo. For all of our history of human rights abuses, Sudan is the only place preternaturals can openly be themselves. And that's the *real* reason my father never rescinded the decree."

Assefa was so tired of this, tired of the inevitable bullshit that came with his name, his family. Tired of not being able to live his life the way he wanted. Tired of the gods shielding full-humans while making their first creations hide in plain sight. It wasn't right. It wasn't fair.

"This country," Assefa continued, "along with the islands of the Caribbean and England, were the residences of thousands of Africans stolen from their homes. Thousands more died on the wretched trek from their villages to the coast and the so-called Middle Passage. Full-humans did that, Sanura. Europeans, with the aid of some Africans, invaded, killed, and pillaged, burning villages and carting off people, destroying families. And for what? Guns? Alcohol? Fabric? Free labor?"

"That has nothing to do with—"

"It has *everything* to do with my family, your family, hell, the history of the entire continent of Africa after the 1600s. They came, they plundered, they took. But it wasn't enough. They wanted more; they wanted it all—oil, gold, diamonds, land. Who do you think stopped them?" Assefa didn't wait for her reply. "*Our kind*, Sanura. For once, preternaturals banded together, interfered in a war between full-humans and prevented colonization."

Assefa shook his head and let out a slow breath. "I don't even want to imagine what Africa would look like today if preternaturals hadn't stepped in, sending the Spaniards, French, and the others back across the Atlantic Ocean."

"So, you think that makes what your father did and does okay?"

"I think," he said, swallowing a growl, "that it makes one cautious, covetous, and protective of their home, their own. Sometimes to the extreme," he honestly conceded. "Not so unlike that Witch Council of Elders you belong to, or that witch- and were-cat-only school of which Cynthia is the principal. Exclusive clubs, as far as I'm concerned. How are they any different from what my grandfather did or what my father continues to support? It's called survival, Sanura, plain and simple."

They glared at each other, crossing arms over chests in defiance of the other's position.

For several minutes, Assefa watched as Sanura ran everything through her psychologist's brain. He could see the different emotions play across her face and feel an invisible wall form between them.

"What else haven't you told me, Assefa of the House of Berber?"

The use of his title to distance them hurt, and he knew that was her intention. He couldn't blame her. Sanura had revealed herself so completely to him during the handfasting ritual. Yet, he'd hid behind old pain and memories. She'd bared her soul to him, and he took what she cautiously gave while not giving equally in return. But her very reaction, her narrow-minded appraisal of his family, and by extension him, was the reason for his silence, his lie of omission.

Assefa braced his back firmly against the wall, legs spread in front of him and crossed at the ankles. He looked like a man settling in for a comfortable little chat with his girlfriend, but he felt anything but. He would've never pegged her to be one to judge without first examining all the facts. Yet, she'd obviously bought into the cable news reports from pundits about the political state of Sudan and the purported villainy of Jahi Berber.

He exhaled slowly, taking stock of his emotions. He teetered on a ledge somewhere between righteous anger and crippling fear. Assefa didn't want this conversation to be the end of them. But he couldn't abandon his family or the truth for the love of a woman who should be able to see *him* for the man he was.

"My father was part of the old military regime that denied people's civil rights and abused their military and political power. But, like me, he was born into it, expecting to fill his father's boots."

Concerned eyes flew to him, the first flicker of hope that perhaps she didn't view him as the son poised to take over for his "despotic" father.

"When my grandfather died, my father was next in line, but he rejected the title of General Supreme. He'd seen too much bloodshed and believed the people of Sudan deserved better than another Berber. But some captains and lieutenants wanted what my father turned his back on. Infighting eventually led to another civil war. The nation was being torn apart. The people cried out for relief from their suffering."

"And the relief came in the form of your father?"

"Yes, he was the only one from the old regime the people thought might do right by them and was strong enough to keep the others in line.

He's a kind, just man, but you wouldn't know if all your information came from biased, misinformed news reports."

"If he's so *kind and just*, why are you here instead of there?"

Good question. The woman was too perceptive by half.

"People expect me to be like him. I'm not. I came here to stake out a life for myself that has nothing to do with being the second son of the House of Berber. I couldn't do that at home. Even the money I used to start my company came from my father. I paid him back as soon as possible, but it's a constant reminder of my dependence on him. To do a good deed, I took questionable funds." He snorted at the irony of it all.

"I haven't taken a penny from him since, and I don't claim the privileges or the scorn that naturally comes with being his son. But he is my father, Sanura, and I love him. He's not perfect, that's for sure, but he *is* my father and, for that, I will never apologize."

His frosty tone chilled the already cool late-morning air.

"I've seen too many of my friends, family, and countrymen die under our flag, and I've no desire to see more. It's not the life I want. My life is here…with you if you still want that."

Her face was unreadable. Definitely an exemplary interrogator she would've been. Or perhaps Sanura had just spent too much time around Mike.

"Look, I'm sorry," he said, sounding too gruff, too raw. "I should've been totally honest with you during the ceremony, but I didn't know where to begin. I was so happy you accepted the Mngwa and the bonding was a success. I convinced myself that nothing else mattered."

Assefa figured this would happen eventually. No matter how hard he tried or how far away from home he went, he couldn't shake the Berber legacy and image. People either wanted to be near him because he was rich or wanted nothing to do with him because they feared or hated his father. He hoped Sanura would prove the exception to the rule, but her eyes made him think otherwise.

"It doesn't matter to me that your father is a dictator or president or whatever he wants to call himself."

She stood and walked away from the bed.

From me and my secrets.

"I wouldn't care if you were rich or poor, and I certainly don't care what animal spirit you possess. I do care, however, about honesty and trust. And while I know in my heart you're an honest man and would never deliberately lie to me"—she paused when she reached the bathroom door— "you should've trusted me enough to tell me the full truth."

"But—"

She held up a hand.

He stayed his words and his frustration.

"You told me to trust my heart, and I did, which is why I'm here with you now. I went out on a limb for you, for us, as I've never done before. And I thought you were on the limb with me. Now I see I was alone, having faith in you when you had none in me."

She took one step into the bathroom, but Assefa's questions halted her. "Would you have given me a fair chance at your heart if I'd disclosed everything from the beginning? Would you have ignored the past misdeeds of my father and his international reputation and seen me for the man that I am and not the man people think I may become?"

She paused for long seconds, dropped her head, and then went into the bathroom, quietly shutting the door behind her.

Yeah, that's what I thought.

Thirty minutes later, Sanura emerged from the bathroom showered, her hair pulled back into a ponytail and moonstone firmly in place. Assefa wasn't in the bedroom, and she was surprised to feel a sense of abandonment. What had she expected? For him to wait, like a lapdog, at the bathroom door to make another apology? She'd walked away from him without answering his question. Correction, she'd walked away, thereby answering his question. *Damn it, he probably now thinks I'm some overly judgmental witch who can't see past her own political ideology.*

She scanned the room in search of her suitcases. Mr. Siddig had placed them in the west corner of the room against an armoire that matched the one Assefa had retrieved his boxers from earlier. Last night, she'd noticed a Post-it note that read, "Welcome, make yourself at home. If I find your clothes here, then I know you intend on staying more than a night."

Assefa hadn't written the note, for he hadn't even been in town for the last two weeks and had no idea she intended to move in with him until he'd already taken off on his Alaskan assignment. Besides, her special agent had too much class to write his feelings on a Post-it. No, that had to be the idea of…well, she didn't know, probably Mr. Siddig or Mrs. Livingston. But the words and sentiment were all Assefa's.

She hadn't unpacked last night. Was she planning on staying more than a night? Had her feelings about Assefa and their future together changed? Did she even know what future she wanted with him? Sanura had too many questions, just too many damnably complicated questions for one morning. Shaking her head, Sanura grabbed one of her rolling suitcases.

She rummaged through the largest of the four cases until she found the ingredients to make a decent outfit. It was an atypical June day in Virginia, with storm clouds threatening overhead and a cool wind cutting across the Potomac. So, Sanura dressed in comfortable flare-cut black jeans, a short-sleeve, baby-blue shirt, and a black pair of easy-on, easy-off recovery tennis shoes intended for versatility, comfort, style, and durability. Perfect for what she had in mind.

Sanura was headed for the bedroom door, intent on exploring the grounds of Assefa's estate, when her cell phone rang. She managed to run to the dark gray leather chair where she'd dropped her oversized pocketbook the night before and dig the phone out before the caller was thrown into voice mail.

"Hi, Cyn," she said, having seen her name appear on the phone's brightly lit screen.

"I need you to come home right away, Sanura."

At her friend's shaky voice, her heart began to race. "Calm down and tell me what's wrong."

"It's Eric; he's sick again and—"

"I'll be right there." Understanding dawned. "Tell Eric I'll be there as soon as I can." She hung up, her face taut and mind already in Baltimore.

Hoisting her pocketbook onto a shoulder, Sanura turned. There stood Assefa, fully dressed and standing on the threshold. She silently walked to and then moved past him and into the outer room, not stopping until she reached the door that led to the upstairs hallway.

"Are you coming?"

He didn't answer right away. Instead, a disturbingly long pause followed. And Sanura didn't even want to know if Assefa had retreated behind his FBI mask, so she kept her back to him, expecting the worst if their eyes met. When he spoke, instead of the frigidity she knew him capable of, his voice was a languid tide—deceptive in its calm fluidity.

"Be. Sure."

Those two words, she knew, went beyond her single question, her invitation. *Be. Sure.* Yes, he was referring to them and their future as a couple. But, was she sure, could she ever be totally sure of something as monumental as trusting another with her heart?

"I'm sure." She turned to face him. And, thank the gods, he wore no mask, but neither was he smiling. "Are you?"

"Of course." Quick. Certain. The man was always so sure of his mind, his heart.

Well, Sanura could be as well.

"Then let's go."

CHAPTER NINETEEN

Assefa and Sanura sat quietly in the limousine. Neither had said a word to the other for most of the ride into Maryland from Virginia.

Assefa looked at her, and the black leather seat expanse between them. "I think if I was contagious, you would've caught it by now."

Sanura opened eyes that had been closed for the last forty-five minutes, blinking at Assefa as if she'd forgotten they shared the same space. "Ah, what did you say?"

"I was wondering if I smell or have bad breath."

"What are you talking about?"

He gestured to the space between them. "You can be honest. Feel free to tell me I need a breath mint or the use of a stronger deodorant."

"I guess you consider that funny," she said, her lips lifting in a small smile.

Assefa took that smile as a narrow opening and moved closer. "I've been known to be funny occasionally, but it isn't something I've been accused of often. In fact, I've been told I have no sense of humor at all and can be quite anal."

"Now, *that* I believe."

Humor. Much better.

Like any driven agent, Assefa asked the question uppermost in his mind. "How long will you be upset with me? Your silence and distance aren't exactly the way I'd hope to start the new phase of our relationship. Yet, despite that, I keep having the most sinful thoughts every time I look at you." He drew even closer. "Do you want to know what I've been thinking during this ride beyond what I can say or do to convince you to forgive me?"

"I'm no longer upset and wasn't intentionally ignoring you."

Well, Sanura was full of surprises. She'd invited him on her trip, not bothering to tell him why she wanted him to accompany her to Cynthia Garvey's home. After their disagreement, he thought it best to give

Sanura space. So, he'd grabbed a set of clothing and relocated to the bedroom across the hall, where he then showered and dressed. By the time he'd finished dressing, Assefa was done with giving her space. He'd wanted to know whether she intended to stay or if he needed to have Mr. Siddig arrange to have her personal belongings returned to Baltimore.

"Okay, why have you been so quiet then? And why are you no longer upset with me?" He had to know. It wasn't enough for her to simply admit that she was no longer angry over the secret he'd kept from her. Women, from his experience, didn't work that way. Less than two hours was scarcely enough time for a woman to forgive a man for some perceived transgression.

"I have a sick friend who needs my help, and I was meditating to focus my thoughts and chi for the work I have to do when we arrive."

"Cynthia's husband Eric," Assefa said, remembering the one-sided conversation he'd overheard.

"He's been sick for a while, and there's a ritual I perform that brings him temporary relief."

"His wife's a witch; why doesn't she perform the ritual herself?"

"She can't," Sanura said without explanation.

Assefa waited for her to elaborate. She didn't. He waited longer. He had nothing else to do, so he could afford the luxury of patience. But Sanura, for all her psychology training, was, in the end, a fire witch. She wasn't rash. But a witch's emotions weren't coiled as tightly as a were-cat's.

"Stop looking at me like that and being so annoyingly patient," she snapped two minutes later, the way he knew she eventually would.

"Would you rather I shook you until you told me the rest?"

Sanura considered him, eyebrows arching at a charming angle, front teeth gently biting her lower lip. "Anyway," she said with a huff of mild annoyance, "I discovered a long time ago that I can cast spells and perform rituals other witches cannot."

"That's because you're the fire witch of legend. So you should be able to do things other witches cannot."

"Do you really believe in the prophecy?"

"All I know for sure is that your unique hair and eye coloring matches the paintings I've seen of the fire witch of legend on the walls of the two ancient temples for Oya in Meroë."

"But does that make it true?"

He shrugged. "I don't know. But in my line of work, there's no such thing as coincidence."

"Hell."

"Yeah, hell."

A long pause invaded the limo again, and he pondered what it would mean to them and the world if the prophecy came true. Nothing good ever resulted when two powerful witches and their familiars battled. Worse, for all the faith Assefa had in the existence of gods, he didn't trust any being who wielded absolute power. Lord Acton had it right. Absolute power did tend to corrupt absolutely.

Sanura shifted her body so that she faced him. "We do have enough time for me to explain why I'm no longer upset with you if you still want to know."

"I haven't changed my mind about wanting to know."

"I thought about the questions you asked me before I went into the bathroom. While I'd like to think I would never judge someone based on the actions of another or media propaganda, I'm not entirely sure. Witches conceal their identity because they fear how they'll be treated…or rather mistreated. And what you did wasn't much different from what I do when I wear my moonstone." Sanura took his hand in hers. "I'm going to tell you something that I've never told anyone, not even my mother or Cyn."

Her hands were soft but also unnaturally warm. The heat radiating from them seemed to reflect the nervous haze shimmering in her faux brown eyes.

"Ever since I was born, with red-gold hair and green eyes, I've been tagged with the Fire Witch of Legend label. I was constantly the center of attention, treated as if my every word and deed were spun gold. As a kid, all the attention made me feel special."

Assefa knew all about feeling "special."

"My parents didn't treat me like that, of course, but they couldn't control how others viewed me."

"And how did they view you?"

Perspiration now moistened his hands, the heat stronger but not yet painful.

"As if I was their savior, Oya reborn in witch flesh."

"A heavy burden for a child."

"It was, but I never truly felt special. I felt like a fraud, a freak, and I was positive that everyone had it wrong. Sure, casting spells came ridiculously easy for me. By age ten, I could outcast all my teachers. By fifteen, my skill surpassed most of the members of the Witch Council of Elders."

"Except your mother's."

She released his hands. Thank the gods for that because Sanura's fire spirit was too close to the surface. From how she stared at him, Assefa didn't think Sanura was aware of the fact.

"How did you know my mother is a member of the Council? I never told you. Did she?"

Gods, did the witch think all there was to being a special agent was shifting into a fierce beast and clawing a perp to death?

"Makena is a much stronger witch than I'd initially given her credit for being. She's also proud and protective of her only child. I can't see her allowing anyone, not even your governing Council, to make decisions for and about her daughter without an equal voice."

Not that Assefa could imagine Makena Williams cowing to a decision she disagreed with, at least not when it came to Sanura. But she and Sanura had also managed to contact and warn dozens of witches while he'd hunted the adzes. Only someone with Council connections could work so fast and effectively. He didn't think Makena ruled the Council. Being a judge took up too much of her time to do both. Still, Assefa speculated her position had to be no less than second-in-charge. How far her influence and power extended, Assefa had yet to ascertain.

"When did you surpass your mother in magical ability?"

"Not until I turned twenty-one. In many ways, she's a better practitioner than I am. I'm more...more..."

"Brute strength," he offered.

She sighed. "Yeah, that's as good a descriptor as any. But Mom is all finesse and controlled power."

Assefa wondered about Sanura's maternal grandmother. If she was, as he suspected, a powerful witch like her daughter and granddaughter, that was even more proof that Sanura was the fire witch of legend. But she had to know that already.

"Anyway, by the time I turned fourteen, I was bombarded by pubescent were-cats."

Assefa almost laughed at her put-upon expression. What had she expected? Sanura was a gorgeous woman. He could only imagine how adorable she had been as a teenager. What red-blooded were-cat wouldn't have been sniffing around her?

"I guess if I'd had any guy other than Eric as my best friend's boyfriend, it would've taken me longer to realize why so many boys were interested in me."

"You can't really blame them, Sanura. When we reach that age, all we can think about are breasts and ass and which girl won't put a hex on us if we try to kiss her."

She rolled her eyes. "You're such a male."

He winked. "I think I proved that quite thoroughly this morning."

She blushed. The witch was beyond adorable, and he wanted to cover her rich lips with his. So he leaned in to do just that, already tasting their heat. But then she said, "Eric overheard a few of the boys talking at lunch."

That stopped him. "What did they say?"

Briefly, she cast her eyes down and away before meeting his eyes with the words, "They said I was Oya reincarnated. That I was a goddess, and every goddess needed a loyal cat at her side."

Not a mean or malicious sentiment. But not what a teenage girl wants to know about the young cats pursuing her.

It all made sense to Assefa now. "That's why you've only dated full-humans because they don't know who or what you are. Because such a male could never truly understand you, would never expect more from you than you were willing to give. And a full-human male would only see the human Sanura you revealed to him, not the fire witch of legend to be cherished and worshipped as a goddess instead simply treated as a person, a woman."

"Yes." Within that three-letter word, Assefa heard the echo of pain and regret. "Assefa, I do know how it feels to be treated as an object, sought after, and judged for the wrong reasons. I understand how that can make you leery of others' intentions and question your own sense of self-worth. I realize how it can make you guarded and how difficult it is to lower the walls you erect around yourself."

Sanura caressed his cheek with a tenderness Assefa never wanted to live without. "You're your own man, beloved, and I would never assess your character based on who or what your father is or was. I want nothing from you other than your heart, which, admittedly, is far more precious and fragile."

Assefa, rarely at a loss for words, didn't have a ready or easy reply. The woman had quite effectively silenced him, no small feat. But he could smile, and he did. He had chosen wisely, Assefa Berber, not the gods.

"We have, I realized while showering, too many challenging things in common."

Too true.

"We're powerful beyond what is considered normal. We're stubborn and value our own opinions above that of others. We have trust issues and walls that need dismantling. We—"

"Stop there. You're listing all the reasons why we shouldn't be together."

She undid her seat belt and then slid close enough to…Sanura kissed him, wet and with a whisper of wantonness. "No, you aren't contagious, smelly, nor have bad breath. And you can keep your smutty daydream to yourself."

Assefa grinned. "You *were* paying attention."

"I'm a teacher, Special Agent Berber; I know how to multitask."

Assefa ran his hand up her thigh, inwardly groaning that Sanura had decided to wear pants for the first time since they'd met. *Oh, all the things I could do to her if she wore a sexy skirt.* "If you don't want to hear it, I could always show you." His hand found the juncture of her sex. One finger rubbed, searching for the heat he was becoming to know so well.

"Mmm, gods, don't do that," Sanura said with a reluctance that stroked Assefa's ego. "It'll have to keep." She pointed to the brick house they were now parked in front of. "We're here, and we need to be focused."

"We?" He didn't understand what he had to do with whatever ritual she had in mind.

Siddig opened the door and let them out on the street's curbside.

"I don't know how long we'll be here," Assefa said to his driver, a middle-aged but still dangerous African golden cat. Dahad Siddig was loyal, an expatriate who, like all of Assefa's friends, had followed him to the States, their allegiance to the man he'd grown into, not to the man-child he'd been at his father's side.

"Why don't you use the time to"—Assefa lowered his voice—"visit that wind witch girlfriend of yours you think Zareb and I don't know about."

Casting a quick glance in Sanura's direction, Siddig cleared his throat, dark eyes shining with were-cat anticipation. "Well, umm…I think I might just do that, Mr. Berber."

"Good, I'll call you when we're ready to leave."

The grateful driver slid back behind the wheel of the limo. Assefa winked at him. "Have fun, Dahab. Take your witch wherever you'd like, on me. Just keep your cell phone close."

Siddig's short nod was enough. The man closed the door, and Assefa stepped away from the vehicle. Ignoring the curious onlookers, Assefa watched as Siddig pulled away from the curb and drove down the street, making a left when he reached the bend in the road.

The block the Garveys' house was located on was pleasant. Cars lined both sides of the one-way street. The front lawns were small but serviceable, and the sounds of laughing children on bikes and scooters filled the air.

Assefa smiled while watching the children play, enjoying the cool spring day. Privately, hoped he and Sanura would someday have children of their own. But that was a wish he knew to keep to himself. She may have forgiven him, but as she'd said, they both had walls. For all she'd shared in the limo, Sanura was still hiding behind a wall. Only time would tell if she would willingly tear it down or allow it to keep him from her.

Before Sanura could ring the doorbell, the front door to the Garvey's home opened. "By the gods, girl, I'm so glad you're here." Cynthia's blue eyes sparkled with a water witch's determination and a wife's fear. Saying nothing more, Cynthia grabbed Sanura's hand and dragged her into the house and up the stairs.

"Okay, I guess I'll get the door," Sanura heard Assefa mumble. Then he followed them, his footfalls nearly inaudible on the wooden steps.

Cynthia led them to the master bedroom. Eric lay curled in a ball on the bed, the green-and-gray sheets in wild ripples around him as if he couldn't decide whether he wanted them on or off. His chest rose and fell with unusual effort, breathing forced, skin pasty, light-brown hair sweaty and matted, eyes closed in a fitful sleep.

"How long has he been like this?" Sanura moved farther into the room, kneeling when she reached the bed and placing a hand on Eric's trembling chest.

"Almost a day. He thought he could weather it and asked me not to let the family know. After what happened with Gen, I've been so preoccupied with taking care of her that I didn't notice the signs of distress. I should've noticed before it got this bad."

"It's not your fault," Sanura tried to soothe. "Eric knows the signs better than anyone. Unfortunately, his stubborn and protective nature kept him from sharing what he views as 'his burden' with you." She raised her eyes from Eric and met Cynthia's across the bed. "You did the right thing calling me when you did." *Before it was too late. Hope it isn't already.*

Cynthia said nothing, just stood there in her jeans and T-shirt, dreadlocks curled about her face and shoulders. She made quite the pretty mid-day Saturday picture, the sun shining through open blinds, illuminating Cynthia's misty azure eyes.

"Do you have everything I require?" Sanura asked, then glanced around the room, seeing signs that Cynthia had done some timesaving prep work.

"I keep all the requisite supplies on hand. As you can see, I've already sanctified the area. Give me a minute, and I'll get the stuff."

Upon entering the room, Sanura had not only noticed a bedridden Eric but white candles placed in the four cardinal points of a chalk-drawn circle. The magical circle she now knelt in.

When Cynthia made her way out of the bedroom, Sanura noticed that Assefa had not only stayed on the other side of the room but that he was silently edging toward the door. "Don't go. I need you to join me in the circle."

"This is obviously private. I don't even know why I'm here. Maybe if you told me his condition, I could let you know if my company has developed something for the affliction. But, beyond medical assistance, I don't see how I can be of help."

"If there were ever two people who needed to communicate more than the two of us, I would like to meet them," she said, smiling, despite the serious nature of what lay before them.

She reached out a hand to him. He came, first taking the offer and then kneeling beside her. "You're my familiar now, Assefa, and there's a lot you need to learn for us to perform the level of magic we're capable of engaging. Do you remember when I said I wasn't intentionally ignoring you in the car?"

"Of course."

"Well, I was thinking of several spells I learned from an old grimoire my grandmother gave me on my eighteenth birthday. I memorized all of the spells, years ago. Yet, I've had luck with only a few. If we are who everyone seems to believe we are, together we should be able to unlock every spell in that book."

"I know what I said in the car, Sanura, but what if what we've been raised to believe is false? What if we aren't the chosen ones but mere flukes of nature?"

She'd asked herself the same question. And while she wanted nothing more than to be let off the prophecy hook, Sanura knew Eric needed the power of the fire witch and cat of legend, not the feeble attempt of two above-average "flukes of nature."

"I don't know, Assefa. But what we'll attempt today will prove or disprove the legend. I'm sure neither of us wants to experience the Day of Serpents, to be the chosen ones."

"But for your friend," he said, nodding to Eric, "you'll pray that we are."

Yes, she'd prayed in the car, one life versus that of thousands, maybe millions, if the prophecy came true. It wasn't rational, she knew. But love and family and loyalty rarely were. That was what Assefa had tried to get her to understand this morning. She didn't fully then. She did now.

"I have everything you need, Sanura," Cynthia said, reentering the room, her arms full.

"Are you ready, Assefa?" Sanura asked.

"No, but I suspect that doesn't really matter."

His feelings did matter. But, no, she would proceed despite his apprehension. *I have no real choice.*

"Like with the handfasting, I'll guide you. If we work together, trust each other, we'll save Eric and free his inner cat."

They were confidently spoken words, incongruous with the heart that beat far too rapidly and the body that began to sweat. And she knew her familiar could detect it all. But Assefa said nothing. For that bit of silent support, Sanura was grateful. And this time, she wouldn't let her familiar down. She would be the witch she needed to be. *For him. For myself. For Eric and Cynthia.*

Sanura took Cynthia's small basin of water and placed it beside Eric's bed. She dropped dry lavender blossoms saturated with jasmine and peppermint oils into the oval-shaped bowl. Then, closing her eyes, she said a silent incantation that caused the water in the bowl to swirl in a counterclockwise direction, imitating the movement of her right hand.

"Do it now, Cyn."

Cynthia took several cotton hand towels and dipped them in hot water, soaking them thoroughly. With Assefa's help, Cynthia lifted and removed Eric's sweaty undershirt, giving her an unobstructed view of his upper torso onto which she placed the towels. Once that task was done, Cynthia covered the wet cloths with two large, dry towels, locking in the heat and moisture.

Sanura rested one hand on Eric's towel-covered chest and reached her other one out to Assefa.

He took her hand. With that one unequivocal gesture, Assefa had given her more than she'd ever allowed herself to take from a lover. *Absolute trust. Faith.*

"What do you need me to do?"

"I need the strength of your Mngwa."

He cut his eyes to Cynthia, back to Sanura, and then lowered his voice to a husky whisper. "You want me to change here? In front of your friend?"

She stared at him. Gods, the man was funny and undeniably cute when being so proper. *As if I would ask him to get undressed in front of another woman, even Cyn.*

"I don't expect you to make the physical transformation."

"Then what?"

"My goal is to manipulate the blood clotting his body and force it into a normal, fluid state. I'll begin with his lungs and then move to other parts of his body. Once that's done, I'll…" She paused and looked at Cynthia. "I'll transfer a portion of your chi into Eric. This will strengthen his body, so he can survive the night and the following ritual."

Cynthia's face registered confusion.

"We can't keep doing this, Cyn. I've been able to keep him alive for the past two years, but the time between each treatment has gotten shorter."

Eric and Cynthia had only been married four years. Her friend knew her husband was slowly dying. Still, like most spouses, she lived in a constant state of denial, the reality being there was little Cynthia could do but watch and pray and temporarily forestall the inevitable.

Death did not have to claim Eric. Maybe they now had a real fighting chance that only came along every five hundred years.

"I will explain my plan to the two of you later, but right now, I just need you to do as I say and trust I know what I'm doing."

Sanura had performed the blood-thinning ritual dozens of times, but she'd only ever subjected Eric to level one of the spell. Level three, the more effective and dangerous level, required a strong familiar, which up to a month and a half ago, Sanura did not have. Meaning that Sanura never actually performed any of the higher-level spells in her grimoire. She fought to shrug off the weight of responsibility on her shoulders and the self-doubt riding her like a debilitating omen. Instead, she focused on the power within and the job only she could do.

"This is one hell of a way to test our bond."

Sanura squeezed Assefa's hand. "I know." *I'm sorry.*

Sanura nodded to Cynthia. "If you're ready, Cyn, take hold of my familiar's hand, then hold the hand of your familiar."

Cynthia did so, and Sanura completed the circle when she reached for and found Eric's right hand.

Without saying a word, they all closed their eyes. Their combined magic began to swirl and form the longer they held hands. Sanura felt a familiar wave of water witch magic mere seconds before the unique signature of Cyn's protective shield formed around them. It was Cynthia's job to sustain the integrity of her field, no matter what transpired within, and to keep the magical line of communication open between Sanura and Eric. Eric was Cynthia's familiar, and as such, her bond would be used to open Eric up more fully to the influence of another witch.

Sanura took a deep breath to calm her nerves, then gave her full concentration to the level-three blood-thinning spell. Her grip on Assefa's left hand tightened as she sent a wave of magical energy through him, testing the strength and preparedness of his aura. They had never done this before. Perhaps if they'd had time to experiment, to learn more about how to work together as a magical team, the bolt of untamed fire energy wouldn't have hit Assefa so hard, doubling him over in obvious pain.

CHAPTER TWENTY

Assefa gritted his teeth and forced himself to relax and absorb the magic. He tried to remember his teachings from Mistress Kemraha, an elderly priestess assigned to him as a child to help guide him in the mystical ways of his people. She'd taught him all she knew of witches and their familiars, but up until this very moment, he hadn't had the opportunity to test the validity of most of her teachings. Nevertheless, Assefa was a good student and learned his lessons well. As Sanura continued to pump more energy into him, he recalled what to do.

He knew there were three layers to his aura. Once a witch made a cat her familiar, an additional layer formed while the other layers took on aspects of the witch's aura. In turn, the cat transferred a portion of his aura to his witch. In the fourth layer of his aura, the energy from the witch was supposed to be stored. The more energy the familiar could hold, the stronger the spell the witch was able to cast.

The key was for the familiar to manipulate the energy by absorbing it correctly, using the connection with his witch through the other three auras to maintain her, give her strength, and, if necessary, take her pain. In return for the familiar's strength and protection, the familiar was shielded, through the witch-cat bond, from the magic of an equally or less powerful witch. This bonding of auras also protected the familiar from magical manipulation by other preternatural creatures like the siren Assefa had recently killed in Alaska.

He felt the warmth of Sanura's magic move throughout his body as intimately as when they made love. He didn't fight the sensation. Instead, he let it consume him. Once he did so, he shifted the power and control of the magic from Sanura to himself. Assefa massaged the energy, twirling and twisting until he settled it securely in his fourth layer.

Sanura sensed when Assefa had control over her magic and knew she could proceed with the ritual. She first concentrated on safely thinning the blood clots closest to Eric's heart and lungs. Like any combustible fluid, Sanura could control blood through her magic. She squeezed her friend's hand and then opened her eyes. With her second sight, she could see into him with X-ray-like vision.

She could clearly see the impediments to his breathing. One by one, Sanura focused on each of the threatening clots, incanting as she worked. She pulled energy from Assefa, who slowly released precisely what she needed without flooding her with too much. As the minutes ticked away, they found their rhythm, Sanura able to dispatch one clot after the other, a laborious, grueling process.

Eric's body was riddled with clots, prompting Sanura to take extra care. So she did, unhurriedly moving from one vital organ to the next, unwilling to miss a single clot. With unwavering effort, she thinned the clots, then replaced a portion of Eric's depleted magical energy with Assefa's healthier, much stronger chi.

Exhausting, but she had Assefa's strength to keep her going.

"Like water that flows from a stream, be not still. Like a tide that rises from the depths of an ocean, be not still. Like raindrops descending on the earth from the heavens, be not still. Be not still, flow freely and give life. Give life and be not still," Sanura commanded tiredly, ending the nearly three-hour ritual.

They released each other's hands, and Cynthia recalled the force field. The water witch's tired blue eyes stared down at her husband, then they lifted to Sanura and Assefa. "He's asleep, and his breathing is normal. You two did it. Thank you."

Assefa's supportive arms caught Sanura before she sank to the floor, the witch, unsurprisingly, drained after what she'd just done. He wasn't exactly full of energy himself. Holding her weight, he steadied her as they walked out of the bedroom, down the stairs, and into the

Garveys' living room. Leaving her on a sofa, Assefa went in search of a kitchen. A few minutes later, he returned with a cold glass of water.

"Here, drink this." He held her shaky hands while she devoured the water. "Would you like another?"

"No, but thanks."

Taking the glass from her hand, he placed it on the marble-top end table before sitting next to Sanura and pulling her to him. "I've never seen a witch do anything like that before, and I've seen plenty of unusual stuff working for the FBI."

"I've never done anything like that before," she admitted and then rested her head on his shoulder. "I didn't know I could, not truly. Something is happening to me. I viewed Eric's blood as lava and manipulated it the same way I would the molten rock—a basic earth spell with a twist."

He gave her a reassuring kiss on the forehead. "I know, sweetheart, something has happened to the both of us since the handfasting. We've gone so far beyond what other witches and their familiars can do together."

"Your eyes turned red," Cynthia said as she entered the living room, Assefa having heard the creak of the bedroom door when she'd closed it and her steps when she'd descended the stairs.

Sanura raised her head from Assefa's shoulder and gave Cynthia a questioning look. She then turned her skeptical eyes toward him, expecting, he assumed, for him to deny or confirm Cynthia's statement. But, before he could do either, she swung her gaze back to her friend.

"What are you talking about?"

Cynthia sat on the loveseat across from the sofa where Sanura and Assefa were seated. "Your eyes turned fire-engine red during the ritual. We've performed that ritual dozens of times, yet, that has *never* happened."

Assefa cautiously observed the longtime friends, knowing better than to get between two women. Besides, he was a visitor in the Garvey home and didn't know her friends well despite his relationship with Sanura. Yet, Cynthia had a valid point that he'd intended to broach with

Sanura as soon as she regained her strength. Cynthia Garvey, however, had beat him to it.

Cynthia gave Sanura a thoughtful look, furrowed her brow, and then sat forward on the loveseat. "We've never done *that* particular version of the ritual, have we?" Her voice was accusatory but not harsh.

Sanura shook her head, and Cynthia reclined back in the chair, her blue eyes still on her friend. "What did you do that would cause your eyes to change colors like that? In fact, what occurred during your hand-fasting that would allow you to use Assefa the way you did?"

Her voice had pitched a bit higher, a slight tremor she couldn't hide from his cat sensitive ears.

Sanura didn't have a chance to answer before Cynthia plowed on. "You performed, by all accounts, a magical operation on Eric, didn't you, Sanura, without even asking me?"

Her hands balled into fists, a vein in her neck strumming thick and fast, blue eyes bright and dangerous. Shit, he would be damned if they put him in a position to break up a fight between two powerful witches. He would gag them before he allowed one spell to be cast.

"Yes, I did," Sanura answered, apparently unfazed by Cynthia's bout of anger, making Assefa think this was par for the course with them. Observing the standoff, Assefa thanked the gods he had only one sister.

"He would've died otherwise. I had no choice. Eric still may not survive the night, so I had to transfer a fraction of Assefa's chi into him."

There was no hint of apology in her tone, although perhaps there should have been. Cynthia had a right to know what Sanura intended to do to her husband, even if it was in his best interest.

"You know I would never hurt Eric or risk his life, but—"

"I know you wouldn't, Sanura," Cynthia interrupted, her eyes calming, body relaxing, the brief spike of magical tension he'd felt receding. She ran her hands through her golden-brown dreadlocks, twisting one finger around one, stopping at the decorative cowrie shell on the end. "Between the attack on Gen and Eric's worsening condition, I'm just a little worse for wear."

"I get it. Eric is your mate, and his condition is tenuous. However, we have to make sure he makes it through the night, and if he does, come morning, much of his strength will return, and we can all discuss part two of my plan."

"There's a part two to all of this?" Assefa asked.

"Ah, yeah, but that's for later. I don't want to put the prayer before the offering," Sanura responded with an air of reserved caution.

Witch clichés, Assefa thought with disdain. His sister was full of them, whipping one out at the oddest times.

"So, this was what you were thinking about on the ride here? This is what you meant when you said you were meditating?"

"I had a lot on my mind, Assefa. I didn't have time to go through it all with you before we arrived. If I recall correctly, you were preoccupied with your dirty little thoughts."

"Okaaay, I'm still in the room unless the two of you want me to leave so you can pick up wherever you left off in the car."

They really were like sisters because Sanura didn't seem the least bit embarrassed. Not the way he knew she could be, so shy and discomforted at times.

"Did you see them change as well?" she asked him.

Ah, they were back to the red eyes.

"They were red, just as Cynthia said."

"I could see inside Eric as easily as I see the two of you now. Of course, I've used my second sight before, like all mature witches, but the results were never like they were today."

"You remember the day you were given your handfasting robe the same as me, Sanura. Your grandmother didn't select the tri-element design randomly. Oya worked through her, guiding her hands. You're a fire earth witch. Now that you've found your familiar, all of your latent powers will come into focus," Cynthia stated as if it were a given. "When we were kids, you acted like nothing was special about you, as if you were just like the rest of us, but that was never true. What you did today couldn't have happened if you weren't on the path the elders have spoken of since your birth."

Sanura's face revealed nothing but exhaustion. Not resignation, nor disagreement, not even annoyance. No wonder she sought escape through her moonstone and the dating of full-human men. Even her best friend treated her with reverence.

Cynthia studied them, her regard pensive. "You two are on a mutual journey, and the sooner you come to terms with it, the sooner you can prepare yourselves for what's to come."

Assefa did not like the casual way Cynthia accepted his and Sanura's fate. His friends and family were no different. Five hundred and the twenty-ninth year was what the Sudanese prophecy proclaimed. This year was the twenty-ninth of his and Sanura's births, Sanura's birthday only a few weeks away, while his was in September. If the Day of Serpents was a forgone conclusion, as Cynthia Garvey implied, it would happen before the end of this year. Before or after he turned twenty-nine, he didn't know. That could give them three months to prepare or no time at all.

She stood. "Thank you. I'm in your debt." Genuine. Humbling. Then Cynthia grinned, a bit of the devil shining through. "You know, Sanura, you used to be so rational and predictable before hooking up with Assefa. Now, you've moved to Virginia, shacked up with a guy you've only known a few weeks, and flawlessly performed an advanced-level spell right out of Nowa's shrine."

Assefa grimaced at the archaic witch saying. Even Najja didn't use that one.

"I think I like this new spontaneous side of you, sis." She then swept from the room, her words, "I'm going to check on my husband. The two of you should rest," trailing behind her.

Assefa listened to her retreating feet make their way down the hall and back up the stairs. Cynthia Garvey was an interesting woman, pretty and subtly powerful. She obviously loved and trusted Sanura. In Assefa's world, those were rare and precious gifts, never to be taken for granted.

"How is it that Cynthia and Eric, who can't be older than us, become the adoptive parents of a fourteen-year-old?"

"When Mom was a family law attorney, she helped save a lot of children from abusive home life. Eric was one of those kids. Luke Garvey, Eric's father, was a social drinker whose social hour started at seven in the morning and ended somewhere between passed-out o'clock and locked-up thirty. The times when his legs would hold his weight and his eyes could focus, his scorn at his 'shitty life with a whore of a wife and worthless kids who don't do shit but eat and spend my hard-earned money,' was treated with cause to assert his oh so manly prowess. What were a few bruises and split lips between family, right?"

"Guys like that make me want to dish out Sudanese-style justice." Sudan damn sure was no utopia. It had many flaws, but Sudanese men who were foolish enough to take that low road were dealt with swiftly and mercilessly. Not by were-cats. No, Sudanese witches, like Sanura's Witch Council of Elders, took care of their own.

"Dad felt the same as you. So anyway, Eric's mother decided to run. One night after her husband had passed out, she bundled her two boys and a few belongings into her car and bolted. She set out with no destination in mind or even a plan of what she would do once she got away. But she knew she couldn't stay, couldn't risk herself or her sons anymore."

Sanura's eyes radiated with intensity, speaking from the soul as if it were her tale instead of a friend's. Assefa wondered if Eric's youthful plight and Makena's legal work contributed to Sanura's interest in child psychology.

"Eileen Garvey didn't stop running until she'd reached Maryland." Sanura leaned her side against his, her head resting on his chest. "She probably thought the distance would be enough to keep her and her children safe. I can't imagine how frightened she must've been. She is a strong woman, Assefa, beaten down but never beaten. I have always admired Mrs. Garvey. Her witch powers are minor, but she possesses a deeper power."

He kissed the top of her head. He knew that type of power. The kind forged in the unforgiving fires of Hell. He'd seen it on the faces of his countrymen, rising up in revolt against a despotic Berber regime. And he'd glimpsed it in his own eyes. *The day I decided to leave home.*

"Survival instinct, sweetheart. There's no better motivator, except, of course, the protective heart of a mother."

She curled deeper against him, slipping off her shoes before putting her feet on the sofa, her knees rubbing his thigh. It was a nice fit. *A perfect fit.*

"The first thing Mrs. Garvey did, when she reached Maryland, was to seek out the Council." Sanura shook her head. "We're actually listed. If you can believe that."

He could. For the most part, full-humans didn't believe in witches. Sure, books and movies abounded about the supernatural, but no one really believed that stuff. It was just make-believe, right?

"It was after she joined the Council that Mrs. Garvey was introduced to a young Makena Williams, Harvard Law graduate and member of the Maryland State Bar. Mom eventually helped Mrs. Garvey divorce her husband and get full legal custody of Eric and Stephen, not that their father put up a fight for his marriage or his sons. Anyway, it wasn't until his father's death, about a year and a half ago, that Eric returned to California. His mother refused to attend the funeral. And, by then, Stephen wasn't around to make the trip. Even if he were in a position to go with Eric, he wouldn't have. He had long since taken up drinking to give a damn about anyone beyond himself. Like father like son, I suppose."

Like father like son. How many times had he heard that said about him? *Too many, but it's not true. Never had been, never will be.*

"Cyn went with him. It wasn't until he reached his father's San Francisco home that Eric came face-to-face with a half-sister he'd only seen in pictures."

"Garvey remarried?"

"He married a barely legal Chinese immigrant girl. But for all her youth, she understood the importance of family. So a few years back, she contacted Eric. From that point on, they kept in touch. Not often, but she would send him a couple of e-mails or text messages each year, keeping him informed of his father's and Gen's well-being."

Assefa already regretted having posed his innocent question. If he'd known it would lead to a drama from a soap opera, he would've forgone his curiosity.

"From what Gen told us, by the time she came along, her father had given up drinking, and he never beat her or her mother."

"Well, that's something."

"True, Eric was relieved to know his sister hadn't suffered the way he and Stephen had. But Luke Garvey still couldn't manage to stay out of trouble and away from the wrong people. The wrong people like Martin Bamber of the Oakland Bamber crime family."

That name niggled at a memory. He knew the name. The Bambers were—

"They're a family of Golems, strong, street-tough thugs who like fast cars, hot women, and their money paid back on time…and with interest."

That's right. Golems. Smart and business-savvy but ruthless if crossed. *And damn hard to kill.*

"Luke Garvey couldn't pay, so they were dealt with. An example to others, I suppose. He and Fang, Gen's mother, were discovered in an alley. Dismembered."

With that grisly tidbit, Sanura raised her eyes to his.

He frowned down at her. "You really could've kept that depressing story to yourself."

"You asked."

"I know, but next time, just say it's a long story and leave it at that."

"Fine." She shrugged. "You know what he has, don't you?" Sanura asked, casually switching topics the same way she was now casually massaging his thigh.

"Yes, feline thrombosis, a rare blood clotting disorder that impacts were-cats who can't turn into their feline form," he answered matter-of-factly, trying to ignore the pleasurable sensation her hand was sending up his leg and to his groin.

"Being the owner of a pharmaceutical company, I thought you would recognize the symptoms."

Well, not at first. "For about a year now, we've been working on a cure for feline thrombosis, but the best we've come up with is an anti-clotting pill that must be taken twice a day. It's far from a cure, though." But the pill only worked on cats in phase one of feline thrombosis. Eric

Garvey was deep into stage three, the last stage before death. "Your friend's condition is too advanced for anything we've been able to manufacture."

Her eyes didn't register the sadness or frustration he thought his news would evoke. *Interesting.* "You think you can cure him by freeing his inner cat, don't you?"

"With your help, perhaps we can do it."

He thought for a moment, looking out the living room window, seeing a group of boys using the street as a field for their game of touch football. An unexpected wave of homesickness assaulted him, repressed memories of playing catch with his father and brother before his mother died and Razi turned from his protector to his tormentor. He pushed away the unwanted memory.

"I've always known that was the key, but I could never figure out how to get a man who'd lost his ability to shift to reconnect with his inner cat spirit. It's a tricky thing, Sanura, bridging that divide once the connection has been severed."

To his surprise, Sanura kissed his lips. "Thank you for coming with me." His neck came next, wet, soft kisses. "Thank you for trusting me during the ritual." She undid the first three buttons of his shirt, extending her kisses there.

He slid a hand around her waist. "You have an outstanding way of showing appreciation."

She rose onto her knees and straddled his thighs. "I'm sure I can do better than a few kisses."

Yeah, I don't doubt it.

She undid the remaining buttons of his shirt, shoved up his undershirt, and lathered revealed skin with grateful, hot kisses. Then those impatient fingers of hers landed on his belt. His eyes flew to the living room entrance.

"Ah, my witchy temptress, perhaps this isn't the best place for you to show me exactly how much you appreciate my familiar skills."

Murmuring incoherent words against the nipple she was deliciously sucking, doors he hadn't noticed slid from the walls until they met in the center, shutting them off from the rest of the house and providing a measure of privacy.

Nice trick.

Lifting her head, she cradled his face in her hands. "I'll take back my magic now." There was a sensual but also serious note to her voice. Obviously, Sanura still felt guilty about having given him a magical fever. While he never wanted to experience that degree of magical discomfort again, he'd forgiven her for her careless mistake. Everyone made them. *I know I've made more than my share.*

They kissed, and he could feel Sanura's fire magic swirling in him, waiting to be reclaimed by its owner. And she did. The longer they kissed, the more magical energy she sucked out of him and into her. The magic eagerly responded to her siren's call, rushing up and out of him, impatient to please its mistress.

It should've burned. The fire magic, so intense as it made its escape, should've brought fiery tears to his eyes. But Sanura was so gentle, her control over her element masterful. She wasn't all brute strength, as he'd said in the limo. He was wrong, or at least only partially correct. She had a surgeon's touch neither one of them had given her credit for.

Breathless from her relentless kisses but energized from the thought of being inside Sanura again, Assefa picked her up.

Long legs wrapped around him. "Where are you taking me?"

"Just here." He checked the door.

"I magically locked it."

Good to know.

Sanura unhooked her legs and slid her feet to the floor. "I thought we could use the sofa." She fingered her pants. "These seemed like a good idea when I got dressed. But then," she said with a naughty smile, "I wasn't thinking about having sex with you in my sister's living room."

But they were going to, and he damn sure had no intention of getting caught.

"Quickie," he said, then spun Sanura around, her back to him, face to the door. "Put your hands on the door, sweetheart."

She did, oh so willingly.

He unbuttoned her pants and dragged them and her panties down to her ankles. "Widen your stance for me. Yeah, just like that. Damn, you look good. Wish we had longer to indulge."

"So do I." She wiggled that cute ass of hers. "But you can make it up to me later."

"That's a given. Now," he dropped his pants and boxers, dick hard, ready and aching to be inside his witch, "let me sample your sweet magic."

He did, taking her from behind, penetration deep, hips grinding, barely thrusting, and maintaining constant, wonderful contact.

"Next time," he began in her ear, voice low, "I'm going to take my time, do this right."

"Y–you're doing it r–right n–now."

Assefa pushed up her shirt and found a breast. Big and soft. He wanted to taste it, suckle the nipple before gently marking it.

"But I can make it better for you. So much better." He moved deeper into her, Sanura's body taking the whole of him, her curvy hips the perfect love handles.

There was one thing he could do. Now wasn't the time to show her what it could mean to be mated to a were-cat with his particular talents. But they were alone, and he heard no sounds from the main level. He heard nothing in the house but an upstairs television.

Assefa thought about what he wanted to do to the woman he was making love to. He crafted the image in his mind, seeing her, seeing him. *Two of me, one of her.*

"Do you want more of me, Sanura?"

"*Yes*," she moaned, hips pushing back, keeping him deliciously deep.

"Do you want me to taste you?"

"G–gods, yes."

"Then say it with your magic. Let it speak for you."

"I–I don't understand."

"Say it. Ask for what you want, and I'll make it happen."

Her body trembled now, so close to release. But he wanted to do this for her, let her see how fantastic it could be between a witch and her mate.

"Say it, sweetheart, just say it."

He'd barely gotten the words out before he sensed her magic, the temperature in the room increasing. Then she said the words he'd hoped she would. "Please taste me."

That was all it took. The erotic image exploded from his mind. Their shared magic poured out of him. Leaking cat magic coated him, hardened, and then split, tearing him in half. A writhing puddle of golden magic lay at Sanura's feet, growing, stretching, and taking form until a second Assefa was kneeling in front of her, hands reaching out and finding hips.

"Not possible. Gods, Assefa, that's not possible."

Despite her surprise, Sanura didn't move, didn't push the second Assefa away.

He didn't answer her. Clearly, it was possible, and he didn't want to waste time explaining it to her. Unfortunately, he could only maintain this dual state for a few minutes.

"Fulfill your witch's command," he told his second self.

The second Assefa lowered his head and licked his witch.

Sanura sucked in a breath.

Assefa licked again, deeper and longer, tasting her the way she'd requested.

Then Assefa began to move again, his thrusts pushing Sanura into the mouth devouring her.

Thrust and lick.

Thrust and lick.

She moaned loudly and then just screamed outright when he kept going. And going.

Assefa hoped Cynthia had the good sense not to come and investigate because he wouldn't stop. It felt too good, and they were too damn close to completion.

Thrust and lick.

Thrust and lick.

"Yes, yes!"

Sanura erupted around him, pulsing and wet and milking him with relentless spasms until he could do nothing but follow her with his own guttural grunts of release.

For several minutes, there was nothing but heavy, breath-catching gasps.

"You've been holding out on me," she rasped, arms at her sides, forehead against the door.

Assefa laughed. "And you never told me you were into threesomes."

They pulled up and adjusted their clothing, then Sanura turned to him after slipping back into her shoes.

"I'm not into threesomes. Besides, I don't think it counts if it's the same man divided in two."

He could argue the point, but it was a moot point since he had no intention of having a real ménage with her and another man.

She wrapped her arms around his neck. "You're trying to seduce me with kinky were-cat sex."

Yes, I am. Seduce you into staying with me forever.

"I love you, Sanura Williams, and I intend to make you my wife."

She dropped her arms. "Your wife?"

"Yes, my wi—"

A girl's scream blasted through the silent house, the shrill cry awaking the beast within.

"Unlock the door," he demanded.

Before he reached it, Sanura already had it open, her movements as quick as his own. Together they ran out of the living room, down the hall, and up the stairs.

Leading the way, Assefa rushed to the master bedroom, only to find Gen and Cynthia standing mutely. Gen pointed to the window in stunned horror.

On the other side of the window, crouched in an oak tree, were a predator's blackened, hungry eyes. *Raven Mocker.* Its soul-stealing gaze was all for Eric Garvey.

CHAPTER TWENTY-ONE

The Raven Mocker was a creature from Cherokee lore and one of the few beings so utterly vile and without conscience that the Preternatural Division of the FBI sanctioned their execution on sight. So now one of them was there, long beak too close to the window, death-black wings in repose, talons digging into tree bark, and its disfigured "human" body throwing off sizzling currents of malevolent energy.

Being the most feared of all demons in Cherokee tradition, Raven Mockers had the power to consume a dying person's soul to sustain their own life. The name came from the beast's immortality, in that its body would never become the prey of scavenger birds such as ravens. An enemy of witches, Raven Mockers tortured and taunted any weakened and dying person, both full-human and preternatural. *An equal opportunity soul-stealer.*

Assefa's hackles rose at the sight of the creature. His Mngwa roared a warning. The cat wanted to be set free, to rip into the predator of souls with claws and fangs.

"I–I came in to check on my brother. Cyn was busy with school work. I thought I could help out."

Then Gen had obviously seen the creature and screamed down the house, bringing Assefa and the witches running.

The last time Assefa had seen Genji Zhou-Garvey, the pretty teen had been flat on her back in a hospital bed, her brother at her side, eyes rimmed red with worry. Now the tables were reversed, but Gen's eyes shone with more than concern. *Horror and fear.*

He was getting damn tired of this, tired of the gods' first creations. *Nothing but predators. Like me.* "I'll take care of it."

"No, wait."

Angry and impatient, he turned to Sanura, claws pressed against the top of his fingers, ready to surge from his skin.

"You can't transform."

"Why not?" Claws broke the skin, sharpened, then lengthened.

"Because, Assefa, how would Cyn and Eric explain a truck-size cat in their front yard? Full-humans can't see Raven Mockers, remember? But they sure as hell can see a 600-plus-pound Mngwa."

Shit. This was why his grandfather had excommunicated thousands of full-humans from the Sudan. It was bloody, cruel, and downright in-humane, but very effective. Unfortunately, full-humans tended to muddy the waters with their fear and ignorance.

"I'm not going to let that thing come in here after Eric or one of you women. I have to do something. For whatever reason, traditional witch magic isn't very effective against Raven Mockers. It can stun but not permanently incapacitate."

"I didn't know that. I don't remember ever learning that," Cynthia admitted, the first words she'd spoken since Assefa and Sanura had rushed onto the scene. The woman looked like nothing more than a walking zombie, ready to drop where she stood. He wondered when she last had a good night's sleep. *Probably not for a long while.*

"What about my powers?"

Assefa swung his gaze to Gen, a reedy teen with intelligent brown eyes, straight black hair, and a scent that confused him. "What powers?"

Gen suddenly seemed less sure of herself, her eyes darting between Assefa and her sister-in-law. Her straight black hair was neatly pulled into a ponytail, and her red and white anime character shirt made her look younger than her fourteen years. But, teen or not, if she had a plan for dealing with the Raven Mocker, Assefa wanted to hear it.

"It's all right, sweetheart. Assefa is like family. You can trust him with your secret." Cynthia stepped closer to Gen and then placed a re-assuring hand on her shoulder.

"Okay, good, then I'll be back." Gen ran from the bedroom. Neither Sanura nor Cynthia followed. Well, Assefa would be damned if he did nothing while a teenager handled the Raven Mocker alone.

"You two," he said over his shoulder, trailing Gen, "keep an eye on that thing. I'll see what Gen's got up her sleeve and if she needs my help."

Assefa followed Gen into a home office—chair, bookshelves, and a desk cluttered with paper. The room was located at the back of the house, an alley separating the home on the Garveys' street from their neighbors on the next street.

He watched as Gen climbed out of the sole window in the room and onto a ledge. She used the ledge as leverage and swung onto the nearby tree. The thick, gray bark of the eighty-foot tree was sturdy and easily supported the teen's weight. Its green, oblong-shaped leaves masked her movements. To his surprise, she expertly maneuvered the tree limbs like a tightrope walker until she reached the low part of the roof onto which she jumped.

Curious, Assefa easily copied her moves, not allowing her to get too far ahead of him.

They scaled the roof until they reached the top of the house, over which they could see the Raven Mocker still crouched in the oak tree.

"Watch this," she whispered, then took a deep breath, and two fangs, not visible before, slid from her gums. Gen reared back like a cobra and spat a milky white substance at the Raven Mocker, her trajectory straight, aim true.

It landed a dead target to the eyes that had peered up at them a second too late. The creature flinched, shaking its feathered head. Gen struck repeatedly; each shot a sniper's perfect score.

Assefa could see the venom burning into the Raven Mocker's barely-visible human flesh, feathers black and covered with venom, soaking through and eating at it, an acidic assault the soul-stealer couldn't evade unless it risked leaving its perch to deal with the unusual witch.

He watched, amazed, as Gen, with steely purpose, kept up the offensive.

"You got this?" She gave him two thumbs-up. "Good, keep your distance. I'm going to check on the women, see if they've devised a plan." Gen's venom was nothing more than a distraction, a painfully annoying distraction, but inconsequential in the long run. They needed a better plan, preferably one that ended with the Raven Mocker's overdue death. *If I only thought to bring my gun.*

"If that thing comes after you while I'm gone, retreat first, then scream for me." And the hell with what the full-humans saw. Assefa would end this the way he already should have. *The things a familiar does for his witch.*

With one last look, Assefa left the Raven Mocker to Gen. He wouldn't be long. Assefa would not permit Gen to be attacked by another monster.

"I don't suppose you have a gun in this house?"

Sanura and Cynthia jumped, turning away from the window when he entered.

"By the gods, Assefa," Sanura said, hand going up to her chest, covering her heart, "give a woman fair warning next time."

"Do you, Cynthia?"

She, too, looked startled to see him. "Do you?" he pressed.

"Ah, no, sorry."

He hadn't really thought the Garveys would keep a gun in the house. Witches and were-cats rarely relied on conventional full-human weapons to safeguard them. He, on the other hand, used whatever worked.

Assefa pointed to the Raven Mocker but spoke to Cynthia. "You were watching that thing when I entered. Keep watching and let me know if it does anything other than try to shield itself from Gen's attack."

Assefa glanced at the bed. Eric Garvey was still in a post-surgery sleep. Good. *One less thing to deal with.* He gestured to Sanura, and she came to him.

"We haven't thought of a plan yet if that's what you want to know."

That was what he wanted to know, the most critical question, but not the only one. "Gen has snake fangs. How is that possible?"

"Her mother was bitten by a cerastes snake when she was pregnant with Gen. As a witch, the venom couldn't kill her, but it did—"

"Guys, we have to help her." Cynthia had their attention. "I don't know how much longer Gen can maintain that attack level." They joined her at the window. Cynthia reached down and found Sanura's hand. "But you could vanquish it. You can send that monster to another dimension. Now that you have your familiar, you are what we all knew you would become."

There was that damn reverence again. No wonder Sanura found it difficult to take someone else's counsel. Besides Makena, everyone in Sanura's life expected her to have all the answers. Even Mike relied on her to help him solve some of his cases.

The women stared at each other, a silent communication that was, to say the least, unsettling in its still intensity. Especially since Assefa figured he wouldn't like whatever the witches were planning.

"You're asking me to attempt a dimensional transference spell?"

"Yes, I know what's at risk, but—"

"While it's doable," Sanura said, thinking over the suggestion, "I've never actually performed such an advanced-level spell. If I screw this up, even a little, I could send myself into the dimension instead."

Scheming witches were the most dangerous predators, and anyone who thought witches weren't predators didn't live long enough to make that mistake twice. Cynthia and Sanura were crazy for even entertaining such an ill-advised idea. Assefa could suddenly envision them as reckless teens experimenting with unsanctioned spells in Makena's basement.

Assefa didn't bother raising the obvious flaws in Cynthia's suggestion. But, clearly, they both knew them, and while Sanura appeared initially shocked, she now seemed onboard with the ludicrous idea.

"Cynthia's right. Gen needs our help. We can use the sacred circle from earlier. It needs to be refreshed, but we don't have time for all that."

Sanura released Cynthia's hand and grabbed one of his, pulling him into the circle with her. They sat crossed-legged, facing each other and holding hands. She was loyal to the end, even if it meant risking her soul. It was actually the best…only plan they had. *If it works. If the crazy woman doesn't displace herself in the process.*

"Gen doesn't have much time, so this will have to be quick, Assefa. Sorry, but I don't have time to slowly push the energy into you. You'll have to take it all at once."

He knew that.

"If I pump your body with too much energy too fast, I could hurt you. That's the last thing I want to do, but I don't have much of a choice." She closed her eyes and took a deep breath. Then, opening them, she gave him a reassuring smile. "I trust you can make the proper adjustments and hold the magical energy as expertly as you did earlier."

"I know what to do. Just get on with it before I change my mind and hunt the bird my way."

Water witch magic shot through the room, spiraling outward.

"Hurry up. I just encased the bastard in a force field when he started to go after Gen, but it won't hold it for long."

Sanura closed her eyes, and Assefa readied himself to absorb her energy. Sanura's magical energy slammed into Assefa like a tidal wave hitting an embankment. The energy was wild and forceful, but like a great practitioner of Tai Chi, Assefa yielded to the magic, letting it flow through him, taking minimal impact. He dispersed the energy into the proper aura. He was ready, and he prayed she knew what she was doing because, the in-love fool that he was, if the witch screwed up and ended up in another dimension, he would challenge Sekhmet herself if it meant getting his Sanura back.

She began the dimensional transference spell, her magic spiking a moment before the words, "Leave this place, disturber of time and space. Leave this place, consumer of hearts and souls. Leave this place, consecrator of lands and lives. Leave this place and never return."

As she repeated the spell, Sanura envisioned the dimension to which she wanted to send the Raven Mocker. It was dead and dreary, home to massive volcanoes that spewed lava and acres of Weeping Willows that rained fire onto a charred ground of screaming souls, their eyes hollow, faces dulled echoes of the past, bodies alight in an endless chain of fire. Assefa saw it all as clearly as if it were his vision, their familiar-witch bond growing each time they shared magic.

Cynthia screamed, "Stop, Sanura, stop!"

But it was already done.

They opened their eyes and followed Cynthia's horrified gaze to the window. A burned body…a burned Raven Mocker slumped against the window.

Sanura pushed herself off the floor and ran to the window.

The Raven Mocker was charred everywhere Assefa could see, covered in a thick layer of what appeared to be hardened lava. Contorted in a mangled mess, its wings were split, and its beak was torn back and open as if a scream had died in its throat.

Of all things, the eyes were the most haunting, for they were the only part of the creature not covered in blood and lava. No longer black with the soul lust he'd seen earlier, the creature's orbs were now metal gray. *More human, less monster.*

"I killed it," Sanura gasped, the shock and disbelief wafting from her a near-tangible thing. "I can't believe I killed it."

She extended her hand toward the window, her fingers touching the glass pane and stroking with a feeling of sorrow he both saw and felt. Assefa took her shoulders and turned her away from the gruesome sight. She shook. Small tremors of fear and panic pulsed through her and into him. He held her to him, wishing he had the power to magically calm her the way he'd seen her do for Elizabeth Ferrell and Cynthia. But all he had was himself, his body, his heart, his love.

"What did Aunt Sanura do to it?" Gen asked when she reentered the bedroom. Cynthia answered, but Assefa was too preoccupied with Sanura's state of mind to care how she explained the unexpected turn the spell had taken.

Assefa spoke softly to her until her trembling decreased and then stopped. Once he felt she had her emotions under control, he said, "You must free them."

Sanura raised her head, tears threatening but holding. *That's my witch. Keep it together.* "To release the souls, sweetheart, you must completely destroy the Raven Mocker. That's the only way to kill and free those who fell prey to its terror."

Sanura shook her head and tried to push away from him, but Assefa refused to allow her to draw into herself. He did enough of that for both of them.

"You may not have meant for that to happen, Sanura, but it's the only way. That inhuman, soul-stealing parasite out there has taken, for probably centuries, what doesn't belong to it. Each soul a Raven

Mocker consumes becomes trapped inside its body and held there, an unwilling, terrified hostage." Assefa cupped her face and held it up, encouraging her to maintain eye contact, compelling Sanura to see his faith in her. The faith they all had in her.

"We have the power to set hundreds of souls free, Sanura, and we can't shy away from it because it'll destroy one worthless life. The Raven Mocker may have been human once, but it gave up its humanity in exchange for immortality. Such godly 'gifts' don't come free. They come at the suffering of others." He whispered in her ear, "I know as a doctor you believe all life is sacred, but sometimes, sweetheart, you have to put things in a cost-benefit equation—one life for hundreds of terrorized souls. You do the math and see if you don't come up with the same bottom line as me."

Sanura may have been present when he and Mike killed the adzes, but she didn't play a direct role in their deaths. So in her mind, she could probably distance herself from their fate. But the Raven Mocker would be different.

"You have to do it, Aunt Sanura."

Assefa let Sanura go, and they all faced Gen.

"You didn't see those dark eyes. I did, and I can tell you there was nothing inside but the hunger and need to feed. If we let it go, it may not kill Eric, but it will definitely find the next person hovering on the edge of life and death and make the decision before the Grim Reaper gets its turn at bat. That burnt chicken is a wacko, and I vote with Mr. Assefa to take it out." Gen placed hands on nonexistent hips. "I know Baltimore is home to the Super Bowl Ravens, but this is ridiculous."

"Look, Sanura, you've sheathed its body, but it's not dead. You need to cast a spell to free the tortured souls and…and…well, hell, I don't know what comes after that," he admitted.

"Neither do I," Sanura agreed. She looked at Gen, still fired up from her confrontation with the Raven Mocker, and then back at Assefa. "She's had so much pain in her short life, forced to grow up too fast. Eric's the only blood family she has left, and I won't let that thing kill him."

"There's my stubborn witch." He kissed her cheek. "We can do this."

Before Assefa could suggest Gen leave the room, Cynthia was already pushing the disgruntled teen into the hallway. "Aw, come on," was all he heard before Cynthia closed and locked the door.

Cynthia turned to Sanura. "Do you know a spell to set the souls free?"

"I don't know how I did *that* to it."

"I believe your spell was altered slightly because of the unique character of the target," Assefa hypothesized aloud.

"What do you mean?"

"It's just a theory, Sanura, but I think you performed the spell the way it was written in your grimoire. I've heard of circumstances when a witch's spell reacts differently depending on the physical or spiritual make-up of the intended target."

"I don't understand."

"Neither do I," Cynthia said, her arched eyebrows matching Sanura's.

"All I'm saying is that I believe an intermediate step was needed before Sanura could vanquish the Raven Mocker to another dimension because…" He paused, trying to piece together all the bits of information into a logical, complete puzzle. "What dimension were you going to send it to?"

"You saw what I saw. I didn't conjure that image from memory." She wrapped her arms around her and hugged herself. "I've never seen or read about such a place, yet it appeared in my mind when I began the transference spell, and it refused to go away, sucking me in deeper." She shivered. "But it felt vile. I wanted the spell to be over, so I could disengage."

He'd only seen the visions. Nothing else of the dimension had touched him. *But it had touched her, made her shudder, recoil, and remember the wisp of malevolence.* And that was it, the key. "Innocent souls cannot go into a Hell dimension."

Silence. Contemplation.

"I think I understand. So, the spell I cast adjusted to this fact and put the creature into a state in which I could first free the souls, then—"

"Then you can send its soul-stealing ass to the Hell dimension where it belongs," Cynthia finished.

"Exactly." Now they were getting somewhere. "Do you think you can free the souls?"

The lava encasement around the Raven Mocker was beginning to melt. If they were to do this, it had to happen now. Assefa pulled Sanura down onto the floor. "I don't mean to rush you, sweetheart, but that's going to be one pissed-off demon if it gets free."

Apparently, that was all the motivation she needed, for Sanura hastily grabbed his hands. "Since you still hold some of my magical energy, that's one less step we need to take."

Once again, Sanura closed her eyes and started incanting, her voice strong and polished, her magic even stronger. "Be at peace, lost souls of heaven. Be at peace, sacred spirits of old. Be at peace, watchers of life and death. Be at peace and find freedom's gate. Be at peace, for I release you back to the earth, water, fire, and air."

Assefa watched, his eyes riveted to the window and the abruptly morphing sky.

Lightning crackled, brightening the evening spring sky.

Boom.

Boom.

Boom.

Thunder roared. Sanura repeated the incantation, louder and with a might that stirred his Mngwa, raising gooseflesh and calling to his magic.

"I release you. Be at peace."

Boom.

Boom.

Boom.

The sky was on fire. Streaks of red-and-gold met white-and-blue. The red-and-gold didn't stop. It kept spreading, spiraling upward and outward, matching each thunderclap with its majestic light, its blatant magical path.

"I release you. I. Release. You. I. Release. You!"

Glowing white specks began appearing in the sky. One. Five. Twenty. Fifty. More. More. More.

The red-and-gold streaks ascended to the heavens. The white specks followed, clustering together in a blazing white ball of euphoric energy. Eyes transfixed, Assefa was convinced he saw clouds part and let the souls enter. It was the most beautiful phenomenon he'd ever witnessed. Then, as each lost soul found its way home, a peaceful silence befell the urban city for a timeless, magical moment.

Then it was all gone. No thunder. No lightning. No white specks. No red-and-gold streaks.

Sanura did it. But she wasn't done. Her eyes flew open, and she spun toward the Raven Mocker. "Be gone, demon, from this place. Travel on the Devil's breath of fire and find your home among the wretched of the earth."

The lava sheath erupted into magical flames of fire witch retribution, consuming the Raven Mocker's hybrid body until all that remained were ashes where the soul-stealer had once been. Then, with a fortuitous spring breeze, that too was lifted and carried away, leaving a vacant spot where the soul-stealer had been.

Assefa smiled at his incredible witch. "You're a dream keeper, Sanura. Langston Hughes had no idea."

She returned his smile, though hers was weak. The woman had to be exhausted, running on magical fumes and willpower. She needed sleep to rejuvenate her mind, body, and spirit.

Clearly, Cynthia had the same thought. "There's a guest room next door, Assefa. Why don't you help Sanura to the room before she passes out?" Then, pushing a stray dreadlock out of her eye, she unlocked and opened the bedroom door.

Assefa lifted Sanura into his arms, over her protest that she could manage. *Stubborn woman.*

Waving off the flood of questions coming from Gen, Cynthia walked the short distance to the guest room. He followed. Cynthia pulled down the sheets, and he laid Sanura onto the bed, her eyes already closed.

Assefa felt a hand on his shoulder and turned to see Cynthia gazing at him. "She's tenderhearted."

"I know."

"And powerful."

"I know."

"And she's afraid of losing control."

He knew that as well.

"Of her fire spirit."

Assefa wasn't blind or a fool. Sanura could've annihilated the adze with one well-focused fire spell, incinerating the bastard as soon as it showed its nasty face. Instead, she'd run, giving it a chance to harm her…kill her. Makena had told him that Sanura had received training beyond that of an ordinary witch, yet she displayed none of that special training the night she played bait. She'd kept a firm grip on her fire spirit, delivering a halfhearted wind attack to the adze instead of unleashing the fiery spirit within. Yes, Assefa understood all of that. What he didn't understand was why Cynthia Garvey was—

"She's also afraid of losing her heart." *Her what?* An unsure hand took hold of his. "You're just as tenderhearted as Sanura and equally as powerful. But you won't lose control of your cat spirit." Her hand squeezed his, an unexpected affection that touched and confused him. "But you've already lost your heart to her. I could see that when we met at the hospital. And I can see it every time you look at her, speak to her, touch her."

Cynthia released him and stepped away, her words of, "*She's also afraid of losing her heart,*" refusing to do the same. "She won't…" Cynthia glanced down at a prone Sanura. "Just guard your heart, Special Agent Berber. I would hate to see it get burned." She exited the room then and closed the door behind her.

"Hate to see it get burned."

Assefa cataloged that bit of unasked-for water witch advice, locking it away with his own nagging thoughts that, yes, his fire witch would someday scorch his heart to the core.

He removed Sanura's shoes and pants and covered her with a light-weight cotton blanket that was folded at the foot of the bed.

Assefa cut the light off and started to leave the room when a tired voice said, "Don't go."

He quickly took stock of the situation. Eric was still asleep and breathing normally. The Raven Mocker was no more, and Cynthia could take care of anything while he and Sanura got a few hours of rest. He reluctantly admitted that he was also tired. Holding and manipulating witch magic was draining, especially since it was such potent witch magic. The fact that Sanura was still growing in her power-set was a sobering thought.

Giving in to his common sense, Assefa removed his shirt and pants and placed the folded clothing beside Sanura's on the dresser. He curled behind the woman he loved. *The woman who will burn my heart?*

Sleep didn't come right away for Assefa, but when it did, he found himself on a precipice surrounded by red-gold flames, his chest open, heart gone, and soul torn asunder.

CHAPTER TWENTY-TWO

Sanura opened her eyes. Her nightmare of a reborn and bloodthirsty Raven Mocker lingered from her dream state to her waking mind. It was only a dream. She knew that, but her heart still pounded and her eyes searched the dark room.

While witches couldn't see as well in the dark as were-cats, they had far better night vision than full-humans. What she saw, the familiar red underbrush wall print in a three-sectional design and the rich, dark finish of the dressers, mirror, and nightstand, Sanura knew she was in Cyn's guest room, a room she'd slept in many times. The memory of Assefa caring her into the room, undressing her, and then joining her in bed began to work through her foggy mind.

She recalled it all now—Eric's fever, the Raven Mocker. *The emancipated souls*. Sanura had done that. She'd released so many souls, given freedom to the enslaved—a glorious feeling. But she'd also sent the Raven Mocker to some unnamable Hell dimension, her magic guided, *manipulated. By my fire spirit. My other half.* That, too, had felt glorious. The truth sickened her.

Disgusted by her own weakness, Sanura turned over in bed. Assefa slept soundly beside her. Her heart swelled at the sight of him. Sanura loved Assefa, from his intelligent, brown eyes to his expensive leather loafers. And every sweet were-cat inch of him in between.

With a solitary finger, she touched his strong jaw. Then, unable to resist, she kissed his cheek, just a peck.

He sleepily turned and pulled Sanura to him. "Go back to sleep. It's still early."

Sanura shook his left shoulder. "Wake up, it's time."

Assefa drew her closer, groggily searching for and finding her lips. His tongue peeked out and slid over closed but tempted lips. She knew better, she really did, but Sanura opened her mouth, accepting his tongue and giving him her own. For a minute, she let herself enjoy the feel of his powerful body against hers, the tongue that explored, the hands that caressed, the pelvis that pulsed and rubbed, threatening her plans and lucidity. Then, with the fleeting strength of a drowning victim lunging for the surface, Sanura pushed at Assefa, breaking the plane and taking in mouthfuls of air.

"I didn't wake you for this."

Assefa rolled annoyed eyes to the clock on the nightstand, then pinned her with a heated gaze. "It's two o'clock. There are only two things I'm interested in doing this time of morning"—he fluffed his pillow—"and, apparently, one of them is off the table." More fluffing. "I'm going back to sleep." He gave her a chaste kiss on the cheek, then rolled over and away from her.

"Men," she huffed and then threw the blanket off him, revealing a white, sleeveless undershirt and bed-wrinkled, white and blue boxers.

"Damn it, Sanura," he snarled, voice low and dangerous. "What do you want from me so early in the morning, if not sex?"

"Does everything with you have to be about sex?"

"You're kidding me, right?" He popped up in bed. "This coming from the same woman who initiated sex in her best friend's living room while there was a minor one floor up."

Sanura blushed. At the time, Gen hadn't crossed her mind. All she could think about was how turned-on she became when they comingled their magic, stirring a sexual craving for the man and his magic. But that was a side effect of the bonding she wasn't yet ready to admit. Besides, with the superior way Assefa stared at her, she would not be copping to that anytime soon, no more than permitting herself to be goaded into a pointless argument.

Instead, she scampered out of bed, opened the bedroom door, and exited. Two minutes later, she returned to the room, closed the door behind her, and flipped the light switch on. "Everyone is asleep."

"Of course, they're asleep. It's too early to be up and about. Tell me what this is about so I can go back to sleep."

Sanura sat down on the bed, ignoring Assefa's displeased grimace. "It's time for us to complete the ritual and free Eric's inner cat."

"It's two o'clock." Assefa glanced at the clock again and corrected. "It's two-ten, for Sekhmet's sake. Wake me in four hours, then I'll be ready to listen to your plan." He groped for the flat sheet and covered himself.

"It's now or never, Assefa, so wake your grumpy butt up and help me."

"Has anyone ever told you you're bossy in the morning?"

"Has anyone ever told you you're a whiny baby when you don't get enough sleep?" she countered, then poked him in the side.

Without warning, Assefa jumped up and pinned her to the bed. His big body held her down, her arms above her head in an unbreakable vise. "I wouldn't be so ill-tempered if you'd woken me properly."

Assefa had caught her unaware, but she wouldn't be cowed by his arrogant masculinity, so she struggled.

He laughed.

He was much stronger than she, but that didn't stop her from putting up a fight. He loosened his grip, allowing her to push and pull herself free, only to be trapped again in his debilitating grip. He did this several times, permitting her to taste freedom only to snatch it away at the last minute.

"You don't fight fair," she panted, her attempts having done nothing but work him between her legs, his hardness grazing her damp panties. And he made sure every squirm of her hips left him in the right spot, tempting her with his delicious weight and thick arousal.

"You wake me before the sun is up with a teasing kiss, not to play my favorite game, but to help you with a ritual. Now who doesn't play fair?"

The way he had her splayed, thighs open, arms hoisted and held above her head, body half-naked, she felt like a movie trope virginal heroine offered up to a so-called pagan god. Under different circumstances, Sanura would play the role of damsel in distress until she was sweaty, sated, and virgin no more.

Sanura smiled at Assefa, knowing he had shaken off most of his initial irritability. He only needed a few more minutes of banter and would be in the proper mindset for what she had in mind.

Deliberately, she raised her hips. Just a fraction, but it was enough. Her wetness connected with his hardness.

Assefa moaned.

She did it repeatedly, rocking into him, a shallow penetration, their underwear an artificial barrier. Yet it still felt good. So good, in fact, that Sanura had nearly forgotten her ploy. That was until she felt Assefa's grip on her wrists loosen and then fall away, sliding to her panties and—

The incantation she'd been holding burst from her mouth. He paused, his wily fingers so close to her moist heat. *Sorry, baby, next time.* Sanura flipped Assefa onto his back, then quickly recited the second half of the spell.

She now straddled his thighs. Inordinately pleased with herself, she winked at her special agent before bestowing him with her best mocking smile.

No matter how hard he tried, he couldn't move, and he tried damn hard, his biceps flexing in the most arousing way every time he did. As did the vein in the center of his head, the one that tended to appear whenever he was…well, *excited*, or in this case, frustrated.

"You can't break the spell, so you might as well give up."

He glared at her when neither his legs nor arms obeyed his commands.

"You wicked little witch. I'll make you pay for this once I'm free." His eyes flashed Mngwa gold, and she couldn't help but wonder if she'd gone too far. But he was still hard under her. Surely that meant he wasn't as upset as he seemed.

"Well, you have to obtain your freedom first." Sanura poked him in the chest. "You fell for a level-one binding spell, Special Agent Berber. Just admit I won, and I'll release you."

"You didn't win. You cheated." He growled and tried to lift his hips and buck her off him. No success.

"Sore loser." Sanura poked him again.

"Stop poking me, woman. Those twiglike fingers of yours hurt."

"Then admit defeat so we can move on." She leaned over him, their faces inches apart and the temptation to kiss and lick his pouting lips so strong.

"You need to stop provoking me, Sanura. I don't think I like this side of you. It's extremely unbecoming."

"What side, baby, the winning side?" she taunted, not fooled by his feigned insult.

"Do you treat all your lovers like this or only the ones who try to have sex with you at two in the morning?"

Lover. The word didn't adequately capture what they were to each other. She didn't know what word did, but "lover" was far too tame, shallow, and *temporary.*

She grazed his lips. "You're the only man I ever wanted to bind, and I hope we can play this game again when we get home." Sliding her tongue over full, supple lips, she played and teased before saying, "I release you. You're bound to me no more."

An inexplicable pinprick of pain struck Sanura, going straight to her heart as she unwrapped him from her spell, giving Assefa his freedom, his leave of her. The biting ache grew, sinking in deeper when the last tendrils of the spell coiled back into her, separating Assefa from Sanura. The pain, a magical foreboding of events to come, to dangers yet revealed, a warning from the fire spirit and to the woman.

Even though his body was now his own, Assefa didn't move. Neither did his witch. "What's wrong, sweetheart?" The way she stared down at him made his gut clench. She appeared on the verge of tears. He didn't understand the mood swing. Assefa wasn't truly upset with Sanura. Perhaps she thought he was. "Tell me."

"It's nothing."

A lie.

He did move then, forcing her to do the same. They sat in the center of the bed, facing each other, no more playful humor between them, just a witch's lack of trust.

"Okay, I'm awake, and you have my attention. What do you need me to do?"

"We need to complete the second half of my plan."

"Wait a minute. You told Cynthia you would go over part two of the plan with her and Eric in the morning. So now you're planning on doing it behind their backs?"

"Don't look at me like that. I don't have a choice."

"You have a choice. You don't have the right to make decisions for other people."

"That's not what I'm doing. Eric can't know, and Cyn would disapprove."

"So, you've decided that the all-knowing fire witch of legend has the right to do whatever she wants regardless of anyone else's thoughts." Assefa stood, the cool from the floor doing little to dull his heat. "You're a doctor, Sanura. You know about informed consent. Yet you trampled over it with the first ritual, and now you intend to do it again."

"It's not like that. You're acting like I want to perform the ritual behind my friends' backs. I don't. If there was another way, I would gladly take it."

"You can't have it both ways. You can't eschew being the fire witch of legend in one breath while acting like an omnipotent goddess the next."

She jumped from the bed, all long limbs and angry eyes. "That's not what this is about. And don't you dare compare me to a goddess. I'm nothing like them."

Perhaps not yet, but someone was working damn hard to ensure she tapped into her new power base. And the opportunities, of late, abounded. Assefa would have to be a fool not to question all the preternatural crap that kept finding them, creating situations where they felt compelled to combine their magic into a fighting force. *Raven Mockers are rare, but one managed to find its way to the Garvey's home when Sanura and I were here.*

The special agent didn't believe in that level of coincidence. Of course, it didn't help that Sanura found it far too easy to ignore the opinion of others in favor of her own. That kind of thinking was a slippery slope. He wouldn't let Sanura go down that path.

"Tell you what, explain the ritual to me. If, after hearing the details, I agree that Eric and Cynthia shouldn't be told, I'll help you. If I disagree, then you accept my decision. You'll tell the Garveys and let them decide how they'd like us to proceed."

She rolled her eyes at him. "I don't like your FBI attitude, Special Agent Berber, nor the way you negotiate."

"But do you agree?"

She plopped onto the bed. "Do I have a choice?"

"Not if you want my help." He sat next to her. "Either we're partners, or we're not. A witch doesn't dictate the terms of the witch-familiar relationship, nor the familiar. I won't tolerate anything less than full equality between us, a respectful partnership. Do you know how to be a partner?"

Assefa already knew the answer, but Sanura's truthful words of, "I've never tried. Not truly," gave him hope. *I'll teach you.* He extended his hand, palm-up, to her. "Are you willing to try, willing to learn?"

She pressed her palm into his, and he circled her hand with his fingers. "I'll tell you everything, Assefa. I'll leave nothing out, and we'll make this decision together. Fair enough?"

He nodded. "Fair enough."

CHAPTER TWENTY-THREE

Eric Garvey awoke from what felt like a fever-induced sleep. His mouth felt desert-dry, lips cracked and painful, the tongue he slid across them doing nothing to alleviate his discomfort.

A sliver of moonlight eked through the raised Roman shades, partially illuminating the darkened room. The smooth whirl of the ceiling fan sliced through the air, bringing with it a cold breeze that chased Eric's exposed legs.

He sat up, then looked down to see he only wore a short-sleeve, black-and-red firefighter T-shirt that read, "When others run out, we run in," and a pair of matching shorts with a raging fire on the thigh and the letters EMT on a fire hose surrounding it.

A sense of unease coursed through him, hotter than any fire he'd ever fought. Needing the comfort his wife always afforded him, Eric reached for Cynthia. Cold, smooth sheets met him. She wasn't there.

Eric frowned, got out of bed, and headed for Gen's room. He knocked first, waited thirty seconds, and then went inside. Her bed was empty, neat, and tidy as she left it every morning before leaving for school. He glanced about the room in search of…well, he didn't know what he was expecting to find. His eyes settled on the clock on her desk, the blinking red numbers the only light in the room.

Eric hustled back into his bedroom and looked out one of the windows. He saw no one on the dark street. The street lamps were out, leaving the neighborhood eerily quiet. Like his own home, no other house he could see had lights on. The Dorseys and Watsons, directly across from him, had their porch lights on past dusk on a timer, like his own. Yet their homes were just as black and oddly bleak as his.

He turned from the window, his heartbeat picking up pace, his mind whirling with confusion and concern. *How is Gen's clock working? Was there a power outage? Did it only affect part of the house? Where in the hell is my family?*

Eric shoved his legs into a pair of faded blue jeans and covered his chilled feet with socks. He cautiously took the steps downstairs, trying his best to see in the dark house. When he reached the bottom step, he noticed a dim light coming from the den. The door to the room was closed, but the light shimmered like a teasing homing beacon from the two inches where the door ended and the hardwood floor began.

Creeping to the door, his heart pounded, compelled forward by the urge to locate his family, to get answers for all the strange shit that had happened since he'd awoken. Finding the wall, he slid along it. His feet hit something long. Eric bent, both hands going to his feet and searching. He lifted the object, knowing what it was. *Cynthia's umbrella. Great, Eric, your family could be in trouble and all you got is a pointy umbrella.* Yeah, that was all he had. He held tightly onto it.

He turned the knob and pushed the door, leading with the umbrella. He peered into the room and didn't know whether to be relieved or afraid. It was empty. He shook his head, realizing the horrific image he'd created in his mind wasn't before him. *Thank Ra.* But he was no closer to finding his wife and sister.

Frustrated, Eric walked out of the den, his steps soundless. He headed to the front door, unlocked it, and walked outside. His car and Cynthia's car were parked in the driveway. He went to them, touching the hoods of both. *They're cold, so where in the hell are the girls? Shit, shit, shit. I get sick for one night and lose track of my goddamn family. What in the hell is going on here?*

Eric ran back into the house, slamming and locking the door behind him. He stumbled to the den and picked up the phone, cursing himself for not thinking to use it earlier. *Mike will know what to do. He can find them. Or Sanura. Or Makena.*

"*Fuck.*" Tension pulsed in his neck, the phone failing to register a dial tone. "How in the hell can there be electricity for the lamp but none for the phone, and they're in the same damn room?" Eric hurled the phone across the room, smashing it against the wall. Bits of plastic and metal fell to the floor, but he was already out of the room to care or notice.

Maybe I can find my cell phone. It has to be in the bedroom some-where. Eric started for the stairs when a sound stopped him cold. He turned around, listening, and then followed the low but consistent noise. An unexpected sound in an otherwise comatose house was coming from the basement. *Shit, why didn't I think to look down there?*

As quietly as possible, Eric moved down the hall and to the door that led to the basement. Then, thinking better of it, he went to the kitchen, found a butcher knife, and dropped the umbrella he'd been clinging to. Palming the handle of the reassuring weight, he returned to the basement door, opened it, and descended the stairs.

Once on the steps, the sounds were discernible now, and they sounded like…*groans*. He reached the bottom of the landing, walked three steps, and—Pain slammed into his head. Eric dropped to his knees. Something hit him again. Head spun, eyes shut, and face hit the floor. Then he felt himself being dragged by one leg, darkness and fury clawing at him, pulling him under.

He went.

Pain. His head. His neck. Eric's eyes flew open and pain seared through him. A warm liquid ran down the side of his head, to his ear, and onto his neck. Then, pain exploded behind his eyes, a stabbing pressure that made him want to cry out.

He fought the cranial assault, pushing the ache away. The swinging ceiling bulb was now on, and Eric could see his bloodstained socks. Willing his neck upward, Eric lifted his head, focused his eyes, and saw them.

His wife and baby sister sat no more than fifteen feet in front of him, tied to separate chairs. Their legs and feet were bound, and they weren't moving. Hell, he wasn't even sure if they were breathing. He went to move, only then realizing he was also tied to a chair. *Dammit.* Desperate to reach them, Eric fought against the ropes, twisting and turning, cutting and tearing flesh. He didn't care. He had to get them all out of here before—

"Don't bother trying to escape," a sinister voice came from the shadows.

Eric stopped struggling and peered in the direction of the voice. He squinted, unseeing, and cursed his human-level vision. The damn disease had stolen every part of Eric that made him a were-cat, *a real man*, even his enhanced senses. Now that he needed them the most, now that his family needed his cat within…

"Show yourself, you son of a bitch. Or are you too afraid to face me like a man?"

A harsh, derisive laugh had Eric's heart jumping into his throat.

"You, Mr. Garvey, are a charlatan, like all the rest. Husbands, fathers, boyfriends, and brothers all think they can protect their women and children from what lurks in the shadows." The interloper laughed again, then slinked into the gloomy light hanging from the ceiling.

Eric could now look upon his tormentor, and what he saw disturbed him more than anything in the world. The intruder leaned down to Eric, only four repulsive inches from his face.

"Recognize me now, little Eric?"

"It can't be," Eric said, with a violently painful shake of his head, wishing the horrifying sight away. "You're in prison. I made sure they locked you up for what you did to those women, you sick motherfucker."

"Well, as you can see, no prison can hold me." He sneered down at Eric. "I've come for my due."

The asshole turned away from Eric and walked toward Cynthia and Gen, their heads hung low, shoulders slumped, hair shielding their faces like a foreboding curtain to the entrance of a house of horrors. He reached Cynthia and slowly slid his hands up her thighs, a hardhearted snake with foul intentions.

"Stay away from my wife, Stephen. Stay the hell away from her, you monster, before I—"

"Before you do what, baby brother? What do you think you can do to me that you haven't already?"

Eric's older brother sniffed the air like the depraved predator he was. "You're pathetic." Stephen ran one pasty hand through Cynthia's heavily coiled locks before jerking her head up. "You can't even shift to protect this hot wife of yours."

He could see his wife's face now. Mouth gagged, eyes glistening with terror. Her teary ocean-blue orbs looked directly into his enraged gaze. His insides boiled with fury and fear.

Stephen smiled at Eric. His twinkling blue eyes and handsome face always masked his true nature, a demon lurking behind the man. "I had to gag the little bitch. She tried to cast a spell, and well…you know how I hate it when they try to fight back."

The rage grew, burning Eric from the inside out when he noticed blood running from Cynthia's nose and mouth and a puffy left eye that would be closed come morning.

"Damn you, Stephen, let my family go. This is between the two of us. Just leave them out of it."

"You don't understand, baby brother. This involves them inti-mately. I've spent the last two years in jail because of you. You could've saved me."

"I tried to save you, but you wouldn't stop. What kind of man would do what you did to those women?" *Thank Ra Gen wasn't around back then. Out of Stephen's reach. But not today. Fuck!* "What was I sup-posed to do?"

"You were supposed to stand by me, watch my back like any good brother would."

"You're a lowdown, filthy rapist, for Sekhmet's sake. I couldn't support that. No real man does that kind of cowardly shit to women. No man I want to call brother."

"Is that why you sent Mike after me? Is that why you let him beat my ass and haul me off to jail like some kind of common criminal?"

"You *are* a criminal. You hurt people. You didn't give a damn about anyone but yourself. I couldn't get you to stop, to turn yourself in."

"You were just upset about Rachel," Stephen casually threw out, as if what he'd done to her was of no import.

A snarl gathered in Eric's throat, a fierce rage rapidly reaching the tipping point. "She was our *friend*, damn you. Sanura and Cynthia's friend. *Your fuckin' witch to protect.* A piece of shit familiar you turned out to be. Rachel's never been the same, and it's your damn fault."

"No, baby brother, I think what you meant to say is that it was your fault. You can't save them all." He glanced at Cynthia. "And you won't be able to save her either."

"Please, don't do this. Cynthia's my wife, your sister-in-law. Don't do this to her. I'm begging you." Eric renewed his fight against the ropes. Skin tore. Blood spilled. *Can't let this happen. Won't let it happen. Not again.*

"If I recall, Eric, I begged you to keep my secret."

Eric ignored the madman because, dammit, Gen was crying. And no wonder, glassy, brown eyes peeked through black hair, watching as Stephen focused his lascivious attention on Gen's sister-in-law.

Still fighting against the bindings that kept Eric from his family and Steven upright and alive, Eric's eyes fell to his wife. Radiant and courageous, she stared back at Eric with far too much concern for him. She closed her eyes once, twice, three times. Each time opening them and then stared back at him before closing them again. His cat roared, and the man swore. Eric knew what Cynthia was doing, what she wanted him to do. It made him feel like a worthless lump of male nothingness.

But fuck that. Eric Garvey wouldn't close his eyes to spare himself while his wife was raped by his damn brother. What kind of man did she think she married? *A man who hasn't been able to shift for two years. A man who's wallowed in fear and guilt for far too long. A man who hasn't acted like much of a man at all, relying on his wife and friend to take care of him.*

Stephen ripped Cynthia's blouse, sending buttons flying, revealing a white laced bra with pink roses. He licked his lips at the sight of her. "Oh, yeah, your wife's so damn hot. Too fine for a wimp like you." He slid a finger under a bra strap, caressing, playing, and then tugging. "I'm going to enjoy this, and you'll watch, knowing there's absolutely nothing you can do to save her."

Eric's heart stuttered, then stopped. In slow motion, the scene played out before him. Stephen grabbed her breasts. Stephen ripped her bra. Stephen untied her legs. Stephen yanked off her pants.

Stephen.

Stephen.

Stephen.

The boiled rage detonated, shattering Eric's senses and his beast's cage. The lumbering snarl grew into an incensed growl. The roar ripped through Eric. A howl of repressed were-cat magic followed; an animal too long denied its freedom. That, too, soared to life, stretching, tearing, and clawing its way to the light, forcing its own rebirth.

When Cynthia's tear-filled eyes slammed shut with defeated revulsion, he was by his witch's side, his cougar knocking Stephen away from his wife.

Before the bastard hit the floor, the cougar was ripping into him, white fangs gleaming sharp and lethal.

The magnificent roar of a proud cougar brought Sanura back. The joyous sound slammed into her, breaking her waning concentration. The spell slipped away. Her magic dispersed.

Sanura blinked away the residual image of Eric's cougar. "Can you hear them?"

"Of course. Eric's purring now, and Cynthia is crying. Should we check on them?" Assefa glanced at the wall separating the guest room from the master bedroom.

As much as Sanura wanted to see Eric's tawny-colored cougar, now wasn't the time. "No, they need time alone. Besides, I thought you were sleepy."

"Do you think I can go back to sleep after what you just put me through?"

"What I put you through?"

"Don't give me that innocent tone. You just had me pretend to be a psycho rapist."

"But—"

"*And*…I had to allow Eric's cougar to damn near rip my heart out."

"Did you get hurt?" she asked with a conceited grin, just to annoy her prickly agent.

"That's *not* the point, Sanura, and you know it." Assefa rubbed his chest, the place where Eric's virtual cougar had clawed at "Stephen."

"It's exactly the point. Your Mngwa is too strong to allow harm to come to you in a magic-induced dream. You're the only one who could've gotten through to him. I couldn't maintain the integrity of the illusion and pretend to be Stephen. As it was, I kept screwing up the lighting. I needed you, Assefa. Partners, just like you said."

"Yeah, well…next time you get to play the psychopath. Better yet, let us never do that spell again." Assefa rose from the floor and helped Sanura to her feet. "I don't think what you did is a cure."

"It may not be the cure you envisioned, my narrowed-minded chemist, but it's indeed a cure. Feline thrombosis is not a disease of the body but of the mind. It may have physical symptoms, but the cause is psychological in nature. Until yesterday, I thought of it as a physical condition only. I didn't understand Eric's rapid descent over the past couple of weeks until I put all the pieces together. I should've thought of it before."

"Thought of what?"

He gestured for her to precede him onto the bed. She did, sliding over and leaving him space to join her. Covers came next. Assefa tucked them into their hips, backs pressed against pillows and head-board. Despite what he'd said about not being able to sleep, the spell had drained them both, a typical byproduct of strong magic use.

"What is your greatest fear?" she asked him.

Assefa gave her question a few seconds of thought before answering. But when he did answer, it was exactly as she'd expected. "Not being there for the ones I love. Not being able to protect those nearest my heart." He stared at her then, his chocolate eyes filling with under-standing. "You're a damn excellent psychologist, Dr. Williams."

"It took me long enough to figure it out."

"Sekhmet endowed warlocks with the ability to protect the females of the species by giving us the spirit of cats. But, for those witches that we love, if we cannot shield them from harm, what good is our inner cat?"

"Precisely." She found his large hands and wrapped hers around them. "Two years ago, Eric tried to stop his brother from pursuing Rachel, Stephen's familiar and our friend." She'd told him this before they began the ritual when he agreed that Cynthia and Eric couldn't know. He hadn't liked the idea of deception, but he could see the logic behind her scheme. "Stephen was Rachel's familiar, but she didn't want him as her mate."

The older Garvey brother was too much like his father. But even Mr. Garvey hadn't stooped so low as to sexually violate three witches.

"One witch, then two, reported her assault to the Witch Council of Elders. Stephen argued that the sex was consensual. The Council asked them all to submit to a magical lie detector test. The women agreed, but Stephen refused. Eric tried to talk to him, to convince his brother to take the test and submit to whatever punishment the Council ordered."

Sanura kissed the palm of one hand, allowing him to twirl her hair with his other. She wondered if Assefa knew how much he did that, how often he reached for her when they were doing nothing more than talking. But she'd noticed every subtle touch, every sweet attention.

"Stephen eventually went rogue, and no one could find him. Mike searched but turned up nothing. Not until Rachel." That had been an awful night, Rachel's internal bruises uglier and more lasting than the ones on her arms, thighs, and neck. But she'd called Eric and Mike after the assault. "I thought Mike was going to kill Stephen. He nearly did. And Eric just watched. I can't imagine how he must've felt, seeing the aftermath of his brother's brutality."

"Eric blamed himself for what happened to Rachel?"

She hadn't realized exactly how much. "He did, and it wasn't until today that I started to connect the dots. Within two months of Rachel's rape, Eric started manifesting symptoms of the disease. I believe the adze's attack on Gen is what triggered his sudden decline in health."

"I remember how Eric looked at the hospital. I'd never seen a man simultaneously look sad and angry. While all of us were angry with the adze, Eric was angry with himself for being unable to prevent what happened to his sister."

Sanura kissed his palm again, then the knuckles of the same hand, a reverent gesture she hoped he would understand. "My getting hurt by the adze was no more your fault than Rachel being raped by Stephen was Eric's fault. But, unfortunately, he didn't understand this, so Eric became sick and almost died due to misplaced guilt."

When Assefa made to withdraw his hand, her grip tightened. Sanura wouldn't let him retreat from this, not physically, not emotionally. If he could call her on her too-independent nature, she could call him on this. "You carry the weight of the preternatural world on your big shoulders. But your heart is even bigger, and the burden you harbor there heavier."

"Sanura, I—"

"No matter how mighty and intelligent you may be, there will always be events and people beyond your control. You must accept this simple but difficult truth and learn to forgive yourself."

"A doctor who makes house calls," he said, in what Sanura's come to recognize as his flirty tone. *One of his many masks.* "Do you have any idea how much I love you?" She loved him as well, but he was trying to distract her. He was good at that. Good at cutting off conversations he'd rather not have. Yeah, well, she was having none of his special agent tricks. This was too important. *He's too important.*

"I love you too much to allow you to keep blaming yourself for my injury." She gave him a stern look and injected a fierceness in her tone he couldn't miss. If she had to, Sanura would be the domineering goddess he'd accused her of being earlier. "I *never* want to have to do to you what I just did to Eric. I've known him since middle school, and it nearly broke my heart to use his love for his sister and wife to terrorize him into reconnecting with his cougar spirit. Gods, I never want to do that again, and I damn sure don't want to do that to *you.*"

He said nothing, just returned her unblinking stare. Then he sighed. "Berber men—"

"I don't care about Berber men. I only care about Assefa. But, if you want us to be partners, you must also be willing to accept my counsel, to understand that even the cat of legend can't be there for everyone. Nor is he responsible for his witch's every scrape and cut."

Sanura crawled into his lap, feeling warm and sheltered when his muscular arms encircled her.

"I noticed you said 'understand' instead of accept."

He would. She'd spoken deliberately. "I know you can't accept such a truth, but you're too smart to miss my logic. But you're also stubborn." Sanura grasped his face in her hands. "Don't be stubborn, Assefa. Not over something as important as your mental health."

He didn't try to pull away this time. Instead, he kissed her nose, then her lips. It wasn't a passionate or heated kiss, but a kiss of love and tenderness.

"I won't." He hugged her again before settling them entirely under the covers. He said nothing more because no more words were needed for a man like Assefa Berber. He didn't lie, didn't say what he didn't believe, or made promises he couldn't completely commit to. So when he said, "I'm proud of you. You're an unbelievable woman," Sanura couldn't help but turn in to him, her eyes shamefully moist, face buried against his neck.

Woman. Everyone else only saw the fire witch of legend, a goddess made flesh. But Assefa, the second son of the House of Berber, a government-trained agent, a were-cat of immense power, saw the woman.

"You're such a girlie-girl, Sanura." He stroked her hair.

"I know."

"And you're getting me all wet."

"I know."

He kissed the top of her head. "I'm beat."

"So am I."

"I'm even too tired to make you pay for using sex to distract me for your binding spell."

She laughed. "Just admit that I outsmarted you."

"I will when you admit that you're into threesomes."

"I'm not. I just…well, you were just…I mean, the two of you…Stop laughing."

CHAPTER TWENTY-FOUR

"You're welcome, Eric. You don't have to keep thanking me. Yes, I will give Assefa your best. Yes. Yes. All right, I promise the five of us will have dinner together next weekend if you get off the phone and get some rest. Love you, too. Bye."

"That's the third time he's called since we left his house. To say he's grateful would be an understatement." Assefa sat in their oversized bed, the elegant coral bedding surrounding him exquisite and undoubtedly expensive.

Sanura crawled into bed and sidled up next to her familiar. "I don't care, as long as he stays healthy. Eric's the brother I never had. I don't know what I would do without him." *Or you*, she silently added.

"Dear friends are hard to come by," Assefa said. "When we're fortunate enough to find them, we need to hold them close to our hearts and never let go."

Sanura started tracing circles on Assefa's bare chest, teasing him with licks to his lips when he peered down at her. "What about lovers? Boyfriends? Familiars?" She kissed his muscled chest between each word, a wet punctuation mark. "They're even harder to come by, especially in one man."

"Have you found the one man who can fill all those roles to your satisfaction, Dr. Williams?"

"I have"—kiss— "and I intend to keep him close and to never let him go. Now," she said, her tone serious, eyes lifted to Assefa's, "if I could only rid myself of an uptight, too-smart-for-his-own-good werecat posing as a full-human FBI agent."

"Damn you, woman, and your mouth." Assefa snarled. Then he attacked. Wicked fingers found sides, back, and legs.

She howled. Laugh tears bubbled up, uncontrollably and free. More tickling and even louder laughter followed, Assefa relentless in his assault. "Stop, stop," she screamed, gasping for air. "I give up."

"You don't know when to give up."

He moved his assault to her exposed feet.

Sanura wailed. Giddy and happy, she squirmed from one side of the king-size bed to the other in a futile attempt to free herself from Assefa's determined hunt.

"I see I have to show you who's boss," Assefa said, his laughter reverberating through the large chamber. He lightly swatted Sanura on her bottom before he resumed his tickling onslaught. "This is payback for this morning, my kinky witch, and don't even think of trying that binding spell on me again."

Sanura did, but as soon as she parted her lips for the incantation, Assefa captured them in a domineering kiss. Every time she tried to cast the spell, his lips were there first, sucking the words from her mouth, stealing her breath. His magic was powerful, intoxicating, and so utterly masculine. It made her feel weak, strong, and loved.

The strength of it overpowered Sanura, causing her to writhe in ecstasy, scream in pleasure, and cry in wonder. His unique brand of magic rivaled hers, and she accepted the defeat with grace and dignity. Well, as graceful and dignified as any woman could be naked and sweaty, sounding like a devoted Orioles fan whenever a batter hit a home run.

After they both regained their composure and redressed, Assefa whispered into the darkness, "I want to be more than your lover, boyfriend, and familiar."

"You already are. You're bound to me as I am to you."

"I know, but I want you to be my—"

"Shh, go to sleep. The future will take care of itself. Besides, I'm exactly where I want to be. No one can come between us." *No one better try*. Her fire spirit hissed from a secret, dark place within Sanura, a place that held the witch's greatest fears.

Assefa awoke to the most alluring song he'd ever heard. The notes were crisp, deep, and hypnotic. The tantalizing melody forced him out of bed and to his feet. The pull of the harp strings on his body was strong, but his mind resisted. Slowly, he walked to the bedroom door toward the enticing song. He stopped. His mind yelled at him to proceed no further.

Cautiously, his Mngwa roused, shaking its mane and snarling a warning. Keen were-cat ears detected the slither of female tongues.

The beast's warning grew.

"He's fighting us."

"No male can resist us, sisters. We must work together to bring him to us."

"Ah! Sconvolta nell'ordine eterno" from Gioachino Rossini's *Semiramide* intensified to a beautifully deadly pitch, its tone sweeter, more inebriating than before. The sweeping melody took Assefa on an inglorious musical journey at a heart-stomping rate. The pulse, pulse, pulse of the crystalline, high soprano voices pushed down on him, moving from a low C to a high F.

Against his will, Assefa plodded along, a zombie prodded and controlled by a powerful necromancer. Walking through the kitchen, Assefa's trembling hand opened the sliding glass doors that led to his backyard. The acres of grass and shoulder-height shrubs sculpted in a nature-defying square design met his glazed-over eyes.

The crisp night air from the Potomac River chilled Assefa, who wore only a black T-shirt and green boxers. His mind knew what was happening, but his body was his enemy. Yet Assefa fought every inch of the way, mind versus body, will versus instinct, anger versus fear.

Never before did he have to battle every muscle and molecule in his body.

Tonight, he did.

He fought to still his legs. But it was no use. With each forced step he took, the music strengthened. The aria thrummed between the two American Dogwood trees at the end of the natural, flat stone path that led to the river. The white, hanging blooms served as the background for three operatic divas, his backyard their stage, or rather, their Convent Garden.

The women stood shoulder-to-shoulder, mouths wide and eyes brilliant in their vicious intent. Each woman radiated a stage presence worthy of a Maria Callas understudy with unmasked contempt and illusions of being the next *La Divina*.

Waist-length, rich auburn hair, hazel eyes, and bright oval faces covered in taut, white porcelain skin hovered like impatient hyenas, waiting for the prey to enter their melodious trap. He already had.

Damn them.

But their Botox-free, twenty-something beauty, along with the modern clothing of capri pants with matching feather-print sleeveless tops and jeweled leather sandals, belied their two centuries' worth of man-killing experience.

His Mngwa smashed into him, a desperate attempt to break the spell.

Slam.

Slam.

Slam.

The confines of the cat's cage shook but didn't open.

Assefa's mind flashed to the division's profile of four murderous women—sirens.

Blood-bonded females who appear to range in age from 20 to 30. Works at or frequent bars, nightclubs, and other public facilities where men congregate in search of female companionship. They are proficient in using knives, organized and cunning in hiding and disposing of bodies, and very mobile. They do not select victims from the same locale more than once. They are preternatural serial killers who kill not for revenge, glory or notoriety, but for an innate need to subjugate men. They will kill again.

The three sisters increased their deceptively sweet music, singing in perfect harmony. The song was enchanting, and so were they. So enticing, Assefa's entire body desired more, and he continued to walk farther away from the house and into the waiting arms of the three siren sisters.

"Yes, that's it. Come to us, you piece of weak, male flesh," the tallest and oldest-looking siren sister hissed. The other two never wavered, pressing the song deeper into his psyche.

The oldest siren pulled a dagger from somewhere near her waist. The gold casing glistened in the moon's rapturous light, the sheath as fatally stunning as the bearer. Sirens were known as much for their beauty as for their hatred of men. But this man, who they were slowly pulling in like a rebellious dog on a chain, held a special place in their blackened hearts. Assefa understood this and knew why the women were at his home. Why, after so many years, so many kills, would they risk their freedom, their very lives, by daring to come to the residence of a were-cat FBI agent?

I killed one of them—the missing contralto in their bloody opera.

"Assefa!" Sanura screamed, waking herself from a nightmare. "Damn it." She jumped out of bed, looking frantically around the bedroom but knowing he wasn't there. Her dream had shown her the danger. Their shared magic pounded against her aura, demanding action.

Not taking time to locate shoes or throw on something over the short-sleeve, black sleep shirt she wore, barefooted, Sanura ran out of the suite, down the hallway, the steps, and out the back door, following Assefa's aura signature. Once outside, she catapulted her body through the debilitating darkness, long, exposed legs tracking her special agent. His Mngwa roared inside her head, his beast calling to her fire spirit.

Assefa was in danger.

She ran faster, fear and rage guiding her movements.

Sanura reached a clearing and saw Assefa walking morbidly toward three women. She could now hear singing. The tortured melody curled its way through trees, wind, and distance, reaching her like a cross-country slap across her sweat-moistened face.

She had a better sense of Assefa's inner turmoil at this closer range, a discordant note against a battered violin. He was resisting the women, but it was a battle he couldn't win—wasn't made to win, his XY chromosomes an unwilling conspirator.

"Zareb and I tracked the youngest siren to Anchorage," Assefa had told her on the drive home this afternoon. "We followed the siren into a house and found her with him."

In the limo, he'd pulled her close to him, Sanura resting her head on Assefa's shoulder. It had been one of those embraces in which the holder needed more comfort than the held. Sanura hadn't minded, especially after he'd described the scene.

"The victim, Jason Vaughn, the homeowner, was tied like an out-stretched starfish to his bed." He'd stroked her hair and then closed his eyes. She waited, and after a heavy sigh that lifted his chest and her head, Assefa continued. "She'd already drugged him with her song. There's no other way to explain how a woman, who barely reached the five-foot mark, could subdue a man who exceeded her by a foot and a hundred pounds. He was naked, legs and arms apart and tied to a four-poster bed."

"Was he alive?" she'd asked, assuming the worst.

"Barely. His breathing was weak, and blood stuck to him like snow to dying winter grass. Through the bloody mess, I couldn't see a single cut or puncture wound on his large frame, except those sprinkling his face like chickenpox. Those were clear, little knife wounds to his cheeks, chin, and forehead. One, two, even ten would hurt, but nothing more. But there had to be dozens of them, shallow cuts intended to humiliate and torture, drawing out the game of dominance sirens like to play. Eventually, they tire or become bored, swatting the man around as if he were nothing more than a squeaky cat toy to their vicious, predatory paws."

The image had made Sanura shiver, and she shivered now, but with fury instead of shock. She'd be damned if she let Assefa end up like that poor, brutalized guy in Alaska. Even if she had to—

Heat and protectiveness shot through her, and Sanura ran the last few feet, separating her from the women who would dare to threaten her man. A spell lingered on her lips.

The oldest siren faced Assefa. "You'll submit before I kill you. They all do."

"Never!" he spat through clenched teeth, face as defiant as Sanura had ever seen it.

"I don't know how you've kept us at bay this long, but you'll be mine." The siren's eyes flicked a dangerous grayish-blue, and her tongue came out to lick sultry, red lips.

"He'll never be yours."

Reaching them, Sanura glanced at the emotionally battered Assefa. A siren's song drained men not only of their free will but their physical strength as well. Worst yet, it could cause brain damage.

The siren nearest Assefa looked at Sanura and laughed mockingly. "Oh, I see now," she said, returning her cruel gaze to Assefa as if Sanura were of no relevance, "you have a little witch protecting you. Well, no matter, you'll be mine, one way or another." Then the mad cow grabbed Assefa, slanted her mouth over his, and kissed him, taking what wasn't hers.

The firestorm began to grow. The heat raged, and Sanura fought for control, which Assefa always seemed to have. The control she knew she must maintain if she were to save Assefa and herself.

The siren smiled at Sanura, beautiful and vindictive. "See, no man can resist our allure. His desire to be with us is what pulled him from your bed and into my arms. He belongs to us, little witch, and your presence here is unwanted."

Sanura mumbled the last lines of her spell.

The siren laughed again, then, with a wave of a manicured hand, she signaled for her sisters to attack.

They didn't move.

She gestured again, waving wildly and with annoyance.

Nothing.

"Get her!" she shouted.

Sanura's mouth lifted in a satisfied sneer. "They can't move, and if they try, the binds will tighten. The more they resist, the tighter the binds will become. The binds can feel like thick ropes, silk scarves, barbwire, or whatever I choose, siren. Either way, their fate is in my hands. Now release my familiar before you really piss me the hell off."

Or my fire spirit comes out to play.

Sanura breathed heavily, trembling with the effort to stay her anger, to keep her fire spirit calm and inside. She at least had control over two of the three sirens. Partial control, anyway, for the two bound sirens still sang. Their voices no longer carried the compelling strength of the notes from earlier, but it was still effective, keeping Assefa planted and under their spell.

She didn't want to hurt them, even though they'd come there to seek their revenge on Assefa. Sanura prayed the threat she'd just made would be enough to curb their bloodlust. Yet, they maintained the poisoning cadence of the song, Assefa's features slack, eyes beginning to fade into bleakness. *Gods, no.*

A forceful wind blew in from the river, whipping around the sirens in a feverous gallop of cold, icy air. Sanura chanted. Her mouth moved, but no words were heard over the top of the howling wind. The ground began to tremble beneath the siren that had kissed Assefa. Yet, the woman didn't waver, her legs steely, her hand still fiercely wrapped around the handle of the dagger.

"What kind of witch are you?" the siren asked, a slither of fear housed in her tone, eyes becoming grayer, pupils dilated, focused on Sanura.

No longer so irrelevant.

"The kind of witch that'll crush anyone who attempts to take what's hers." No bluff this time, just unvarnished fire witch truth. "He belongs to me. Now release my familiar, and I'll spare your life."

The siren glanced at her sisters. The binds cut ever tighter into their clothing, their pale skin. Blood streamed down their arms, legs, and from mouths that still sang. The notes, still magically deceptive, struggled past quivering lips. Then she looked at the man who had killed the youngest of them. Then, finally, she met the hardened gaze of Sanura, whose reddish-gold hair blew like wildfire in the wind.

Sanura could see some sadistic streak of realization pass her eyes and knew, in that instant, the siren comprehended the extent of the bond she shared with Assefa. Sanura's magic and their bond protected him from the likes of such creatures. That one siren Assefa had tracked to Alaska and killed wouldn't have been able to use her melodic, manipulative wiles on him as she'd done so many others. This would've made her an easy target for the special agent, not even requiring him to shift into his feline form.

In a blinding rage, the siren's eyes turned battleship gray, and she unsheathed the dagger.

She flew at Sanura.

Long, wide, white wings flashed in the darkness. They hadn't been there a second ago, but they were present now, allowing the siren to dive toward Sanura like an eagle after a field mouse.

The siren sliced at the air, screaming at Sanura in a foreign language. Sanura ducked, just avoiding the wild lunge. She made to cast a binding spell, but the siren plowed into her, knocking the wind—and the remainder of the spell—out of Sanura.

Now several feet in the air, the siren held onto her waist, then drove Sanura to the ground. The carpet-looking grass did not absorb her fall. The witch's back and head slammed into the hard ground, sending jolts of pain up her spine and out her eyes.

She had no time to think, only to react.

The siren came at her again, demonic wings fanned out, the torn shirt from her transformation gone, white-pink breasts swaying.

Sanura rolled, the agile siren passing overhead. The edge of her right wing caught Sanura's bare leg. A thin line started where her sleep shirt ended and extended to her knee. Blood flowed, hot and wet, the cut more painful than it looked, deeper, too.

Then the siren was back, the sparkle from the polished knife dull compared to the shine in the siren's murderous eyes. Sanura attempted a faint move to her right, but the siren was there. Instinctively, Sanura raised her arms to block the attack, screaming when flesh met steel—flesh losing. Another cut, more blood, and a smiling siren.

Sanura stumbled back, using her hands and arms defensively.

Block. Strike. Blood.

Block. Strike. Blood.

Block. Strike. Blood.

The siren's arrogantly wicked smile grew every time she scored a blow and Sanura screamed. Sanura's mind raced, while uncontrollable emotions flowed through her. *Must focus on a protective spell. Can't let her keep cutting me.*

She was losing, bleeding, and those sirens were still singing. The pulsing beat was a wretched symphony—Lady Macbeth of the Mtsensk District—the growling siren hunting her Katerina Lvovna Izmailova, a woman who took a lover, killed her husband, and spent his money. Karma got her in the end, an icy river her reward.

There had to be ice in the siren's veins. Blood, pain, and death key ingredients in her sadistic pleasure stew.

Bleeding and exhausted, Sanura stumbled, and the siren advanced. She grabbed Sanura's hair and drove her to the ground again. Sanura's vision blurred, and weird sparkling lights formed. But she didn't have to see to know exactly where the siren was. The woman straddled her chest, legs pinning Sanura's arms to her side.

The witch began a chant. She had to get the homicidal bitch off her.

The knife slid to her throat.

Sanura stopped mid-spell.

The siren sneered down at her. "I'll enjoy slicing off bits of your pretty little face. Then I'll drag you before your male, so he can see how hideous you are. But I won't kill you." The siren licked her lips as if the prospect of mutilating Sanura was a treat she couldn't wait to devour. Perhaps it was. "No, I won't kill you. Instead, I will make you watch what we do to him. He's a big, strong man. I wonder how many cuts it'll take to make him scream, make him drop to his proud were-cat knees and beg for mercy. I bet not as many as you think. Men simply aren't that tough."

The blade dug deeper, just piercing Sanura's skin. Blood trickled down her neck.

"I think I'll take the tongue first. You have a smart mouth. And while screams are my favorite music, I prefer baritone to contralto."

The siren replaced the knife with her hand, long nails digging into Sanura's throat, the pressure forcing her mouth open on a ragged gasp. The blade came to her mouth, sliding over her lips and teeth.

"No!" Sanura screamed. But it was too late. *Too late for me. Too late for the siren.*

The knife pierced her tongue.

Blooded spurted.

The siren cackled.

Sanura's magic erupted, twisting and twirling and then spiraling upward and outward. An inferno unleashed. Rage and heat mingled in a fire spirit cocktail that promised doom and death. *To the siren. To them all.*

Then the blade was gone. The crushing weight on her chest and arms had also vanished. Sanura opened her eyes, fire flickering around the edges. An inhuman snarl followed.

She stood. And with her movement, the winds returned, howling and squealing. A frenzy of invisible arctic binds held its prize aloft. Red eyes lifted and narrowed on the screaming form dangling fifty feet above her.

White wings battled, seeking freedom. But none was to be found. *Not now. Not ever. Too late. Tried to warn you.*

Sanura lifted her hands to the sky, connected with the electromagnetic energy, and let the power flow into her, become one with her.

Now!

Thunderbolts materialized and vaulted through the clouds, bringing the dark sky to life with their heated beams of light. Sanura flung her arms wide, a general commanding her troops. Off they went, spreading outward and locating their targets.

Boom.

Boom.

Boom.

Lightning.

Raw, unleashed fire witch of legend magic.

Boom.

Boom.

Boom.

There were shrieks of horror and pain but no aria, just the strangled cries of three dethroned divas.

Sanura's hate-filled gaze watched as the sirens burned, their corpses falling with a defeated *thunk*. Her lightning flames retreated, the smell of ozone left behind, a remnant of death in the sullen night air.

For minutes, or perhaps only seconds, Sanura couldn't move or think. But her fire spirit danced and giggled in exultant satisfaction. She no longer felt cold, achy, or entirely sane. Instead, Sanura felt warmth radiate from within, a cauldron overtop of simmering heat.

Dazed, Sanura barely registered when Assefa slumped to his knees, body giving out now that the sirens no longer controlled him. She rushed to his side and aided him to his feet.

"Are you all right? Did she cut you? Is there anything I can do for you?" Without pause, the questions kept coming, rolling from Sanura in a fluttering wave of rushed words and heated concern.

He wrapped his heavy arms around her neck. "You saved my life," he breathed, voice shaky. "No man, full-human or preternatural, can ignore the call of a siren. It took three of them to get me this far, and still my mind remained my own. That shouldn't be possible."

Yeah, they'd been saying that a lot lately. Clearly, they needed to redefine their definition of "possible." But, by the gods, her special agent sounded uncharacteristically tired and weak. She held him tighter.

"I told you we are bound to each other." She kissed his forehead, forcing back her fire spirit's vicious satisfaction at having meted out the ultimate justice.

"And I belong to you?"

"Yes, and I belong to you."

He ran his eyes, then his fingers over every tear in her sleep shirt. "There's blood on your arms, hands, and legs. She cut you. I heard you scream. Yet"—he touched her shoulder— "I see no injuries."

Sanura had fractured her leg when she'd jumped out of a tree in her backyard when she was ten. At age twelve, she'd cut and scraped her knee while running in the rain. When she was twenty, she'd dislocated her shoulder while sparring with an overzealous lion shifter. Not one of those incidents resulted in the type of miraculous healing she'd just experienced. *What in the hell?*

Sanura shrugged. "Were-cats can heal themselves. Maybe I got some of that ability when our auras merged." Of course, she'd never actually heard or read of that happening. But it was a reasonable explanation. It sure beat the one flitting around in her paranoid brain, saying her fire spirit had taken control of her, cast a rejuvenation spell, and healed Sanura. That damn sure shouldn't be possible. Yet …

They walked in silence until they reached the back door, Assefa leaning heavily on Sanura, a sign his body needed time to recover from the magical assault. Once there, Sanura paused before going inside. Looking back toward the three bodies, shame and regret filled her, her fire spirit controlled and locked away.

"I've never killed anyone, Assefa." Sanura fought the urge to cry at what she'd done.

"I know, sweetheart." He pulled her inside the house and locked the door.

Forty minutes later, after showering, Sanura stood in front of a full-length mirror. She had appraised her body for the slightest nick. There had been none. Not even the cut to her tongue. There was nothing to remind Sanura of what had happened this night.

Nothing but my memories and nightmares. Always the damn nightmares.

They settled back into bed, Assefa too weak for Sanura's liking. But he was a proud man. She wouldn't insult him by bringing undue attention to his temporary state. "It's never easy." He wrapped her in his arms, holding her when she should've been holding him. "Killing is never easy, Sanura. I wish you didn't have to experience it."

She wished the same.

"Something has happened to me, my magic," Sanura confessed. "I didn't mean to kill those sirens. It just happened. I was so afraid they would hurt you and so damn angry. I've never been that angry before, and I…I—"

"Shhh, don't say it. If you didn't kill them, they would've killed us. I know it's not your way, but sometimes our choices are already made for us, and we simply act."

His words rang true, but she wished it wasn't so. In less than twenty-four hours, she'd vanquished a Raven Mocker to a damnable Hell dimension and killed three sirens. All Sanura's actions were in self-defense or in defense of another. But did that truly make such violence acceptable? What was she becoming, and how could she stop it? Could any of this madness be halted? Sanura didn't know.

Sanura raised her head from Assefa's shoulder. "I think it's time for part two of the handfasting ritual." It was a spur-of-the-moment decision. She probably should've thought it over first. But she'd heard what Cynthia had said to Assefa. And her sister was wrong. She had no intention of hurting him, of burning his heart. She was just…well, that didn't matter.

The way he stared at her, with shock and disbelief, said he hadn't expected her suggestion, that perhaps he had the same concerns about their relationship as Cynthia. Sanura would have to have a word with her and Mike about sticking their noses where they didn't belong.

His smile was tentative at first. Yet it broadened the longer she held his gaze, not backing away from her words. "Sounds perfect, my life-saving witch." He grinned with anticipation. "Do I get to see you in that itsy-bitsy bathing suit again?"

She smiled at Assefa, feeling better about her decision and ignoring the anxiety that always accompanied her thoughts of bonding with a man who had the power to know her as well as she knew herself, a man she couldn't hide her true nature from, a man who would eventually force her to face her silent demons or risk losing him forever.

"What about the sirens? We can't just leave their bodies out there like that."

"Zareb will take care of them. I called him when you were in the bathroom. He's en route from Richmond International Airport. ETA—forty-five minutes. I also had Mrs. Livingston check on Siddig and the other were-cat house staff. They are more friends than staff, despite the odd jobs they do around the estate. They are groggy from the sirens' song but otherwise unharmed. I'll personally check on them in the morning. They're my responsibility, as much as they think I'm theirs."

Sanura understood. Her father had felt a similar sense of responsibility for those who'd worked for him—from the groundskeepers and maintenance workers to the managers and leasing agents of his apartment buildings. So she would go with Assefa tomorrow, meet the were-cats whose welfare he cared so much about.

"Come on and get under the covers, sweetheart. The air is on, and that nightgown, sexy as it is, cannot be warm. That's right, let me warm you. No need to use fire magic when you have a were-cat's natural warmth to heat you."

She did, snuggling close and inhaling deeply of her familiar. "Who's Zareb?"

"I told you about him. Remember? He's my best friend and partner. He lives in the guest house by the pool. I left him in Alaska to deal with the siren there. Now, he'll have to deal with the three here. Disposal is one of his many talents. Though, I probably should not have added that last detail from the nauseous look on your face. It's all right. Zareb will take care of everything. No worries."

Sanura nodded, remembering Zareb with only the slightest of recognition. She usually had a better memory, but she'd had a long day. And if pressed right now, she probably couldn't recall her bra or panty size.

"I told him all about you. He said he couldn't wait to meet the woman who tamed me in less than two weeks." His hand began a scalp massage, and she closed her eyes. "He also said that no witch's bond was strong enough to shield her familiar from a siren's musical lure."

"Really?" Her eyes popped open. "Then I guess he's the perfect man for the cleanup job."

Mild laughter followed, the kind that was more tension-relieving than spirit-lifting, for nothing was amusing about what she'd done.

Assefa hugged her closer to him. His reassuring heartbeat pumped strongly under the cheek pressed against his chest. Sanura shut her eyes again. Then, slinging one arm over Assefa's middle, she held him with fierce, burning possession. She willed his masculine strength into her, praying his soothing murmurings of, "I've got you. It'll be all right," would stave off the nightmares, and the creature that lurked behind her eyelids, looking frighteningly like her fire spirit—a burnished Phoenix with firestorm wings and a golden tail.

A half-hour later, Assefa slept but Sanura was still awake, listening to him breathe. Gods, she almost lost him tonight. *Almost lost myself.* Her hand went to his chest--over his heart. *Strong, but not invincible.* "I love you. And I'll never let anyone hurt you again. Not even if I have to become my worst nightmare."

EPILOGUE

"They are almost ready, Sekhmet," Yemaya said, waving a hand to clear the sleeping image of Assefa and Sanura over the horizon on which the goddesses perched. Their forms, if seen from below, looked like heavy gray-and-white soapstones in the form of Zimbabwe Birds, standing proud and tall, guarding the walls and monoliths of the ancient city of Great Zimbabwe.

"I know. Our fire witch did well. But she needs to fortify herself if she is to beat Mami Wata's water witch. She is too sentimental, and that will lead to her demise," Sekhmet said with the impatient roar of a lioness. "As it was, I had to give her a little push with that Raven Mocker. Show your fire witch exactly where to send the demon. She is too soft. Except when it comes to her mate, then she is the fire witch of legend we need her to be."

"Leave Sanura to me. You worry about your Mngwa."

"My Mngwa is all I knew he would be—fierce, loyal, and capable of much more. But we have no more time to prepare them. Your daughters are ready, and we can no longer deny them."

"You are right. The time has come. We have shown Sanura and Assefa the path, and they have conquered many of their fears."

"But not all of them."

"No, Sekhmet, not all."

"And what of their faith?"

"Their faith is stronger than they know."

"But not yet strong enough."

"No, but they are yet babes, my friend."

"Yes."

"Their bond will face a great many challenges, Yemaya. The beasts will come and test them."

"I know. Now let us begin."

They held hands and, in unison, said, "Goddess Oya, we release the binds that shackle you to the ocean's floor. Goddess Mami Wata, we release the binds that shackle you to the ocean's floor. Go forth and find your champions. Go forth and remind the world that Gods take many forms and features. Play your game, and when it is done, return to this place of slumber, place of serenity until you are called forth once more in another five hundred years."

The world's oceans erupted, geysers spouting thousands of feet into the air, covering landmasses with salt and silt. Bringing life and destroying crops, homes, and people, the goddesses were free and in search of their witches.

THE END

RAVEN MOCKER

SIREN

AOZE

USA TODAY BESTSELLING AUTHOR

N.D. JONES

N.D. Jones, Ed.D., is an award-winning African-American female author who has achieved USA Today bestselling status for her captivating Black Fantasy and Paranormal Romance novels. Residing in the heart of Maryland with her loving family, N.D. is a trailblazer in the literary world of Blacks in fantasy.

Driven by a passionate desire to introduce more positive, sexy, and multi-dimensional African-American characters as soul mates, friends, and lovers, N.D. embarked on a remarkable journey of her own. Determined to address this challenge, she took it upon herself to redefine the narrative.

N.D. has an impressive portfolio of series that reflect her dedication to bringing diversity and depth to the romance genre. Her works include the enchanting fantasy romance series "Forever Yours" and the contemporary romance trilogy "The Styles of Love." Moreover, she has authored three thrilling paranormal romance series: "Winged Warriors," "Death and Destiny," and "Dragon Shifter Romance," along with two captivating fantasy series: "Feline Nation" and "Fairy Tale Fatale."

OTHER BOOKS BY N.D. JONES

Winged Warriors Trilogy (Paranormal Romance)
Fire, Fury, Faith (Book 1)
Heat, Hunt, Hope (Book 2)
Lies, Lust, Love (Book 3)

Death and Destiny Trilogy (Paranormal Romance)
Of Fear and Faith (Book 1)
Of Beasts and Bonds (Book 2)
Of Deception and Divinity (Book 3)
Death and Destiny: The Complete Series

Forever Yours Series (Fantasy Romance)
Bound Souls (Book 1)
Fated Path (Book 2)

Dragon Shifter Romance (Standalone Novels)
Stones of Dracontias: The Bloodstone Dragon
Dragon Lore and Love: Isis and Osiris

The Styles of Love Trilogy (Contemporary Romance)
The Perks of Higher Ed (Book 1)
The Wish of Xmas Present (Book 2)
The Gift of Second Chances (Book 3)
Rhythm and Blue Skies: Malcolm and Sky's Complete Story
The Styles of Love Trilogy: The Complete Series

Fairy Tale Fatale Series (Urban Fantasy)
Crimson Hunter: A Red Riding Hood Reimagining
Bearly Gold: A Goldilocks and the Three Bears Reimagining

Feline Nation Duology (Urban Fantasy)
A Queen's Pride (Book 1)
Mafdet's Claws (Book 2)

Fantasy in Black (Coloring Books)

Spread Your Wings and Fly: Black Women Fairies Coloring Book
Be UnBound: Black Men Angels Coloring Book
The Beauty of Black Mermaids Coloring Book
Black Superheroes Coloring Book

Fairy Tale Fatale (Dystopian Fantasy)
Crimson Hunter: Red Riding Hood Reimagined
Bearly Gold: Goldilocks and the Three Bears Reimagined

www.ingramcontent.com/pod-product-compliance
Lightning Source LLC
Chambersburg PA
CBHW021106110726

47900CB00007B/2063